How to Get a Literary Agent
in *Two Murders or Less*

By Ellie Burmeister

How to Get a Literary Agent in Two Murders or Less

Mirth Press
PO Box 231137
San Diego, CA 92193
www.mirthpress.com

ISBN-978-1-936869-01-5
Library of Congress Control Number: 2011927884

Cover designed by Scarlett Rugers Design
www.scarlettrugers.com

First Edition

10 9 8 7 6 5 4 3 2 1

For all the struggling artists
who fear they'll never catch a break.

People in glass houses shouldn't stow bones. So the killer brought his victim to a cemetery. The beams from his headlights shot through the fog between the trees, bathing the willows in rays of pearly violet. The beauty of the scene could not have escaped his notice as he carried a cardboard box that contained the shards of charred bone that was all that was left of the beloved girl. There would be no gravestone for this dead lovely.

The killer set down his burden and yanked a newly planted pink rosebush out of the ground, setting it upon the frosted grass with far more care than he'd shown the box of shattered remains. He drew a trowel from his belt and thrust it into the pit that he'd exposed within the violated flowerbed. Once he had excavated a fair amount of soil, he lifted the box and poured the contents into the hole where the blackened bits rattled together like a haunted chime. Satisfied that the box was empty he tore the cardboard into strips, which followed the bone shards into the grave. He stripped off his undershirt and his pants for burial as well. The final item into the pit was the trowel. He pushed the hill of soil in with his hands before restoring the defiled rosebush. What dirt wouldn't go into the pit he scattered about with his foot.

Thus relieved of his burden, the killer knelt beside the improvised grave and rubbed his hands compulsively through his hair, as if trying to scrub all memory of his grisly deeds out of his mind. Although he didn't make a sound, his cheeks were puffy and streaked with tears. His mouth moved only a little. Perhaps he spoke to himself, or to her, or to whatever god he believed in.

But even as he wept, his eyes glowed with a grim satisfaction. He'd gotten away with it. The body, the evidence, the alibi – he had calculated every last detail so that nothing would be suspected of him.

He didn't know there was a witness.
      -Prologue, Houses Made of Glass, *by Jonny Goodsnuff*

Part 1
Prose and Cons

Chapter 1

If there's one thing I've learned from this whole ordeal, it's never marry one of your idols. It doesn't end well. And when the man in question is internationally renowned suspense writer Jonny Goodsnuff? Well, then you're likely to end up with a bullet in your head. Or at the very least, a cell on death row.

I never wanted to get mixed up in any of this. I just wanted to get a novel published. And toward that end I had paid my dues, working two or three jobs at a time to put myself through Youngstown University so I could get that oh-so-valuable degree in comparative literature. I had written eight manuscripts, each better than the one before it. I attended countless local writing conferences and seminars to learn the art and science of mystery writing well enough to attract an agent. But what sort of agent would want to fly out to a dreary little nowhere-town in the Midwest looking for the great American novelist? A high-powered agent would much rather jet off to a conference at a paradise vacation spot like Malibu, California, so that's where I was headed.

I looked at my little dog-eared postcard, with its sandy cliffs surrounding sapphire-colored waters while I waited for my manuscript to finish printing. I wasn't going on vacation. This trip was all business, so I didn't even bother to pack my bikini. But I packed all my good designer dresses, and when I finished, the closet was nearly bare. It was a sorry sight, but I'd always preferred quality over quantity, and nearly every spare penny I'd earned since college had gone into my writing.

Once my manuscript and my laptop were packed, I locked the tiny studio apartment that might have been chic if I lived in New York City. But this was Ohio. And a bad part of Ohio at that.

I wheeled my suitcase past derelict houses tagged with gang symbols, and apartment complexes with iron bars on the windows and feral cats digging through the dumpsters. It was almost midnight. Nearly everything I owned was in that suitcase, but I wasn't afraid. I'd lived in that apartment since I was seventeen. As long as I stayed in the well-lit areas I'd be fine. Still, I wore baggy jeans and a football jersey, put my hair in a thick braid, and scowled like a Viking. No point in tempting fate.

I'd been promised a ride to the airport from my least estranged ex-boyfriend, who shall remain nameless. Because frankly, if any of my exes were worth remembering, I probably wouldn't have much of a story to tell.

He was supposed to pick me up, but I'd dated him for his looks, not his reliability, so I worried that he might be asleep. As I neared the Victorian style house he sublet to between seven to twelve college students, I realized that sleep would have been impossible. I could feel the bass from his stereo from half a block away.

A typical Friday night at the flophouse. This sort of frat boy lifestyle was charming four years ago, when he was actually still in college and not bordering on thirty. But then again, I was twenty-six and still worked the same Lancôme counter I'd manned since I was seventeen, so who was I to judge?

I pounded on the door and he answered in a dirty T-shirt and jeans, holding a can of beer. "Oh shoot, Blondie. I forgot. Let me get my keys."

I pointed to the beer in his hand. "How many of those have you had?"

"Just a few." The hot stink of weed reached my face before his words did. Drunk and stoned on the night he promised to drive me the airport. It was a painful reminder of why I'd turned down his proposal of marriage during my high school graduation ceremony.

Trouble was, he fit this neighborhood a lot better than I did. He'd learned to make the best of it, while I was still foolish enough to believe that my life might turn out to be a fairy tale: A beautiful romantic fairy tale like *Cinderella*, and not some dreadful morality tale where the girl dies cold and alone like *The Little Match Girl*.

I'd told myself time and time again that I'd been born in the wrong place and the wrong time, and certainly to the wrong family. But this conference could fix all that. Assuming I managed to get there.

I yanked my suitcase from his doorstep and walked away.

"Come on, Amanda, you're such an old lady. I've driven with more alcohol in my system than this and I've never had any trouble."

Oh, now that was reassuring. "Forget it. You're an idiot. I'm calling a cab."

I walked past the cluster of cars in the driveway so that I could open my cell phone, but I closed it again when I saw my friend Courtney, a woolly haired biology major, lounging in the backseat of a corroded Honda and reading the calculus textbook propped on her knees.

A kindred soul, no doubt in need of some peace and quiet. I rapped on the window, and she looked up from her studying.

"Hey, Court, sorry to bother you, but if you give me a ride to the airport, I'll let you crash at my place for the weekend."

She opened the door and moved into the driver's seat. "Get in."

I hoisted my suitcase into the back and belted myself into the passenger seat. "Thanks. You're a lifesaver. I'll give you my key. Just leave it with the manager when you're done."

She waved it off. "Don't worry about it. I'll head over to Starbucks after I drop you off."

"Oh," I reached in my purse. "Let me give you some money for coffee."

"I said don't worry about it. This will be my good deed for the day."

I made a mental note to do something nice for her when I was rich and famous. I suppose I should have felt relieved, but even then, I could somehow sense that a drunken stoner ex-boyfriend was going to be the least of my worries on this trip.

CHAPTER 2

A freak thunderstorm in Dallas had delayed my connecting flight. Although it gave me enough time to change into a dress and heels, I had only ten minutes to get to the conference before the interviews began.

As I dragged my suitcase into the hotel lobby, I wanted to check out the grandeur of the marble-lined lobby of the Hotel Cortez, but the tinkling of a fountain set amid potted ferns and wrought iron banisters reminded me, like the ticking of a chess clock, that I didn't even have time to go to my room to stash my luggage. The conference brochure said to be on time for the interview sessions and I hadn't even picked up my badge and itinerary, so that took precedence. After all, who would want to represent a writer who couldn't meet a deadline?

As I approached, the girl at the conference registration table looked up from the graphic novel she was reading. She was tiny, with hair cut into a short brown wisp. Under her tank top there were neither bra straps nor any discernible need for a bra. She wore a tutu and I might have mistaken her for a child if not for her facial piercings and the many tattoos that decorated her right arm from wrist to shoulder.

"Name," said the urban pixie, in a bored tone that I felt did not convey the respect owed to a woman in an Italian mini-dress.

"Amanda Anderson."

The girl set her book down and went over to a laptop where she typed as if she'd never seen a computer before.

"I don't mean to rush you, and I know it's my own fault that I'm late, but I've just flown out from Ohio on a red-eye, sat in a taxi for an hour, and the conference has already begun. I've saved for years for this and I don't have a lot of money."

She looked up. "Ah, sweetie, that's the saddest thing I've ever heard. Don't you know that this conference is a total sham? Run by crooks, and frequented only by the foulest dregs of the industry? I'd advise you to ask for your money back, but we don't give out refunds."

I clenched my jaw. Why would she say such a thing? Even if it were true, knowing that didn't do me any good. I tapped on a placard announcing

Jonny Goodsnuff as a special surprise guest. "I fail to see how a bestselling author could be considered one of the foulest dregs of the industry."

The girl glanced over the sandwich board. "Oh, him. Turns out he was already staying at the hotel, and Mrs. Brasher talked him into doing a couple of seminars. I met him and he seems like a nice guy." Her voice dropped to a whisper. "Just don't ask him what he's working on. That question makes him absolutely insane."

"Why would that make him insane?"

She shrugged "If you figure it out, let me know."

I gritted my teeth. "Hurry please. I'm missing the commencement speech."

"I wouldn't let that bother you. It's just a loser pimping his book with a fake-ass motivational speech about how if he can make it, so can you. It's the same speech every year. Only the author changes." She tapped at the keyboard. "Anderson...Anderson..."

A sturdy matron with horn-rimmed glasses and a badge marked "Event Organizer" emerged from behind me and jammed her thumb at the screen. "Anderson. Right here, Ivy, under A. She gets a blue badge."

"A blue badge, Mrs. Brasher? Are you sure about that?"

"Yes, Ivy, give Ms. Anderson her blue badge and her packet and send her on her way." The woman grasped both of my hands in her own. "Welcome, my dear. It is such an honor to have you here. I do hope you enjoy your visit. If there's anything I can do to help you, you'll let me know, won't you?"

"I guess," I said, taken aback by such overt hospitality.

"The commencement is in the ballroom, through that door. If you rush you may be able to catch the end of the keynote speech."

I glanced at the closed door. Knowing my luck, it would be the one closest to the stage and I'd disrupt one of the very agents I was trying to impress. When she went off to help someone else, the imp Ivy flashed a morbid smile usually reserved for ladies with their skirts tucked into their pantyhose. Something was going on, but I didn't have time for speculation.

I tore open my envelope and pulled out my itinerary. Inside was a thin slip of red paper.

LAST MINUTE CHANGES. AGENT HARALD GREENE IS SUFFERING A SUDDEN ILLNESS AND WILL NOT BE ABLE TO CONDUCT HIS INTERVIEWS ON SATURDAY. ALL PARTICIPANTS WHO REQUESTED INTERVIEWS WITH MR. GREENE FOR SATURDAY ARE TO REPORT TO THE CONFERENCE DESK WHERE THEY WILL BE ROUTED TO OTHER

AGENTS. NO REFUNDS WILL BE OFFERED AT THIS TIME. MR. GREENE IS UNDER A
PHYSICIAN'S CARE AND IS EXPECTED TO RECOVER BY SUNDAY.

I guess my luck was not so bad after all. I'd considered requesting an
appointment with Mr. Greene, but in the end I selected other agents. It
seemed that after such a rocky start, at least the day wouldn't get any worse.

Then the door opened and the attendees poured out. Writers in suits,
writers in jeans, writers in dresses, writers in costumes. Big writers, small
writers, old writers, young writers. Writers with gray hair, writers with
no hair, writers with hair in shades that nature never intended. They all
came pouring out. Hundreds of them. I wondered how any ballroom
could possibly be large enough, and they still kept coming. A stampede of
budding literary minds had the same genius idea I had and descended on
Malibu, California in search of their big break in publishing.

What were the odds that a simple Midwestern girl like me could make a
lasting impression on the dozen or so agents in attendance?

Answer: not good.

My first appointment was with a Ms. Judy Simons, who turned out to be
a well-dressed woman in her thirties with graying-brown hair and a tastefully Parisian-looking scarf. She gushed profusely about how much she
enjoyed my first ten pages and how she couldn't wait to read the rest. But
when I held the manuscript out to her, she wrinkled her nose as if I was
offering her a sandwich that I'd already taken a bite out of. She told me to
e-mail it to her, since she didn't have room in her luggage.

I rushed over to tell Ivy, because frankly, I had to tell someone.

That's when I learned that Judy Simons had a reputation as a "non-
responder." Apparently, that's the sort of agent who claims she loves your
writing so you'll feel like you got your money's worth, but after you send
her your manuscript, you'll never hear from her again. A group of Ivy's
writer friends decided to test the theory with the worst samples they could
come up with. One wrote a haunting love story, but drew a bunch of
x-rated cartoons all over the margins of page eight to see if she gets that
far. The mad cartoonist won her agent's choice award that year, proving
that either Judy Simons never gets to page eight, or she really has a thing
for the Smurfs.

The next few interviews were less colorful. Some agents liked my descriptions, but not my dialogue. Some liked my dialogue but not my descriptions. Some thought my work was too original, some thought it wasn't original enough. They all thought the manuscript was too long and urged me to trim it down to three hundred pages at the most.

The more I heard, the more heartsick and disillusioned I became. I felt myself weakening, but then again I was still dragging my suitcase, and I hadn't eaten that morning. The conference included breakfast, but since I was late, I'd missed it. Lunch wouldn't be served for another hour. But I was too nervous to eat since my final appointment for that day was with Gertrude Hastings, who Ivy assured me was "one crazy bitch."

I entered a teak-paneled meeting room and a tiny old woman with close-cropped white hair and a purple caftan smiled up at me. I'd expected an ogre, but she looked like Jimmy Carter in drag. Seeing that she clearly had not bathed in the lifeblood of unpublished authors, I breathed a sigh of relief.

"Ms. Hastings?" I extended my hand.

She took it and squeezed with surprising vitality. "You must be Amanda. It is so nice to meet you, please have a seat."

As I sat, she reached into her macramé satchel and pulled out a folder containing my sample pages. I waited while she stared at it with a confused expression as if it had suddenly materialized out of thin air. She glanced up at me.

"I'm going to be perfectly honest with you. I found this to be well written and it held my interest, but there is nothing exactly like it on the shelves right now."

"Well, that's good, right?"

Ms. Hastings frowned. "No that's not good. How am I supposed to sell a book that hasn't been written before?"

I blinked, certain I'd misheard. "I'm not sure I know what you mean."

She took a deep breath and spoke slowly. "Publishers don't like to take risks. You are unpublished. Therefore when they ask me how many copies of your book will sell, what am I supposed to tell them?"

I felt like I was in the middle of a verbal minefield. I was afraid to speak, but I couldn't just sit in this chair and not answer until my time ran out. "You could tell them that nothing in life is predetermined. There is risk in all ventures, but the work is strong, so they should put their faith into it."

Ms. Hastings nodded, and my heart roared. She liked my answer.

"When were you born?" she asked.

"I'm twenty-six. I'll be twenty-seven in about four months."

"No, I need to know your date of birth."

"September fifth?" I knew when I was born, I just didn't know why she was asking.

"You're a Virgo. That's an Earth sign. I'm afraid this isn't going to work. I can't sign you."

I wondered if this was a joke but she looked deadly serious. "You're rejecting me on the basis of my horoscope?"

She gave a look of pity. "I'm sorry. You're a good writer. But I can't change what's written in the stars."

I felt weak. "Oh, come on, you can't possibly believe everyone who was born in the same week I was is having the same luck right now. Please, I beg you. If you think my work is good, give me a chance."

"Very well, I'll give you one shot."

It took all my composure to keep from squealing and clapping my hands together, until she reached into her bag and drew out a deck of cards. She fanned them in her hand and then held them out.

"Pick a card."

I hesitated then drew a card and placed it face down on the table in front of me. She flipped it over and revealed a drawing of a woman with a baton in each hand, surrounded by a garland of snakes.

"Is that good?"

She jabbed it with her finger. "That's the Fame card. It is the highest ranked card in the deck. It signifies success. This card guarantees great fortune to whomever is lucky enough to draw it. Unfortunately for you, it's reversed."

"Reversed?"

She snatched the card and replaced the deck in her bag. "When a card is reversed it takes on the opposite meaning. That means you will never amount to anything as a writer."

I sat there as her words ripped my heart to shreds. "It didn't look reversed to me."

"Trust me, when I flipped it over it was reversed."

"Well, then, maybe it's you who will never amount to anything as a writer." I smiled at my simple attempt at levity, until I saw the murderous glint in Ms. Hasting's eyes. Her fingers hooked into claws around the table and a blue vein rose out in bas-relief against her rapidly flushing forehead.

She gave me one last venomous look before she pushed back her chair.

"You know what? I don't have to take this from you! I was going to try to be nice, but since you aren't taking this seriously, I'm just going to spell it out for you: no publisher is going to buy your book. And seeing as how you're more interested in smarting off than in being published, I'm leaving."

She got up and stormed out of the room in a huff of purple caftan with a full two minutes left in my appointment. Two minutes is a long time when you've paid for ten. I just sat there unsure of what to do.

I really did need a pastry and as soon as possible. When I stood up, I noticed a card had dropped onto the floor. I picked it up. It depicted three gray and naked people standing in shallow graves, their arms outstretched to a floating angel playing a trumpet. I shuddered and left it on the table.

I wheeled my suitcase to the hotel's coffee shop and peered at the selection. They had the full spread: muffins, Danish, éclairs, and my personal favorite, iced cinnamon rolls, still warm from the oven and dripping with white-frosted goodness. Even more seductive was the lemonade machine. Its motor hummed out its siren song as slices of lemon and perfect little cubes of ice danced an aquatic ballet for me in their tank of shimmering topaz. Normally, I don't even like lemonade; I'm more the margarita type. Nevertheless, what I needed at that moment was a tall dewy glass to drown my sorrows—as soon as I'd checked into my hotel room and dropped off my luggage.

By the time I'd returned, the line in the coffee shop stretched out the door. Everyone must have gotten out of their interviews at the same time and had the same thought I did.

And the closer I got, the more apparent it was that the line wasn't moving. Several people in the queue mumbled in frustration, and one poor soul was even pacing back and forth like an expectant father.

Normally, I would've just joined the pack and suffered in silence, but my meeting with Ms. Hasting had put me in a rare temper. I marched past the line to see what the trouble was.

I should have known. Ivy was leaning on the counter in her tank top and tutu and holding a paper cup. Behind the counter, a boy shrank in terror under his paper cap as a muscular behemoth of a woman with a badge that read "Sherri" stood with her arms crossed staring daggers at Ivy's tattoos.

"I'm the manager. You wanted to talk to me?"

"Your employee made a mistake," Ivy said. "Could you please void the register?"

"Now why would I do that?"

Ivy proceeded with the explanation. "I came in here a few minutes ago and I bought a cup of coffee. I set my laptop down at one of your tables, I took a sip, and then I noticed that the cup felt a little light. I lifted the lid and saw that your boy had only filled the cup three-quarters of the way. No problem. It was an honest mistake. I walked back to the counter and asked him to top it off, which he did, but then the idiot rang me up for a refill."

"And?"

"And nothing. Please void the register so I can get back to my laptop, which is currently unguarded."

"No," Sherri said. "You're paying for the refill."

Ivy scoffed. "Like hell I am. Re-fill implies that cup had been filled at one time, which I assure you, never happened. I never got what I paid for."

At our backs, the line was turning feral, but the amazons at the counter didn't seem to notice or care.

"You admit you drank out of the cup. Therefore, you accepted the transaction. Since you want more coffee, you are legally obligated to pay for a refill. Otherwise I'll have no choice but to call hotel security and report you for shoplifting."

Ivy's cheeks went crimson. "You do that and I'll sue your huge ass out from under you."

Meanwhile the counter boy was slinking away like a lizard who'd detached its tail and hoped no one noticed amid all the thrashing. Poor boy, it was probably his first job out of high school and here were these two harpies, scaring the ambition right out of him.

"Excuse me," I whispered to him. "How much is it for a refill?"

His face lit up at the mercy in my voice. "It's fifty cents."

Fifty cents? Two women were locked in mortal combat over fifty goddamned *cents*? Don't get me wrong, I was as broke as the next starving artist, but if I were to threaten legal action, it wouldn't be over the type of money that rolled when I dropped it.

I barged my way into the melee. "Hello, Sherri. I'm Ivy's friend Amanda. I'd be happy to pay for her refill, as well as a medium glass of lemonade and that cinnamon roll right over there."

The boy took my ten-dollar bill. Behind me, I could hear the contented hum of the line, now that order had been restored and it was moving again.

I dropped a dollar into the boy's tip cup for good measure before I pulled the last bit of paper from the straw and took my first victorious sip. It tasted like heaven.

I expected Ivy to be annoyed and a little angry with me for getting involved like that, but she let out a relieved sigh and leaned in close.

"You know, I swore I'd kill the next bitch that called security on me, and that woman was making it way too easy. Thank you for saving her life."

I shrugged. "I'm always happy to help out when I can." And if I managed to cut to the front of the line to get my lemonade and my sweet roll, so much the better.

She pointed her coffee cup at the table that held her laptop. "Come sit with me. I'm dying to know how it went with Hastings."

"Traumatic." I said as we slid into the seats, "I'm trying to repress the memory of it even as we speak."

Ivy's eyes lit up. "Do tell."

"She had me pick a tarot card, and I drew Fame, reversed."

"Does that mean you'll be infamous or unfamous?"

"It doesn't mean anything. It's just a piece of cardboard with a cartoon printed on it. Speaking of which, she dropped one of her cards."

"I told you she wasn't playing with a full deck. She's never been quite right in the head since she was abducted by aliens back in '03."

"You're joking, right?"

"She blogs about it." Ivy narrowed her eyes at me. "Don't you screen your agents?"

I narrowed my eyes right back. "Don't you?"

She smirked. "If by me, you mean this den of thieves that employs me and their non-existent screening process, I would like to say that there are many fine conferences that make dreams come true. Unfortunately this isn't one of them."

I felt my face go red, but I doubt she noticed since she'd set her cup to one side and pecked away into her laptop with one finger.

"What are you working on?"

"I'm writing my first novel. I'm about ten pages into it, but I need to have it done by March of next year. Typing is a lot harder than I thought it would be."

"Well if you think typing is hard, just wait until you have to talk to agents."

Ivy didn't even look up from her keyboard. "I'm not getting an agent."

I felt a flush of superiority wash over me. "So you're going the vanity press route? Well good luck with that, because I hear that you'll never get your money back."

Ivy looked up with her mouth pinched into a vaguely guilty expression.

I raised the straw to my lips. "I suppose you have an angle?"

"My angle is that I already have a three-book deal from Castlegate Press."

I removed the straw from my mouth to keep from swallowing it.

"How is that possible? I heard that publishers won't even look at you unless you have a top agent, and no top agent will sign you unless you have a completed manuscript, and even then it has to be brilliant."

Ivy nodded. "That's one way. The publishing industry is like a convenience store. The front door has locks, cameras, and an angry foreigner watching your every move. But if you go around to the back, you'll find a door that's propped open with a bucket."

"But...you don't even know how to type."

Ivy finished her coffee. "It's like this: I'm an art student over at City College. I do a cartoon about my job called *Confessions at the Piercing Pagoda* for the school paper. It just so happens that one of the interns at Castlegate also goes to City and brought a paper to work with her. An editor saw it, and the next thing I knew, I got a call asking if I'd be willing to convert my observations into novel form."

I buried my head in my arms as I lost the will to live.

Ivy touched my shoulder. "Hey, sweetie, are you okay?"

Was I okay? Let's see: I'd just spent the past ten years of my life writing a trunk full of novels while working multiple dead-end jobs to put myself though college. I'd dedicated three months to learning to write a query letter, four months to learning to write a synopsis. I'd spent my entire life's savings on a ticket to this con-job, only to be baited and bullied by what Ivy had informed me were the dregs of the industry. And why? Because I believed I needed to do this to have the tiniest fragment of a chance of getting my foot in the door.

And yet there I was, sharing a drink with a girl barely out of high school who got hit by a multi-book contract that just fell out of the sky.

Ivy gave me a guilty smile. "If it makes you feel any better, it isn't a very good contract. I'm still working here, aren't I?"

"That's completely beside the point. I'd pay them!"

"You really want an agent that badly?"

"More than anything."

"I can get you an agent."

"Really? Just like that?"

Ivy packed up her laptop and nodded. Her eyes were bright with mischief, which made me a little uneasy. "Does this agent have a name?"

Ivy lowered her voice. "I'm fairly certain that Harald Greene will be dying to sign you, after I have a quick word with him."

As wonderful as that sounded, I was beginning to question her sanity. "Harald Greene? But isn't he already dying of some illness?"

"That's what he told Mrs. Brasher. But I heard him tell his cell phone a different tale. See that bar?"

Ivy pointed across the corridor to the shamrock emblem of the Irish pub called *The Rogue's Tavern*, where I could barely make out a soccer game commencing on the big screen over an oak bar decorated with ferns.

"Yeah?"

"He's in there right now, watching the game. He never intended to be sick, but he had no way of knowing that his team would make the playoffs. As far as I'm concerned, that's embezzling. As an employee of this conference, I have a moral obligation to make his life very unhappy, unless he gives us a good reason not to."

I sucked in a deep breath. "But that's blackmail."

Ivy smiled. "I prefer to think of it as two wrongs making you a writer."

"Thank you, I appreciate that, I really do. But I don't want an agent that lies, and drinks before noon, and weasels out of his business commitments to watch the big game."

"I take it you haven't met a lot of agents?"

"Look, a thief is a thief. If he's an embezzler, how can I trust him with my royalty checks?"

Ivy looked at me as if I'd gone insane. "You don't sign the contract. You just wave it in the face of the agent you really want."

"Huh?"

"Let me break this down for you, Princess Blue Badge. Right now, you're an unpublished author trying to get an agent. That's like a chess geek trying to get a date with a cheerleader. You have to figure they'll all say no, just on general principle, but it's a lot easier if everyone thinks you've already got one interested in you."

"Hey, I'll have you know that I was a cheerleader, and there were some really hot guys on our chess team."

Ivy smiled in admiration. "Well, good for you. You just went up another notch in my estimation." She glanced at the bar and then grabbed my wrist. "And speaking of hot guys, do you see what I see?"

Her full attention was drawn to the bar. Or more specifically, the bartender. The dark, lanky, heavily-tattooed bartender. Even from a distance, I could tell he was wearing thick eyeliner as he polished a glass and returned Ivy's gaze across the corridor.

"The greaseball bartender? He looks like a hobo."

"He looks like a hot hobo, which is exactly my type." Ivy packed up her laptop and slung the case across her chest like a bandolier. "Now if you excuse me I'm off to meet the father of my children."

She drifted toward the bar as if caught in a magnetic field of physical chemistry.

What a crazy girl.

CHAPTER 3

There was time to kill before lunch so I attended a lecture called *Social Networking and Marketing Using Facebook.*

If the instructor was to be believed, publishers have no marketing budget and instead rely on their authors to do their own publicity. And 'publicity' in this context meant shedding all vestiges of pride and dignity in front of as many people as possible so that complete strangers will take pity on you and buy your book.

Make friends with all your friends' friends and tell them to buy your book. Look up long lost lovers and tell them to buy your book. Crash weddings and funerals and tell people to buy your book. Strike up friendships with creeps who are sending you pictures of their junk and tell them to buy your book. Turn every social interaction into a venue you can use to sell your book. You aren't you anymore; you're a vehicle for your book. Heaven help you if you disappoint the publisher who took you in when nobody else wanted you.

I thought back to a sad documentary I once saw on teenage runaways who came to Hollywood looking for fame and fortune only to be brainwashed by pimps on Sunset Boulevard. It made me feel dirty then and it made me feel dirty now. After hearing that talk, I wasn't sure that I wanted to be a writer anymore. I saw a middle-aged woman with a decidedly Victorian flair record furiously into her chintz notebook. I got a sudden vision of her working a stripper pole in her orthopedic bra and granny panties and had to look away.

At this point, it was lunchtime. With a heavy heart, I made my way back to the ballroom, where attendees pushed their way along sideboards covered with turkey, roast beef, and vegetable sandwiches, while soft drinks chilled in tubs of ice near the plastic cutlery. I scanned the room, looking for Ivy. I found her at a table sitting with the bartender. Like most people in the room, he was wearing a white conference name tag. I found it highly improbable that he was a paying attendee and I couldn't help but smile.

She saw me, pointed to the bartender, and gave me a wink and the a-ok signal before she made beckoning motions to join them. As I reached for a turkey sandwich and a Diet Coke, the conference organizer, Mrs. Brasher, appeared in front of me.

"Oh, no, Ms. Anderson, that isn't for you." She pulled the items out of my hands, placed them on the table, and led me by the arm. "We have a place for you in the other room."

"What other room?" I glanced back at Ivy.

"White badges eat in the white room and blue badges eat in the blue room." Mrs. Brasher said.

"But I want to sit in here."

"That's very noble of you Ms. Anderson, but rules are rules. Once you're done eating, you can come and go as you please."

That seemed like a pretty silly and arbitrary method of running a conference lunch. I shot a quick apologetic glance to Ivy and her friend. Mrs. Brasher slid open a door and I saw where she led me.

The blue room was far smaller than the white room, and hung with blue curtains and a crystal chandelier. A single circular table was covered with a blue linen tablecloth and set with real flowers. The occupants of the table sat in the traditional male-female seating arrangement. They greeted me with warm smiles as Mrs. Brasher directed me to the single empty seat, situated between a bronze-haired young Adonis in a suit, and an older yet ruggedly handsome gentleman in a polo shirt and khakis. Both men rose until I took my seat.

I picked up the knife next to the dinner plate. The weight of it impressed me. "I guess we've been invited to the captain's table."

Several people gave me a polite chuckle, although their smiles stopped far below their cheekbones.

"How witty," said a waif-thin woman in a man's suit and a black pageboy haircut. "Are you a writer?"

I gave her a polite little geisha-laugh of my own, but the others didn't seem to see the irony in her statement. "Why, yes," I stammered to help her keep face. "I am a writer."

"Well, what do you know?" The older gentleman in the polo shirt to my left said. "I'm a writer too. Two writers at a writer's conference, what are the odds?"

This got a polite laugh from the other side of the table as a waiter served the salads. I noticed marinated straw mushrooms and baby asparagus mixed in with field greens. I looked up with alarm. "We're not going to be charged for this, are we?"

This got another laugh. A ghostly pale blonde in a black chiffon dress leaned forward. Her wrinkled mouth puckered as she strained to read my badge. "Amanda Anderson, you are a delight."

"That's my name too," the woman with the black hair said. "Amanda Andersen. Only my family is originally from Denmark so we spell Andersen with an E."

I turned to the gentleman in the polo shirt. "I actually get this quite often. You wouldn't think that Amanda would be so common for women named Anderson, but parents seem to like the alliteration."

He smiled at me, and the corners of his eyes actually did wrinkle with genuine interest.

The Adonis on my other side cleared his throat. "Ms. Anderson, you mentioned that you are a writer. How many books have you written?"

"Too many," I said.

"And how many is too many?"

"At least seven or eight. But the first three weren't any good."

"You're very modest," he said. "After delighting in your wit and charm, I can't assume that they are anything less than wonderful."

If that's the case, I thought, he must be too easily amused. Though I smiled at the compliment, and when he smiled back, I could see the light of the chandelier gleaming upon his perfect teeth.

"So what is the title of your latest?" the other Amanda asked.

"It's a thriller called *The Ice Cathedral*."

"Yes, I think I've heard of it," said a bald man in a cable-knit sweater, "I believe it was a best-seller not too long ago."

As I finished my salad, I hoped he was wrong since I liked that title and didn't want to change it.

"And what about you?" I asked the Adonis. "What do you write?"

"I'm not a writer," he said. "I'm an agent."

"Oh." I stole a glance at his badge. Jake Spenser. I knew the name. He had made the top twenty agents list in my genre four years in a row. I'd just wasted a month's wages having my heart broken by lesser agents for fear that I'd appear invisible to an agent of his stature, and yet here we were, dining together under a glimmering chandelier.

"So, who is your agent?" Jake asked, as if to confirm that this was all too good to be true and I was going to wake up at any moment.

"I don't have one," I said.

"Oh, I admire that," The Amanda in the man-suit said.

"I do too," said the man in the cable-knit. "It really is so brave of you to blaze a trail all on your own."

"Actually, I do want an agent," I said. "That's why I'm here. I'm hoping to find one."

At my right, the Greek God Jake reached into his pocket. "Let me find my card. I know that you're probably swamped with offers, but I really hope you won't sign with anyone before you talk to me." He held up one hand and like a conjurer, a gold monogrammed business card appeared between his fingers.

I glanced at it for the briefest of moments before resuming eye contact. He looked deep into my eyes. "You are exactly the sort of author I represent. It's just a feeling right now, but my feelings are never wrong. Moreover, I can see in your eyes that you feel it too. We have a connection, you and I. A bond of sorts."

His finger caressed my wrist so lightly that nobody at the table would have noticed, but I felt it. My God, did I feel it.

"We are like a pair of kindred souls, and I can say from what I heard that you are really something special. You want to go to the next level, and I'm ready to take you there." He took my hand and folded my fingers around the card. "Call me, and we'll have the talk. Don't wait. I may not be able to sleep until I hear from you."

I felt my heart flutter and the older gentleman laughed. "And if after *the talk* you find that this bozo isn't to your taste, give me a call and I'll set you up with my guy, who could mop the floor with this slick-talking gigolo."

The younger man gave him a bitter look, but we all faced the waiter when he arrived with a cart loaded with our entrées. I hadn't gotten a straight answer as to who was financing this meal so I greeted the medallion of beef with its swirl of béarnaise sauce with mixed emotions. However, any hesitation I had vanished as soon as I had my first forkful. The chef had charred it perfectly. It was so tender that my knife sank right through and it practically dissolved in my mouth. The others seemed to share my appreciation. Everyone except for the gentleman in the polo shirt on my left.

I pointed to the filet that lay in front of him, untouched. "Are you a vegetarian?"

"Hardly," he said. "I'm just a man with too much sense to put undercooked food in his mouth. And far too much sense to send a dish back to be doctored by the kitchen staff. I intend to grab a plate of ribs after this. Would you care to join me?"

I gave him a coy look. I couldn't deny that he was handsome, in a devil-may-care way, but he was also old enough to be my father. "One lunch a day is enough for me, but thank you."

He seemed to take it in stride as he reached for the breadbasket. I turned to the dreamboat agent on my right, but he had the back of his head to me and was engaged in conversation with the woman on the other side of him. I turned back to the gentleman in the polo shirt.

"So you mentioned that you already have an agent?"

"Jeremy Stonewall Kendal. The best in the business. I can't say that he put me on the map, since I did that on my own, but he did untie me from the barrel they had me over while they were screwing me."

I laughed. "So you've been published by a mainstream press?"

"I take it you didn't pay attention during my keynote speech? Or to any of the New York Times Best Sellers lists for the past ten years?"

I stole a glance at his name tag, and then hyperventilated like a schoolgirl at a pop concert.

"You're Jonny Goodsnuff! THE Jonny Goodsnuff!"

"So I assume you have heard of me?"

"Heard of you! Everyone has heard of you! You're famous! Everyone, he's famous! He's like Stephen King famous! I can't believe they let people get this close to you." I knew I was annoying everyone with my fawning, but I just couldn't shut up.

I suddenly understood why the peasants in the middle ages collected relics of their saints. I just wanted to tear off a piece of his shirt and carry it around so that some of his success would rub off onto me. I turned to the others at the table and they were all staring back at me as if I'd just lost my mind. I suppose that in a way I had.

Jake frowned in annoyance. "You seem awfully star-struck for a writer with so many published novels under her belt."

"Oh, I haven't had anything published yet. That's why I need an agent."

The man in the cable-knit looked at the other Amanda and they nodded. Then the others at the table also nodded in some sort of telepathic agreement. "I'll be right back," the other Amanda said as she rose from the table.

She was out the door as the waiter wheeled in a cart with slices of cheesecake and cups for espresso. As they placed my slice in front of me, I saw that it was topped in a sauce made with figs stewed in port. My mouth watered and I almost forgot that I was sitting next to a celebrity. I raised my dessert fork, but lowered it as the others stared at my dessert like it was a ticking time bomb that might go off at any moment.

"Is something wrong?" I asked, but they remained silent. Maybe they expected me to say grace? Then I realized they were probably just waiting for the other Amanda to return. I set the fork down and the door burst open. Mrs. Brasher entered the room with Amanda Andersen at her heels.

"Miss Anderson, where did you get that blue badge?"

"You gave it to me this morning. Remember?"

"And why would I do that?"

"You told your assistant to hand me a blue badge, and when she questioned it, you repeated it to her. I didn't understand the significance of the blue badge versus the white. I still don't."

"The white badge is for paying attendees. The gray badge is for agents and editors. The blue badge is for industry executives, top grossing agents, and world-renowned authors. There has been a misunderstanding."

"It's okay," I said.

"No it's not okay. You need to leave this room at once." Before I could say anything, she grabbed my plate of cheesecake and dumped it into the bussing cart. I was unable to speak, so I just sat there, senseless at the waste of such a decadent dessert.

"Now, Miss Anderson. Leave. I told you that you can't be in this room."

As I stood up with as much dignity as I could muster, Jake Spenser placed one hand on my arm. "Amanda, wait."

When I turned toward him, his eyes were cold. "Can I have my card back?"

I ripped up his card into little pieces and flung them in his face before I strode out of the room.

Outside, the attendees were still in the main dining hall, chatting over freshly baked cookies. I searched the room for Ivy and her new beau, but they'd already left. I sighed and grabbed an oatmeal-raisin, which would have been delightful if I wasn't still in mourning for the slice of fig cheesecake.

Most of the tables were either crowded or empty, so I sat at a table half-filled with Sherlock Holmes re-enactors.

"Excuse me," said a woman in a deerstalker. "This is our table."

"Screw you and the dray-cart you rode in on." I stood and gave them a gesture that I'm sure they found anachronistic, before I took my sad little cookie to an empty table. This was shaping up to be one of the worst days of my life. And I'd had some pretty bad days. But none were quite so public. Or expensive. I couldn't believe I'd flown out all the way from the Midwest just to be disillusioned and humiliated. I was only dimly aware of the slice of fig-topped cheesecake that slid in front of me.

"I thought you might need this." World-famous writer Jonny Goodsnuff slid into the seat next to mine.

My heart brimmed with gratitude, but I was afraid to show it, just in case the universe wasn't through having its little laugh at my expense. "You don't want it?"

"I never eat dessert on an empty stomach. That's how people my age get fat."

I speared the fork into it before he had a chance to change his mind. "Shouldn't you be in the VIP room with your friends?"

"They're not my friends. These people out here are my friends. The paying public. The ones that line up outside the bookstores at midnight so they can read my latest novel before their coworkers spoil it for them. Without them I wouldn't have a job and neither would any of those people in that room. I think they forget that sometimes. I'm sorry that you were treated so badly back there."

"Don't worry. It wasn't nearly as mortifying as being snubbed by The Baker Street Irregulars."

Goodsnuff laughed, but then his face became serious. "You mentioned that you're a writer. What sort of stories do you write?"

I sighed and mashed at my cheesecake with my fork. "The novel I'm pitching is a thriller called *The Ice Cathedral*. It's about a plane that crashes with a serial killer on board, so my heroine has to try to get the other survivors, including a wounded air marshal, to safety. Pretty stupid, huh?"

"No, that sounds like pure genius."

I felt myself blushing. "Do you really think so?"

"I know so. You managed to touch upon a unique plot that taps into every sort of conflict. Your protagonist has to battle a serial killer, the elements, the Grim Reaper, and I assume her own insecurities as well as a budding romance with the air marshal – which, if it doesn't exist really should. I'd guess that once someone began reading this, it would be a difficult book to put down."

"I wish I could find just one agent that agrees with you."

"Well, times are tough. When's the last time you've seen an overnight success come out of a major publishing house? You just need to stick with it until you catch a lucky break." He rose. "Now if you'll excuse me, I'm going to grab a real lunch so that I can get back in time for my next seminar. Are you sure I can't interest you in a plate of spareribs?"

"Sorry, I make it a point never to eat with my hands on the first date." I spoke without thinking and then blushed when I realized how forward that sounded, but Jonny didn't seem to notice.

"Do you have a copy of my latest novel?"

I felt myself go redder as I shook my head. It wasn't until that moment that I realized that I'd never actually read anything he'd written. But his attention was on his satchel as he dug out a hardcover book. On the red cover, the words JONNY GOODSNUFF jumped out in marquee size letters, and printed below it, like an afterthought, was the title: *The Limits of Risk*. I took in the minimalist cover with its three bullets in a simple stripe of white before he flipped it open. "I'll even sign it for you so you'll have something to show your grandkids."

He quickly scrawled something onto the inside cover before he closed it and surprised me with a kiss on the cheek. "Enjoy the rest of the conference. I sincerely hope that we'll meet again."

I waited until he was gone before I opened it to see what he had written.

Room 345. Any time after 10:00p.m. tonight. Don't knock, just enter.

CHAPTER 4

It was 9:45PM. I lay in my bed, counting the tiles in the ceiling and wondering what to do.

It wasn't that I was afraid of being seduced. I wanted to be seduced. Especially by a living legend like Jonny Goodsnuff. I wouldn't say I was exactly promiscuous, but I did have my fair share of college flings: romances that I knew wouldn't survive the end of the semester, or even the end of spring break. Add to that the guys who said they'd call but didn't, the guys I'd caught walking with their fiancées, the guys who couldn't start it, the guys who couldn't finish it, the guys who finished too quickly or not quickly enough for me...

Needless to say, if Jonny Goodsnuff proved to be a disappointment he'd have plenty of company, and I'd still have a fantastic story to tell my grandchildren.

But with everything that had gone wrong on this trip, I couldn't see how this could possibly go right. I tried to imagine the worst that could happen and had visions of the paramedics asking me what I was doing at the exact moment Jonny Goodsnuff suffered his massive heart attack.

No. That was just silly. Bad luck didn't breed more bad luck. Not unless my irrational superstitions kept me locked in my room all night. I got up from the bed to get my one good cocktail dress. I took one look at it dangling from its hanger before I came to my senses and left it in the closet. No sense in going to Jonny Goodsnuff looking like a call girl.

But I did make an extra effort with my makeup, and brushed my hair out until it shimmered before pinning it back into what I knew was a sexy ponytail. I left my room, locking the door behind me, and walked until I was outside room 345. I raised my fist to knock, until I remembered that Jonny had written not to do so.

I pushed the door, which creaked open.

Inside, I saw a room that was significantly larger than my own, but still not nearly as grand as I'd want to stay in if I were an author of Jonny Goodsnuff's caliber. From the open door of the bathroom, I could hear the tinkling of the shower.

"Amanda, is that you?"

"It sure is."

"I'll be out in a minute. I wasn't expecting you so soon."

I looked at the clock on the nightstand. It read 10:13PM. There was a gift basket next to the clock, and on the desk was an electric typewriter with a thin stack of paper next to it. I paused when I heard the shower stop. But then the bathroom door closed and I heard the buzz of the hairdryer, so I picked up the stack of papers and read the first line.

People in glass houses shouldn't stow bones.

Cute, I thought, then shrieked as Jonny snatched the manuscript out of my hand.

"What are you doing!" He screamed. "Don't touch that!"

Too late, I remembered Ivy's warning about how jumpy he is about his manuscript. I backed against the dresser as Jonny advanced. He wore a towel and his eyes were wild, like a rabid animal's. That should have been all of the warning I needed to bolt from the room and have nothing further to do with him. But to be honest, his reaction wasn't that different than my own whenever I caught a hot guy I'd just hooked up with snooping around on my laptop.

"I'm sorry. I know that's none of my business. I didn't mean to pry, I just wasn't thinking."

That didn't seem to mollify him in the slightest. "What did you see!"

"Nothing, I just read the first line."

Jonny stared at me as if deciding whether to believe me. He studied the first couple of pages, then yanked the half-finished sheet out of the type-writer and put the entire stack in the room's safe.

He tested it to make sure it was locked, and then drew a deep breath. "I'm sorry I snapped at you like that, but nobody is allowed to look at that, not even my agent. Right now, he's shopping it to our publishers even thought he has absolutely no idea what it's about. It's vitally important that this manuscript remains cloaked in absolute secrecy until it's finished."

"I understand," I said. "Do you want me to leave?"

"Not at all." He gave me a sad look. "Do you want to leave?"

I shook my head. "Not at all."

He went to the room's mini-bar. "May I offer you a drink?"

"I'll take gin and tonic, if you have it."

"All I've got is Scotch, but it's the good stuff."

"I'll take a Scotch then."

He poured a couple of glasses, and I sat on the edge the bed and took a few sips. I was never a fan of Scotch, but seeing as how I was with Jonny Goodsnuff in the flesh, and very nearly in the buff, I needed something to steady my nerves.

"So." He stood in front of me. "Did you bring your manuscript?"

I clutched the glass in both hands. "My manuscript?"

"Your manuscript. I thought maybe you came up here to show me your writing."

"Oh," I said. "I'm sorry. I guess I misunderstood."

He smiled and flung away the towel. "Well then, I guess I can drop the pretense and get down to business.

I averted my eyes before I could get a good look. He leaned toward me, and I drew back. He tried to kiss me and I twisted my eyes shut and sat there shaking.

Maybe I was still frightened. Or maybe it was because he was old enough to be my father. Or maybe I was worried that I'd do something else wrong. Or maybe the thought of me and Jonny was just too intense to handle. My intuition was warning me to run away as fast as I could. All I knew was that I wanted to get back to my room, but not if it meant I'd never see him again.

"You're afraid."

"I'm sorry," I said.

I heard Jonny reach for the towel and I opened my eyes as he wrapped it around his loins.

"Don't apologize. I think it's charming. You wouldn't believe the number of sluts that I have hurling themselves at me. It's refreshing to meet an old-fashioned girl who knows how to act like a lady."

I didn't know what to say to that, so I said nothing.

"Do you like me?"

"I like you. I just don't think I'm ready for this."

"I can take you home. Or are you staying here in the hotel?"

"I'm in Room 207. I have the room until Monday."

"So does that mean that you'll be at the conference tomorrow?"

I nodded.

"Well then, I guess I'll see you tomorrow. Oh, and Amanda? If you have any plans for dinner tomorrow you might want to break them."

CHAPTER 5

I woke before the alarm feeling bright, sunny, and ready to take on the world. I gave Ivy a cheery good morning as I passed her desk on the way to the breakfast room.

"Hey, how did it go with you and your bartender?"

Ivy gestured to her tank top and tutu. "I'm still wearing the same clothes as yesterday, aren't I?"

"I thought maybe that was your work uniform."

"With the night I had last night, maybe it should be. I think he's the one. He brought me back to his apartment and he has the most amazing book collection. But enough about my conquests. Did you have any luck in the VIP room?"

"Before or after Mrs. Brasher realized that she'd made a horrible mistake and threw me out?"

Ivy cast her eyes down. "Sorry about that. I knew that she was confusing you with Amanda Andersen the filmmaker, but I'm not one to stand between a struggling artist and a free steak luncheon. I should have known that no good would come of it."

"Oh, don't be sorry. I'm sure I'll laugh about it someday. And it wasn't a total disaster. Tonight I just might get lucky after all."

She lowered her voice to a stage whisper. "Really? Come sit with me. I want to hear all the dirt on the VIPs."

Normally, I don't like to kiss and tell, but Ivy had taught me everything I knew about how publishing really works, so the least I could do is dish a little dirt in her direction.

"Well," I settled into the chair next to hers, "we all got along great when I was an internationally renowned author. They laughed at all my jokes and Jake Spenser even offered to sign me, work unseen, based on this amazing connection we had."

Ivy brought her hands to her cheeks in mock outrage. "No! He gave you the pimp talk?"

"That he did. Then someone realized that they had one Amanda too many and she went for Mrs. Brasher, who came in and pulled the cheesecake right out of my hand. Then Jonny Goodsnuff took pity on me and gave me his. We hit it off quite nicely. In fact, he invited me up for a nightcap."

Ivy bounced up and down with delight. "Oh, you whore! Did you do it?"

"Go up to his room for a nightcap?"

"Yes, that too!"

I gave her a coy glance. "I did have the nightcap, but I think we both chickened out on the sex. I'm going to try again tonight."

She reached her tattooed arm into her purse and pulled out a business card. "If I don't see you again, call me. I need to know if you got lucky. With the agents and otherwise."

I took the card, which featured a cartoon pagoda surrounded by pink and purple cherry blossoms. The words IVY JOIE - SENIOR HENNA TECHNICIAN appeared in faux kanji. "Is this a real card?"

"The name is real. What's sad is that Ivy is short for Ivory. Ivory Joie. Doesn't that sound like it was taken straight out of a Victorian porno?"

"I was thinking multipurpose dish-soap."

Ivy laughed. "That's what happens when your parents name you when they're still in high school. You'd better get going before all the good pastries are gone."

I entered the ballroom, which was well stocked with croissants, bagels, and the aroma of freshly roasted coffee. The VIP table, complete with its blue cloth and floral arrangements had somehow migrated into the southeast corner of the mess hall, where a chef was preparing fresh omelets for the people who had merited their blue badges. Jonny Goodsnuff saw me and winked. I smiled back.

I took a coffee and a croissant and sat at a table to look over the schedule. Today was a short day. The convention closed at two o'clock and we were on our own for lunch. I had only one appointment left so I looked at the workshops. At nine, Gertrude Hastings was teaching a class on channeling our goddess power. I put a big X through that box. Another lecture was giving a talk on how to do an effective book signing. I was still a few years away from needing that one. The only other class was called "Rudiments of Grammar."

Profound sigh. Grammar school it was.

I looked up and saw that Jonny Goodsnuff was glancing over at me and he grinned when our eyes met. I felt a wave of euphoria pass over me as I looked over the next batch of classes.

The eleven o'clock selections were a little more interesting. "Understanding how an agent manages his time and your money." That one looked promising, until I saw it was taught by Harald Greene. If Harald's clients understood how he spent his time and their money, he'd probably end up behind bars.

"How to get an agent's attention." I checked quickly to see if Ivy was teaching that one, but no such luck.

"Mastering the Art of Suspense with Jonny Goodsnuff." I felt my heart go pitter-pat as I drew a heart around that box instead of a circle.

The post lunch seminars were nondescript. They were either Q&A sessions or impromptu readings. I guess they figured that most people would want to take a long lunch or catch an early flight.

The lecture on grammar turned out to be amazingly informative, but the workshop with Jonny was far better. Not that I can remember a word he said. I was too preoccupied with trying to laugh at all of his jokes while my eyes conveyed the appropriate amounts of both intelligence and longing.

Every so often, our eyes would meet and he'd go red in the ears, as if there was any doubt in my mind whom the teacher's pet might be. I felt tingles of delight go through me, and it was all I could do to keep from leaning over to the girl next to me to tell her that I'd almost seen him naked.

After the workshop concluded, he stopped me in the hall. "What do you say we skip the rest of the conference and run away together?"

I clutched my notebook to my chest like a naughty schoolgirl. "I'd love to but I have one last agent interview."

"Call my room as soon as you're done. Don't forget I'm treating you to a night on the town."

"Now how could I forget a thing like that?"

To be honest, I hoped he'd talked me out of staying at the conference. With the way things were going, a hot date with Jonny Goodsnuff was going to be the only thing that made this trip worthwhile. But I couldn't dismiss the possibility that the next agent might fall in love with my book.

One glance at her told me that wasn't going to happen.

The agent was Elaine Spiranova, an older lady who looked as crusty as hell. I could see that we would never be friends or sit down over a couple glasses of wine and discuss what we were wearing the next day. I sat with my chin in my palm and felt jaded as I watched her read all ten pages and asked me for a summary of the plot. Then she shrugged.

I sighed. "What's wrong with it?"

"It's flat. There is no life to it. You write as if you were giving the pre-requisites for a course in organic chemistry. It would be different if you had some solid ideas buried in there, but do you realize how many books are written with the same kind of characters and plot?"

"I was told by another agent that it might be too original."

She nodded. "That may seem like a contradiction, but it is not. As a debut author, you have very few opportunities available to you in today's market. Regrettably, your skill is years away from being front-list, so your only option is to pare this down and sell it as a genre piece."

"Worse novels than mine get published every day."

"Yes, by established authors with followings. The deeper problem is that you lack a platform. You're counting on readers to discover you by acci-dent, and that probably won't happen."

I remembered the speech I'd recently dismissed on the marketing power of Facebook, which now didn't seem so shady and sordid after all. "So you think I should build an online following before I attempt to get this published?"

She shook her head. "No, that will eat up all your time and might get you sales in the hundreds. You'll need them in the tens of thousands. If I were you, I'd put this manuscript in a drawer and work on something else. Something more topical. If you can latch onto a subject of broad appeal, like a celebrity scandal or a tale of true crime, your readers will find you. Assuming a better known author doesn't beat you to market."

She replaced my unmarked materials into their folder. "Your writing has potential so I suggest you revisit this once you are better established, but I don't see this as a viable debut novel."

"That's interesting, since I was guaranteed an offer of representation, but I thought I'd take a day or two to think it over."

"I wish you luck then."

Our time ran out and I just sat there. Ivy said an offer would make me more attractive, yet she still wasn't interested, so my world became a cold and bitter place.

But that didn't mean I was giving up. There had to be a way.

CHAPTER 6

I suppose you could say that my date with Jonny began the moment I returned to my hotel room. I'd planned to touch up my makeup and pull a brush through my hair before changing into my red chiffon dress. Those plans went straight out when I saw an exquisite champagne satin gown laid out on my bed, as smooth and shimmery as a cool crystal stream.

When I read the label, I sucked in my breath. Valentino. I could sell everything I owned, including my car, and still not have enough money to afford the garment in my hand. At the foot of the bed was a pair of creamy Tuscan gold leather stiletto heels. Size seven. I'm a size eight. Not that I'm complaining.

So much for a quick change before dinner. I had a soak in the tub before I pinned my hair into a French twist, and pulled out my makeup kit to give my face an appropriately smoky evening look. I'd just pulled on the dress when the phone rang.

"Hello, Angel."

I couldn't help but smile. "Is this my fairy godfather?"

"More like your Prince Charming. I take it you like your presents?"

I blinked. Presents? I assumed the outfit was a rental. "Isn't floor length Valentino a little generous for a first date?"

"Babe, you ain't seen nothing yet. Prepare yourself for the night of your life."

I tugged a shoe onto my foot. It was a little tight in the toes, but the leather molded to my foot like a second skin. "I don't even get a little hint?"

"No hints. Just get dressed and come outside."

I stamped the other heel into place. "How will I find you?"

"I'll be waiting in the Jaguar."

As I walked through the hallway in my silk dress I could feel the stares of men as they peered at me over the shoulders of their wives. Not that I could blame them, or take all of the credit. Any woman would have been stunning in that gown. It was draped tastefully low in the front, scandalously low in back, and with a kick pleat to allow my legs to move. Had it been a cheaper dress in the same cut and style, I might have been mistaken for a high-end escort. But the cut was so exquisite that the overall effect was ethereal and unattainable, like a goddess from Mount Olympus. I didn't ask the men in the elevator to hold the door for me. I didn't have to.

I made my way out of the lobby and into the cool afternoon breeze and found the Jaguar. Jonny Goodsnuff emerged and opened the passenger side door for me. He was wearing a tuxedo and his mouth hung open.

"A tuxedo, Mr. Goodsnuff?"

"Please, Amanda," he said. "We are long past the misters. Just call me Jonny."

"I can't get over how amazing you look," Jonny said as we drove away from the hotel.

"It's the dress."

Jonny shook his head. "It's not the dress. When I met you yesterday, I couldn't stop thinking about how sweet and charming you are. But tonight it's like you're a whole other woman."

"I'm a professional makeup artist, so I know a lot about facial contouring. But the real secret is in the eye-makeup. Just open any tabloid magazine and you'll see the starlets have the cat-eye look, even if they're just going to the supermarket. The trick is to sweep the liner and shadow a quarter inch past the lash line, because there isn't a woman alive who doesn't look amazing—"

I stopped when I noticed that he wasn't paying attention. Great. A few minutes into the date and I was already boring him with shoptalk. I decided to change the subject. "Have you settled on a title for your next book?"

"It's called *Houses Made of Glass.*"

"I like it," I said. "What's it about?"

His face took on a look of foreboding and I remembered this was a taboo subject. "Sorry, I misspoke."

"Look, if I told you, I'd have to kill you. I know that's a cliché, but in this case it really is true."

I let out a deep breath. "Forget I asked. To be honest, I'd be a lot happier if you didn't ruin the surprise."

Jonny chuckled. "Babe, you just said a mouthful."

For a guy who didn't want to talk about it, he wasn't being very discreet. It was time for another change of subject. "So…want to hear what this latest agent had to say?"

"Absolutely."

I told him about my conversation with Elaine Spiranova, and to my surprise, he let out a belly laugh. "You see, that's the problem. Nobody takes risks anymore. Everyone just wants a free ride in a bandwagon, and those are a lot easier to spot from the back than the front."

"You don't think she's right?"

He snorted. "No, I think she's a myopic parasite like the rest of them. Of course she wants nothing to do with you when you're broke. Agents can smell money. Once you hit the best-seller list she'll be on her knees, apologizing for not giving your work the attention it deserved and begging for another chance."

I forced a smile, grateful that he was so supportive. But the truth was, she'd read ten pages of my work and he hadn't. While he lessened the sting, it allowed me to see that her advice had some merit. The paying public would probably be a lot more interested in a juicy tell-all about a hot date with Jonny Goodsnuff than in any of my serious novels. Not that I had any intention of writing one. At that point, I still had my soul.

For the rest of the ride, Jonny didn't grill me with small talk, which I felt was for the best. I certainly didn't want to tell him about my family, other than to say I was born in Ohio and was an only child. Not that I'd been abused or anything. I'd had a perfectly normal childhood, maybe a little too sheltered and a little too spoiled. Until I was about sixteen, and my father lost some money that wasn't really his to invest, and left town after draining all our bank accounts, including my college fund.

After that, my mother and I moved into an apartment, and she stayed out with her increasingly sketchy boyfriends, until one turned her on to heroin. After that, she no longer cared if she had a boyfriend. She didn't really care if she had an apartment either.

Aside from all that, what was there to talk about? My dead-end job? My godforsaken neighborhood? My ever-changing circle of friends—who had the annoying habit of moving far away and losing touch because they had been smarter about choosing their life's ambitions? My life bored even me. It would sound downright pathetic to a big star like Jonny Goodsnuff.

The car stopped. "We're here," Jonny announced.

A valet took the car and all I could see was a hundred bright flashes. Jonny offered me his hand and I stepped onto a red carpet, while photographers surged behind a velvet rope to get our picture. I took Jonny's arm and forced myself to smile and look straight ahead, despite the blinding flashes going off in my eyes. The path led into a huge auditorium filled with techno-music as a DJ clamped one hand over his earphone as he pumped his other fist in the air. Giant video monitors showed alternating images of flowers and exotic animals that morphed into beautiful painted women.

"Is this an award show?" I asked as we moved through a room filled with A-list actors and actresses. It was like being in a wax museum, but with figures that moved around and talked to one another.

"No, I'm afraid it's merely a charity auction. I agreed to this months ago. I hope you aren't too bored."

"Bored? Are you kidding me? This is amazing."

Jonny led me to a neon colored bar, where a herd of tiny Hollywood debutantes sipped brightly colored cocktails. Although we'd never met, I knew all their names. I lost the power to do anything more than smile and nod, and to my surprise, they smiled and waved back at me.

"I'll have a Scotch," Jonny said to the bartender. "Amanda, what would you like?" He must have realized that I was paralyzed from the jaw down. "Give me one of those green drinks with the slice of apple in it."

I took a sip and quickly regained the power of speech. "Is your life always this glamorous?"

"I'm afraid so. Personally, I prefer quiet, but seeing as how my books are all that's keeping my publisher in the black, they like to put me in the public eye every so often."

"I think it's wonderful."

"That's because you're not from around here. Eventually all these parties start to look alike and you recognize these functions for the ridiculous time drains that they really are." He gave me a small smile, "But I'm starting to see that it's all different with a beautiful girl on your arm. I feel like I'm seeing what you're seeing, and it's making it all fresh and new for me again."

I picked up on his hidden meaning. "You don't date?"

"I don't have time to date," he said. "Women throw themselves at me, of course, but these days you never know who you can trust. Every so often I'll meet a lady I'd like to call more than once, but I can't call every night, so eventually they get frustrated and find someone else."

"Oh." I tried to sound sympathetic but he must have mistaken my tone for concern. He took my hand and looked deep into my eyes.

"It would be different for us, Amanda. You're a writer. You understand what it's like to be a slave to your typewriter. To cancel plans because your agent might be trying to call you. To have to break off a tender moment to write something down so you won't forget it."

He stepped forward bringing his face close to mine. "I know we've just met but I feel like I've known you for a very long time. I'm becoming very fond of you. Maybe a little too fond, too quickly, if you know what I'm saying."

I touched his lapel. "I'm becoming very fond of you as well."

I thought he was going to kiss me, but instead he took my arm.

"Come," he said. "Let's see if we can find anything interesting at the auction tables."

We walked over to a long row of gift baskets, placards, and pouty models in simple black dresses showcasing designer jewelry. I stopped in front of one model dangling a cascade of chunky oval crystals from her willowy neck. As I approached, she held out her necklace so I could get a better look. I picked up the clipboard in front of her. The current bid was $50,000. I put it down like it was radioactive.

Jonny glanced at the necklace. "If you want it, just say so."

The thing was, I really didn't, so the offer made me uncomfortable. I'd always been a giver, not a taker. My favorite thing about the holidays was the satisfaction of finding the perfect gift for someone else. I'd never had a lot of money, but my list was small and intimate. To see a man offer that much money for a girl he'd just met was a little frightening to me.

Then I noticed a poster of the ocean at the other end of the table and made my way over there as if I was under a spell. I'm not sure what item it was supposed to represent. A sailing trip, a dinner, or a stay in a hotel most likely. Or it might have been something inappropriate because Jonny was giving me the oddest look.

"I have that image on a postcard," I said. "I keep it by my laptop to give me inspiration. If you really want to buy me something, buy me the ocean."

"Have you ever seen it?" Jonny asked. "Have you stood there and looked out at the ocean?"

I shook my head. "No, but it's always been a dream of mine."

"You have to see the ocean." Jonny glanced at his watch and then grabbed my arm and ushered me to the exit. "We have to hurry."

"We're leaving? Just like that?"

"Don't worry about it, we'll come back. This thing is going to drag on all night, but we've only got about two hours of daylight, and you really have to see the Pacific while the sun's still up."

I looked down at my gown. "We're really not dressed for the beach."

Jonny shrugged. "There is no experience on earth that's better than seeing the ocean for the first time as an adult. I saw it when I was in my forties, and I'm not ashamed to admit I cried like a baby. I know what I'm talking about. This will change your life."

This is going to sound stupid, but there was nothing that could have prepared me for my first sight of the ocean. Nothing. No picture, no post-card, not even television. None of those things gives you a sense of the way the salty wind stays on your lips and in your hair, or how the foam swirls as the waves lap the shore, or the way that the sunlight dances in the blue waters as it churns through the windswept cliffs and the golden sands.

But the most awe-striking thing was how very big the ocean was. Beyond the rolling surf, the blue water just stretched on forever without end, meeting the sky at a horizon so far off that I could make out the curving of the earth.

Even in the Valentino dress, I had to feel the sand under my toes, to have the water dance over my feet. I gave my shoes to Jonny, hiked up my skirt and went to where the sand grew hard and soggy. A wave crashed a few feet away and a ripple of foamy water came toward me. It sloshed around my ankles and I screamed at how icy cold it was as it splashed up past my knees. I ran back to Jonny. He caught me in his arms, laughing with a joy that matched my own.

There was a sense of peace that I'd never felt before as I realized how very small and achievable my dreams were. Anything was possible in a world that held such beauty. I had an overwhelming desire to pack up my things, quit my job, and sit here and write novels until I was amazingly successful. I was caught in a dream and I knew it. Even Jonny seemed to know as he caressed the curves of my body and whispered in my ear. "I told you this would change you forever."

I leaned back, and we kissed. He held me and for a long time we just stood there and kissed to the rhythm of the shrieking gulls and the crashing waves. Maybe he had taken liberties. I didn't care. He had shown me the greatest miracle of my life, so as far as I was concerned he was a sorcerer who had me under a spell.

Under the circumstances, isn't it only natural to fall in love?

CHAPTER 7

My euphoria lasted until dinner, while we waited for the waiter to take our order. Jonny had taken me to an exclusive cliff-side restaurant with a giant aquarium filling the far wall. Our booth was made of plum colored leather. Jonny smiled at me and I forced myself to smile back. The menu I'd been given didn't have prices printed on it, but I guessed that Jonny's did from the way he was holding it close to his chest like an especially good poker hand.

I still couldn't help but wonder why he'd go all out like this for a girl he'd just met. I began to worry that he needed a kidney, and I'd wake up in a tub filled with ice.

"Evening, Mr. Goodsnuff," said a young waiter with slicked hair and an apron. "Shall I start you off with a Scotch?"

"Yes, please. Is the shark steak good tonight?"

"It's inspired."

"I'll have that then, well-done with the string beans and scalloped potatoes. And also a side of stewed mushrooms."

"Excellent choices. And for the lady?"

I folded up my menu. "I'll have the crab cake appetizer, served as an entrée, and a glass of water."

"She'll have the crab cake appetizer, served as an appetizer, and the Lobster Thermidor. And we'll each take the suggested wine pairing served with the entrees."

"Very good, sir," the waiter said as he took our menus and retreated to the kitchen.

"Jonny," I said in a stage whisper.

"You do like lobster, don't you?"

"This is too much."

"If you're concerned about the calories, I intend to help you with the crab cakes."

"That's not what I meant, and you know it."

Jonny took my hand. "I wouldn't worry about the bill if I were you. It's not as if I'm paying for any of this out of my own pocket. I'm going to send all the receipts to my agent and he'll forward them to my publisher for reimbursement."

"And they'll cut you a check? Just like that?"

"They'd better, or else I'll tell him to walk out of the contract negotiations and go somewhere else." He gave my hand a gentle squeeze. "I wouldn't feel badly for them if I were you. They've been screwing me for decades. I blame my last agent, he was a true birdbrain. My new guy? Now there's an artist! He could sell you your own car and you'd be laughing on the drive home about how you got the better of him."

"That must be nice." I didn't add that it was unlikely I'd land an agent from this conference without stooping to blackmail. "I assume you come here often?"

"Once a week, at least. I have a sprawling Presidio estate about ninety miles from the city, but I spend most of my time at my private beach front bungalow only a few blocks from here. That's where I stay when I'm writing."

"If you live so close, why did you take a room at the hotel?"

He pondered this question for far longer than seemed logical and then shrugged. "That's a long story. The short answer is that I was hoping for some peace and quiet. But I never stopped to consider that I'd be mobbed by networking parasites. Or that I'd find a girl like you."

I found myself blushing. Jonny released my hand as a platter appeared covered in edible flowers, drizzles of tangerine sauce and wasabi mayonnaise, and two crab cakes the size of silver dollars. He dredged one through the sauce and popped it into his mouth.

I sliced mine into slivers as he continued talking.

"Baby, why do you want to be a writer? It's a terrible life, and it never gets any better. You think it's bad now, but this is nothing. Once you get a book deal, you'll never have a moment's peace. There's a reason so many bestselling writers are drunks and addicts. It's not because they started out that way, that's what this business does to people."

His voice was so tender, so sincere, that I found myself falling for him all over again. "You seem to be doing pretty well," I said.

"That's because I've been doing this for three decades. And the first two were no picnic, especially since everyone was getting fat off my books but me."

He paused as the plates were cleared, and the table was reset for the main course.

"I come from a simpler, more lucrative time. Nowadays, expect a lot of pain for very little gain. It will take years for you to hit the big time, and once you do, all the parasites will get in line to screw you and take your money. And that's if you're successful. If you're looking to get rich, you're better off buying lottery tickets."

I shook my head. "I'm not doing this for money. I'm doing this because I've got an inexhaustible gold mine of stories in my head that I know people will want to read."

I expected him to laugh at my naivety, but instead he nodded. "Yes, I know what you mean. That's how I started out as well."

The food was divine, but I didn't expect anything less. Halfway into the meal Jonny looked up at me. "Do you mind if we play a game of truth or dare? Only without the dares?"

Oh, I thought. Here is where the date gets awkward again. "What fun is that?"

"We ask each other a question that we want to know the answer to but might be considered rude to ask on the first date, the other person either has to give an honest answer or say none of your business."

"Okay." I tried not to look nervous. I hoped he wouldn't ask about my family, but he did give me the option of declining to answer.

"You start."

I took a deep breath. "Is Jonny Goodsnuff your real name?"

"Yes and no. There is a different name on my birth certificate, but I had it legally changed after I sold my fifth novel under that pseudonym. My birth name was one of those unwieldy Polish things that could earn you about a thousand points in Scrabble." I watched as the plates were cleared and the dessert setting and tiny crystal port glasses were set out. "My turn."

I looked up, afraid of what he might ask. I'd hoped it would be whether I'd go to bed with him, since I'd already decided I would, and nothing so far was enough to make me change my mind.

"Are you a real blonde?"

I blinked. I found the question to be odd. Not offensive, just odd. Boys have asked me if I was blond all over, or if the curtains matched the carpet. But those guys were idiots, Jonny was a renowned artist.

"Yes, I am."

"Did it get darker as you got older so you have to touch it up with highlights?"

"No, it grows out of my head this color. My great grandparents are from Sweden and I get it from my mother."

"Amazing," he said. "It's so rare to find that shade of flaxen as it occurs in nature."

"It's not so great. I've always envied the bottle blondes with their alluring dark eyes and rich complexions. I can't leave the house without penciling in my eyebrows and slathering on mascara or I look like a ghost."

Jonny's eyes glazed. I was boring him again. It seemed strange to me that he fixated on my hair, but had no interest in my makeup. It was a relief when the server set out the platter of pineapple, kiwi, pomegranate, and figs, along with a bottle of port.

I waited for Jonny to prompt me for another question but he didn't say a word.

Chapter 8

We got back to the hotel at around midnight. Jonny and I began making out in the elevator as soon as the door closed. I was still giddy from the strong wine I had with dessert and as we kissed, his lips were as soft as rose petals and his tongue still tasted of tropical fruit. I was incredibly turned on, and I could tell he was too, but when I rubbed my body against his in a suggestive manner, he pulled away.

"Bad girl," he said. "You need to behave like a lady and keep some mystery about you for the second date."

"We don't have time for a second date. I have to be on a plane to Ohio tomorrow morning."

"What's in Ohio?"

"My car, my apartment, my job…"

"…your husband, your boyfriend."

I shook my head. "It's like you said, the writer's life doesn't leave a lot of time for romance."

Jonny stepped away from me. "I'll give you my cell phone number. Call me when you get back to your room and give me your flight information so that I can write it down. Then I want you to call me from your departure gate. I'd like to make sure that you arrive safely for your flight."

"Why not come up to my room?"

"Not this time, Amanda. I don't do one-night stands with someone as special as you." The elevator door opened at my floor and he kissed my hand. "Call me, Amanda, don't forget."

I left, watched the door close, and stood there for several minutes. Despite his words, I was sure that I would never see him again. That within a week he would have forgotten all about me.

The thought of it was nearly unbearable.

It was with a heavy heart that I lay my Cinderella gown into my suitcase. My sad little chiffon dress went on top of it, looking very much like a homely stepsister. I didn't have a chance to wear it on this trip. I'd probably never have a chance to wear the other one again. But it would look magnificent in my closet.

I left the hotel in my old football jersey and jeans. It felt a bit awkward to be dressed so causally after such a magical evening, but I still had stabs of pain in my toes, so I was happy to be wearing sensible sneakers with nice pillowy socks. My makeup was minimal and I'd pulled my hair back into a braid. Nobody held the elevator door for me this time.

In the taxi I stared at the rows of palm trees that we zoomed past on the road to the airport. I sat in silence and reflected on how I'd been ruined for other men. No matter how hard the next guy tried, he'd never be able to compete with the amazing night I'd shared with Jonny. Maybe that had been his intention all along. Maybe he was a tease, and it was enough for him to know that I'd dream of him every night. How many others were there? How many girls were lying in their beds right now pining over his memory?

When I arrived at the airport, I was tempted to get back into the cab and tell the driver to take me back to the hotel. But I realized that would be foolish. I had no money for a second ticket, and no guarantee that Jonny would still be there. So I forced myself to go forward, through the check-in, through security, and to the gate where my flight would leave in about two hours.

I sat and sighed and watched the people around me who were lost in their laptops and newspapers as we waited for the plane that would whisk us away to the Midwest, where I'd return to my makeup counter and my dreary little apartment while I charted a new course for my writing career.

A few people chattered into their cell phones and I remembered that I'd promised to call Jonny. I pulled out my phone and selected his number, grateful for this last little bit of contact before I flew out of his life forever.

"Hey, baby," he said after the third ring. "It's about time you called. I was getting worried that you didn't want to speak to me anymore."

"What do you mean? My flight doesn't leave for another two hours. I just got here."

"Yes, I can see that."

"Huh?"

"Turn around."

I spun and saw Jonny walking toward me.

I rose to my feet. "Jonny? You're not supposed to be back here. This area is for passengers only."

Jonny held up a ticket. "Someone has to help you pack."

"Pack?"

As Jonny reached me, he took my hand and dropped to one knee. "Amanda Anderson. I know this is insane, but will you marry me?"

My hand flew to my mouth. Jonny Goodsnuff wanted to marry me? Out of all the women in the world, he picked a simple Midwestern girl with no family to speak of and barely a penny to her name?

It was unreal. I had to speak quickly, before he had a chance to change his mind.

"Yes, Jonny! Yes!"

The other passengers cheered as I leapt into his arms and we kissed each other madly.

If they'd only known that we'd met that weekend, and that we only had a single date, and that the only thing he cared to know about me was my true hair color—then perhaps they might have held their applause.

Part 2
Mrs. Goodsnuff

CHAPTER 9

I was flying, both emotionally and literally. Outside, the canopy of clouds nestled like a fluffy white blanket below the plane and the sun beamed through the window, sending up sparkles from my brand new cushion cut diamond ring. Of course, Jonny had upgraded my ticket to first class, and I nestled in the plush seat while the flight attendant refilled my champagne flute. It was more luxury than I was used to, and I felt uncomfortable in my Levis and jersey. Especially with Jonny in his tailored suit seated next to me. I looked over and saw he was scrawling something into a spiral bound notebook.

"Are you working on your novel?" I asked.

He nodded without pausing.

"I have a laptop you can use. Let me get it down for you."

He snorted. "No, thanks. I won't use one of those. All of the great novels were either typewritten or done in longhand. Computers promote laziness, and lazy writing is what is killing the publishing industry. Good writing is hard work and it needs to feel like hard work."

"Okay," I said. Not that I agreed. As a girl, I'd bought a typewriter from the Goodwill for a dollar and I hated it. I saved every penny I could to buy a laptop. Now I had a whole disc of novels that I'd typed up the lazy way and I loved them unconditionally, the way a good mother should. But it seemed a silly point to argue over.

He called for the flight attendant to bring him another Scotch. "So, what do you think about having the honeymoon in Paris?"

"A honeymoon in Paris? I can't imagine anything more perfect."

"I was hoping you would say that." He pulled a pair of tickets out of his breast pocket. "I booked our trip, departing in one month. That should give you just enough time quit your job, move out of your apartment, and gather up your loved ones for a massive impromptu church wedding."

Oh, dear. Here it comes. "Actually, I was thinking it might be more romantic if we eloped."

"Eloped?" Jonny raised one eyebrow. "I thought all the girls your age wanted storybook weddings."

"Well I don't."

He stared at me as if I just sprouted a third eye in my forehead. "Why don't you want a wedding?"

I felt a sick knot forming in my stomach. I knew this was all too good to be true. I wondered if he'd get second thoughts about marrying me, and if he'd let me keep the ring. "Weddings just seem like a big waste of money to me. Why spend all that money on flowers, cake, and champagne for a party where we don't even get a chance to relax?"

"But what about your family? Surely your parents should show off their little girl, who's all grown up and getting married to some big shot."

I sipped my champagne as I pondered the best way to explain that both my parents were felons. For a moment I considered telling him that I was an orphan, but that was too easy a lie to get caught at. Besides, I didn't want to start my married life by spinning a web of falsehoods. So I told only as much of the truth as I thought I could get away with. "I don't think my parents would be able to make it to the wedding."

"And I sense that your parents won't be able to make it because you don't want them there."

"That too."

Jonny closed up the notebook. "Listen, if you're worried that I'm some snob who is going to reject you because your father is a janitor and your mother walks about in a muumuu and hair rollers, you need to know that I spent the first thirty years of my life sharing a mobile home with three other people."

I swallowed hard. "I'm not ashamed. I just don't want my family at my wedding. I don't believe that they'd be happy for me."

Jonny lowered his voice. "So you hate your family. Why?"

"It's nothing like that. It's just that..." (I'm the product of a fugitive and a junkie. For the past ten years they've wanted nothing to do with me, but that may change when they find out I've married a famous guy with money.)

God, how could I say that in a way that wouldn't send him running as soon as we reached the terminal? I should have told him everything, but instead I chickened out. "My mother is a very jealous woman and she doesn't seem to like me very much."

That seemed to work. Jonny took my hand, his eyes glowing with sympathy. "Don't be sad. I'm sure your mother loves you very much, in her own way. She just resents you for taking her youth away from her. My late wife Diana was the same way. That's why, no matter how busy I get with my writing, I make sure that my two girls know how much their daddy loves and cherishes them."

"You have children?"

"I assumed you knew that since I always dedicate my books to my two little angels. Is that going to be a problem for you?"

"No, I think that's wonderful. I've always wanted children. Do you have any pictures?"

Jonny opened his wallet and pulled out a snapshot of himself as a younger man, smiling proudly as he held an infant in his arms while a toddler in pigtails buried her face in his pant leg. "That's Misty and the baby is Lulu."

"They're beautiful."

Jonny put the photo back in his wallet. "Well they're quite a bit bigger now, but that's how I still see them. So you like kids? Good. Then there remains just one last issue to be ironed out before we take this plunge." Jonny's face went grave.

"What's that?" I said, suddenly apprehensive.

"The prenup."

"Oh," I said.

"I don't want one, but my agent is going to insist. He's a real shark. When he sees you, he's going to think you are just some silly gold-digger who chases after old geezers like me for their money. Normally, I'd just tell him to go to hell, but I'm not a person so much as a corporation, and corporations have to protect their assets, if you know what I mean."

"I understand. I'll sign whatever you need me to."

"Even if it means that you get absolutely nothing unless we stay married for five years?"

I nodded. I didn't care about his money. I was only too happy to sign an aggressive prenup, just to prove to the world that I was marrying for love.

I found someone to assume my lease, and sold the car to Courtney the biology major for only a little more than the balance of the car loan. I could have gotten more for it but I owed her big time, and it's not as if I needed the money. Meanwhile Jonny holed up in a hotel, hard at work on his novel.

It didn't take long to pack—most of what I wanted to take with me was already in my suitcase. I suggested we push the date forward, but Jonny refused to be rushed to the altar. He also refused to be rushed into the sack, claiming that he didn't want to sully things by jumping the gun on our honeymoon. That sounded romantic to me, so I simply sat in my adjoining suite at the hotel and counted off the days like a kid waiting for Christmas.

At long last, the big day arrived. The judge preformed a quick ceremony and I was officially Mrs. Amanda Goodsnuff. We took a taxi to the airport and boarded the plane to Paris. It was my first trip to a foreign country and I couldn't help but grip my husband's hand in anticipation. The plane landed in the dark of night while rain poured from the sky in sheets. We rode the Metro into the city and Jonny took me to a restaurant that he assured me was one of the best in Paris.

I was underwhelmed. My chicken was greasy, the clotted cheese sauce smelled like old socks, and everything was salted to a point that I no longer consider edible. However, Jonny seemed to be in ecstasy, and this was our wedding night, so I forced it down as best as I could with large swallows of wine and San Pellegrino. Unfortunately, there was a rough taxi ride to our hotel, so as soon as we reached the room, I rushed to the bathroom and puked into the bidet.

I thought that might have put Jonny off, but he petted my back and told me that it was only natural to be a little afraid on my wedding night.

Once my stomach settled, I showered, fixed up my hair and face, and changed into my honeymoon lingerie before presenting myself to my husband. He took one look at me, thrust the notebook off to one side, and beckoned me to join him in the bed.

That night we made love three times, and I finally knew why he wanted to wait.

Jonny was small. Very small. A lot smaller than I'm used to, and I'm not used to big. I'm used to average. And Jonny certainly wasn't average. Jonny was little. I'm talking Italian Renaissance statuary little. He began tiny and at the very peak of his excitement, he grew to slightly less tiny.

But I was so turned on that it didn't even matter.

The next morning Jonny took me to the Louvre. The sun shone through the glass pyramid, and bathed the area in a prism of colored light. I wore a yellow sundress and Jonny wore a pair of tailored slacks and a charcoal-colored polo shirt. We held hands as we walked through the museum, sharing what we knew of the story behind each masterpiece we recognized.

Then his phone rang. He looked to see who was calling, and his eyes lit up in a way I'd never seen before. This alarmed me, seeing as how we were newlyweds. I could only hope it was one of his daughters calling to see if we arrived safely.

He released my hand and wandered away. "Hey there, buddy! It's about time you called…No, you're not interrupting anything. I'm just walking the new wife around the museum."

"Jonny, who are you talking to?"

He waved his hand in my direction as if he was swatting a fly. "So, how was your flight…? What? The hospital! Christ, man, you're killing me! You'd better find a doctor who can get that under control…Yes, yes, I suppose I'll just have to hold her at bay until they release you."

I bristled. "Excuse me?"

He mouthed the words "not you" at me before he turned back to the phone. "Okay, give me the address and tell her I'm on my way. But this is coming out of your fifteen percent….Call when they let you out so I know you're okay. Ciao."

"Who was that?" I asked as he closed up his phone.

"That was my agent. He was supposed to meet with our publisher to discuss a distribution deal, but he had a massive asthma attack and stopped breathing. He's at the hospital so I have to keep her amused until he gets out."

"Don't they know you're in Paris right now? On your honeymoon?"

"Of course they know, who do you think is paying for this trip?" Jonny said. "Why do you think I couldn't push the wedding forward? I'm supposed to meet with them tomorrow night to sign a distribution deal, and it's not every day you get to take a romantic honeymoon in Paris on someone else's dime."

I didn't say a word. I couldn't. I was stunned into a state of paralysis.

"Here, have some money to tide you over for today." He pulled a wad of euros out of his wallet and clasped them into my hand. "Make sure you return to the hotel before nightfall, because I hear this place becomes a den of pimps and white slavers after dark. I guess being from a barbaric nation filled with guns and lawyers does have its advantages, eh?"

It sounded as if he was joking, but I didn't think it was funny. He kissed me on the corner of the mouth. "I'll call you as soon as I can, babe, but don't think that you have to wait up for me."

"Jonny?" I'm ashamed to admit that I followed him to the door.

"It's all part of the price of fame and fortune." He circled back and took

me into his arms for one last embrace before he backed away, blowing me
kisses until he vanished out the exit.

I spent the rest of the morning wandering around the museum. It was
impressive, to be sure. But I quickly learned that even the greatest museum
in the world isn't that much fun when you're all alone.

The streets of Paris were a little more entertaining. Contrary to what I'd
expected, the people I met were friendly and spoke a good deal of English.
The vendors weren't the slightest bit grateful when I laced the conversation with my smatterings of high school French, and begged me to stop
murdering their native tongue.

On the train ride back to the hotel, I sat with a group of waif-thin
students in skintight sweaters, jeans, and bike shoes who were delighted to
discuss their favorite American television shows with an actual American.

The conversation got me curious about the state of French television. As
soon as I was back in my room, I stripped down to my bra and panties,
crawled into bed, and clicked on the TV.

The first show appeared to be a grainy soft-core porno. A pair of beautiful
young people seemed to be making love, but it was hard to tell since all
of the action was filmed from the shoulders up. Then the girl put on her
tennis dress and went to talk to her grandparents for about ten minutes.

I was curious as to when there would be more action, but that didn't stop
me from changing the channel to a beautiful couple, without so much as a
trace of fig leaf, caressing in a garden in front of an apple tree and a serpent. I
thought it might be a high budget porno, but it turned out to be a commercial for chocolate candies. The station itself featured music videos.

I surfed over a housewife doing her laundry in nothing but a pair of white
sneakers, and I finally found an American sitcom, dubbed over in French.
It was a show I'd seen a hundred times before, with actors in their thirties
pretending to be teenagers. The dubbing added a whole new dimension
to the show. The plucky heroine's nasally whine had been replaced with
a sultry whisper. The love interest had a deep husky voice, and even the
creepy stalker character was now a hot throaty baritone. I knew the episode
by heart, but it still sounded like they were all trying to seduce one another.
It was funny that with all of the actual smut on TV, this was the show that
was making me hot. I switched off the television and hoped that Jonny
would be back soon.

I must have drifted off to sleep, because I woke to the sound of footsteps.

I sat up, intending to give Jonny a lecture for staying out so late, but then sank back down with my heart in my throat when I realized that the man in the room with me wasn't my husband.

The intruder was wearing a hat and an expensive looking trench coat. Thankfully, he had his back to me, but even so, I saw that his frame was too tall and too thin to be that of Jonny Goodsnuff. He ran his gloved hands over the surface of the desk, knocking the few small items to the floor. One of Jonny's Scotch glasses fell on something else with a shatter. The intruder spun to face me.

I lay as still as I could, pretending to be asleep, and watched him through my lashes. A heavy scarf obscured the bottom half of his face so I could only see his eyes. He stood there and looked at me for about fifteen seconds before he turned around again and reached for my suitcase. In an instant, he had it open, and was shaking out its contents. My exorbitantly expensive dress slithered out onto the floor, but I didn't care. There was nothing in that suitcase that was worth more than my life. As he reached for Jonny's suitcase and fumbled with the clasp, I decided I'd make a run for it.

No sooner had I raised myself up than the intruder spun around and pulled the scarf from his face.

"No, please, don't bother getting out of bed."

I froze, frightened out of my wits. I tried to scream, but my throat wouldn't work. My heart was beating so hard that I could feel it bruising my ribcage.

"This will only take a minute. I'll take what I need, and then I'll let you get back to sleep."

I sank down into the bed and cowered while the intruder resumed pillaging our belongings. He'd showed me his face. That meant he was going to kill me. First, I'd be subjected to God knows what. I could just imagine the headlines back home: *Local Girl Makes Good – Only to be Brutally Murdered by Hotel Room Rapist.*

Suddenly he stopped and turned to the door. I could hear Jonny humming a tune as the doorknob began to turn. The intruder's eyes narrowed and his right hand clenched into a fist.

I summoned my nerve for one last act of heroism.

"Jonny! No! Stay out!"

The door burst open and Jonny leapt into the room with his arms spread wide. "Stonewall, my man. Come over here and give Jonny some love."

Chapter 10

The man called Stonewall gave Jonny only a brief look before he resumed his ransacking. "We don't have time. I have to fax the contract to New York within the next ten minutes or the deal is off."

"You mean this contract?" Jonny reached into his breast pocket and pulled out a folded piece of paper.

Stonewall snatched it out of his hand.

"Sorry about that, buddy. Right after we hung up, I remembered that I had it with me the whole time. I tried calling you, but you didn't answer your phone."

"I turned it off. I didn't want to wake Amanda." Stonewall reached for a black bag he'd set by the door. From it, he pulled out a fax machine the size of a three-hole punch. Then to my utter and complete outrage, he sat on the bed and set it up on the nightstand.

Jonny went for his Scotch bottle and stared forlornly at the broken glass on the floor. Meanwhile, I just sat there with my arms folded, wondering why it didn't occur to either of them to let me get up and put on a robe. Fortunately, they both appeared to be oblivious to my presence in the room.

"You broke one of my Scotch glasses," Jonny said.

"Can't talk right now," Stonewall said as he hooked the phone cord to his fax machine. "Not unless you're willing to go back to the bargaining table and renegotiate your ten million dollar advance because you couldn't get your signature on the contract before the deadline."

Jonny waved his hand, "Big deal. So I lose an advance. All that means is that the publisher won't be making me an interest free loan of my own royalties. Don't worry—you'll get your paws on your fifteen percent eventually."

Stonewall fed the paper through the machine. "It's not the money, and you know it. It's the hype and the publicity that comes with a publisher making an eight figure investment in a book that nobody knows anything about."

"Hey, all anyone needs to know about this book is that it's going to make history. This book is going to hit the world like the next Krakatoa, and then your puny little eight figure advance is going to look like chicken scratch."

"I'm glad you're so sure of yourself," Stonewall said and packed up his things. "Fortunately, the fax went through, so we won't have to find out."

Good. He was leaving.

"Don't go," Jonny said to my complete chagrin. "Stay and have a drink with me."

"I couldn't," he said, and I hoped he meant it.

"No, please. You only just got here."

Stonewall set the bag down. "I suppose I can have just one."

He pulled a chair up to the table and Jonny poured him a glass of Scotch and then toasted him with the bottle. "Cheers." Jonny drank right out of it before setting it down and smacked his lips together. "I haven't heard you say much about Marlene lately. How is she? Still as fat as a house?"

"I wouldn't know," Stonewall said. "We got an annulment three months ago—right after her psychic told her that we were father and daughter in a previous lifetime."

Jonny chuckled. "Jesus Christ, Stonewall, what are the odds?"

"Pretty good, I'd say, seeing as how I'd slipped that psychic an envelope full of cash."

Jonny slapped him on the shoulder. "My God, you are too much! Did you hear that, Amanda? Leave it to Stonewall to find a way to toss his bitch wife out on her fat ass and make her think it's all her idea."

"Gosh, Jonny," I said. "If I ever get fat, are you going to toss me out on my bitch ass?"

"Hell no, because if you gain as much as fifteen pounds, I'll have your jaw wired shut."

Stonewall had the good manners to look uncomfortable. "Jonny, you can't talk to your bride like that."

"Why not? Seeing as how you just faxed over ten million reasons for her to just lie there and take it."

Those words felt like a slap in the face. I bit my lip, as Stonewall looked over at me.

Jonny grabbed his arm. "Hey, don't worry. Amanda already knows my sense of humor."

No, actually I had no idea. I certainly wasn't expecting to hear this sort of talk from the charming man who'd swept me off my feet only a few weeks ago. And just why the hell was he apologizing to Stonewall and not me?

Stonewall glanced my way again and stood in a flash. "You know what? I think I'll just leave so you two can recover from your flight. We have a big day ahead of us. It was nice to meet you, Amanda."

I just sat with my arms crossed over my chest and didn't say a word.

As soon as he was gone, I picked up a throw pillow and hurled it at Jonny. He swatted it away. "Jesus, what the hell was that?"

"That's what I want to know—what the hell *was* that! 'Hey Stonewall, I see you've broken into my hotel room and scared my wife half to death. When you're done sifting through her dirty underwear, why don't we all hang out together, even though she's half-naked with morning breath and bed head, because that wouldn't be uncomfortable in the slightest!' I'm surprised you didn't invite him into the bed for a threesome, or was that why you were plying him with alcohol?"

"For your information, I told him to come in here because he needed the contract."

"And it never occurred to you to call and let me know he was coming?"

Jonny took a deep breath, and when he looked at me, his eyes were tender. "Oh Christ, I forgot. I'm really sorry about that, Amanda."

"And what's with all the misogynistic fat jokes?"

Jonny took my hands into his and held them. "Baby, listen to me. Jeremy Stonewall Kendal is the best agent in the world, because he's a total shark. He's my friend but he's not a trusted friend. I can't let my guard down around someone that ruthless and cunning."

"He didn't seem that ruthless and cunning to me."

"Of course not, because he's the devil. He likes to pretend that he's a nice guy, but you can't let him fool you. Think about it. Could a nice guy get an eight-figure deal for a book he knows nothing about? And that's just for the North American print rights. Tomorrow Stonewall's going to trick some nice old lady out of a truckload of euros." He pulled me into his arms. "I can't let him see my weaknesses, and right now, you're my only weakness."

I felt myself slump against him more out of exhaustion than anything else.

"When this book comes out I'll get you a solid gold toilet, and you can wipe your ass with hundred dollar bills, but in the meantime, I'm under an insane amount of pressure. I'm going to have to play some games you won't like, so you have to promise me that you'll be a good sport for the next few months, no matter what I do. Promise?"

"Fine," I said. But I was terribly uneasy about what it was I was agreeing to.

CHAPTER 11

When I woke the next morning, Jonny was already gone. There was a stack of euros on the nightstand, right next to a note written on hotel stationery. I held it up so that I could read it in bed.

I'm with Stonewall. We'll be out late. Have fun without me.
– Love Jonny

Oh, great, my husband left money on the nightstand and was spending our honeymoon with another man. What *wasn't* wrong with this picture?

I reached for the guidebook and was disappointed to learn that most of the tourist attractions were closed because it was a Monday. I decided that I'd put Jonny's pile of money to good use by doing some shopping. I found the cutest boutique, but many of the outfits that I liked were too tight in the bust. The tops were designed to give the illusion of a bosom, rather than actually accommodate one. I thought back to the chain-smoking students with their long hair and skeletal frames, and realized that by Parisian standards, I was positively corn-fed.

Talking to those youngsters had been the highpoint of the trip. It was ironic that I'd spent the last five years looking for peace and quiet so that I could work on my novels, yet now I felt pathologically lonesome.

And then I remembered that I was supposed to be on my honeymoon.

I found a few cleavage-inducing dresses, as well as some cute sweaters and jeans with French writing embroidered on the pockets. As I walked down the streets with my bags of shopping, I became aware of how the charm seemed to have faded from the city. The day before, I was enchanted at how chic and regal everything was. Today it all seemed drab and dingy.

The buildings were a uniform shade of dove-gray. Was this how it always looked? Were my eyes too full of stars to notice it before? Or was there still magic that I couldn't see because I was blinded with annoyance with my absentee husband?

I searched for a cafe for lunch and my phone rang.

"Jonny? Is that you?"

"Hi baby. I figured you'd want me to call, so I'm calling."

"Well, you've got perfect timing, I was just about to get lunch. Are you close by?"

"Afraid not. I'm with Stonewall. We're working out a deal. I'll probably be out past midnight. Don't forget to get back to the hotel before dark."

"I know. I know. I've been doing some shopping. I just bought the cutest dress. It's white with little red swirls that look like cherries–"

"Have to go. Stonewall needs for me to sign something. Don't forget to pack tonight, since we're flying home at nine tomorrow morning."

"What?" Several pedestrians turned to see what I was shouting about, so I spoke with my jaw clenched to keep the volume down. "You never told me we're leaving tomorrow morning."

"I'm pretty sure I did, babe."

"Oh, you most certainly did not! I think I would have remembered being told my honeymoon would consist of three quick shags, a home invasion, and whole lot of nothing else!"

A petite young woman with a lapdog smiled warmly at me. I hoped she didn't know a word of English.

"Look, I can't really talk right now. Stonewall is breathing down my neck and giving me the 'get off the phone signal' from across the room." I was so piqued I barely caught the physical impossibility of that statement. "Don't worry, babe, I'll make this up to you. There will be other trips when I don't have the fate of the literary world clamped down on my shoulders. All right?"

"Oh, all right," I said.

"Love you, honey, gotta go. Bye."

I hung up the phone, cursed the heavens, and headed for an obvious McDonald's clone. After all, I still hadn't gained my international palate, and I was curious to try some French fries that had actually been fried in France. It turned out to be just like American fast food, only I had to pay extra for the catsup and the soda was the size of a Dixie cup. There were no refills. I asked.

Back at the hotel, I found the novel that Jonny had given me, and it suddenly occurred to me that I'd still never read anything that my husband had written. I drew a bubble bath, settled into the tub, and cracked open *The Limits of Risk*.

What I read filled me with dismay.

The writing was bad. Very bad. The nicest thing I could say about it was that a child in the third grade wouldn't have to open a dictionary. This was unfortunate, because what I was reading certainly shouldn't be accessible to someone with an eight-year-old's level of comprehension.

The story began with our macho hero arriving in Thailand with his posse of foul-mouthed friends. At the hotel pool, he spent three full pages watching a pillow-lipped Asian beauty with cantaloupe-sized breasts jump off a diving board and only three sentences seducing her. Judging from the way she ripped off his clothes and gobbled his massive crank, it was probably two sentences too many.

I wasn't sure what happened next, because at that point, I'd flung the book across the room. This was what the people wanted? Really? There were enough knuckle-draggers roaming the bookshelves to justify an advance check with so many zeroes on it? Meanwhile I couldn't even *pay* agents to look at my work.

After my tantrum, I rose from the tub, donned a robe, and resumed reading on the bed. I was being unfair. The book would get better. It had to. Maybe I'd hit his one bad patch and the rest of his work was beyond amazing. But I didn't get more than ten pages into it before I heard a knock on the door.

"Just a minute," I called out.

Jonny was back early, thank God. I looked over at the vanity table and contemplated putting on my makeup before I opened the door. It was probably a bit much considering that I was still in my bathrobe, but if Jonny was half as shallow as his writing suggested, I was going to have to stay as refined as a geisha until our third child was born.

I stepped toward the vanity, but the pounding intensified.

"Hold on!" I shouted and went the door without even combing my hair. If the sight of my straggly blond locks was a bit too honest for him so early in our marriage, then it was no less than he deserved.

I threw open the door and jabbed Jonny in the chest with my finger. "You know something? You've got a lot of nerve pounding on the door like that when I've been waiting for you all day."

Only it wasn't Jonny. It was Stonewall.

I recognized him right away even though he looked a lot different out of his housebreaking clothes. He wore an immaculately tailored suit, and he actually wasn't a bad looking guy. I'd assumed from his voice that he was about Jonny's age, but he looked a lot younger, with a thin nose and dark-blond hair that had been slicked back until there was just a little bit of curl to it. That hair and the long cut of his clothes, combined with his big caramel-colored eyes gave him the illusion of youth, but then I noticed the faint lines under his eyes and realized he only looked young. That was all I had time to notice before he spun around and stood with his back to me.

With great trepidation I looked down to examine the state of my robe. It had fallen open just a little, but, to my relief, everything that he wasn't supposed to see was still covered in an only slightly risqué x configuration, flashing a bit more sternum and kneecap than I normally show, but not even remotely pushing the envelope of G-rated attire.

And yet here was the world's most ruthless agent, giving me the Lady Godiva treatment.

Oh, for crying out loud.

"Give me just a minute," I said and closed the door to his back.

I opened it a few minutes later wearing jeans and a sweater. By then he was facing the door again. "Hello, Mr. Stonewall. Can I help you with something?"

"Where's Jonny?"

"Huh?" It was all I could manage.

He entered the room and sat down on a chair. "He called to leave the name of the cabaret, but the message was garbled so I couldn't make it out. Do you know where we're supposed to go tonight?"

"No, why would I?" It wasn't as if I was invited. "Didn't you two gentlemen discuss this while you were gallivanting about all morning?"

"Gallivanting? I just woke up a half hour ago."

I stood there blinking. "You—just woke up a half hour ago?"

Stonewall must have mistook my stunned disbelief at my husband's deceit for reproach. "I didn't go to bed until about ten in the morning. I had to jab myself with a syringe of stimulant yesterday and it's very hard to sleep after something like that. I've been in my room all night talking with our people in New York and Asia."

I got Jonny's note and sank into a chair.

I'm with Stonewall. We'll be out late. Have fun without me.
— Love Jonny

Son of a bitch.

We weren't even married a week and he was already sneaking out and lying to me. Fortunately, Stonewall's attention was on his PDA-style cell phone.

"Never mind, he sent me a text," he tapped into his phone. "Yes there it is. *Chez de Poupée*. It's off in the forest, about an hour's drive from here."

He got up and I waited for him to leave but he just stood there staring at me.

"You're not going to the cabaret dressed like that, are you?"

I'm sure that if Jonny wanted me there, he would have invited me.

Then again, he never said I couldn't go.

"Give me five more minutes."

We drove through the woods in Stonewall's rented Mercedes. Well, actually, he drove. I just sat there in my cherry-dotted dress looking out the window and feeling about as awkward as I did when Tyler Johnson took me to my first homecoming dance in his Dad's pickup truck. The scenery was beautiful. Even in the dark, the cute little cottages with their hay-covered roofs and their diamond pane windows looked like they were right out of a fairy tale. But I wanted to share this with my husband, not his agent. I struggled for something civil to say.

"Nice watch."

He smiled. "Thank you for noticing. It's a Breguet."

"I've never heard of a Breguet. Is that like a Rolex?"

He cringed a little. "I suppose you could say that a Breguet is very much like a Rolex. Just like you can say that a diamond is very much like a cubic zirconia."

Now it was my turn to cringe. "Pardon me. I was just asking."

He looked at me and shrugged in a manner that I supposed was apologetic. "I'm exaggerating, of course. A Rolex is a very fine high-end watch, but as far as I'm concerned nothing tops a Breguet in terms of style or substance."

"That's good to know," I said. To me a watch was a watch. Either it told you the correct time, or it didn't.

He sighed. "So, Jonny tells me that you're a writer?"

"Why do you ask? Are you looking for more clients?"

"Have you sold anything?"

"Not yet."

"Then, no, I'm not looking for more clients."

I clenched my jaw. "Well then maybe you shouldn't have brought it up."

"I'm just trying to make conversation."

I turned in my seat. "Okay, if you're so interested in making small talk, let's hear everything my husband has said about me."

"He said you're the best wife a man could ask for and that he's lucky to have met you." He looked over to see my reaction. Those words should have warmed my heart, but instead my blood still boiled. Why? Because I'd married a fraud. The most benign explanation was that he was a pathological liar. I didn't even want to consider the alternatives.

At last, we pulled into a complex in the middle of nowhere. Stonewall parked, then opened my door from the outside. As I walked, my heels slipped about in the gravel parking lot and he took my arm to steady me. I tried to free myself, but he kept a grip on me until we were back on solid ground. As we walked side by side, an older couple gave us a knowing smile. I made a face at them.

Outside the building, a playbill showed a collage of women in bikinis wearing entirely too much makeup. Stonewall gave a hundred euro bill to an old woman in the ticket booth. She nodded and gave him two tickets.

"You're holding a business meeting in here?"

"Does that bother you?"

"No, I just think it's weird."

"Good, I'm glad you understand," he said. When he opened the door, I was assailed by a blast of noise, light, and smoke. In the chamber beyond was a topless cabaret. Bare-chested women in top hats and fishnets formed a chorus line in the background while a buxom woman with big hair, big shoes, a big feather boa, and absolutely nothing else was practically making love to a chair as a crowd of chain-smoking drunks screamed out encouragement in a variety of foreign tongues.

At that moment, I hoped that an earthquake would strike and level that room to the ground with everyone in it.

I'm no prude, and it was all pure burlesque, so nothing on that stage bothered me. What bothered me was that my husband sat there and watched the show with a prune-faced woman in a low-cut dress and a Cleopatra haircut. He didn't seem to mind that her long red fingernail was tracing a figure eight on his forearm.

For a moment, I couldn't breathe. I just stood there and watched the man I'd married being caressed by another woman. Then I turned and ran back into the parking lot.

"Amanda!" Stonewall cried out as he chased after me, but I didn't stop running. I had to lose myself in the woods. I didn't want anyone to see me cry. He caught up with me while the gravel mired my heels. "Amanda," he grabbed hold of my wrists. I struggled to get away.

"Let me go!" I broke into sobs, "My husband lied to me. He said he had a meeting with his publisher, and instead I catch him at a strip club with some old whore!"

"Amanda, it's not what you think. That old whore *is* his publisher."

I stopped struggling and stared up at Stonewall with my mouth hanging open.

"I'm really sorry—I thought he explained all this to you."

"He's never explained a damn thing!"

"Amanda, when a person gets to be as big as your husband, this business gets dirty. They liquor you up, and then they offer you hookers, and fancy cars, and bags of cocaine—all to put you in the proper frame of mind to sign a deal with the devil. You have absolutely nothing to worry about. Jonny's been playing this game too long. He's smart enough to pay just enough attention to make her think that her tricks are working."

"Well if Jonny's so good at dancing with the devil, what the hell does he need you for?"

"I'm the angel on his shoulder who gives him an excuse not to take her candy."

He released me, and I wiped my nose. "I'm not going back in there. Take me back to the hotel."

"I understand how you feel, Amanda, but I can't do that."

"Take me back to the hotel!"

Stonewall looked deep into my eyes. "I wish I could, Amanda, but if I don't get in there right now, this is all going to turn into a complete disaster."

"And you don't think stranding Jonny's defenseless young bride in the middle of the woods in front of a drunken hootchie-kootchie show won't turn into a bigger disaster? Take me back to the hotel!"

I expected an argument, but he just stood there staring at me. "Fine. Let's go." He reached for his pocket like he was getting his keys, but then without warning he lunged and pinned my arms to my sides.

I kicked at him as he dragged me to a taxi, where a hirsute cabby was eating a sandwich and dropping bits of ham and cheese onto his lap. When I saw an ominous looking scar stretched down his face, I fought harder, but Stonewall forced me up against the car.

"Excuse me, sir, do you speak English?"

The cabby smiled like a predator and Stonewall crumpled a few bills into his hand. "This lady needs a ride to her hotel. Be sure she gets there safely."

I screamed, but Stonewall opened the door, pushed my head down, and literally flung me inside before slamming the door shut. The inside of the cab smelled like a basket of dirty laundry. I spun and lunged for the door, but it was locked from the inside.

Stonewall knelt toward the driver. "Drive, please."

As the car moved, I screamed profanities at Stonewall until I saw his form retreat back into the theatre. I slumped down into the seat and wiped the tears from my face with the back of my hand.

The cabby gave me a knowing look. "Is that your boyfriend?"

"Why don't you shut the hell up," I said.

I wish I could say that it made me feel better but it didn't.

It was nearly midnight when Jonny returned to our hotel room with a dozen roses and a box of chocolates. I sat up in bed and put aside his consistently awful novel.

"So how was your date with your agent?" I asked with as little venom as I could manage.

"Baby, he said, laying the roses across my lap. "I've got a confession to make. I lied to you and it's been eating at my gut all day. I just hope you can forgive me, but I'll understand if you can't."

Just one confession? It had better be long and detailed. "Okay, let's hear it."

He sat on the bed and took my hand. "Baby, I didn't spend the day with my agent. Last night I really needed to do some typing and I didn't want it to wake you, so I booked another room. It was just going to be for a few hours, but I was getting so much done that I wrote you that note. Then I called Stonewall and told him that I was spending the day with you and couldn't be bothered."

"Oh?"

"I told myself that as soon as I got back from my meeting I was going to tell you the truth."

"And how was your meeting?"

Jonny shrugged as he took off his tie. "The same old, same old—Roasted goat with some aging jezebel and then off for an evening of sexual harassment at the cabaret while some former-soviet nudie girls prance about on a stage with their goodie-slots spackled over."

I rolled my eyes. "You poor thing. That must have been quite an ordeal."

Jonny unlaced his shoes. "Yes, well, we'll see how much you like it when your books start selling like hotcakes and they decide to send in the gigolos."

"So…did your agent put you up to this?"

Jonny paused a bit too long. "Huh? What does Stonewall have to do with anything?"

"He came by tonight, so I already knew a lot of what you've told me right now. I thought he may have warned you to bring flowers to take the edge off your crabby wife?"

"Now that you mention it, he did drop some subtle hint or two along those lines, but he didn't need to." He gave me the box of chocolate. "I went out shopping for these long before I met with him."

I tried to give them back. "I'm not touching those. I might gain fifteen pounds and I don't want my jaw wired shut."

Jonny chuckled. "Don't be like that, baby. You'll find these don't have any calories."

I tore open the box, and my mouth fell open. There weren't any chocolates. Nestled in each paper cup was an article of jewelry—a string of opal beads that could have paid my rent for three months, a ruby tennis bracelet worth more than a semester of student loans, star sapphire earrings that meant I'd never have to panic about "final notice" envelopes from bill collectors…

I grabbed a tanzanite ring, pulled it onto my finger and admired it in the lamplight. The jewels he bought impressed me. Not because they were costly, but because there was no way that he could have obtained them since my surprise visit to the cabaret. He had to be thinking of me the whole day. Wondering what I might like, and trying to find little gifts as tokens of his esteem for me.

Okay, to be perfectly honest, I was also impressed by how expensive they were.

"You like them, don't you, baby?" Jonny said. "And that's just the beginning." He reached into his pocket, pulled out a wad of papers, and flicked them at me one by one. "French language rights – one million euros. German language rights – one million euros. Spanish language rights, half a million euros. Italian language rights—only a quarter of a million euros. They aren't that into me. But do you know what this means?"

He took hold of my face and held me by the cheeks. "It means we're filthy rich in a half dozen different languages."

CHAPTER 12

The few hours that remained of our honeymoon went without any major mishaps, so I was feeling pretty good as Jonny's Jaguar wove through the hills north and east of Los Angeles on the way to my new house. It was a perfect cloudless day and sunlight poured down onto the grassy peaks dotted with white rocks. We were getting along great, and he assured me that everything would be wonderful now that he and his man Stonewall had gotten the grueling contract negotiations out of the way. Now he could focus on me, on his family, and on finishing his novel.

"I can't wait to meet your girls," I said.

"You'll love them. They're such perfect angels and completely devoted to their daddy."

"I hope they like me too. I intend to spoil them rotten."

"Lulu will like that. She loves getting presents. Especially when they're all pink and sparkly or worth a lot of money."

"I'll do my best to explain I'm not trying to take the place of their real mother."

"Oh, I think they're old enough to know that, seeing as how they're both in their thirties."

"What?" I said, grateful that I wasn't the one behind the wheel. Had I been driving we probably would have crashed through the guardrail.

Jonny beamed with pride. "I see you're surprised that a man who is as young and good looking as I am has two daughters who are that old."

No, I was surprised that two daughters that old were still living at home with their father. "So I take it they're not married?"

"Ha! Are you kidding me? Unfortunately, they take after their late mother in the looks department. Don't get me wrong, they're great girls, but they'll never win any beauty contests." He bowed his head. "My poor dead Diana, loyal as a dog, and twice as ugly. And that was before she got fat. But don't you worry, Amanda, you've got good genes. That's why I married you."

He tried to take my hand, but I pulled it away. I thought he'd loved me for my mind, but what the hell did I know?

"We'll be home in a few minutes," Jonny said. "The estate is just around the corner."

I breathed a sigh of relief. Until we rounded the corner.

The first thing I noticed was the ramshackle mansion behind a rusted gate that jutted up from a yard choked with weeds. Above the stone lions and the peeling paint, a flag fluttered from a rusty flagpole at the very pinnacle of the crumbling architecture. I watched the flag unfurl and saw, to my horror, that it was a Nazi flag, complete with a swastika.

Jonny's words came rushing back at me. *Are you a true blonde, Amanda?* I reached for the door handle, certain that death from tumbling out of a speeding car was far preferable to whatever fate awaited me in that compound. The door had power locks, preventing my escape.

"Amanda? What the Hell? Oh, no, you don't think…" He pulled over by the side of the road, threw back his head, and laughed. "Amanda, that's not my house. That's Fritz, the neighbor."

"The…neighbor?" In the screen door, I could see a silhouette holding a shotgun. I'd hoped that it was a mannequin, strategically placed to scare away intruders. Then the shadow retreated into the house.

"You didn't think…Do I look like an Aryan superman to you?"

"No. But neither did Hitler."

"Good point," he conceded. "But you should know that I'm a public figure. The tabloids would eat me alive if I owned a house like that." He continued driving. At last, we reached his estate, and I had to blink to convince myself that it wasn't an illusion. Behind the seven-foot gate, the driveway seemed to go on forever, until we reached a multilayered Greek-inspired mansion. In front of the house, a fountain sent jets of water streaming up from the mouths of marble mermaids.

As the Jaguar crunched the gravel in front of the house, the front door opened and a woman who was shaped like a bowling pin ran out in black satin pajamas. Clearly, nobody had ever told her that bright red hair didn't look good on women with dark olive complexions, she was sporting a catsup-colored bowl cut. "Poppy!" She screamed with her arms open wide.

Behind her, a more sensibly dressed plastic surgery junkie pursed her overstuffed lips between windswept cheeks, and scowled at me with green eyes below a permanently-pressed forehead.

Don't get me wrong, I have nothing against excessive plastic surgery, as long as it makes people happy. But this woman looked like she'd never been happy a day in her life.

"Amanda, this is Misty," he said, pointing to his cosmetically enhanced offspring. "And this–" he pointed to the eggplant-shaped one "–is Lulu."

"Poppy!" Lulu squealed. "What did you bring me from France?"

Jonny put his arm around my shoulder. "I brought you two girls the nicest gift of all—a brand new mommy."

Misty and Lulu sneered at me and Jonny laughed. "I'm just kidding. Your presents are in the trunk."

The women ran to the car like two cats who suddenly found that there was food in their dish, and Jonny led me into the house with its marble floors and cherry-wood paneling. "This house has an indoor pool, sauna, and a Jacuzzi. However, you use them at your own risk because Misty has staked that out as her own territory. If you sneak in a swim while she's out drinking, it might be better not to tell her."

He pointed forward. "Straight ahead is the formal dining room. Francois, our chef, serves meals at nine, noon, and five-thirty on the dot. But don't you worry. If you miss a meal, he's been instructed to leave a tray by the door, just like room service. Lupe is our maid. We have another woman come in once a week for the dusting. The garden is beyond the dining room. I don't even know the gardener's name. He might not even have one. It hardly matters as long as the hedges stay trimmed."

He pointed to the stairs. "Upstairs are four bedrooms. Misty's is the largest—don't ask. Lulu's has the best view. However, ours has the biggest television set. At the end of the hall is my office. You'll find I'm in there eighty percent of the time. You'll also find that the door is locked eighty percent of the time. Don't knock, it's completely soundproof. And don't ask for the key. If I wanted anyone to have it, they'd have it. The phone in there blocks out everyone but Stonewall. If the house is on fire, you can call him and then he'll call me. If the house isn't on fire, you're not to call him. Understood?"

I thought of Stonewall cramming me into a cab with a potential axe-murderer. "Oh, don't worry."

"Good, because he's a busy man, and so am I. There is a tennis court and a putting green out back. Misty might play with you, if you ask nicely. Don't bother asking Lulu. She's not much of an athlete. Glandular problem and fibromyalgia, her doctor says. She had to go through five doctors until she found one that would say that." He laughed. "She works out every Wednesday with her personal trainer. Not that I've seen any difference, she still has an ass like a beanbag chair. But it does her world of good to have a

Latino man with a chiseled body pay attention to her once a week, even if I'm paying through the teeth for it."

I was a little disgusted to hear him talk that way about his own daughter. I hoped to steer the conversation to her career, or her hobbies, or her talents or other fine qualities. "So how does she spend the rest of her time?"

Jonny looked at me as if I spoke in tongues. "Hell, I don't know. She reads her tabloids and talks to strangers on the Internet. Beyond that, your guess is as good as mine. Anyway, I have to make some calls and work on my book. I trust you can find your own way upstairs. Remember dinner is at five-thirty."

He gave me a quick kiss on the cheek and retreated to the study. I drifted to the family area where Misty and Lulu sat on a leather couch and stared at me like a pair of nervous shopkeepers.

"Hello ladies," I said. "I'm Amanda. I'm a writer, just like your father."

"Are you a gold-digger?" Lulu asked without guile.

"No, Lulu, I'm not a gold-digger. I met your father at a conference and he swept me off my feet. I think it was love at first sight for both of us."

She fixed her beady eyes on me. "Did you sign a prenup?"

Lulu was starting to remind me of a squirrel—fluffy and harmless-looking until you stared long enough to detect the rodent glint. Misty gave Lulu a venomous look and then reached for a cigarette, lit it, and turned her green eyes back to me, clearly awaiting an answer.

"Yes, Lulu, I did sign a prenup. If I divorce your father, I get absolutely nothing."

"What about when he divorces you? Like he did with our mommy? Do you get anything then?"

Divorced? Jonny said he was a widower.

Misty blew out a plume of smoke. "Don't mind her, Amanda. She has absolutely no social skills due to the fact that she's mildly retarded."

"I'm not retarded!"

"I wouldn't be so sure about that. Has the old man had you tested?"

Lulu sprang up from the couch and ran to the hall wailing "Poppy!" like an ambulance siren.

Misty tamped out her cigarette. "Oh, crap, now we've done it. It would be best if we went outside for a few hours."

"Your father is in his study and he assured me that it's soundproof."

"It's soundproof, but not Lulu-proof. She can scream the paint off the walls when she gets going."

Misty rose from her seat. "So, do you golf?"

"I've tried a few times, but I'm terrible at it."

"Good," she said. "Then it won't be hard to beat you."

Misty raised the flagstick while I stood just outside the green. "The key to chipping is to try not to hit the ball. You want to hit the ground just behind the ball, and let the tremor bounce the ball onto the green."

That didn't sound right, but I clenched the club she'd handed me and struck the grass with it, just as she said. To my surprise, the ball hopped up and rolled toward the hole, stopping just about eight inches away. Misty gave a polite clap. "Excellent shot. You're not bad, you just need lessons."

Her words were kind but her eyes were hard. I couldn't shake the feeling that she was trying to gain my trust so that she could lure me into the woods and make me disappear.

I looked back at the house, and in a window, I could see Lulu sobbing on her father's shoulder. Jonny was petting her head and rocking her gently.

"Isn't that just the most disgusting display you've ever seen?" Misty said. "I notice she never gets this upset when the old man is away at the beach house, the fat fraud. I wish she would choke on a cupcake and die so I don't have to share a roof with her anymore."

"If she annoys you so much, why don't you just move out?"

She set down the flagstick, picked up her club, and tapped her golf ball straight into the hole from about two feet away. "You'd like that, wouldn't you?" She asked in a voice that was neither mocking nor serious. "Wouldn't it be great if Misty was completely out of the picture while Amanda and Lulu fought over her father's fortune? Sorry, but I've been kissing his ass for too long to just give up without a fight."

"I told you, I didn't marry Jonny for his money."

"Right. Would you have agreed to marry him if he was a janitor instead of a famous novelist?"

"I love your father for who he is. If he were a janitor, he wouldn't be the same person."

"He was a janitor when he married my mom."

I had nothing to say to that, and Misty gave me a half smirk in victory. I had to admit that she had a point. Not about my wanting his money. But had I not been so starstruck, I might have paused to consider the consequences of marrying a man I knew so little about. I sat on a bench under an elm tree. "What was your mother like?"

Misty's eyes softened for just a minute, but were hard again when she sat next to me and crossed her leg over her knee. "She was an immigrant and she had one of those noses with a bridge that sticks straight out of your face instead of sloping down. Lulu ended up with Dad's face and Mom's figure. I got Mom's face and Dad's figure, and it took doctors four hours and half the cartilage in my ears to straighten out that mess. But Mom wouldn't let them touch hers. She claimed it was her Nana's nose, and it reminded her of the Old Country." Misty shook her head sadly. "She had the heart of a peasant, the poor dumb fool. I don't remember too much because she died before I was ten."

"Jonny told me that he's a widower, but Lulu mentioned that your parents divorced?"

Misty sighed. "It's a long story." She looked at the window. Jonny held the still sobbing Lulu, "but I think we have time: My parents met in high school and eventually they married. Neither of them could afford college so they cleaned hotel rooms until I was born. My dad spent his nights working on his novels. Eventually one got published and he landed a three book deal. The trouble was that he had two years to write two more novels, and not nearly enough advance money to feed a family of four. My mother persuaded him to stay home and write, while she took a second job. By day, she'd clean hotel rooms and at night, she washed dishes at a local diner. Every night she'd bring home huge plastic buckets filled with the soup of the day and anything else they were planning to throw out. Her hair and clothing smelled like grease, but I think despite that, she really enjoyed those days."

She glanced at the house. "Then times got good. Dad was finally able to support the whole family with his writing. We moved out of the trailer and into a decent house. But for some reason, Mom was unhappy. They began fighting. One day, she took us out of school, brought us to an apartment, and told us she was working things out with our father. Right after that, he filed for divorce."

She shook her head. "She didn't even want a lawyer, while he got the best money could buy. The judge awarded her custody and the merest pittance in terms of child support. My father's books were bringing in money hand over fist, and yet we were living on leftover soup again. When she realized what she had done, she locked herself in the bathroom, put a gun in her mouth, and pulled the trigger."

I touched her shoulder. "How horrible. I'm so sorry."

Misty shrugged, and stared right into my eyes. "I'm glad she did it. I'm proud of her. Dad didn't mistreat her, so walking out was just stupid. If she hadn't killed herself, he wouldn't have taken us back. He'd have been free to start another family with a more attractive woman. In a few years he would have forgotten all about us, and then we wouldn't have all this, now would we?"

I sat there, chilled to the bone. Misty meant it—she seemed utterly convinced that her mother's suicide was the ultimate manifestation of a parent's love for her children.

Dear God, what had I married into?

CHAPTER 13

As soon as we got back to the house, I claimed I had jetlag and barricaded myself in my bedroom. Jonny had sent Misty to her room without dinner for upsetting her sister so Lulu probably thought we were conspiring, but that couldn't be helped.

The bedroom was nice, in a masculine, hunter sort of way. The walls were paneled in knotty oak and the bedspread was done in a pattern of green and burgundy. I closed the drapes so that I wouldn't have to look at the neighbor's fluttering swastika right outside the picture window. I would have liked to come down for dinner and draw a hot bath, but Misty's story rattled me so much that I was determined to focus on my writing. I set up my laptop and searched the web for reports of missing women, hoping to find an unsolved murder or two that I could crack wide open and jump-start my career as a novelist.

The stories were sparse. There were several disappearances, but the reports didn't have many details. That made sense. The police played things close to the vest so they could trap suspects into sharing details about the murders that were not available to the general public. Not that there was any great mystery to it, most of the time the killer would turn out to be an uncaring husband or a vengeful ex-boyfriend. The parade of sad tales and battered corpses got to me after a while and made me a little paranoid that my marriage was a cautionary tale in the making.

I was beginning to have serious doubts, and this troubled me because I vowed that when I got married, it would be for life. I'd intended to take my vows seriously. And yet here I was, married to a stranger.

But what grounds did I have for leaving? That my husband was a busy man and I wasn't the center of his universe? That he sometimes talked like a caveman, which I might have picked up on if I'd gotten to know him a little before I married him? As far as I could tell Jonny didn't engage in self-destructive habits, so unless he cheated on me or struck me hard enough to leave a mark, I couldn't justify walking out.

And if I did leave, where would I go? It wasn't as if I had a bustling support network or even a penny in my own name. If Misty was to be believed, any split from Jonny wasn't likely to be amicable.

I flopped down on the pillows and gazed at the two framed photos on Jonny's nightstand. One was a studio portrait of Jonny and his two daughters from when they were in their early teens. The girls were wearing puffy shirts and I recognized Misty from her description of her mother. Actually, I thought her old nose was cute and it gave her face a lot of character, but I could see why it bothered her. The boys I went to high school with generally didn't date girls for their character.

The other photograph showed Jonny and Stonewall seated on mats in a Japanese tea-house surrounded by hostesses in kimonos. Jonny was holding a slightly oversized check for one million dollars in one hand and pointing at it with the other. I was willing to believe that my husband kept that photo by his bedside because of the check, and not his boyfriend, since it wasn't a very flattering picture of Stonewall. He really did look ruthless in that picture. He was holding a cup and looking straight into the camera, but his big eyes were narrowed and he wore an arrogant frown. It looked like he was criticizing me. I slid his half of the picture behind the family portrait.

I really needed to hear a friendly voice. Trouble was, I didn't think the gang back in Ohio would have much sympathy for how alienated I felt in my huge California mansion while they were sleeping three to a room and skipping meals to afford textbooks.

It was time to make more friends. I grabbed the phone and searched through my purse until I finally found the card I was looking for: *Ivy Joie - Senior Henna Technician*

Well, she did say that she wanted to know how my date with Jonny Goodsnuff had turned out.

Ivy picked up on the third ring. "Yellow."

"Hello, Ivy. I'm not sure if you remember me, but my name is Amanda Anderson. We met at a writing conference about a month ago?"

"Amanda!" I was gratified that it was a full-throated shout and not the helium-pitched phony-squeal that I myself have been guilty of so many times in the past. "I'm so happy you called, did you get an agent?"

"No, not even close. How have you been?"

"Oh my God, Amanda, you won't believe half of the amazing crap that has happened to me since we parted. You know Zachary? Zachary Calvin? The guy I was seeing?"

"You mean the bartender?"

"Yeah, him. Well I told you that he was the one. I wasn't kidding. We like all the same shows, we listen to the same music. It's like we have the same soul. I can't keep my hands off him, and he feels the same way about me. He told me that he loved me on the second date. Can you believe it? We've never fought, not even once, and believe me, that's saying something because I fight with everyone."

"Wow, that's great," I said, genuinely relieved to hear that not all relationships end in tears.

"Anyway, I asked him to run away with me, and he said yes. A friend got us jobs on a cruise ship, but I learned my line editor has a roommate who owns an art gallery and they loved my illustrations. They asked if I wanted to do a show and I said 'um…YES' so I've been painting all month and then Zachary got a call offering him a job working on a missile defense system."

"A missile defense system? He's not tending bar there, I hope."

"No, didn't I tell you? Zachary is a genius. He's got a PhD in nuclear physics. I call him Doctor Calvin because I can't get over the fact I'm dating a doctor. The only reason he was working the bar is because jobs at his level are hard to find. A twenty-one-year-old with a PhD is still only twenty-one, and most interim employers aren't looking for boy geniuses with visible tattoos. Anyway, I know it's not cool to brag, but I can't help it. We're renting a house with a white picket fence. But enough about me, how did things go with Jonny Goodsnuff?"

I took a deep breath. "We had this amazing date. Then when I went to the airport, Jonny showed up and proposed to me. We just got back from our honeymoon in Paris, and now I'm in his huge house about ninety miles northeast of Los Angeles."

Ivy sighed. "Okay, you win."

"Trust me—it isn't quite as magical as it sounds. It all happened way too fast, and now I'm starting to wonder if I did the right thing by marrying a guy I barely know."

"Oh, come on. The guy's a celebrity. Everyone knows him."

"Not well enough to marry him, I can tell you. I'm starting to see a side of him that's making the words *no-fault divorce* sound pretty attractive."

"Well that's what you get for marrying a bestselling author. They get smooched on the southern hemispheres so often that they act like a higher life form. It *is* an act, you know, a big bluff to hide the insecurity. Don't cut him any slack, men like that are overgrown children. Just don't forget to keep the spark alive. As long as you're having fun in the sack, isn't that all that really matters?"

"Yeah, sure." I liked Ivy, but not enough to reveal that my husband's wood was more like a splinter. "Now that I'm a Californian, is there any chance you'll want to hang out?"

"That would be great. Unfortunately my license has been suspended, so you'll have to drive here to get me."

"I'll see when Jonny needs the car and we can set something up."

"Sounds like a plan."

"Great, I'm looking forward to it." I hung up, feeling pretty good now that my social batteries were recharged. I was still smiling when Jonny walked in.

"Who were you just talking to?"

"My new friend Ivy. We met at the conference."

"You mean that short girl that's all tattooed up like a circus freak?"

"Yes," I said tartly. "Her."

Jonny went over to the window and threw open the drapes before he stretched out next to me and turned on a boxing match on a huge television set. I gazed out the window, but the neighbor's swastika, fluttering in the moonlight, marred the view. I sighed and curled up under the comforter.

"So why didn't you come down for dinner?" Jonny asked.

"I was feeling tired from the flight."

"You didn't seem that tired a second ago. Did Misty say anything to upset you? Because she does that, you know. She's a great girl but she can be really hurtful at times. I didn't get a damn thing accomplished today because of her antics."

"I wouldn't push that all onto Misty. Lulu had a hand in it, too."

"Well, Lulu's different. She's sensitive."

"Sensitive? Or spoiled?"

Jonny clicked off the television.

I crossed my arms over my chest. "All I'm saying is that Lulu seems capable of surviving just fine when you're not around to defend her from her sister."

"Yes, well Lulu has it rough. I hate to say this about my own child, but she's got absolutely nothing going for her. She doesn't have her sister's trim figure, or her smarts. So I have to pay her a little bit of extra attention to bolster her self-esteem."

"And you don't think that Misty mistakes this extra attention for favoritism, and lashes out at Lulu because she's jealous?"

Jonny turned over on his side. "Look I'm really sorry you had to deal with all that your first day here. They're great girls, but they can be a handful when they want attention. I blame their mother. Her suicide really messed them up. Children love their mothers unconditionally, but Diana was a cruel, narcissistic woman who could never be happy unless everyone around her was miserable. I tried my hardest to get them away from her, but back in those days, it was impossible for a father to get custody of his kids." He sounded sincere, but I still wasn't sure how much I believed him. "I've tried my best to make it up to them by giving them a happy, carefree life, but I can't deal with them right now."

He turned down the family portrait, which revealed Stonewall and his judgmental gaze. I turned and looked out the window. Jonny leaned over and stroked my hair. "I have to find a quiet place to write. How would you like to go off and live in a hotel for the next few weeks?"

"Didn't you say you had another house on the beach?"

"Yes, but we can't go there."

"Why not?" I asked. "It's always been a huge dream of mine to live by the beach."

"I don't like the neighbor. He's a real weirdo."

I tore my gaze from the Nazi flag. "You have got to be kidding me. We're sleeping next to the Fourth Reich, but you won't take me to your beach house because you don't like your neighbor?"

"I'm not going to talk about it," Jonny said. "Suffice it to say, he gives me the creeps."

"And you don't think it's a bit weird that you own two houses and yet you can't think of a place to stay?"

Jonny sat up, and I flinched because I was afraid that I'd made him angry. But instead he seemed startled, as if the thought had never occurred to him.

"Very well," he said. "If you want to go to the beach house, we'll go to the beach house. I'll pack up the Jaguar and we'll drive out there tomorrow. But I don't want you talking to the neighbor. You can wave or smile and say hello or goodbye, but that's it. No conversation."

"Why not?"

"I just told you. He's a weirdo. His wife went missing, and if you're not careful you might go missing too."

I recalled the faces of the missing and murdered women I'd seen during my research and a chill ran through my body, but at the same time a morbid little voice in the back of my mind told me that a wife-killing neighbor might make a good topic for a novel. "A missing wife? You mean as in, missing and presumed dead?"

"No," Jonny said. "Nothing like that. He's just weird."

"Fine, I won't talk to the neighbor. Which house? The one on the right or the left?"

"The one on the left when you're facing away from the ocean." He rested back on the pillows with an anxious look on his face. "The one that's shaped like the back half of an Aztec pyramid."

I tried to settle into a comfortable position, but Jonny still looked stressed. I reached over and nestled up against him. "You know, if you think he's done something, you can always phone in an anonymous tip. You could claim you're a concerned friend and you haven't seen her in a while."

Jonny rolled his eyes. "I told you, it's nothing like that. They broke it off and I wasn't that surprised. He's an obnoxious nutjob, but I know for a fact his wife is even more messed up than he is. Look, it's not that big of a deal. I just don't like them. And I certainly don't want you mixed up with people like that."

"Good." I nestled into the pillows. "You worried me there for a second. I'm glad it's nothing serious."

"And I suppose I should tell you what my novel is about." It seemed like an odd change of subject, but I was too tired to comment. "It takes place in Asia and is about an ambassador. I draw deeply upon several ancient myths. However, you're not going to say anything to anyone, not even my agent. There are millions of dollars at stake so I need this book shrouded in absolute secrecy until it hits the presses. Have I made myself clear?"

"Yes, my love."

I fell into a deep sleep, content that he trusted me with a secret so close to his heart that he hadn't even told his beloved Stonewall.

CHAPTER 14

It was love at first sight. As we drove along the coast, I could see a massive glass and chrome structure rise up in the distance, with recessed lights along the overhanging roof, illuminating the house and the rustling date palms that surrounded it. It towered over the neighboring houses and the interior façade glowed golden beige. The top level was a dining room. It had turquoise chairs and a glass table in front of its one opaque wall tiled in sea green glass. The rest of the walls were crystal clear and the view must have rivaled the finest oceanfront restaurants anywhere in the world.

I perched up on the seat of the Jaguar and pointed. "Tell me that's our house."

Jonny sighed. "That's our house."

"Are you just saying that?"

"No, I'm not just saying that. That really is our house."

I let out a scream of delight and bounced up and down in my seat like a kid seeing the Matterhorn after a long drive to Disneyland. Jonny rolled his eyes and kept driving. We reached the house and he pulled into a hidden ground-level garage, and parked the car.

"We're home," he said. His voice was glum. I barely noticed since I was in the throes of ecstasy. The house even smelled right, like a subtle mix of leather, eucalyptus, and new car.

"How do we get inside?"

"The elevator is to your left."

Elevator? Oh, my God. In the span of a single month, I'd gone from a tenement apartment to a beach house with its own elevator. I looked and saw the brushed aluminum chamber, beckoning me to my new life. I had to fan myself to keep from fainting.

"The buttons on the walls are for the intercom. If you ever need to speak to me when I'm in another room, press the big square button. But don't abuse it while I'm writing or I'll have it disconnected." He chuckled. "I'm just kidding. I'll just hit the mute button right below it."

I was flying so high I didn't even give him a dirty look.

Jonny grabbed our suitcases from the trunk and led me to the elevator. The door opened to a palatial living room with a turquoise leather sectional surrounding a glass table. A lavish bar was visible as was a fireplace made of white stone. Lighted niches were filled with exotic bits of sculpture, mostly made of blown glass. The walls seemed to be covered with cream-colored suede. I touched it to see if it was a faux finish. It felt like velvet.

"Oh, Jonny. Pinch me so that I know this isn't a dream."

"Am I to assume that you like it?"

"Like it? There is not a word in the English language that can describe what I'm feeling right now."

"Come upstairs and I'll show you the living quarters." I followed him upstairs to a nearly featureless guest room that was all white. White walls, white bed, white carpet—the only color in the room was the crystal bowl of ultra-realistic looking silk roses on a glass end table. Normally, I'm not a fan of plain white rooms. They remind me of hospitals. But this room was so chic that I wanted to scream. I sat on the bed and sank into about a foot of down. A window overlooked the psycho-housing half-pyramid home next to ours.

Jonny beckoned. "If you're wondering where to put your things, come. I'll show you the walkthrough closet."

I rose and he opened a pair of folding doors to reveal a closet that was the size of my old apartment back in Ohio. Jonny had his things hung up and was using most of the cabinets and shelves for storage, but I didn't mind. I could shop every day for five years and still not fill the remaining space. On the other side was a huge travertine-lined bathroom with a Jacuzzi tub and a shower that looked like a small grotto.

"This is our master bath. When you need to dry off, press this button," Jonny hit a switch as my hair and skirt flew about as jets of hot air assailed us from every angle. "The chute here leads to the laundry room in the basement. There are no servants. You'll have to do your own wash. Here is our bedroom," he opened a door to another room decorated with some fairly good paintings in the style of Monet and Matisse. Velvet curtains framed a balcony that held a fancy telescope with a lens as thick as a coffee can. From the angle, I guessed that the only stars Jonny gazed at were the ones staying incognito at the luxury resort down the road from us.

"Upstairs is the dining room that you saw from the street."

"Where is the kitchen?" I asked.

"The kitchen is behind the garage."

In the basement? "That seems like an odd place for it."

"People who own houses like this don't cook their own meals."

"Oh," I said. Obviously, the house was built before people discovered that cooking could be a form of relaxation and entertainment.

"You don't like it?" Jonny asked.

"No, I love it. I was just expecting the kitchen to be closer to the dining room so that we can talk to guests while we're cooking."

"Let me make some calls and I'll get you your kitchen."

"No, really, please don't. It's great as it is. I love this house so much I don't want to change a thing. Putting in a new kitchen would be like adding recessed lighting to the Sistine Chapel."

"I don't mind, I'll call someone and have a new kitchen for you within a week."

"No, Jonny. I don't want one. If you'd like, you could get me a fondue pot instead. That way we can hold dinner parties without having to bring the food up from the basement."

That night we curled up in front of the fire in our magnificent new bedroom and sipped champagne before retiring to the bed. The evening was perfect. Who needs a honeymoon when their home is Shangri-la? For the first time in my married life, I was content. I felt that old magic again. Maybe I hadn't been a fool for marrying in such haste after all. I could hear the songs of angels in my ears as I drifted off to sleep.

How was I to know that this house was a deathtrap?

CHAPTER 15

When I woke the next morning, there was no water. I'd sent my sleep-wear down the chute, entered the shower, turned on the tap, but nothing came out. I stood in the grotto and waited with my arms crossed, wondering if this was some sort of futuristic plumbing that required special training to operate, but the tub didn't work, and neither did the sink.

I pressed the button for the intercom. "Jonny? I can't get any water. Is it because you were away? Would you like me to call the city and have them turn it on for us?"

"Don't worry about it, angel. I've got it all under control."

"Good, because right now I'm standing in the bathroom, completely naked, and I could really use a shower."

I heard deep masculine laughter coming from the other side of the intercom. It didn't sound like Jonny. It didn't sound like Stonewall either.

"Jonny, is there someone in here with us?" I wanted to dart into the closet but I was afraid to leave the room until I knew where our guest was. "Where are you at?"

"We're in the dining room. Don't worry about the water. I had it shut off so the contractor could install some new pipes. Guess who is getting that new kitchen that she wanted?"

I muted the intercom, so he couldn't hear me swear. How many times had I told him that I didn't want a new kitchen? Was it four times? Five? Yet here I was, trapped without water in my palatial bathroom while workers took a sledgehammer and a crowbar to the exquisite glass-tiled wall of my formal dining room.

Couldn't he have waited until I'd had a chance to set foot in it?

I told myself not to be so ungrateful—this was his house long before it was mine, and he was doing this for me. I dressed in the closet and took the elevator to the basement to find some bottled water so I could wash up a little and brush my teeth.

The kitchen was dank. Just a poorly lit prep area with a battered metal table, an oversized refrigerator, and wire racks stacked with tin cans and nonperishables. Maybe Jonny did have the right idea. I felt a profound pity for the previous generations of servants who had been consigned to this dungeon when there was so much natural and man-made beauty surrounding it in all directions.

Once I was combed and cleaned and had my daytime face on, I took the elevator up to the dining room. Jonny was standing at the glass table next to a sweaty man with black stubble, and they both straightened up and leered at me as I walked in.

Jonny nudged the workman. "So what do you think? Huh? Pretty good for an old goat my age, eh? Turn around, baby, and let him see you from the back."

Unless this contractor was Michelangelo reborn, there wasn't anything to be gained by Jonny's macho preening. So much for Jonny's claims that he had to act like a jerk to keep Stonewall in line. I now saw that he got infused with a misogynistic energy whenever there was another man in the room and I felt sick in my soul.

"I'd like to help you with your designs for the new kitchen."

Jonny nudged the other man. "That's great baby. Why don't you just lean over the table and tell us what you want done."

The workman cocked his head to the side, as if trying to take me in from a different angle. Everything about the situation made me feel queasy. "You know what? I'll go work on my writing."

"You do that, babe."

I set my laptop on the coffee table in the glorious new living room. Jonny had his typewriter on the writing desk, but I didn't mind. I prefer to write lying on the couch with the laptop in front of me.

I opened a text file to start a new novel, but then just stared at the blank page. What was the point? I had already written eight novels, each as good as I could possibly get them, and none would ever find a home. Try as I might, I couldn't find a story that would put me on the map. So I wasted a couple of hours surfing the web before I rose and hit the intercom switch. "Jonny, I'm going to go for a swim."

"You do that, babe."

I went back to my room and changed into my bikini. The beach must have been exclusive since it was fairly deserted for such a beautiful but slightly overcast June morning. I dropped my stuff onto the beach and ran into the blue water that lapped up against the sand with a froth of white foam at the crest of each wave. As I entered the water, I could taste the spray of the salt upon my lips. Soon my troubles were lost in the sound of the crashing waves and the screeches of the circling gulls.

This is the life, I thought, as I wove to keep my footing in the drive and push of the currents. But then, like Lot's wife, or Eurydice of the Greeks, I made the mistake of looking back.

I saw my magnificent new glass house, sparkling like the jewel of the neighborhood. Since it was daytime I didn't need the floodlights to see the cratered ruin of my formal dining room. And standing in the foreground, like an actor on the stage, was Jonny's contractor.

He was leering openly at my brine soaked breasts and buttocks. I hugged myself and waded deeper into the water until it covered me to my neck, but he just drank from a beer can and cocked his head to the side to get a better view. I waited a few minutes for him to get back to work, but he showed no intention of doing so.

The tide started to pull so I stomped out of the water and onto my towel. I looked up and he was still staring down at me. From this angle, I could only see his head. I began to worry where his hand was. I shook the sand from my towel, wrapped it around my waist like a sarong, and walked back into the house.

When the elevator door opened in the living room, I heard the clack of Jonny's typewriter. He sat at the desk with a bottle of Scotch and a can of baked beans with a spoon sticking up from it. He stopped typing when he saw me.

"Jonny?"

"Yes, babe?"

"I feel like going for a drive. I'm going to take the car. Is that okay?"

"No, it's not okay. That's a goddamned Jaguar down there, not some beat up Civic."

"Yes, well I'm your goddamned wife, not some teenage daughter who just got her license."

"Amanda, nobody touches my car but me. If the Virgin Mary herself came down from heaven and offered me everlasting salvation, I still wouldn't let her touch my car."

"Oh?" I put my hands on my hips. "You wouldn't let Stonewall drive your car?"

"Don't be ridiculous. Stonewall wouldn't be caught dead in a Jaguar."

I stepped away, then thought better of it and turned around again.

"Jonny, I need a car. I had a car just a few days ago, but I sold it and gave you all my money. You owe me a car."

"Fine, I'll buy you a brand new Lexus. Later. Right now I have a ten million dollar novel to write, which I'd be able to do a lot faster if I didn't have to deal with your constant interruptions or this new kitchen that you absolutely had to have."

My jaw dropped. Was he trying to upset me, or was he really that delusional?

"Jonny, how long are we supposed to wait until we have running water again?"

"I don't know. It will be off for at least a week while the plumbing is rerouted."

A week? "And what are we supposed to do for basic hygiene in the meantime? Jonny, I haven't had a proper bath in three days."

Jonny pursed his lips. I steeled myself, expecting a lecture, but instead he shrugged. "You just got back from the ocean."

"Oh, great, so you're telling me that we have to live like castaways because some shifty-eyed troll has set up camp in our dining room?"

"I'll handle this."

"Then handle it. I don't know how much money you're paying this guy, but I don't see what he's doing to earn it. Sure, he'll shut off the water and trash the place the moment you hire him, but I didn't see him making any progress while he was ogling me on the beach just a few minutes ago."

"That's your opinion. I think he's doing a fine job."

"Yes, but once your Scotch-and-bean breakfast finishes working its way through your digestive tract, we'll see what you think about his fine work then."

"I'm way ahead of you," he said. "And if you must know, there is an outdoor shower on the beach not too far from here. You can use that until I get the indoor plumbing situation straightened out."

A public shower? Perfect. "Jonny, you really expect me to pack up my entire beauty regimen and shower in front of the entire world? Do you think my hair grows out of my head this shiny and manageable? I use a lot of different conditioners."

Jonny raised his voice, but only a little. "Amanda, baby, I really don't ask all that much of you. You don't work. You don't have any responsibilities. You said yourself this is the house of your dreams, and now here you are, bitching because you have to take one or two steps across a pristine beach every morning."

He shook his head and went back to his typing. "Jesus Christ, when did you get to be such a nag?"

I thought about Jonny's words as I stood in my bikini and shampooed my hair in the shower next to the cinderblock toilet cabana. Maybe he was right. Maybe I wasn't the same sweet gracious girl he thought he married. As I looked at the sun dancing on the water, I reflected on how happy I would have been if someone told me a few months ago that this was going to be the worst of my problems.

Granted, I would be mortified if they could see me now, furtively sneaking soap under my bikini to get clean. Nevertheless, I couldn't deny that Jonny had given me a lot in a very short time while asking for nothing in return, and all I ever did was look for things to be negative about.

Maybe I just needed to stop complaining and learn to count my blessings. I gazed about for witnesses and then slathered deep-conditioner into my hair. I reached for my shower cap. I had to leave it on for at least twenty minutes to trap my body heat, so I could get the maximum body and shine from the conditioner.

Unfortunately, a cute guy came by after only five, carrying a surfboard and looking far hotter than any man had a right to look now that I was a lawfully married woman.

I yanked my cap off and did my best to rinse away the goo.

God, how do I describe this guy? He was slim and bronzed with just a hint of golden glint in his hair, no doubt from spending hours in the sun. He was young, with muscular limbs that were well-showcased by his sleek one-piece spring suit. He had a narrow but well-chiseled face that could rival any in Hollywood, from this era or any other. The worst thing of all was his award-winning smile, which regarded my basket of beauty supplies with obvious amusement.

He planted his board in the sand next to me. "That's an awful lot of product just to get the salt out of your hair."

I did my best to smile. "Sadly, this is my morning shower. I live a few houses down, but the water's been shut off." I would have pointed to my house, but thankfully, the cabana obscured it from view. I say thankfully, because if I couldn't see the house that meant the shifty-eyed handyman couldn't see me. "We're having a kitchen built onto our dining room."

"Oh, you must have moved into Goodsnuff's old place. I hadn't seen him for a while, but I wasn't aware that he'd moved. You wouldn't happen to have his forwarding address, would you?"

"Oh, no, he still lives there. With me. I'm his wife. Amanda. Amanda Goodsnuff," I held out my hand for him to shake.

"Lance. Lance Archer. Pleased to meet you, Mrs. Goodsnuff." Then he looked away. "Would you mind if I went over there and used the nozzle on the other end of the shower area? To rinse off? I can wait if you'd rather."

I shrugged. It was charming to see a guy this good-looking act so shy, "It's a public shower, go right ahead."

He walked over and turned on the water and tested it with his hand. Then, to my utter shock and amazement, he unzipped his spring suit and peeled it down to his waist, revealing a perfect set of pectoral muscles and six-pack abs.

I felt my legs go weak and I had to stagger back against the wall of the shower to keep my balance. Fortunately, he didn't notice, since he had his eyes closed as he arched his back to rinse his face under the jet of the shower. To me, adultery was one of the most evil things in the world and certainly something I would never engage in. Even so, it was all I could do to keep from pulling that zipper down the rest of the way and tugging that suit around his ankles while he still had his eyes closed.

Fortunately, I'd regained both my footing and my composure by the time he opened one eye.

"So, Mrs. Goodsnuff. What is it that you like to do?"

"Huh?" I felt myself blush.

"You know, for work, or for a hobby…"

"Oh, I'm a writer, just like my husband."

"No kidding? So am I."

"Really? Which genre?"

Now it was his turn to blush. "I've gotten about eighteen books published under the penname Prudy Newcastle. Perhaps you've heard of them?"

Of course, I'd heard of Prudy Newcastle. I'd even read a few of her books. They were the sort of chaste romances with all the good parts ellipsed out and left as an exercise for the reader. I'd always thought she must be a white-haired lady in a chintz dress and a purple hat, not some strapping young buck who was making me think impure thoughts while we shared a shower.

"You're Prudy Newcastle? No way."

"I'm afraid so. I never really set out to be a romance writer. I wanted to do thrillers, just like your husband. But I couldn't sell anything, so my wife suggested that I do a formula romance to get my foot in the door. The trouble with having your foot in the door is that you sometimes end up getting stuck there."

My face fell. "Oh."

"It's not so bad. I have a huge following of great fans who buy my books as soon as they come out. Besides, my job makes people very happy, and not everyone can say that. So really, it's all for the best."

I didn't tell him that I was more disappointed that he was married and off the market. But then again so was I. So he was right, it was all for the best.

He shut off his water and retrieved his board. "It was very nice meeting you, Mrs. Goodsnuff. Oh, and if you ever need to shower in private, you're welcome to come over and use one of mine."

"Really?" The mere suggestion of it made me tingle.

"Sure, and bring your husband. In fact, you should tell Jonny that the two of you have an open invitation for dinner at Lance Archer's place. I'm an excellent cook and it will be nice to have company for a change. I tend to be very introverted and melancholy, and if I don't make an effort to be social I end up retreating into hermit mode."

"I thought you said you were married?"

"My wife and I are going through a rough patch right now..." He sighed. "Who am I kidding? She's left me. I only found out about it by the note she left and the empty closets. It seems that I'm too boring for her. She went to where the action is."

"I'm sorry." I didn't ask if there was anything wrong with her eyesight, but that was certainly what I was thinking.

"I keep thinking that it's some terrible joke, but it's been over a month now and she hasn't even called to tell me where she is or what the next step is going to be." He gave a half smile. "And now I'm doing it again, burdening you with my problems before we've even gotten to know each other."

"I don't mind." Actually, he was so attractive that he could probably recite the Oxford English Dictionary and I still wouldn't mind.

"Tell Jonny I'm expecting the two of you for dinner this week and I won't take no for an answer. We haven't spoken in a while. I'm looking forward to catching up with him."

"That sounds great," I said. "I'm sure he'll be thrilled. Especially since our dining room is lying around in pieces."

"Again, it was great meeting you, Mrs. Goodsnuff. I look forward to having you over. And if your husband is too busy, feel free to stop by for a coffee or a glass of wine."

What a nice guy. I tried not to giggle as I watched him carry his board toward my house. As he neared it, he looked over his shoulder and gave me a wave before he entered the house next to ours.

The house that looked like half of an Aztec pyramid.

The one that allegedly housed the psycho neighbor.

Fortunately, he turned around before the blood drained from my face.

CHAPTER 16

I waited for Jonny to take a break from his typing to fix a sandwich in our dungeon-level kitchen before I approached.

"I've just met Lance Archer on the beach."

Jonny stopped scraping mayonnaise from the bottom of a jar. "Damn it, Amanda! I told you not to talk to him!"

"Well that's easier said than done, seeing as how I have to walk past his house every time I need to wash up or get a bucket of water. He seemed nice."

Jonny's head bobbed about. "Of course he did. What did he say?"

"He said he'd like us over for dinner soon."

Jonny snorted. "I'll bet he'd like that."

"He also told me about his wife."

"Oh, really? Did he tell you all about what a crazy freak she was?"

"No, he just said that he came home and the closets were cleaned out and there was a note, saying that she was leaving him because he was a bore."

"Yeah, I suppose so," Jonny said in a snide voice.

"Jonny, is there something I should know about our neighbor?"

Jonny spun and stared into my eyes. "I've already told you everything you need to know. He's a weirdo, I don't like him, and I don't want you to talk to him. Ever. In fact, if I ever see you talking to him, I'll drive you to the airport and put you on a plane back to Ohio. You're not to say another word to him. Not even to tell him that you can't talk to him. Especially not to tell him that I don't want you to talk to him."

"Why not?"

He looked away. "He's exactly the sort of freak of nature who keeps trying to get his name into the papers, that's why. I've got a blockbuster release coming out in just a few months, and the last thing I need is for you to say something foolish in front of that weirdo. If you see him coming, I want you to turn around and walk the other direction."

"Okay, but I think you're making a big deal out of nothing."

"I'm not making a big deal about it. Just don't talk to him."

I poured myself a glass of orange juice and went up to the living room. Maybe Jonny was telling the truth. Or maybe there was something more sinister afoot that Jonny just didn't want to get involved with, and if I could get to the bottom of it, might be my ticket to fame and fortune as a writer.

In the living room, I turned on my computer and did a quick Google search for the name Lance Archer. There were matches, but it quickly became clear that these were for different people. So much for wanting his name in the paper. I pulled up Facebook and MySpace. Again, no hot surf-god images appeared.

I took a sip of my juice and did a search for Prudy Newcastle. There were many matches there. Books, fan clubs, etc...I found her main homepage and brought up her biographical information. A glamour photo of an older woman with synthetically browned hair appeared on the screen, along with her life story and photos of her husband, two adult sons, six grandchildren, three cats, and her vegetable garden.

Maybe Lance Archer really was crazy.

There was a number at the bottom to reach her management—for serious inquiries only. I picked up the phone and dialed. A thoroughly bored male voice answered. "Pennyroyal Promotions, representing Prudy Newcastle. How may we help you?"

"Um, yes, I was wondering if you could help me with a phone number I've misplaced. It's a friend of mine. His name is Lance Archer?"

"I'm Lance Archer, who's this?" There was a pause at the other end. "Mrs. Goodsnuff, is that you?"

My heart skipped a beat and I slammed the phone back down on the cradle without thinking. Oh, crap, it never even occurred to me that the webpage was just a front. I had to find a way to fix this before he walked over here and told Jonny I tried to call him. I picked up the phone and hit redial.

"Mrs. Goodsnuff?"

"Hi there. Sorry about that, but I've been having trouble with this phone. It keeps cutting out unexpectedly," I added, just in case Jonny walked in and I had to hang up again.

"You've found my webpage, I presume?"

"Yes. I forgot to ask for your number so I tried to get it in a roundabout way. You must think I'm awful."

"Well, I could call you out on your devious behavior, but seeing as how you managed to find me through my web-page of lies, I don't think that I'm in much of a position to judge."

I couldn't help but smile. "So where did you get the photos to use for

Prudy Newcastle?"

"That's my Great-aunt Penny. When I told my family that I needed a jacket photo for my first romance novel, she offered me hers. Nobody knew that it was going to be a big deal back then."

"I'll bet she gets hassled a lot."

"She complains, but I can tell that she loves the attention. It isn't every day that a lonely old woman can't get young girls to stop talking to her at the grocery store."

"That's too funny. So why not route your calls to your real agent?"

"I haven't got one."

"You don't have an agent?"

"That's the beauty of the romance genre. You don't need an agent to get started. You just call up the publisher and they send you a tip sheet on what they do and do not want you to write."

"No agents, huh," I said. "Maybe I'll write a romance."

"Ah, careful. If all goes well you'll end up contractually obligated to finish a book every three months, and then there goes your marriage. Speaking of which, what did Jonny say about dinner?"

I felt my lip twist. "Well…I'm sorry but Jonny's been busy and I haven't had a chance to talk to him yet. But now that I have your number, I'll call you just as soon as I've asked."

"Great. I can't wait to have you two over."

"Sure. Bye now," I said.

No sooner had I hung up than Jonny walked in. "Ask me what?"

I screamed and nearly sprang from the couch. "My God, Jonny, don't sneak up on people like that. You scared the life out of me!"

"I'm sorry." His eyes were big and warm, just like they were when I fell for him. "So what did she want?"

"Who?"

"That tattooed chick you just got off the phone with, I assume that's who you were talking to."

"Oh, Ivy." I felt just rotten about misleading him like this, but what else was I supposed to say? Emily Post didn't exactly write a chapter on how to conceal an accidental and purely innocent conversation with a potential psychopath from your husband. "I was wondering if I could invite her and her boyfriend over for dinner and a tour of the house."

"Of course you can, baby. Just be sure to explain to them that I'm on a tight deadline and you'll have to entertain them on your own until dinner." He sat at his typewriter then looked up at me. "And I'm really sorry that I've been so short with you lately. I've been thinking about it, and you make a good point about needing a car. This weekend, after I've finished the chapter I'm writing, I'm going to go right out and get you a Lexus."

I never did get that Lexus. I'm sure that Jonny was sincere when he told me he was going to buy it, but the drama that followed purged all thoughts of car shopping completely from my mind.

Ivy and her boyfriend agree to come over, but the day got off to a bad start. I went up to the dining room to have a look at the progress before the handyman came in. Unfortunately, that unsavory character was already there. He held a wrench, puffed out his cheeks, and lowered his eyebrows at me. Otherwise, the room looked no different than it did the day before. I backed out and took the elevator down to the kitchen so I could get some plastic jugs to fill with enough water to cook a pot roast and do the washing up afterwards.

Ivy arrived that afternoon and introduced me to Zachary. He turned out to be a great guy, despite his scruffy haircut and mascara. After only a few minutes of talking to him, it was obvious that he was smart, funny, down to earth, and completely devoted to Ivy. It did my heart good to know that there were some fine men out there with deep souls and a healthy respect for women, even if none of them had ever been interested in dating me personally.

I showed them around the house and led them into the kitchen where the smell of the roast filled the air. The three of us were playing beer pong on the stainless steel food prep table when Jonny walked in.

"What are you doing?" Jonny asked.

"We're playing a drinking game," I said. "Would you like to join us?"

Jonny looked over Ivy and Zachary and took a deep breath. "Amanda, can I talk to you in private?"

I didn't like the question. It sounded rude. "Whatever you have to say, you can say in front of my friends."

"I was going to say that I'd like it if the woman I married showed a little class and stopped playing carnival games on the kitchen table."

I gave him a warm smile because I sincerely hoped that he was trying to be funny. "Well, I would have preferred to play on the dining room table, but it's currently buried under power tools and bits of broken tile. Jonny, I'd like you to meet my friends Ivy and Zachary. As I told you before, Zachary is a doctor of physics, and Ivy is an accomplished artist."

Zachary straightened up and held out his hand. "It's nice to meet you, Mr. Goodsnuff. I've read a few of your books and it's just amazing to be able to meet you in person."

Jonny stared at his hand as if it was a moldy dishrag, and then shook it reluctantly. Ivy watched with an expression of heartache.

"So you're a physicist, huh? Shouldn't you look smarter?"

Zachary's smile vanished. "I don't know what you mean, sir."

"I mean, come on, your hair's a mess and you're painted up like a fairy! Shouldn't you be wearing glasses and a pocket protector?"

"Sure, Chief," Zachary said. "If this was still 1978."

I laughed aloud and it sounded a little weird because nobody else made a sound. They all just turned and looked at me as if I was drunk in church.

"Jonny, Ivy is having a gallery show tomorrow night, and just for fun, all of her friends will be dressing up. The men have to wear long coats and the women will wear wigs. I've already told her we'd be there. I think it will be great, and we'll really enjoy it."

Jonny's lip curled. "First cups and balls, and now dress-up games. What are you, five?"

I felt myself flush to the roots of my hair. Ivy hopped off the counter. "You know what, Zachary? I think we'd better get going."

I forced another laugh. "Don't be silly. You promised you'd stay for dinner."

"Amanda, if your friends have somewhere they'd rather be, I think we should let them go."

Ivy came over and tapped my arm. "It's a lovely house, Amanda. We'll catch you later."

As I watched them leave, I had the horrible realization that I might never see them again. Jonny opened the oven. "Something smells good. What's for dinner?"

My hands shook with rage as I grabbed the glasses off the table and dumped them out into the sink. I had to keep my hands busy to keep from picking up the carving knife and ramming it between Jonny's shoulder blades.

"I made pot-roast with fingerling potatoes and baby carrots. Since I was cooking for four people, you should have plenty of leftovers."

"Don't take that tone with me. They left here of their own free will."

"After you went out of your way to make them uncomfortable! How could you humiliate Ivy like that? You must have known how proud she was of her gallery showing and you made it into a cheap joke."

"Well then maybe you should find some friends that aren't so easy to make fun of."

"You mean like your asthmatic fancy boy you call your agent?"

"Hey, you leave Stonewall out of this!"

I threw the dishrag in the sink. "Oh! So you're allowed to trash my friends, but I'm not allowed to trash yours?"

"That's correct, because unlike your friends, Stonewall isn't one of life's losers."

"Well, then, since you love him so much, maybe you should have married *him*!"

"Maybe I should have! Then at least I'd have someone intelligent to share dinner with!"

I just stood there and stared at Jonny with my mouth hanging open before I reached for my purse.

"Amanda!"

"Eat by yourself. I'm leaving you."

I ignored Jonny's protests as I stormed out of the house and into the night air. The sound of surf served as a soundtrack for my life crashing down around me. My worst fear had been confirmed—I'd married a Neanderthal. One that pretty much admitted he loved his agent more than he could ever love me. Not that I thought there was any funny business going on between them. In a way, that would have been easier. Then I could claim he tricked me, and none of this would have been my fault because Jonny had needs that I could never satisfy.

As I walked down the boardwalk, I glanced back once, just to make sure that Jonny wasn't chasing after me. He wasn't. I kept walking until I entered a bar and grill. College students filled the booths. A perky young waitress approached. "How many this evening?"

"One," I said.

"Right this way, ma'am."

Ma'am? Since when did I become a ma'am? I followed her to a round raised table, flanked with two high stools. I would have rather sat at a booth, but those were packed with people, so I was stuck at the table like an exhibit on display.

Behold, the lonely newlywed, married only a week and already filing for divorce.

I took out my cell phone and dialed Ivy.

"Yellow," she said.

"Ivy, this is Amanda."

"Hi, sweetie. I hope you don't take this the wrong way, but I think your husband is a total douche bag."

I laughed. "Sadly, I don't disagree."

"Does this mean that you'll still come to my art show tomorrow?"

"Does this mean you'll still have me?"

"Geez, of course, but I think that from now on we should hang at my place."

"Oh, I hear you."

"Mrs. Goodsnuff?" I looked up and saw Lance Archer. He smiled that hundred-megawatt smile and suddenly the world didn't feel like such a dreary place after all.

"Got to let you go, Ivy."

"Bye, sweetie. Call me later."

I turned the ringer off as I smiled back at Lance. "Hi, there."

"Imagine, both of us choosing the same place and the same time. Is your husband joining you?"

"No," I said. "And I'm not sure that won't be the permanent state of things."

"Did you have a fight?"

"More like an epiphany."

"Oh." Lance gestured feebly toward the table. "Do you mind if I sit here?"

"Please do." As he sat, I noticed that a sorority girl with jet-black hair nudged her friend at another table while the other girl sat speechless, lost in a fantasy no doubt inspired by Lance's rugged shoulders.

"I think you have some admirers at the table behind us."

Lance glanced back and shrugged. "You were saying that you were having trouble with Jonny?"

I shook my head sadly. "I don't think we're meant to be together. I'm a Cosmo girl and I suspect that he wants some old-fashioned floozy who will look good on his arm while he goes out carousing with his Neanderthal friends. We seemed to get along great while we were dating, but now that we're married, everything I do meets with his disapproval. And, sadly, the feeling is totally mutual."

"Maybe things will work themselves out."

"I doubt it," I said. "He just humiliated me in front of my friends. I really resent that the man I married sees me as a fixer-upper. I don't intend to reinvent myself just to suit his outdated world view. The only reason I even hesitate is because I don't want to have to give up that beach house, and the fact that I'd stay with someone for a house bothers me a little."

"Well, if it makes you feel any better, I'd hate it if you left, too."

Those words sent a flutter through my body.

The waitress appeared. "Do you know what you'd like to order?"

"What's good?" I asked Lance.

"They're famous for the grilled mahi-mahi."

"I'll have that then, and a rum and Coke, with the meal."

"And for you sir?"

"I'll have the mahi-mahi, but with a bottle of your house ale."

"Coming right up."

After she left I leaned toward Lance. "So what do you think I should do?"

"I think you should wait until Jonny is getting ready for bed and tell him what you told me—that you're deeply in love with him, but you're worried that you're disappointing him as a wife."

"Huh?" I don't know what I'd expected him to say, but that wasn't even close. "I'm not sure that I agree with you. I've dealt with narrow-minded narcissists like my husband in the past, and in my experience when you start accepting responsibility for their failings, they never let you hear the end of it."

"Yes, but were any of these people professional novelists?"

When I didn't answer, he reached for his wallet. "Here, let me show you something." He pulled out a photograph and gave it to me. It was a black and white close-up of two children. On the bottom was written LANCE – AGED 6. LORI ANNE – AGED 7. The little boy was pillow-lipped and stared into the camera with a Gerber Baby expression. The girl had long dark hair and had her head thrown back in laughter.

He tapped the figures. "That's me, and that's my wife Lori Anne. We lived next door to one another, but I knew even as a child that she was the girl for me. The original was in color, but it hurt too much to look at it. I've changed it to black and white to remind me that she's part of the past."

The food arrived. The fish was served with a side of citrus rice, a bed of beans, and a small wedge of pineapple. After we had a few bites, I prompted Lance to continue his tale.

"We dated throughout high school and all the other kids thought we were the perfect couple. She was captain of the flag girls, so I joined the football team. She sat with the popular kids so I sat there, too. We were crowned homecoming king and queen, and we dominated half of the yearbook our senior year. But then we graduated and I couldn't bear the thought that we might be accepted into separate colleges, so I asked her to marry me."

"And she said yes?"

He nodded. "Our families were overjoyed. Her parents paid for a huge fairy tale wedding and invited over a hundred people. My parents paid for a honeymoon in Hawaii and set us up with a furnished condominium to help get us started. I didn't feel comfortable supporting a wife on charity, but we were still kids and I couldn't find a job that would pay a living wage. So I took up writing and got my first novel published at nineteen."

"Congratulations," I said.

He gave me a faint smile. "At first, life was perfect. We moved out of our little condo, into a house in California. I did that for Lori Anne and I thought it would make her happy, but it didn't. Where we're from, Lori Anne was something special, but in the city, she was just another small-town girl. She complained constantly so I had to zone her out. At that point Prudy Newcastle was becoming an industry and I'd learned that being a novelist is its own special kind of hell."

"Really," I said. "Because that's the sort of hell that I'm trying desperately to get into."

"Writing is probably the one profession that gets harder rather than easier after you pay your dues. You have to keep proving yourself over and over again. Each new book has to be better, because heaven help you if your latest book sells one copy less than the one before it."

He took a large swig from his bottle before continuing. "I'm contractually obligated to produce four books a year, and I used up all the good ideas I had before I finished the third book. My days are spent sitting at my computer, frantically typing out whatever images pop into my head in the hopes that I can build a cohesive story around them later. I had to ignore Lori Anne, and Lori Anne is not a girl who likes to be ignored. She wanted to go out every night and do things, just like we did in high school. I tried, but I couldn't enjoy myself and that upset her. So she'd complain so much I had to wear earplugs while I was writing."

That conjured up an image of Lulu beating on the door of her father's study. I took a sip of my drink to chase it away.

"Soon I was bringing in advances in the high six figures, so we moved to this beach house. That seemed to make her happy, for a few days. You see, I like to surf, but Lori Anne has very fair skin that burns easily. Soon she was twice as bored and upset as she had been before. Therefore, I made the biggest mistake of my life. I, an alleged authority on romance, bought a book on how to have a better marriage."

"Oh, dear," I said.

Lance nodded solemnly. "It suggested that the key to a happy marriage is the freedom to pursue outside interests. I encouraged Lori Anne to get a job and develop a life of her own outside of the marriage. Looking back now, I realize that's probably the worst advice you can give a couple whose relationship is already on the rocks."

"So what happened?"

"Lori Anne stopped complaining. She was happy, so I was happy." He looked down. "How was I to know it was because she was screwing her boss? Her fat, much older, married boss. I didn't find out until I came home to an empty closet and a note explaining why she'd rather be his kept woman than stay with me for even one more day."

"Wow," I said. "That must have been harsh."

"It destroyed me, Amanda. I've loved her my whole life. I don't know how to live without her. I keep waiting for her to come back, but it's been almost two months and I haven't heard from her, so I'm starting to realize that might not happen."

He looked so upset that I couldn't help but reach out and touch his arm. "Hey, I'm sorry. But if that's the way she feels, you're better off without her."

He gave me an imploring look. "Please, give Jonny another chance. Don't break his heart. Do you know what he's working on?"

I shook my head. He waited for me to speak, but I didn't intend to do so.

"Well, knowing Jonny Goodsnuff, it's probably something dark and violent and that's putting his head in a bad place. Now might not be a good time to suggest ways that he can be of service to you. But if you let him know that you're willing to do whatever it takes to make him happy, he'll take the hint and start treating you as well as you deserve."

I nodded, even though I did not intend to follow his advice.

We finished our meal and Lance gave the waitress his credit card. "I've got this."

"Thank you," I said.

"No I should be thanking you. I've never spoken of my problems with Lori Anne before. It actually feels really good to get this all out into the open. Give me a call later and let me know that you've worked things out."

He leaned over and gave me a kiss on the cheek. The feel of his lips lingered for several hours.

Chapter 17

As I walked home, I could see the silhouette of the handyman peering down at me from the remains of our dining room. I didn't even care. I just wanted to retrieve my laptop and then get a good night's sleep before I plotted my escape. When the elevator opened into the living room, I saw my husband typing away next to a portable toilet. The kind they keep at country fairs and construction sites. I didn't even say a word. I just grabbed my laptop, went up to my room, and got ready for bed.

Jonny was up a few hours later. His hair was oily and he smelled like a goat.

I turned over on my side. "I think it might be a good idea if I slept in the guest bedroom."

"You do that."

I picked up my laptop and left for the one room of the house where I could get away from my husband and his plumbing issues. The guest room was cool and inviting like an oasis, but I couldn't sleep, not with the view of Lance's house outside my window. I kept thinking about the story he told me. It certainly painted a damning portrait of his wife, but she wasn't around to defend herself, so I couldn't be sure how far his recollections could be trusted.

I reached for my laptop, brought up Facebook, and typed in the name LORI ANNE ARCHER.

A match came up right away. All I could say was wow.

She'd set up her profile as public so I was able to see everything, and I do mean everything. Well, almost everything. Her avatar photo was an up-the-miniskirt shot where she'd thrust out her derriere to give the photographer a good view of her French-cut white panties. The caption read "My best side."

That photo and the lewd remarks in barely literate English were like something out of a Fellini movie. I suspected this might be another of Lance's carefully staged web hoaxes, but Lori Anne had seventy-five friends. I didn't check all of them, but I did click on enough to confirm that they all had families, careers, and social circles that didn't revolve around the Archers.

Then there were the pictures. All of the other photos in her album showed her dressed as Bettie Page for a costume party, complete with a leopard print bikini, fetish boots, and in some shots, a ball gag. Even though the airbrushed makeup hid her freckled complexion, I could see she was a grown-up version of the little girl from Lance's photo. She had her head thrown back in that familiar expression of laughter as a partygoer in a gorilla suit and a diaper carried her around. The name tagged for the photo confirmed my initial hunch that the man in the costume was not her husband.

In another photo, she posed with her arms around a sexy witch, whose innocent expression told me that she was unaware that Lori Anne's tongue jutted to her ear in a sexually suggestive manner.

Really, Lance? Your wife acted out like this in public, and it never occurred to you that your marriage could benefit from a little more 'us' time?

The photos were dated Halloween from the year before. There were no recent photos. There were no status updates since early February. This concerned me, since before then she'd left a comment on her Facebook page on a nearly daily basis. Yet according to Lance she must have walked out on him sometime during the early May timeframe.

So what happened to March and April?

Maybe Valentine's Day was when her boss began filling her void?

Or maybe she simply no longer wanted to be known as Mrs. Archer? I wished I knew her maiden name. I returned to her friends' profiles and scanned for a listing for a Lori Anne with a different surname. I'd clicked on fifteen profiles before I gave up.

I glanced at the window, which offered a view of the top of Lance's beach house, and let out a sigh. So close, yet out of reach. I looked out the window to see what I could see. To my surprise, the tiers of his house were made of glass so I could see down into a few of his rooms. Just like looking into a dollhouse. His living room was white, with sparkly granite floors and mahogany-colored leather couches that formed a U around the fireplace. A bronze carousel horse reared up near the bookshelves by a computer hutch desk along the far side.

In the tier above that was an outdoor gym, complete with a fire pit. I could see Lance stretched out on a weight bench, pressing what I guessed to be about a hundred and fifty pounds. His muscle shirt had crept up to expose just a little bit of his flat belly. A trail of fine dark hair led from his navel to his shorts.

I felt a sudden urge to go over there and straddle him as he worked on his weights. I forced myself away from the window, but only for a moment.

I just couldn't stay away. Lance stopped and looked toward me. I ducked, and then realized that there was no way that he could see inside. From the outside, the window was mirrored both night and day.

Still, he was thinking of me. It was too much. The fact that he'd stared at my window after we'd just had dinner together gave me goose bumps, in a good way. I grabbed my cell phone and headed down to the beach.

I hiked up my nightgown and headed for the water. As the waves sloshed against my ankles, I felt safe to dial.

"Yellow."

"Ivy. I've got a problem."

"So let me see if I've got this straight: you're currently trapped in a love-less marriage with a total pig, whose latest stunt is to set up a porta-potty so that he can crap at will in the middle of your living room, and the only reason you're staying with him is so that maybe you'll have a shot at the hot neighbor, who may or may not be an axe-murderer?"

"Yes, that's pretty much it in a nutshell."

"And exactly how hot is this beefcake neighbor of yours?"

"Have you ever seen the commercial where all the women in the office all get up from their desks and run to the window whenever the cute deliv-eryman comes by?"

"Yeah?"

"He's that hot. He's the sort of guy who looks good in everything and better in nothing."

"And he claims he's Prudy Newcastle?"

"It's true. I called her exclusive management firm and he answered the phone. He could be an employee, but from the looks of his house they must have an amazing benefits package and one heck of a telecommuting policy."

"I'll look him up on Google."

"I've already done that. There's no record that he even exists. But I saw a lot more of his wife than I wanted to see on Facebook."

"Are you sure you got her name right? I don't suppose that he wrote it out for you. I'll bet that I can come up with about a dozen variant spellings for Lori Anne."

"I saw it written on the back of a photo. L-o-r-i A-n-n-e. I'm fairly sure it's two words."

"Let me go to my computer and take a look…"

I paced about on the wet sand as I waited for Ivy's reaction.

"Wow. Just—wow."

"I know, huh?"

"I think you should give your neighbor the benefit of the doubt on this one. Lori Anne is not the sort of girl who could 'go missing' and not be missed by a whole lot of people."

"Except she went from being the life of the party to incommunicado, and nobody bothered to make a comment on her page about it."

"Perhaps we could contact a few of her friends to gather some further insight?"

The suggestion made me nervous, given the amount of snooping I'd done already. "I don't think that would be a good idea. They might notify Lance, and he'd been quick to guess who was studying up on Prudy Newcastle. He's probably half convinced that I'm stalking him already, and I doubt that telling him we're merely ruling him out as a potential serial killer will make him feel any better."

"Then I wouldn't worry about it. If something had happened to her, it would've made the papers. And as a suspense writer you must know the police always badger the husband until he either confesses or proves he didn't do it."

I sighed. "I suppose you're right. Now that we've established that Lance isn't an axe-murderer, I just have to figure out what's really wrong with him."

"Has it occurred to you that what's wrong with him is that there's nothing wrong with him?"

"How do you mean?"

"From what I've seen of your husband, he seems like an insecure little Chihuahua. His car, his phallic-symbol mansion, and his macho tough-guy novels—he obviously has self-esteem issues. Meanwhile he's living next door to some boy-wonder novelist who is younger than he is, hotter than he is, probably richer and more successful than he is—"

"Richer and more successful than Jonny Goodsnuff?"

"Hey, you'd be surprised. Romance readers are insatiable. Jonny's may earn five times more, but Prudy writes ten times as many. Do the math. You don't think that chafes your husband just a little? And to top it all off Jonny's brought home a cute blond pinup girl shortly after Lance's skanky wife put him back on the market...Come on, sweetie, I'm no mystery novelist, but you don't have to be Sherlock Holmes to figure out why your husband doesn't want you popping over for a cup of sugar."

I smiled. "So what should I do? Jonny's making me miserable, but Lance seems determined to patch up my marriage. I'm afraid that if I leave, he'll see me as just another faithless Jezebel and want nothing more to do with me."

Ivy paused. "Sorry, can't help you with that one. All I can say is that if something's meant to be, it will happen. Good luck with whatever."

"Can you ask Zachary to give me a ride to your show tomorrow?"

"Of course. Bye now."

As she hung up, I stood with the water churning around my feet. I looked back and saw my house, with the roof level floodlights illuminating the ruins of my dining room. Right next to it was Lance's house, with light beaming out from its multi-tier exterior.

Houses made of glass, indeed.

I couldn't just walk out of Lance's life. Not without explaining why I couldn't stay. I took one more look before I made my last call for the night.

"Pennyroyal Promotions, representing Prudy Newcastle. How may we help you?"

"Lance? It's Amanda."

"Hey," he said. "Did you work things out with Jonny?"

I bit my lip. I wanted to say no, but he sounded so hopeful that I lost my nerve. "Yes, thank you. I did just what you said and it worked like a charm. But I have a huge favor to ask."

"Oh?"

"We're supposed to go to a friend's art show tomorrow night, but Jonny can't make it. So I was wondering if you could be my chaperone?"

I felt my cheeks burn while I waited for his answer.

"An art show?" Lance said. "Sure, I'd love to. That sounds like fun."

"Do you have a long coat? The men are supposed to wear coats and the women are wearing wigs."

"Nothing I'd wear to a gallery, but I've been meaning to buy some coats anyway. What time should I pick you up?"

A vision flashed through my mind of Jonny erupting like a volcano after seeing Lance show up at our doorstep with a corsage.

"Actually, it would be better if we came and got you."

CHAPTER 18

Zachary and Ivy drove up in their jeep while I was putting on a bobbed red wig. I wore glittery green eye shadow and a silk baby-doll dress with a funky print. I was trying for sultry and mysterious, but ended up looking like the mother on *Bewitched*. Unfortunately, I didn't have time to change.

"Goodbye, Jonny, I'm off on a date," I said to the intercom to assuage my conscience. He didn't bother to reply.

When we arrived at Lance's, he was waiting outside in a black leather coat over a white T-shirt and blue jeans. The coat had a Mandarin collar meant to be buttoned, but then it wouldn't curtain his chiseled physique, so I said nothing. I opened the door and scooted to one side as he slid in next to me.

"Lance, I'd like you to meet my friends, Ivy and Zachary." They looked back and gave a half wave. "Guys, this is Lance, my neighbor."

"Nice to meet you," Lance shook Zachary's hand and gave Ivy's a quick squeeze. As he leaned forward, his leg brushed against mine, in a way, knowing Lance, must have been completely accidental. I closed my eyes and let the shivers travel through my body. When I opened them, Lance was stealing glances at me as if I was the last cupcake on a party tray.

"Is something wrong?" I said.

"You look amazing."

"Ah, thank you, you look great, too."

"No, I mean it. You look incredible. Not that you don't always look nice, but I love the way you've made up your eyes."

"You don't think it looks too sixties-hippie matron?"

"Are you kidding? No."

He stared right into my eyes and it threw me off guard. I wouldn't have known that Lance could be this forward. Had that coat given him a dose of badass attitude? Or was he on social anxiety meds and had taken one too many?

The gallery was in the better part of Santa Monica. Men in Italian suits and women in silk dresses mingled among Ivy's friends in coats and Day-Glo wigs. Within a few minutes, Ivy and Zachary drifted away into a group with multiple facial piercings.

"This drawing is interesting," Lance said as he looked at a spiral pattern of mermaids with fangs devouring fish, and fish with fangs devouring mermaids.

A tall brunette in a Burberry coat and calfskin boots set down her cocktail. "Yes, that one is my favorite too." She stood between us, and placed her hand on his arm. "There's another drawing of a geisha looking into a pond that is quite amazing. Can I show you where it is?"

He looked down at the hand on his arm and wrinkled his nose. "Do you work here?"

"No I'm an art-lover, just like you."

He pulled his arm away. "That's a shame because I was going to ask you to get a drink for my date. Let's go, Amanda."

He led me away, and in the distance, we could see tables offering phalanxes of champagne glasses and platters of cheese, crackers, and dried fruit. Lance gave me a flute of champagne and took one for himself. In the background, I could see a blonde in a spandex dress edging toward us with a hungry look.

He glanced at her as if she was a tiger and pulled me off into a corner. He was standing so close I could feel the heat from his body. I took a long sip of my drink to cool off, but that only made it worse.

Lance glanced at the blonde in spandex, who was still edging toward us. As she walked, her breasts bounced unfettered like two giant hacky sacks. Some men watched, spellbound, but Lance wasn't one of them. A couple passed in front of her, and we slipped through an archway into another part of the gallery filled with ink drawings and velvet couches. On the closest wall was a drawing of a geisha who gazed into a pool at her reflection, which had been distorted to resemble a decaying corpse.

"This must be the drawing that woman was talking about." He leaned over to whisper. "I don't know what it is, but I can't go out in public without being hassled by complete strangers."

I took another sip. "I know why. It's because you're absolutely gorgeous."

He smiled. "Thanks, that's quite a compliment, since it comes from a true beauty, both inside and out. I can't believe how great that wig looks on you."

He touched a lock of the red hair, and even though it wasn't real, I had to hold the glass with both hands to keep them from shaking. As his fingers traveled down the length of it, they brushed against my skin and I felt my legs go weak.

This wasn't the Lance I thought I knew. It was as if he'd taken the night off and had one of the rakes from his novels take over for him. The sort of

arrogant rogue that had to tame Prudy Newcastle's stable of interchange-
able Charlottes, Violets, and Georginas who were forever mistaking their
sexual frustrations for deep-seated loathing. Seeing as how I wasn't nearly
as repressed, I had to steer the conversation to banality, and fast.

"It's been my observation that natural blondes do tend to look good with
black or dark red hair, just like blond hair looks good on brunettes. Gold
hair matches well with tan skin, while bold hair colors go well with light
eyes and porcelain complexions."

I'm sure that would have put Jonny to sleep, but Lance gave me a silly
smile. "Have you ever considered dyeing it that color permanently?"

I laughed. "No way, I'd have to give up wearing pink. Besides, this wig is
not nearly as flattering as you think. I'm wearing a lot of makeup right now."

"Really?" He took hold of my chin and tilted my face about to get a good
look from all angles. "That's incredible. I don't see a trace of it, aside from
the eye shadow, but your face has undergone a complete transformation.
It's amazing."

"Actually, I'm a professional makeup artist. There isn't anything I don't
know about facial contouring."

He raised his eyebrows. "Facial contouring?"

I sighed. "It's about the proper application of cosmetics. You wouldn't
be interested."

"Amanda, you're talking to Prudy Newcastle. Of course I'm interested."

He steered me to a corner done up with red draperies and velvet couches.
We sat with his arm close to mine and our knees touching. I felt shivers at
the proximity but forced myself to concentrate.

"It's simple really. It's all about using multiple shades of makeup to create
the illusion of light and shadow. Light hits the parts of your face that are
most prominent and darkens the parts that are more recessed. Therefore,
to create the illusion of cheekbones, you would start out light at the top
and use foundation and blush that is progressively darker below. The same
principle applies to your nose and chin. A good enough artist can create an
illusion that fools the eye, even in profile."

I thought I might have bored him to death at this point, but he stared
into my eyes with a smirk of fascination on his face. Therefore, he didn't
notice the blonde and her spandex-clad buttocks passing through the
crowd in the distance, but she noticed us and pivoted to approach. As soon
as she entered his field of view, Lance moved closer to me so that our torsos

pressed together.

"I hope you don't mind my sitting so close," he whispered. "But if she thinks we don't want to be disturbed, maybe she'll leave us alone."

I might have said something clever if I'd been capable of speech. Or thought. The feel of his body against mine left me completely intoxicated. His next words worked as an antidote.

"So how are things going with Jonny?"

I pulled back a little. "Great. Thanks for asking."

He grinned and held up one finger. "I hate to say it, but I told you so. Your husband's in a dark place right now. You just needed to give him the opportunity to prove that you had nothing to do with it. Did you ask him how far along he is with his novel?"

"His novel?"

"He is a novelist," Lance said. "I assume he must be working on something. Did he say what his next novel would be about?"

As I studied his rakish smirk, it occurred to me that Lance might be turning on the charm so that he could steal some of Jonny's ideas for his own writing. He'd already said that he had to work all night and write by the seat of his pants.

"That information is strictly confidential."

He waved his champagne flute under my nose. "If I ply you with enough alcohol, you might get tipsy and reveal a plot point or two."

"You're certainly welcome to try."

He raised his glass to my lips and I took a small sip. The more I thought about it, the more sound my theory seemed. Jonny's next novel was sure to be heralded by an enormous amount of publicity and fanfare. If Prudy Newcastle could put out a similar book in the same timeframe, Lance would tap into some of that hype or even steal Jonny's thunder entirely. It was no wonder Jonny didn't want me to talk to him. I wasn't sure if I felt disappointed or relieved.

"Can you keep a secret?" I said.

"Of course."

I tried to think of an outlandish plot, just to test my theory, but I couldn't think of anything crazy enough that it might not be true. I figured I'd better not tempt fate. "Jonny isn't working on anything at all. He's taking a break from writing."

I studied Lance's face to see his reaction. I thought he might be disappointed, but instead he let out a wistful sigh. "Taking a break from writing, that must be nice. Maybe I should take a break as well."

"I think so. After all those novels, you've certainly earned one."

Then I noticed the spandex blonde, crouched for approach. Lance's lip curled in disgust.

"Unbelievable," he said. "Some people just cannot take a hint. I guess we're just going to have to spell this out for her."

I gasped as he grabbed hold of me and pulled me onto his lap so that I was facing him.

"Lance, what are you doing?" As he brushed his hand down my hips to straighten out my dress, I felt a surge of heat travel through my body, making me dizzy. "We shouldn't sit like this."

"What do you mean?" His arms circled my waist and he pulled me closer. Close enough for me to feel that he knew exactly what I was talking about. I immediately went into a panic. Not because I was afraid of what he might do to me. I was afraid of what I might do to him. "I think she's gone. I can get down now."

He gave me a roguish smile. "I can't hear you over this music. You're going to have to lean closer."

I could feel his breath on my lips. I knew what was coming. I knew it was wrong, but I couldn't have resisted even if I wanted to. I bent forward and he cupped his hand behind my head. We kissed, and it was the hottest, most intense kiss of my life. The heat at the junction of our bodies began to ache, and my breath came out in rough gasps. Lance seemed to take delight in my torment. I didn't care. Lust consumed me and I had to have him right there in the middle of the gallery. It didn't matter who saw us. All that mattered was that I needed to take him before I came to my senses and remembered that this was a bad idea.

And then I remembered why this was a bad idea.

I was cheating on my husband.

Many years ago, I made a list of the things I hoped never to do. Adultery was at the very top of the list. Yet here I was, married and sneaking out of the house to be with another woman's husband.

Maybe that other woman had a list as well, before she crossed everything off. Now she was probably going to spend Christmas all by herself in some corporate condominium, waiting for her boyfriend to come back from his ski trip with his wife and kids. The thought worked on me like a bucket of ice water.

I leapt up. "I can't do this."

Lance closed his coat over his middle. He was probably in pain. I felt terrible about that, but not nearly as terrible as I felt about what we'd just done. Maybe Jonny wasn't the best husband in the world. Maybe a divorce was inevitable. That didn't give me the right to go out in public and behave like a whore with a man that he despised.

"I'm sorry." When I realized that wasn't enough, I turned and ran.

I wove through the groups of people looking at drawings until I found Zachary. "I need someone to take me home."

He set down his plate. "Amanda, is something wrong?"

I shook my head. "I just need to go home now."

Zachary looked over and could see Lance. He was standing in an archway with his shoulders slumped and his cheeks flushed.

To Zachary's credit, he didn't ask any questions. He just put his hand on my shoulder and walked me to his car.

When I got home I walked straight into the kitchen, where I pulled off the red wig and tossed it into the garbage. I fluffed out my real hair and wiped off my makeup with a dishrag, which I had to wet with a bottle of drinking water. Even when I no longer saw the makeup in my reflection in the stainless steel table I could still feel it on my face, so I kept scrubbing until my skin felt raw.

The room darkened as Jonny stood in the doorway.

"You're home early. It must not have been much of a party."

I tried to say something, but as soon as my mouth opened, I cried like a baby.

"Hey, hey," Jonny put his arms around me. "What's wrong?"

I looked up at him through my tears. "We have to get divorced. I did something very bad tonight."

Jonny stared at me in pain and horror. "Oh, my God, no. Please tell me he wore a condom."

I stopped crying and pushed him away.

"I didn't do anything that bad."

"Well, then what happened?"

"I let another man kiss me."

Jonny blinked. "You're crying your eyes out because some guy kissed you at a party."

"It wasn't a very chaste kiss."

"And he kissed you? Just like that? You didn't kiss him, or tell him you wanted to be kissed?"

"No, but I saw it coming and I didn't exactly fight him off."

"But you ran straight home and began bawling because you think I'll divorce you?" He laughed and held me close. "Amanda Goodsnuff, you're a rare treasure. I don't deserve a wife as good as you."

I knew he wouldn't say that if he knew the whole truth. "Jonny, it's over. We're not compatible. All we ever do is fight about everything."

Jonny stroked my hair. "We fight about everything because I'm an idiot. I'm sorry. It's just that..." His voice broke. "No girl like you has ever liked me before. You're everything I've ever wanted. You're everything every man has ever wanted. Then I see you goofing around with some guy with tattoos, and something inside me just snapped."

My mouth fell open. "You were jealous of *Zachary*? He's a child! I barely know him. His girlfriend was sitting right there watching us!"

"I know, I know. I probably need to see a shrink. I don't want to, but if that's what it takes to keep you I'm willing to do it because you are the best thing that ever happened to me, and I really do mean that."

Those words touched my heart and I wiped my eyes.

"It's this book. It's making me go crazy. I promised the publishers I'd have it done in time for Christmas, but it's kicking my ass. I don't know why I thought I could write a novel in two months and get a new kitchen at the same time. Would you like me to get rid of my guy and have someone else put it back to the way it was before?"

I nodded. For the briefest of moments I felt bad about having that troll fired. Then I reminded myself he never should have been hired in the first place.

"Then it's settled. No more fighting, and no more books for at least a year. As soon as this one is finished, we'll do all sorts of things together. I want to take an extended honeymoon to see the world. We'll start with the Taj Mahal. Would you like that?"

"I don't care where we go. We just need to spend more time together."

He kissed the top of my head. As we stayed there with our arms around each other, it occurred to me that I had just said all the things that Lance told me to say in order to save my marriage.

The irony of this did not escape me.

CHAPTER 19

I t took three days and four crates of sea-green glass tile to restore my dining room to its former glory. Once the water was running and Jonny was bathing again, I moved out of the guestroom and back into the bedroom.

Jonny was as good as his word. For nearly a month, we settled into a cozy routine. We worked on our writing, and I cooked, and we chatted and had date nights on Fridays. Every Wednesday he'd go out to a local card room to play poker with the guys, and at least once a week he'd have dinner with Stonewall, who I learned to my bemusement had a downtown office a mere six miles away.

They dined at all the best restaurants, and it bothered me that I was never invited. Just like it bothered me that Jonny kept the portable toilet in the living room, even after the plumbing was fixed. But I didn't complain. After all, these were minor annoyances that paled even further in significance whenever I reminded myself that I'd given a public lap-dance to a man that he specifically told me to stay away from.

The only incident of note that happened in the four-week span occurred the day after the party, when Lance approached while I shampooed my hair during my final al fresco shower.

"Mrs. Goodsnuff?"

I tensed in mid-lather but he stayed back, keeping a respectful distance. "I left you some messages," he said. "You haven't returned my calls."

I just stood there with my fingers in my hair. He looked good. The sun shone on his skin and it glowed as if it would be smooth and warm to the touch. His lips were perfect, and now that I knew what it felt like to be kissed by them, I found myself craving them even more. Against my better judgment, I still wanted him. But I also wanted to save my marriage, so I was afraid of anything I might say or do.

Lance took a deep breath. "I'm really sorry about what I did to you in the gallery. It was wrong and I feel terrible. I hope that someday you'll be able to forgive me."

I lowered my hands. "There's nothing to forgive. I could've stopped you if I wanted to. That's why we can't get close. For the sake of my marriage I can't take a chance of anything like that happening again."

"But it won't happen again. I promise. I'm not even attracted to you."

I spat out a mouthful of suds. "What?"

"Did you listen to any of my messages? I've been trying to tell you that I love you, but as a friend. I don't want to go to bed with you any more than you want to go to bed with me."

I stood still, but now I was stinging with anger. It was bad enough that we'd dry humped at my friend's party. Learning that it had meant nothing to him was the perfect cherry on top. If he'd been looking for just the right words to ensure nothing like that could ever happen again, I'd say he'd found them.

However, he kept talking. "You're married to Jonny. I respect that. I'm married to Lori Anne. She's not here now, but she could come home any day, and I don't want to tell her I didn't wait."

I nodded. It made a lot of sense. It didn't make me feel any better about the whole situation, but it did make a lot of sense.

"So when are you and Jonny going to drop by my place for dinner?"

I turned off the water. "I've got to get home now. I'm baking Jonny a cake."

In the reflection of his big glass house, I could see him scowl as he watched me walk. I did my best not to smile.

Then came a Wednesday that wasn't like any other.

It began with a phone call at 5:50AM. I was asleep at the time, but there was no way I could remain asleep with the way Jonny was screaming.

"I told you I don't want any publicity! None! So I open the paper and turn to the book section and what do I see but *this*? What the hell, Stonewall? What the hell!"

I felt my whole body go cold and I hid under the covers. In my mind's eye, I could see a newspaper photo of a mystery couple whoring it up at Ivy's gallery show.

"No, I'm not going to calm down, you sickly bastard! No publicity means NO publicity! So why is there a full page spread in The Times announcing a book I haven't even finished writing yet?"

Was that all? I threw back the covers and crept out of the bed to get the paper. I got close enough to see that there weren't any incriminating photos before my husband snatched it from my sight and threw it on the floor.

"You don't think that saying that I refuse to talk about my book isn't the same as talking about my book? You listen up! I'm going to drive over there and wring your scrawny neck…No, this has everything to do with you, you asthmatic weakling!"

As much as I thought it would warm my cockles to hear Jonny unleash the full force of his wrath upon Stonewall. I had to admit that his rage was a bit excessive. I put on my robe and tried to speak, but Jonny seemed oblivious to my very existence.

"I signed with you because you were supposed to be some sort of genius when it came to contracts! You're supposed to be able to talk your way out of any situation! But you're just another parasite like all the rest of them! You can't even get off a goddamned airplane without turning blue and falling flat on your face! You know what? You're fired!"

He slammed the phone down and glared at me. "What do you want?"

"I think I'll go for a swim."

"Yes, you do that," he said.

As I left the room, I heard something crash against the wall with a shatter and a clang and the ack-ack-ack noise of a phone that had been left off the hook for too long. I struggled into my bikini and rushed to the elevator. I didn't bring so much as a towel. I knew I had to get out of the house as fast as I could.

I'd only gotten a halfway to the water's edge when I saw Jonny running after me. "Amanda!"

I turned. If anything Jonny's face had grown redder and there was murder in his eyes. He wasn't coming after me to apologize. The only thing that kept me from running for the water was the logic that he couldn't drown me if I stayed on dry land.

"Jonny? What is it?"

He took hold of my arms. "What did you do to my car?"

"What do you mean? I'm not allowed to touch your car."

"It's not in the garage!"

"I didn't do anything to your car."

"Yes you did!" Jonny gripped my arms so hard that I screamed in pain. "You took it out last night and you wrecked it! You just left it somewhere because you were too afraid to bring it home after I told you not to touch it!"

"I didn't touch it."

"You liar!" He shook me so violently that my head tossed about. "Where is my car!"

I feared for my life. I screamed and hoped that Lance would hear me and come running out to save me. The shaking continued until Jonny panted and released me. He turned and reached for his cell phone.

"Hello Stonewall...No, you aren't fired—I just said that because I was pissed off. I need you to get here right now."

I rubbed my arms and noticed red circles forming. The sight of it made me cry. I'd promised myself I'd never stay with a man who struck me hard enough to leave a mark. My marriage had to end now. There was no going back. However, a part of me still loved him. I wept until I heard the next few words he said to Stonewall.

"What happened? I'll tell you what happened. *The Dingbat* wrecked my car."

I froze and forgot all about the pain in my arms.

"*The Dingbat*, Jonny? Is that what you and your agent call me when I'm not around?"

"Quiet, dingbat, I'm on the phone."

I had a mental picture of Jonny and Stonewall laughing at me over cups of sake in some geisha bar and my heart filled with righteous anger. Jonny never loved me. I was just a walking blonde joke to him. I'd had Lance Archer's undivided attention, but I'd blown any chance I might have had so that I could provide a font of amusement for my husband and his fancy-pants agent.

I pulled the rings off my finger and hurled them at Jonny. I knew they might be lost in the sand but I didn't care. Those rings meant nothing to me anymore.

Jonny bent and dug them out of the sand. "I'm sorry, Stonewall, but I'm going to have to go inside. Amanda's having one of her infamous little fits again."

As soon as he turned around I ran over to Lance's house and rang the doorbell. There was no response. I jabbed my finger into it a dozen more times before I sank against the door.

I hid there for several minutes in my bikini and buried my face in my arms, unsure of where to go or what to do next. When I looked up, Lance appeared behind me on the doorstep. He was wearing cargo shorts and a black T-shirt, but in my eyes, he looked like an angel.

"Amanda, I was just out for a jog. What's wrong?"

I leapt up and grabbed hold of him. "Lance, please, you have to let me in. Jonny's crazy. I can't be with him anymore."

Lance hesitated a few seconds before he opened the door wide enough for us to enter. "What happened?"

"Someone stole his car. He went crazy and attacked me. Just look at my arms! It's over between us. I'm leaving. I can't waste any more of my life with him."

I would have liked it if Lance had gathered me into an embrace, stroked my hair, and told me that everything would be fine, but he just stood there looking confused. I decided to take the initiative and leaned against him with my face against his chest.

That was when I noticed the bright fuchsia coat draped over a chair next to the sofa. A bright fuchsia *woman's* coat, if that isn't clear enough by the color. There was a black overnight bag on the table beside it.

I pulled away from him. "It seems that I've come at a bad time."

He looked over at the coat and then back at me. "Amanda, please, let me explain."

I shrugged and tried not to sound hysterical. "There's nothing to explain. We're both adults. If you choose to have company, it's really none of my business."

Lance held me close and looked into my eyes. "Amanda, this isn't what you think. That coat—it's my wife's."

"Then Lori Anne came home after all." I tried to look happy for him. "Lance, that's great."

"No, you don't understand. I'm finally getting rid of her things. She's not the one I want. I can't deny it any longer."

I gasped as he forced his lips against mine. It was so rough and so sudden that I pulled back in horror. But even as he tried to be more tender, I found myself recoiling. What was wrong with me? A few moments ago I was practically in tears because I didn't have a chance with him and here I was, blowing it again.

Fortunately, Lance had a better handle on the situation than I did.

"I get it, your husband abused you and now you don't want to be touched. Go tell him that you're leaving him. If he gives you any trouble, you call me and I'll go in there and deal with him myself. You can stay here until you have everything sorted out." Lance looked outside his door. "Did you call 911 before you came here?"

"No."

"There are police outside your place talking with your husband."

I peeked my head out, and in the distance I could see Jonny talking with several uniformed officers and gesturing at the garage. At his side was Stonewall. Damn, he'd gotten there quickly. Fortunately nobody saw me so

I ducked my head back in.

"I think Jonny's asking the cops to find his car."

"Good, then it's probably safe for you to go over there right now to get your things."

"But I don't want anything out of that house."

"Amanda, that man put you through hell. You can't reward him by taking the easy way out. Tell him to his face that you're taking everything that's coming to you. Did that bastard make you sign a prenup?"

I nodded. "Yes. I get absolutely nothing."

Lance frowned in disgust. "You see? That old lecher had one foot out of the marriage before it even began. I didn't make Lori Anne sign a prenup and I certainly wouldn't make you sign one. You go back there and tell him you're leaving him for someone who is going to treat you with the respect you deserve."

"Come with me."

He shook his head. "I have to finish gathering up Lori Anne's things so that I can haul them off to charity. This won't take long. Just give me a half hour. I don't want any trace of her in this house while you're staying here."

He went to the doormat and lifted it to reveal a key, which he gave to me.

"This is yours. If I'm not here when you get back, feel free to let yourself in. And don't be shy about looking around – *mi casa es su casa.*"

I raised my eyebrow.

"It's Spanish. You'll pick it up after you've been in California a while."

I strolled to my former dream home, which by then was swarming with cops. I had butterflies in my stomach, but try as I might, I couldn't get those butterflies to dance a merry jig at the thought that I'd soon be living with Lance.

Sure, I was interested in being with him. But I was newly separated from my husband—as in, just minutes ago. My idea of a courtship involved romantic dinners and long walks on the beach, while our friendship gradually blossomed into something more. I couldn't see that happening if I was sleeping on the couch, fixing his breakfast, and worrying about where I'd left my towels after I showered.

But where else was I going to go? I had no car, I had no job, and the bulk of my support system was thousands of miles away. Not that I intended to return to the Midwest, but I had a feeling that the $500 rent I was paying in Ohio wasn't going to get me much in paradise.

I looked up at the shiny glass facade and sighed. Goodbye, gutted dining room. Goodbye, porta-potty in the living room. Goodbye, woman-hating over-the-hill novelist. Goodbye, snow-white guestroom. I think I'll miss you most of all.

As I approached, Stonewall came toward me.

"Amanda, Jonny has something he wants to say to you."

Jonny stared at his own feet. "Amanda, I'm sorry I yelled at you. I'm sorry I accused you of taking my car. I thought you'd invited your hoodlum friends for a joyride and left it in a ditch somewhere, but the police said the garage was forced open from the outside. I know how much you love this house so you probably had nothing to do with it."

I blinked. That was his apology? My friends were hoodlums, but we *probably* didn't take his car? I let out a profound sigh. "You know what Jonny? I'm sorry too. I'm sorry to tell you that I'm going inside to collect my things because I'm leaving you forever. Actually, I take that back. I'm not sorry in the slightest."

Jonny stood in my path and sobbed. "Amanda, don't."

"I don't think you want to cause a scene, Jonny. Not with all of these cops around. If I tell them how I got these bruises, they'll have no choice but to arrest you for assault and battery. And if you think that an advertisement in The Times is too much publicity for you, just wait until the tabloids learn that Jonny Goodsnuff was arrested for beating his wife."

He moved out of the way and I went into the house. Once I was in the closet I locked the doors, changed into my traveling clothes, threw my suitcase on a chair, and began loading it up with clothing, makeup, and jewelry.

As I packed, I could hear Jonny's voice crackle over the intercom.

"Amanda, please don't leave me. I beg you."

I hit the button to speak. "Don't worry Jonny. I'm not taking anything that belongs to you. We certainly wouldn't want to violate the terms of your wonderful prenup."

"Screw the prenup. I'll tear it to shreds and have Stonewall write up a new one. You'll get everything. I don't care about anything but you, babe. I really mean that. Please, just give me a chance to make this up to you."

I looked down at the marks on my arms. I already knew how this worked. On the first fight it's two bruised arms, followed by tears and a heartfelt apology. On the next fight it will be a black eye, followed by a dozen roses. Then all of the fights after that will involve trips to the emergency room, followed by death threats.

"Sorry, Jonny, I swore I'd never stay in a relationship with a man who hit me hard enough to leave a mark. And unlike some people, I try to keep my promises."

There was a long silence over the intercom and then a different voice came on. "Amanda, this is Stonewall. I know you're upset. You have every right to be, but running off isn't the answer. If you want a trial separation, we can work that out, but I think that it would be in your best interests to explore your options."

My mouth fell open. Jonny was sending his slimeball agent to renegotiate our marriage? Unbelievable!

I stabbed my finger into the intercom button and snarled. "You listen to me, you prodigious fop! I have absolutely no interest in hearing another word that you have to say! So why don't you take your fancy watch and your eight-figure contracts and crawl back to whatever rock you climbed out from under. Because, frankly, you are the bane of my existence and I want you out of here, now!"

"Uh…what?"

It made me smile to hear I'd struck a nerve. "Oh, I think you heard me."

"I'm very sorry that you feel that way."

"Yes, well, I don't know what the customs are like on Planet Macho, but here, women don't care to be referred to as *The Dingbat*."

That got Jonny shouting again. "Amanda! You listen to me." I jabbed my finger into the mute button because I had no intention of doing so. I resumed packing and was finished a few minutes later. By then the house was silent.

I zipped the suitcase and carried it out. I'd left behind the Valentino gown, the outfits I bought in France, and the candy box of jewelry. Lance was purging all his reminders of the past. It was the least I could do as well. When I got to the elevator there was a note on the door.

Call my cell phone. Please. It's important.—I love you, Jonny

I crumpled up the note and threw it on the floor.

When I arrived at Lance's place, I rang the bell. There was no answer, so I let myself in.

"Lance?" I called out.

The house was silent. I set my suitcase against a wall and entered the living room to look around, and then glanced up through the skylight ceiling at my old home. The glass canopy above me let in the daylight, but at night, Jonny would be able to look down and watch my every move. It was a chilling thought. Staying here, even temporarily, was starting to seem like a bad idea for a number of reasons.

I pulled out my cell phone and dialed Lance's number then hung up when I heard a phone ring nearby. Damn, his home phone number wasn't going to do me a whole lot of good right now.

I looked for a phone and found one on an oak writing desk, near a black-and-white photo of his wife and a miniature palm tree planted in a black lacquer pot.

What struck me right away—aside from the fact he forgot to get rid of the photo of Lori Anne—was how tidy he kept his workspace. He left papers out, but they were carefully stacked and aligned at perfect right angles with the corners of the desk. The books on the shelves were free of dust and alphabetized.

I like to keep things neat, but not that neat. I worried that might be a problem.

His phone plugged into the computer. Good, it was one of the modern types, the kind that might forward missed calls to a cell phone. I dialed his number again. The phone on the desk rang. As I waited for it to kick over, his computer made a weird sound and the screensaver flicked off, revealing an opened text document and a thumbnail video of a butterfly fluttering around a cluster of pink roses, filmed from an overhead angle.

It seemed an odd image for a man like Lance, but it probably helped him get in touch with his feminine side, so who was I to judge?

Finally, I heard a click at the other end of the phone. "Pennyroyal Promotions, representing Prudy Newcastle. How may we help you?"

"Lance?"

"Hey, cutie pie, where are you?"

"I'm in your living room trying to figure out where I should unpack my things."

"Oh, sorry. The bedrooms are on the top floor. The master bedroom is on the left, or you can use the guest bedroom if you're worried that I won't be a gentleman. So how did things go with Jonny?"

"He wasn't happy about me leaving, but he didn't make a scene."

"Does he know where you are?"

"Of course not. I'm not going to drag you into this. But I'll need to find a better hiding place."

"Why's that?"

So he didn't know that his spectacular view of the outside worked both ways. If not, I didn't want to be the one to tell him.

"I'd just feel safer surrounded by solid walls. Did I tell you that Jonny had his car stolen this morning?"

"I think you mentioned something like that. Look, I've got to go. I have a bunch of errands to run. I was thinking that this evening we could go out for Chinese and a movie. Sound good?"

"Sounds great," I said.

"If you get hungry before I get home, help yourself to anything in the fridge. I can't wait for tonight. Bye, love."

I dragged my suitcase up two flights of stairs, surprised at how spoiled I'd grown in the short time that I'd owned an elevator. I stashed the suitcase in the guest room. I'd be sure to sleep there until I had a better feel for the true dynamic of our relationship.

Maybe I was just rattled from my fight with Jonny, but it seemed to me that Lance was being weird about all this. I considered calling him right back, but then the temptation to snoop got the better of me. I went into Lance's room and immediately went hunting for his porn. Not that I'm nosy or anything, but if you're going to live with someone, it really pays to take a peek in Bluebeard's Closet to see what level of kink you're dealing with.

I found his magazine collection in a drawer of his chest bed. Maxim, FHM, and other assorted PG-13 rated lad rags: Cherryboy magazines. Evidently, Lance was too strait-laced to avail himself to true smut. In a way that almost made sense. Despite his hot looks, Lance was relatively inexperienced. Unless there was some Mrs. Robinson figure in his past, he'd probably only ever been with his wife.

Indeed, beneath the magazines was a collection of three high school yearbooks from some small town in Iowa. I picked up the most recent and flipped to the senior section.

LANCE ARCHER.

A younger Lance with one tone hair and a boyish crew cut grinned at me. His dress shirt was buttoned to the top button, which made him look a bit square, but he still had the million-dollar smile, even then. I smiled back.

I didn't know Lori Anne's maiden name so I flipped through the rest of the pages until I found her under the K's.

LORI ANNE KOTEX.

Kotex?

The poor thing. No wonder she agreed to become a child bride.

What's worse was Lori Anne was a redhead. I'd gotten the wrong impression from the Bettie Page wig and the black-and-white photos Lance kept of her. Her hair was that dark shade of natural red that appears almost black in the shadows and spiced pumpkin in the sunlight. In her senior photo she wore a black lace and turquoise satin top. The color was stunning with her fiery hair and lightly freckled complexion. I flipped though the yearbooks from the years before.

Lori Anne was popular, so there were dozens of photos, both by herself and with Lance. Beneath the yearbooks were her pageant photos, dating all the way back to kindergarten. She was a redhead in each one.

Something about that troubled me.

Lori Anne was supposed to be a brunette. I was sure of it. I knew I'd made a wrong assumption because her hair looked dark in Lance's black-and-white pictures. However, I couldn't shake the feeling that there was something terribly wrong with Lori Anne having red hair.

Then I remembered that Lance kissed me while I wore a red wig.

Have you ever considered dyeing your hair red, Amanda?

Great. Just great. I wasn't Lance's girlfriend. I was his wife's stand-in. I replaced the yearbooks and slid the drawer shut before I dialed Lance.

"Pennyroyal Promotions, representing Prudy Newcastle. How may we help you?"

"Hi Lance, this is Amanda again."

"Hi, sweet cheeks. I was just thinking about you."

"Yeah, I've been thinking, too. Maybe it would be better if I called Ivy and asked if I could stay with her."

There was a long pause. When Lance spoke again, his voice was slightly frantic. "Amanda, what are you saying? You're leaving me? You don't want to be around me anymore?"

"Lance, maybe I shouldn't move in so quickly. It might be better if we took it slow."

"Why? Have I done something wrong? Did I say anything that upset you?"

"No. I'm just not sure I'm ready to share a roof with another man so quickly."

"You just think that because you're married to a jerk that abused you. He never cherished you. I cherish you."

I twisted my eyes shut. I wanted to believe him. I really did. But I didn't want to make a habit of getting into quickie relationships with guys who were only interested for the wrong reasons.

"Lance," I took a deep breath. "I'm concerned that you still have feelings for Lori Anne."

"I don't. Trust me. She's not the girl I thought she was. She might come back tomorrow, but I won't have her."

I wanted to believe him, but I didn't. Nobody who said words like those to me ever meant them.

I sighed. "Are you almost done with your errands?"

"Actually, I forgot. I have an appointment this afternoon."

Of course, the cynic in me said. At least that would give me time to reflect upon whether I'd just moved from the frying pan to the fire. One minute Lance was cold as ice, the next he was acting like he'd already picked out names for our children. I had to be reading too much into this. He's a friend, I told myself. A hot *married* friend. Nothing more. Though it was clear he wanted more. Except when he insisted he didn't...

What a mess. I needed a clear head so I could think this over. "Do you mind if I have a nap? It's been a rough morning."

"Yes, a nap is good. I think that a nap would be a great idea. I can't wait to see you."

"Likewise," I said and hung up.

I went to the guestroom, locked the door, and stretched out over the covers and allowed myself to drift off to sleep.

I dreamt I was in the bed I shared with Jonny. It was the same scene from this morning, but in the dream he spoke calmly to Stonewall, then hung up, smiled at me, and wandered from the room.

I sat up and checked my arms. There were no bruises. I slumped back and smiled. Jonny hadn't harmed me. We wouldn't have to divorce. Like the philosopher and the butterfly, I wasn't sure if I was really dreaming, or if I'd just woken from a dream about leaving Jonny for Lance.

I drew myself from the bed and went to the steps, dragging my hand against the wall as I walked. The velvet texture felt real enough, as did the carpet beneath my feet.

I made my way up into the dining room. That made it clear that this was the nightmare. The scene that awaited me there was like a hellscape from a Bosch painting. I jumped back as a lizard creature darted over my foot. There was shattered green glass tile all over the floor, but the gutted section of the wall had been replaced with a jagged cave of gray stone filled with rusted grates and cobwebs. I saw what looked like a rotten branch in the alcove, but as I stepped closer I saw that it was the mummified remains of a human arm. The word **PINK** had been carved in runic scratches into the wall behind it.

Pink? What was the significance of the word pink?

I heard a chorus of deep laughter behind me. I turned and saw Jonny approaching, flanked by his agent and his handyman.

"Two months ago Lori Anne Archer disappeared," Jonny said. "Now it's time for you to disappear as well."

Their hands reached for my face and I screamed myself awake.

When I caught my breath, I was back in Lance's guest room. I could see the sun through the open curtains.

"Lance?" I called out. The house was quiet. I got up and checked my cell phone. 2:15PM. There were no messages, no missed calls. I placed the phone on the nightstand and screamed as it let out a loud ring.

I let it ring a few times as I placed my hand against my chest. When my heart was steady, I grabbed the phone.

"It's about time you called. Where are you?"

"Amanda?"

A shock went through me as I recognized Stonewall's voice. I would have hung up right then, but I didn't, because his voice was ragged and it sounded like something was terribly wrong.

"Amanda. I'm sorry. There's been an accident."

I felt my whole body go numb and I almost dropped the phone. There had been an accident and Stonewall was calling me. That meant that Jonny was hurt. Maybe even...

"Stonewall, before you say another word. I need you to tell me that my husband is alive."

There was a terrible silence. I felt myself sinking. "Please, Stonewall. I don't care how bad it is. It doesn't matter if he'll need a wheelchair, or if he's in a coma and his prospects are grim. I just need to know that he's alive."

"Amanda—"

I shouted into the phone. "Tell me that he's alive!"

"Amanda...I'm sorry."

Chapter 20

S tonewall didn't say another word until I was able to speak again.

"He's gone? That can't be right. Are you sure?"

"Yes, I'm sure." I could tell he was fighting to keep his voice steady, as was I. "What happened?"

"Jonny was struck and killed. It was all very quick. The driver sped off and the police are trying to find him. They say that Jonny died instantly. He didn't feel a thing."

Of course they said that. They always said that. It makes it easier for the survivors if the departed never knew what happened. The truth was, nobody dies in an instant. Not as far as I could tell. "Where is he? I need to see him."

"That's not a good idea, Amanda."

I fought back my tears. "You don't understand. The last time I saw him things were horrible between us. I need to say goodbye."

"Amanda, trust me. It's better if you don't see him. He wouldn't want that. Jonny knew how you felt about him, he told me that there is no evil in you whatsoever. Everything is being taken care of. It's better that you remember him as he was."

That made me feel a little better. I wiped my eyes and struggled to think of something gracious to say. "Thank you for calling me. I know this isn't easy for you. I'm glad that he had such a good friend, and that he wasn't alone in his final moments."

"There's something you should know, Amanda. Jonny really loved you. I know he had a problem conveying it, but he was like a whole other person after the two of you met. You made him want to be a better person, and for that you have my sincere gratitude."

My God, I didn't want to hear that. A fresh wave of grief hit me. I found myself choking on my sobs too hard to even say goodbye so I just waited a respectable amount of time before hanging up.

I went back to my house, unable to accept that Jonny was gone. The halls felt unbearably empty, but I couldn't go back to Lance's place. I just couldn't.

It wasn't until I stood in the living room and looked at Jonny's typewriter that I fully realized that he was never coming back. I sank into a chair, overwhelmed with guilt. Not for leaving him, he'd made that inevitable, but he'd tried to apologize for hurting me and I wouldn't let him. He wanted to tear up the prenup and start over, but in my mind, I was already in bed with another man.

We never should have married. Had I ignored his summons at the conference, he might still be alive. Or at least his final days wouldn't have been such misery for the both of us. The last time I saw Jonny I told him that I never wanted to see him again. And now I never would.

I picked up the phone and dialed like a zombie.

"Penny—"

"Lance?" I could barely force myself to sit in this house and say his name, but he'd opened up his home to me so I had a duty to inform him of why I couldn't be there right now.

I heard his sigh of exasperation. "I know, I know. I promised I'd be home by now, but I'm interviewing photographers. I thought it would be quick but these guys can talk and talk—and the funny thing is they're not that good. I don't even own a camera and I know a lot more about composition and framing than these guys do."

"Oh, Lance. He's dead!"

"Dead? Who's dead? What are you talking about?"

I tried to force my voice to be steady enough for him to understand. "Jonny. He's dead."

"What? What happened?"

"He was in a car acc..." I couldn't even get that word out. The hand that held the phone shook violently and my voice became completely choked off. I placed my other hand over my face so that Lance wouldn't hear my sobs.

"Screw the photographers. I'm coming home now."

"No. Please don't."

"It's no trouble. I'll be there in about ten minutes."

"I'm sorry, Lance, but I really need to be alone tonight."

"Of course," he said. "You need time to grieve. I understand that. I'll tell you what, why don't you call me when you're ready and I'll come over there and help with whatever needs to be done."

"Okay."

"You take as much time as you need. I'm not going anywhere. I love you, Amanda."

"Thank you," I said before I hung up. Under the circumstances, I couldn't offer him any more than that.

With that taken care of, I wandered through the living room as dazed as a sleepwalker. I glanced at objects as if I might find something with the power to bring Jonny back to life. I still felt the bruises that Jonny left on my arm, but with him dead, they felt more like Stigmata than the relics of a failed marriage.

I stared down at the glass table and I had a sudden mental imagine of Stonewall and Jonny driving through an intersection while a truck came barreling at them with its horn blasting, right before Jonny's window shattered into a million pieces.

My God. Stonewall had been in a terrible accident, bad enough to kill his best friend, and I'd never thought to ask if he was hurt. He may have been calling from the hospital, drenched in blood that may or may not be his own, and yet I'd been so absorbed in my own grief that I'd hung up on him without expressing the least bit of concern for his welfare.

I barely stirred when I heard the doorbell ring.

I pressed the button for the intercom. "Hello?"

"Mrs. Amanda Goodsnuff?"

"Yes, who is this?"

"Police, ma'am."

I wiped my face. "I'll be there in a minute."

I crossed through the glass foyer and opened the door for the two men that stood on my doorstep. One was an older man in a brown suit. The younger was in uniform and had auburn hair and blond eyelashes. He pulled out a notebook as the older man bowed his head.

"Ma'am, I'm afraid we have some bad news. I'm going to have to ask you to sit down."

"Yes, I've heard. My husband is gone. Please come in."

I led them into the living room. I sank into a chair and gestured for them to be seated on the couch. They remained standing.

"Ma'am, I'm very sorry for your loss and to have to intrude at such a difficult time, but I'm going to have to ask you what you know about the circumstances of the accident."

"I don't know much. At two-fifteen my husband's agent called and informed me that my husband is no longer alive."

"His agent? What is his name?"

Christ. I didn't even know. My hands began to shake again at my utter helplessness so I folded them in my lap to steady them. "We always called him Stonewall. But he was the one who was driving during the accident."

The younger officer looked up from his writing and opened his mouth, but the older officer raised his hand and spoke instead.

"Ma'am. Before we say another word I'm going to have to ask you to tell me to the best of your recollection the exact wording of that phone call."

"He just said that there had been an accident, and when I asked if my husband was alive, he told me he was sorry. Then he told me that Jonny had been killed by a hit and run driver."

"He didn't say anything more than that?"

"That was all I could bear to hear."

The older officer looked over the younger officer's notes. "Ma'am, does the name Jeremy Kendal mean anything to you?"

Jeremy Stonewall Kendal, the best agent in the business.

"Yes, that's him. That's the agent."

"Ma'am, your husband was exiting the Lucky Ace's card room on foot when he was struck and killed by a hit-and-run driver. Mr. Kendal arrived fifteen minutes later. He made a series of calls on his cell phone before we questioned him. That must have been when he informed you of the accident."

Oh, so Stonewall hadn't been in the accident after all. He didn't even see Jonny die. He might have told me so, then I wouldn't have felt so guilty about my display of indifference. "Jonny went to the card room every Wednesday, and Stonewall—Mr. Kendal must have dropped him off there."

"Ma'am, it's routine procedure that we treat any violent death as a potential homicide. Therefore, we're going to have to ask you some very difficult questions."

I settled back against the seat cushion and gripped the arms of the chair. "Go ahead."

"Do you think Mr. Kendal might have played a role in your husband's death?"

I would've laughed if I wasn't so heartbroken. "Certainly not. Those two men adored each other." Maybe a little too much for my liking, but I wasn't going to tell them that. Besides, if Stonewall had killed Jonny they would have noticed the damage to the front of his car, but the officers were probably just following a checklist so I wasn't about to dazzle them with my armchair detective work.

"Do you know of anyone else who knew of your husband's habit of going to the card room on Wednesdays?"

"He didn't make a secret of it."

"Do you know of anyone who would have wished to harm your husband? Anyone who had made threats against him?"

The words brought a fresh wave of tears to my eyes and I had to wipe them away before answering. "No, officer."

"Do you know of anyone he might have recently offended, or made angry?"

"No."

"Any mistresses you know of, or bitter ex-girlfriends?"

I shook my head.

"Was there any aspect of your husband's lifestyle that might have attracted the attention of a criminal element? Such as drugs, gambling, or prostitution?"

"No drugs or prostitutes that I know of. Like I said, he went to the card room every Wednesday, but I don't think he gambled to excess. I think he just wanted to unwind and relax with the guys."

"Did he ever invite you to any of these games?"

"No, officer. I think he saw it as a male bonding ritual."

"Did he call you at any time today?"

I thought back to the note he left me.

"No, officer. He wanted me to call him, but I didn't."

The officer took a deep breath. "Ma'am, I'm sorry, but I have to ask this. Where were you at two o'clock this afternoon?"

Oh, great. Now on top of everything else I was a person of interest. Maybe the only person of interest. I dug my fingers into the fabric of the chair. "I was taking a nap."

"A nap," he said to the younger officer, who nodded. "Again ma'am, this is strictly procedural. Is there anyone who can vouch for the fact that you were taking a nap at two in the afternoon?"

"No, of course not. But I couldn't have had anything to do with a hit-and-run. Jonny and I had only one car between us, a Jaguar, and that was stolen from the garage this morning."

I thought this might change the tone of the questioning, but both of the officers nodded to one another before the older officer continued.

"How did you and your husband meet?"

I gave them the name, dates, and location of the conference.

"Ma'am, what would you say is the approximate value of your husband's estate?"

I breathed a sigh and for the first time in my life I was grateful to be destitute. "I'm afraid I have absolutely no idea. Everything is in Jonny's name, and I signed a very aggressive prenup that waived all my rights to his money unless we stayed married for at least five years."

That got their attention. The older officer's mouth froze as if in mid-thought, and the one taking notes raised his eyebrows and gave him a startled look. I could sense them mentally crossing me off their list of suspects.

"Who do you believe that your husband left his money to?"

"I'd imagine he left the bulk of it to his daughters, but he was at the height of his career and worth much more to them alive than dead."

"So you can't think of any reason why someone would want to harm your husband?"

I shook my head. "Not deliberately, no."

He nodded to the younger officer who folded up his notes. "That will be all, ma'am. You've been most helpful. We thank you for your cooperation and are very sorry for your loss."

I saw them to the door, but as they were leaving I called out to them. "Wait. You said that there was a witness? Do you think you'll catch the guy who did this?"

The older officer frowned. "Ma'am, we're not at liberty to disclose the details of an ongoing investigation."

Of course. I locked the door and took the elevator to the bedroom. Once there I stood in the closet and stared at Jonny's shirts. They still held his scent. I stroked my hand down the suit he wore on the day he proposed. Soon I was too weary to stand and made my way to the bed. I hugged a pillow to my chest, closed my eyes, and drifted away from the horrors of my waking life.

This time I dreamt that we held Jonny's funeral in the desert. An army of mourners surrounded his casket, while winds rippled the sand and blew grains off the dunes that surrounded us. A red carpet led to the mouth of a massive tomb carved out of stone. As I watched the coffin travel over the red carpet, Misty and Lulu crossed in front of me wearing matching black gowns with veiled caps.

"There's nothing in the basement," Lulu said. "Just an empty garage, a laundry area, and a kitchen."

"There is a lot in the living room, but Jeremy says that most of it came with the house."

"Where do you think Father kept his valuables?"

Misty glanced in my direction. "They're probably in the bedroom. You should get up there before Amanda gets back."

"But she's here. I went up there and she's sleeping in the bed. I came down here so I wouldn't wake her."

They both turned and regarded me for a moment before they faced one another again.

"Lulu, you moron! She can hear every word we're saying."

My eyes snapped open and I was back in my bedroom, but I could still hear the voices.

"Even if we whisper?"

"Yes, Lulu, even if we whisper!"

I sat up. The voices were coming from the intercom. That meant Jonny's daughters were in the house. I climbed out of bed and went to the elevator.

When the door opened into the living room, what I saw made my hair stand up on end. I recognized Misty Goodsnuff even though the skin on her face had been freshly peeled and was the color of pizza sauce. She had her hair tucked into an eggplant-colored turban that matched her tracksuit, and the overall affect made her look a bit like a deranged genie from a cheap 70's movie.

Despite the chemical burns that covered ninety percent of her face, she seemed in remarkably high spirits for a woman who had recently been orphaned. At her side was Stonewall, coughing into a handkerchief.

"Son of a bitch!" I screamed.

CHAPTER 21

M isty grinned like a fiend. "Sorry, dear. But right now we have more of a right to be in this house than you do."

I looked down at the stack of boxes against the couch and felt my blood pressure soar to near volcanic levels. "For the love of God, your father isn't even cold yet! Couldn't you have waited before swooping in like a flock of vultures?"

Misty shrugged. "That would have been lovely, but Lulu didn't want to give you a chance to hide any of Daddy's belongings."

I pointed over at Stonewall who'd crept back against the wall. "What's he doing here?"

Misty reached for a box. "When we told him we were coming, he insisted on joining us. Since this house came furnished, Jeremy is here to make sure that we don't accidently take something that belongs to the owners."

"The owners?"

Misty laughed. "You didn't think that Father actually owned this house, did you? This place lists for seven million. Father was rich, but he wasn't that rich."

I looked over at Stonewall who was coughing behind his handkerchief. "Jonny never told me this was a rental."

"Actually, that works in your favor," Misty said as she rummaged through her purse and pulled out a lighter and a pack of cigarettes. "Since the house and most of the items in it did not actually belong to Father, they aren't part of the prenup. So as far as I'm concerned you have full use of the premises until September."

"I would really prefer it if you didn't smoke in my house."

Misty tapped the cigarette on the table and flicked open the lighter. "I'm sorry? Did you not hear a word I just said?"

"Just don't!" I bared my teeth. When I first saw Misty and Stonewall I felt like a wounded, cornered animal. Now I was a wounded animal who was having her corner taken away.

In response, Misty drew her scorched lips back and her eyes flared like a demon's. "You know what? I'm going to smoke this no matter how much it bothers you, and you know why? Because I lost my father today, my only living parent, a man you had just met, what, two months ago? So why don't you just pull that stick right out of your ass and quit being such a bossy little bitch, because if I feel like having a goddamn cigarette I'm going to have a goddamn cigarette!"

Even nearly out of my mind, I had enough sense to back off.

She put the cigarette between her teeth and lit up. I would have thought that smoking would be painful for someone with a recent chemical peel, but Misty Goodsnuff probably lost all sensation in her face years ago.

Stonewall leaned back against the wall, stretching like a cat.

"Fancy seeing you again," I said. "And so soon after I ordered you out. It's been a while since the last time you broke in and ransacked my place while I was sleeping, but I guess Jonny's daughters needed the assistance of a professional?"

"Oh quit being so melodramatic," Misty said over the sounds of her looting. "You should be glad he's here, or this might go a lot worse for you."

"Worse?" I laughed. "What could possibly be worse than this?"

Misty shrugged and turned over a glass sculpture in her nonsmoking hand. "Can I have this one, Jeremy?"

He shook his head.

"You can have the portable toilet," I suggested.

"No," Stonewall gasped out from behind his handkerchief. "It's also a rental."

I shot Stonewall a dirty look while she replaced the glass sculpture in its niche. "Well, what can I take?"

Stonewall pointed to Jonny's workspace and Misty tamped her cigarette out into the Scotch glass on Jonny's desk. I hoped that meant she'd finished smoking, but she immediately reached for her pack and pulled another halfway out.

"Hey, Jeremy. I assume I can help myself to the liquor bottles?"

Stonewall nodded.

I bit my lip. "Oh, by all means, and as long as you're at your father's writing desk, why not help yourself to his typewriter?"

Misty put down her cigarettes to clap with girlish enthusiasm. "Just what I always wanted: the very finest in 1800's technology." She dumped the typewriter into the box, along with everything else within easy reach. Meanwhile Stonewall tried to skulk away. I put my hand on the wall to block his path.

"You know what, Mr. Kendal? I'm really glad that you're here to make sure that Jonny's landlords receive the proper consideration, because nobody seems to give a damn about the widow."

Misty smirked at me before she pulled open a desk drawer. It made a clunking noise and she screamed and leapt back as if a rat had jumped out at her.

"Jeremy, why did my father keep a gun in his writing desk?"

Stonewall and I came closer, and the hairs on the back of my neck stood up as I saw a revolver in the otherwise empty drawer.

Stonewall pushed the handkerchief into his pocket and picked up the gun. He slid out the cylinder and spilled the bullets onto the desk.

Son of a bitch. I'd married a man who kept a loaded gun and didn't bother to tell me about it. I wondered what other horrible surprises were hidden around the house.

And then I realized that I hadn't seen Lulu.

"Misty, where is your sister?"

"She's probably up in your bedroom by now."

My bedroom?

I ran for the elevator with Stonewall right behind me. The door closed and we ascended. I faced forward, because that's what normal people do when they ride in elevators, but Stonewall stood facing me. I moved as far from him as I could get. The close quarters amplified that rasping, and his intermittent cough was really starting to get on my nerves. I worried that the house might be on fire from the way he was carrying on.

"Lulu is not entitled to any of my personal effects, nor to any gifts from my husband. Right?"

He nodded.

"Great, I'm so glad you agree, since I seriously doubt that Lulu knows that."

The door opened and I began calling out to her, with Stonewall right behind me. I didn't hear a reply, but I did hear a rattling coming from the guestroom over Stonewall's wheezing. "Lulu, I know you're in there! I'm coming in."

I opened the door and as soon as I saw her, I could feel the blood boiling in my veins. She was holding my chocolate box of jewelry and was wearing several of the pieces. That wasn't what upset me. What upset me was that she was also wearing my champagne-colored Valentino gown, despite the fact that it was at least six sizes too small for her. The fabric at her ample hips was so strained that finger-sized holes had appeared between the seams and I could see the texture of her skin through the runs in the delicate fabric. The dress was coming apart like the skin of an overcooked sausage. It was by far the nicest thing I'd ever owned, and it was ruined.

The room turned red as something inside me snapped.

"You stupid cow! I'm going to rip your head off!"

Lulu just stared stupidly as if she couldn't understand how anyone could be so mean to her. The sight of it just made me madder. I let out a scream as I lunged for her.

Stonewall tried to hold me back, but it was going to take more than some asthmatic fancy boy to restrain my fury. I'd managed to drag him halfway across the room before he gave up and sank onto the bed.

Unfettered, I went for Lulu's throat.

Lulu grabbed for my hair and we rolled about on the floor, locked in Greco-Roman combat. I'd say that it was a fairly even match. Lulu probably outweighed me by a good fifty pounds, but I was faster, and years of turning cartwheels and backward somersaults in high school had given me a deceptive amount of upper body strength. And while she had the invulnerability of the truly witless, I fought with the strength of the criminally insane.

In the periphery of my vision, I was aware that Misty had entered the room. For an instant, I worried that she might join her sister in battle against their wicked stepmother. However, Misty wasn't even looking at us.

"Jeremy!" She screamed. "Jeremy! Stop fighting, you bitches! I think he's having a heart attack!"

Lulu and I froze, and then we turned toward the bed.

Stonewall looked bad. He was hunched forward with his eyes squeezed shut and his hands were beaded with sweat as they pressed up against his chest, which was bowed out in a manner that hardly seemed natural. The muscles in his arms and neck were tensed as if he was in a great deal of pain, but his torso didn't seem to rise or fall.

Lulu got up and ran to her sister. They held one another as they stared at Stonewall.

I knew CPR from a stint I did working in a rest home, and I'd even had to use it on occasion, but this didn't look like your garden-variety heart attack. It looked more like heart failure. But if this was heart failure, Stonewall should be gasping for air. It looked as if he might not be breathing at all.

"Call 911!" I said as I jabbed my fingers against the side of his neck and felt for a pulse. Given the way he looked, I thought it might be faint or nonexistent. Instead, his heart was racing so fast I could barely tell where one beat stopped and the next began. But it was steady, with no sign of partial or skipped beats.

I had no clue what was going on, or what to do about it. I was lost, and freaked out about that. I needed someone to talk me through this. "Call 911!" I shouted again, but the two just stood there. Maybe they didn't know the number?

Stonewall's fingers were turning an alarming shade of teal. Acute cyanosis. I knew just enough to know that he was asphyxiating. There wasn't enough oxygen in his blood to keep him alive for more than a few minutes. Since his heart seemed to be working, it had to be lung failure. That made sense. Stonewall had asthma.

I thought back to the coughing and gasping that I'd witnessed downstairs. The attack began even then, but I'd been too absorbed my own troubles to recognize his distress, which I had no doubt exacerbated with my screaming and my fighting.

I'd have to do something, and do it quickly. I forced Stonewall onto his back and pushed his mouth open. Then I pinched his nose shut and placed my lips over his. He managed to raise one hand to my face and tried to push me off.

"Stop it, I'm trying to help you!"

Stonewall shook his head weakly and pointed to his ribcage, which appeared swelled like a balloon. I understood what he was trying to tell me. Getting air into his lungs wasn't a problem. He couldn't get it back out again.

I grabbed his hand. "I know you can't talk, but I want you to squeeze my hand two times if you can hear me."

He clenched my hand twice.

"Good. Once means yes, twice means no. Is it your asthma?"

One squeeze.

"Are you going to be okay?

He gripped my hand once. Then a second time.

Crap. I felt tears come to my eyes. "Is there something I can do?"

He clenched my hand, hard.

"What? What do I do? How do I save you?"

He released my hand and reached up. But his eyes focused on something only he could see and his fingers opened and closed as if he was trying to catch something that floated in the air. Misty screamed as he moved his arm about and grasped at nothing. Then his arm fell and his whole body went limp.

"Stonewall?" I placed my hand over his face but I couldn't feel him breathing. I felt for a pulse. It was steady, but faint. His heart had been racing before, but now the beats were growing further and further apart. I knew that meant that his body had given up on trying to get oxygen to his brain and was now shutting down. If anything was to be done, it would have to take place within a matter of minutes, if not seconds.

I looked down and saw that he'd dropped his handkerchief on the floor. I was an idiot. Stonewall had stopped breathing right before I'd met him in France, but somehow he'd managed to survive long enough to get to a hospital. He had said something to me about that, but for the life of me, I couldn't remember what.

"Misty! Where does Stonewall keep his rescue inhaler?"

"Check his pocket. The right one. I'm pretty sure it's the right one."

That made sense if Stonewall was right handed. I plunged my hand deep into the pocket of his trousers and felt around. Misty's mouth fell open.

"His coat pocket, you slut!"

"Oh." I removed my hand and found the inhaler, right where Misty said it would be. I tossed it onto the bed, since I couldn't see how it could do any good if Stonewall wasn't actually breathing. I plunged my hand back into his coat pocket and felt an object that I'd have guessed was a highlighter pen. I pulled it out. The label looked distinctly medical, thank God. That was how he'd survived before. This was his medication in injectable form. It had to be. I yanked his arm out of his coat, pulled up his shirtsleeve, and tapped for a vein in the crook of his arm.

"No, in the neck!" Misty said. "Stick him in his neck! It will reach his brain faster!"

"No! Into his heart!" Lulu said. "You have to stab him in his heart like in *Pulp Fiction*."

I didn't know what to believe so I looked at the label.

WARNING: NOT FOR INTRAVENOUS USE.

Great. We were all wrong. I would have killed him.

I raised the pen and stabbed it through his pant leg, embedding the needle into his upper thigh. All at once, he sat up and breathed out, with the pen sticking out of his leg. I reached for it, but he pushed me away, counted to ten with his fingers, then pulled it out himself. As he gasped for air, his color returned, but now his whole body shook. He rose from the bed.

"Are you okay?" I asked.

Misty pushed past me. "Does he look like he's okay? Come on, baby, let's get you to the hospital."

Stonewall didn't say anything. He just let her lead him out the door.

Before they left, Misty called back at us over her shoulder.

"Nice dress, bitches. I hope it was worth nearly killing a man over."

Chapter 22

The Chinese believed that if you save a man's life he becomes your responsibility forever. I knew the feeling. I spent most of the evening lying on my bed in my lavender pajamas, staring at my cell phone, and wondering if I should check on Stonewall. I was sick with worry, but I was sure that I was the last person he wanted to talk to. And who could blame him?

Jesus Christ, what the hell had I turned into? Misty's parting comment hurt, but I couldn't be mad at her. She had a point. I'd nearly sent a man to the morgue over a dress. A dress I probably would have never worn again. A dress that I'd left behind when I walked out on my husband.

I reached for my laptop and did a quick search on acute asthma, hoping it would make me feel better. What I read curdled my blood. I grabbed my phone and directed it to dial the last person to call me before I had a chance to talk myself out of it.

The phone rang twice. I worried that I might be calling at a bad time. Then I looked at the alarm clock.

3:45AM.

Crap.

If Stonewall wasn't already furious at me for nearly killing him, he was going to be livid at me for waking him in the dead of night. I raised my thumb to hang up, but it cut out in mid ring.

"You've reached Jeremy Kendal," a voice said. It sounded upbeat and fully awake. Thank goodness, it had to be a machine. I'd just leave a message. I waited for a beep, which didn't come.

"Hello, I'm afraid I can't hear you."

"Um, Stonewall?"

"Speaking." The decidedly non-mechanical voice was growing impatient. I wanted to hang up, but forced myself to explain.

"Stonewall, it's Amanda Goodsnuff." My voice shook so much I could barely get the words out. "I had to know you were okay, but I didn't realize how late it was. I'm sorry. I'm going to hang up now and leave you alone."

"Wait."

Damn.

"Don't hang up."

"I'm sorry. I didn't mean to wake you."

"You didn't wake me. You've pumped me full of stimulant, remember? I couldn't sleep right now if I wanted to."

I braced myself for the tirade I knew I so richly deserved.

"Amanda, I'm glad you called. I'm fine, really. I've never been better. The trip to the hospital is just a formality in situations like this one."

I wished I believed that.

"They just did a few hours' worth of tests, then gave me a clean bill of health and let me go. I would have called, but they didn't release me until after midnight and I didn't want to wake you. You haven't been up the whole night, have you?"

I began to cry. "Of course I've been up the whole night! I'm not a monster, you know!"

"I'm really sorry I put you through that."

"What are you apologizing to me for? You're the one who was almost killed."

"That didn't have anything to do with you, Amanda."

"Don't give me that. You were having trouble and I didn't even care. If I'd given you a moment's peace, you could've used your inhaler."

"Amanda, you'd just suffered a horrible loss, and there we were, breaking into your house to take whatever we could. It was cruel and horrible. I should have tried harder to put a stop to it."

"So what? Those were just things. Things can be replaced, but if you'd died, you'd be dead forever."

What he said next surprised me. "Those weren't just things. They were the memories of your happiest times with Jonny." I wiped my nose as I realized that he had a point.

"You had a right to protect what is sacred to you. In any case, you need to stop blaming yourself. This sort of thing happens to me at least once every springtime, I'm afraid."

"But not as bad as that, or you'd already be dead."

I hadn't meant that to be funny, but Stonewall laughed. "Oh, this attack wasn't as sudden as most. I could have easily gone for my inhaler if I wasn't trying to look like a big shot."

I found myself smiling. "You must admit, I'm pretty piss-poor when it comes to administering first aid."

There was a pause. "Amanda, to be honest, I don't remember anything that happened after I got in the elevator with you."

"Because you suffered brain damage?"

"No. No brain damage. I just don't remember."

Good. Then he didn't recall me sticking my hand in his pants. That removed a large degree of awkwardness. "Well, I'm glad to hear you're doing well."

"As I said, don't worry. And don't be upset about the dress. I'll make sure that Lulu buys you a new one exactly like it."

I frowned. "I thought you said you couldn't remember anything."

"Well, I do have this one terrible image burned into my retinas…"

I laughed and rolled over onto my back. "If it's all the same to you, I'd rather have the cash. I sold most of my things, and I gave all of my money to Jonny to put in his bank account, so right now I don't have a penny to my name."

There was a pause. "You're kidding."

"Nope. I'm going to look for a job and it would really help to have a car. I was going to sell some of the jewelry Jonny gave me, but if you could get a few thousand from Lulu, then I could hold onto it for a little longer."

There was a long silence on the other end of the line. "Amanda, Jonny really screwed you with that prenup, didn't he?"

"Oh, well, live and learn. I'm sure he didn't expect to leave me in the lurch like this. Next time I marry some rich old guy I think I'll be a lot smarter about it."

"Amanda. I'm supposed to settle Jonny's estate. I was going to postpone it, but hearing of your circumstances, I think we should settle this right away. Could you drive out to Jonny's estate at three in the afternoon? Do you know how to get there?"

I sat up. "Did Jonny change his will after the marriage?"

There was a sigh. "I'm afraid so. But not in your favor."

"Oh."

"But I'm going to talk the girls into giving you something."

"Oh, I don't think they'll go for that. They don't seem to like me very much."

"Trust me. This is my job. I'm very good at convincing people that they should be reasonable. But it's important that you remain quiet so they don't suspect anything. And I'll need for you to drive yourself there. Do you think you could do that? Can you be there tomorrow at three o'clock?"

"Sure," I said. "I'll rent a car. I've still got my credit cards, and the bills won't be due for a while."

"Great, I'll see you in the afternoon. Not a word from you. Just let me take care of everything."

We said our goodbyes and I hung up and sank back onto the pillow. Maybe Stonewall wasn't such a bad guy after all.

If only I could have held on to that assessment for just a few hours longer.

I arrived for the reading in a simple black dress.

Lulu opened the door. "Why are you here?"

"It's okay, Lulu," Stonewall called out from inside the house in a voice I can only describe as New England prep-school snob. "I asked her to be here."

Lulu stood aside and followed me as I walked into the living room. Stonewall and Misty were sitting with tumblers of Scotch in their hands. Misty had her shoes off and her foot was on Stonewall's knee.

I nodded to them, and when Stonewall looked back, his caramel colored eyes looked as if they were as hard and cold as granite. I took that as my first clue that this reading might not go the way I'd hoped it would.

"Good. We're all here now." Stonewall gathered up his papers. "Shall we begin?"

"Daddy said Amanda doesn't get anything," Lulu said as she took the chair that was furthest away from mine.

"Well, we'll see about that." Stonewall began reading. "I, Jonathan Goodsnuff, being of full age and sound mind and memory, do make, publish and declare this to be my last Will and Testament, hereby revoking any Wills and Codicils by me heretofore made."

He cleared his throat. "Item one: I direct that all my just debts and funeral expenses be paid out of my estate as soon as practicable after the time of my decease."

Misty waved her hand. "Yeah, yeah, get to the good part."

"Item two: To any sons born from my marriage to my current wife I give and bequeath seventy-five percent of the real estate and property herein described and the contents of said real estate if not otherwise disposed of by other Items of the Last Will and Testament or Codicils thereto.

"To my current wife, in the event she produces living children from our marriage, I leave an annual income of ninety-thousand dollars to raise our children until the youngest reaches his or her majority," Stonewall looked up with a gleam in his eye, "contingent upon the establishment of true paternity."

I covered my mouth with my hands, but not before I let out a scream of outrage. So Jonny assumed I'd cheat on him? I won't deny I had my moments of weakness, but for Jonny it was a foregone conclusion.

Misty's lowered the glass from her lips. "It doesn't really say that, does it?" The paper made a fluttering sound as he thrust it out to her. She scanned it with her finger, and when she looked at me, her eyes were two pools of pity in her burned off face.

"Item three: All the rest, residue and remainder of my property, both real and personal, of every kind and description, wheresoever situated and which I may own or have the right to dispose of at the time of my decease, I give, devise and bequeath to my daughters, to be their property absolutely and in fee simple."

"So what does that mean?" Lulu said.

Misty set down her glass. "It means you and I get everything."

"Exactly," Stonewall said. "So shall we divide up the estate?"

For two more hours, I just sat there in shock, while they picked over Jonny's assets like a turkey carcass after Thanksgiving. The two women argued over everything, even things they clearly had no use for, but I noticed that the more something cost, the greater the sentimental value that Lulu placed on it. Misty seemed hell-bent on keeping her share of the estate equal to or greater than the value of Lulu's. Meanwhile, I just sat there, forgotten and neglected, like Cinderella watching her stepsisters get ready for the ball.

Stonewall told me that I had to keep quiet, that he was playing at something. It was quickly becoming clear that what he was playing at was revenge. Against me.

I decided I'd had enough of this shortly after Misty opened their mother's jewelry box.

"I should get the diamonds and you should get the pearls," Lulu said.

"Why's that?" Misty said.

"Because Mother told me that I could have them. I used to dress up in them when I was little and she told me I was her little princess. Those diamonds mean a lot to me. I think I should have them."

"Fine," Misty picked out a rope of pearls, a bracelet, and some earrings from the box. "As long as I get a lump sum of cash equal to the difference in value."

Stonewall closed the box and gave it to Lulu. "Actually, the pearls are worth more. The diamonds are imitation."

Lulu looked down at the box. "Imitation?"

"Diamonds of that size would have cost close to a million dollars, but the pearls are real."

Lulu put the box on the table. "You know what? I actually look better in pearls." She reached for Misty's pile of jewels, only to have her hand slapped away.

I stood up. "Is there any reason for me to be here?"

Stonewall shrugged. "I was wondering when you'd leave."

Bastard.

I snatched my purse off the couch and headed for the door.

Behind me, I could hear Misty. "You know, I feel bad that she came all the way out here just to be humiliated like that."

Stonewall spoke. "Amanda? Please wait. I think Misty would like for you to have something."

Here it comes, I thought. He did have something planned. This whole pompous ass routine was just an act to stir up the dying embers of humility in Misty's charred up soul. The man really was a genius. I forced the smile from my face before I turned around.

"Oh, no," Misty said. "I just said I feel bad, I didn't say she should get anything."

Lulu nodded. "And if she does get anything, it has to come out of Misty's share. I don't feel bad at all."

I thought that Stonewall might mention that she had destroyed my dress so she owed me at least that much, and that I'd given their father all of my money and worldly possessions, but he didn't.

Instead his eyes took on a devilish glint and he chuckled. "Now, now, girls. That's not very charitable. Suppose you were to give her something of purely sentimental value. Something that would mean a lot to her, but absolutely nothing to anyone else."

Misty frowned. "You mean like dad's underwear?"

Stonewall shook his head. "I was thinking maybe something that would be of use to her as a writer."

"Like what?" Lulu said.

Stonewall smiled. "I think you should let her have his typewriter."

What the hell?

"I suppose we could do that," Misty said, and all three of them began cackling like witches.

I felt my face go hot. Of all the cruel jokes that Stonewall could have played this was probably the cruelest. He must have noticed my wrath and gave me a sadistic smile. "And since you're letting her have the typewriter, why not let her have the correction fluid so that she can fix all of her mistakes?"

"Sure," Lulu said.

"And the spare ribbons? Those could be hard to come by for such an old relic."

Misty sighed. "I suppose so, out of the goodness of my heart."

"And the paper?"

"Oh, why not?" Lulu said.

"And maybe even his stapler and three-hole punch?"

"Hey! Not the three-hole punch!" Lulu said. "That might actually be worth something."

"Well why don't you two girls make up a nice big box of writing supplies for your stepmother and send her on her way."

I stood there stewing in my own bile as Jonny's two daughters grabbed a cardboard box and filled it with Jonny's old office supplies. Stonewall leaned back and watched them from a distance, but turned to give me an evil wink. I wanted nothing more than to walk over and slap the smug right off his face.

When Lulu placed a Scotch tape dispenser into the box, Stonewall walked over and fished it out. "Careful, are you sure you want her to have this? Because as soon as she leaves this house, everything inside of this box belongs to her and she doesn't have to give it back."

Lulu took the tape and returned it to the desk. It was a small gesture, but it spoke volumes for their contempt for me. At that moment, I hated them all: I hated Lulu, I hated Misty, and I even hated Jonny. But not nearly as much as I hated Stonewall. I was trembling with rage and shame as he taped up the box and brought it over to me.

"Here you go." He thrust the box into my chest. "You're welcome."

Behind him, Misty and Lulu didn't even bother to hide their giggles. I felt sick with anger. I was ready to drop the box on his foot and leave the house empty-handed, but then Stonewall's eyes softened and his fingers touched mine. He mouthed the words. "Go. Quickly."

I understood at once. He'd slipped something into that box. A pile of money or something else of great value. That's why he pulled out the roll of tape. He had to make it clear that whatever it was, it was something they could never have back. But if Stonewall hid something without their knowledge, wasn't that stealing?

Whatever the case, it wasn't my problem. I had to get the box out of the house and fast.

Jonny's daughters followed me out. They waved goodbye and blew kisses as I loaded the box into the passenger seat of my rented compact. I forced myself to sulk, and I waited until the swastika was no longer visible in my rear-view mirror before I allowed myself to smile.

There was a present for me in the box, and I'm the sort of girl that loves surprises.

Chapter 23

The surprise was, there was no surprise. As soon as I got home I tore open the box and searched its contents. I found one typewriter, four boxes of carbon-film ribbon, a rusty stapler, two reams of unused paper, one-quarter ream of used paper, and a few bottles of Wite-out. The paperclips and rubber bands had come loose and spilled all over the bottom of the box. There was nothing else.

I pulled apart the folds of the box to see if there was anything concealed there. There wasn't. I lifted the typewriter and shook it upside down to see if anything fell out. Nothing did. I sat on the floor and buried my face in my hands. Stonewall's little joke cost me a full day that I could have spent looking for work, as well as sixty dollars worth of car rental fees that I still had no way of paying. I couldn't comprehend how anyone could be so rotten to someone who was so thoroughly defeated.

He must have known how badly I was hurting, especially after the phone conversation from the night before. But I guess that just made it all the more fun for him. In desperation I opened the reams of paper and leafed through the sheets, to see if there was anything hidden between the pages. Nothing.

I looked at the first page in the quarter ream.

`People in glass houses shouldn't stow bones.`

Brilliant, Jonny, pure poetry. I walked over to the portable john and flung all of the paper down the hole. Then I called Jake's Rentals to come get their toilet. I'd had quite enough of Jonny's crap to last me for one lifetime. They gave me back a twenty-dollar deposit. At least that was something.

I had to find a job. Something suitable for a makeup artist or an English major, or failing that I'd be happy with a waitressing job, especially if it was close enough to walk to. But first I had to deal with more pressing matters. When I'd pulled out my cell phone, I saw I had eight missed calls.

The first was from Lance. Staring at his name on the display made me smile, and took away a lot of the hurt. I considered calling him back, but decided against it, on the grounds that I was far too vulnerable not to do something I'd regret in the morning. As happy as I was to know that he was thinking of me, I was in no state emotionally or financially to enter that minefield right now.

The next few calls were from Ivy, which made me realize we hadn't spoken since before Jonny died. She might be freaked out as to why I wasn't answering my phone. I had to call her right back.

"Ivy?" I said when she picked up.

"Sweetie! I heard about your husband on the news. I'm so sorry, how are you holding up?"

"Griefwise, I'm doing pretty well, since I learned that my husband was a contemptible bastard who was just keeping me around for breeding-stock. Financially, I'm a complete mess. I don't suppose you know anyone who is looking to hire a makeup artist?"

"Actually, I have some friends at a local studio. They should be able to pull some strings and get you onto the set. Does that sound like something you would be interested in?"

"Sure. That would be great."

"I'll talk it over with them, but I can just about promise you it's a sure thing. I have to warn you, you won't get the hours you want. They tend to work ten-to-fourteen hour shifts about fifteen days a month."

"That's okay," I said. "I've only got twenty dollars to my name right now, and I need something coming in before the food in my refrigerator goes rancid."

"What do you mean? Your husband was as rich as hell."

I sank onto my rented couch and told her the whole sordid tale.

"Oh, my God. That Stonewall guy sounds like a complete dick!"

"You don't know the half of it. At least he's out of my life now," I sighed. "Is there any chance you'd be interested in buying a typewriter?"

"The typewriter that Jonny Goodsnuff wrote all his novels on? I'll give you two hundred for it."

"Sold. I want it out of my life completely before I get anything going with Lance."

"Is Lance that guy you brought to my show?"

"Yes, that's him," At that moment the landline on the end table began ringing. "Hang on, I've got another call. Wouldn't it be funny if it's Lance?"

"He could probably feel his ears burning. I'll stay on the line."

I picked up the phone. "Hello?"

"Hi, Mom, it's your daughter Misty."

"And your other daughter, Lulu."

Their voices were practically dripping with saccharine, which I took as a signal to get my guard up, and fast.

"What's up?"

"Nothing," they both said at once. And then there was a pause and a *click*.

"Let me handle this, Lulu," Misty said. "Amanda, we're calling to apologize. We both feel really bad about the way we treated you and we want to say how sorry we are."

"Thank you, I appreciate your calling, but I have someone on the other line right now, so—"

Misty cut in as if I hadn't spoken. "It was totally wrong of us. We talked it over and we decided that we want you to have our mother's pearls." *Click*.

Huh? "Well, that's very nice of you both, but I couldn't accept your family heirlooms. Those are meant for you."

Misty's voice took on a tinge of panic. "But we want you to have them! We'll trade them for the box of junk we gave you." *Click*.

I folded my arm over my chest. "What is it exactly that you want out of this box?"

"Oh, nothing. It's all worthless junk," Misty said.

"Then how about if I just come over there and you can give me the pearls, and I'll keep the box?"

"No! You have to give it back! With everything in it!" *Click*

At that moment, I remembered what a clicking noise signified. "Why are you girls recording this call?"

"Do we have to tell her the truth?" Lulu said.

"God damn you, Lulu!" Misty said, and they both hung up.

I went back to the cell phone. "That was weird."

"What was?"

I just got off the phone with the Goodsnuff girls. They wanted to trade their mother's pearls for the box of junk they gave me."

"Maybe our friend Stonewall isn't such a dick after all. He must have hidden something and you just haven't found it yet."

"Or maybe he pocketed a little something for himself and made the girls think that I took it."

"Oh, now that would really be evil." This time the cell phone beeped, indicating that I had a call pending.

"Hang on, I've got another call coming in. I think they're about to try again at this number."

"Call me back as soon as you get to the bottom of this."

"Sure thing. Talk to you later." I changed over. "Hello?"

"Amanda?"

I felt a wave of impending doom sweep over me. "Hello, Stonewall."

"I've got some very good news for you. Things have gone really well, a lot better than I'd hoped. Would you like to hear the details, or should I just get to the point?"

I sucked in my breath. "I think you'd better tell me everything."

"This is how it all worked out: Jonny's daughters called me and wanted to know where the money from Jonny's latest book was. I told them the truth, that the funds were being held in a reserve account pending the delivery of Jonny's completed manuscript—a delivery which will be exceedingly problematic, seeing as how they just gave away the only copy."

The phone nearly slipped out of my fingers.

The only copy? Oh, Christ!

"They asked me to get it back from you, but I told them that was going to be a lot easier said than done. After the way that the three of us had treated you, you'd probably be more inclined to throw it in the trash than to be of any help to us. But I suggested that you might be more amenable if they agreed to give you a percentage."

"A percentage?" I didn't have the heart to tell him that the manuscript he was referring to was currently en route to Jake's Toilet Rentals.

"I suggested that they offer you fifty-percent of the advance, which is what you would have been entitled to if you'd married in California without the prenup. They told me that they don't want to wait. They want their money now. They offered to let you buy the rights to the manuscript from them for a million dollars apiece."

I was speechless, but probably not for the reasons Stonewall suspected. I felt like I was watching a train wreck in slow motion. Only I was the one driving the train.

"They know that it's worth a lot more than that, but they'd rather have their money now and let you deal with the publisher. Long story short, as soon as you sign some papers and return the manuscript to me, you'll be a millionaire many times over."

"That's great," I blurted to keep from screaming in hysterics.

"Here is what I'm going to need you to do—I'll give you the address of my office. It's only about five miles from you so it won't take long for you to drive over here. I'll need you to gather up Jonny's papers and bring the manuscript to me as soon as you can."

No, what he needed for me to do was build a time machine so I could go back and alter history at the precise moment when I turned this dream into a horrible nightmare.

"Amanda, do you still have the rental car?"

I sat in a stupor and watched my life flash before my eyes.

"Amanda, are you still there?"

"I...There's someone at the door. Can I call you back in a minute?"

"I'll wait."

"No it would be better if I call you back."

"Very well, just don't take too long."

As soon as he hung up, I frantically dialed the number for Jake's Toilet Rentals. "Listen, this is really important. I just returned a toilet to you less than a half hour ago. I dropped something inside it. Can you have your truck bring it right back here?"

"No problem. What's the serial number?"

Serial number? "I don't know the serial number."

"It's printed on the rental agreement."

"I don't have the rental agreement. It was my husband who rented it, not me. Can't you look it up in your computer?"

"Sorry. The gal who runs the office is gone for the day. But if you'd like, you can drop by to see if you can recognize it. You'll have to get here within the next half hour because that's when we have them hauled away to be cleaned and sanitized for the next customers."

"How many are there to be cleaned?"

"About twelve or so."

One dozen dirty outhouses for me to poke my arm into, looking for Jonny's manuscript...

"Sir, please. It's an emergency. I accidentally dropped an important document into that toilet. If you could find it and bring it back to me, I'll write you a check for $50,000."

"Document?" The man laughed. "We put a chemical in our tanks that eats right through paper. If it's papers you dropped, they're long gone by now."

I sat on the sofa and rocked back and forth in a crisis of self-pity. "So there's no hope?"

"None. Sorry, ma'am. I wish I had better news for you."

"Well, thank you anyway."

"No problem. Next time, try to be more careful."

I hung up and paced about pulling at my hair with both hands. This couldn't be happening. I couldn't have screwed things up this badly. The worst part was Stonewall was waiting for me to call him back and I didn't know what to tell him. How could I have been so wrong about him? Stonewall wasn't a bad guy. Stonewall was my knight in shining armor. He entrusted me with a $10,000,000 fortune, and I'd literally flushed it down the toilet.

No, not just $10,000,000.

$10,000,000 plus €2,000,000 for the French rights.

Plus €1,000,000 for the German rights.

Plus €500,000 for the Spanish rights.

Plus €250,000 for the Italian rights.

Not to mention the other rights I didn't even know about.

But I knew what that meant.

It meant I'd just screwed myself in a handful of different languages.

And then an idea came to me. It wasn't a very good idea, but at that point, a bad idea seemed better than no idea at all. I pushed back my hair, took a deep breath, and called Stonewall.

I forced myself to smile in case he could detect it in my voice. "Hey, Stonewall, sorry to keep you waiting. Where were we?"

"I was just going to give you directions to my office so that you can bring me the manuscript and sign a contract with Jonny's estate. The rest will have to wait until the publisher assigns a ghostwriter to finish the book for us."

"Actually, about the manuscript..."

"Yes?"

I stretched out on the couch with my feet up and broadened my smile. "Jonny's already finished it."

There was a long pause, and I held my smile even though my distress was burning a hole in my stomach. When Stonewall spoke, his voice was full of skepticism. "The draft I saw looked as if it was a hundred and fifty pages long at the very most."

I had my answer ready. "That's because I'd finally talked Jonny into joining the twenty-first century. He completed it on my word processor. We thought that since you had to work such a tight deadline it would be nice to surprise you with an electronic copy that you could just e-mail over to the publishers."

He didn't sound convinced. "When I dropped him off at the card room, he told me that it was only halfway finished and it was going to take him at least another month or two."

Fortunately my mind was racing, so an answer came quickly. "That's because he thought he'd have to retype the portion he'd already completed on his typewriter. I'm afraid my husband didn't have a very good grasp of technology. He didn't realize that I'd already fed those pages into my scanner and even finished up the proofreading."

For a moment, the phone went quiet and I bit my lip in worry that he'd see through my obvious lies.

"Amanda, are you near your computer?"

"I sure am."

"Then why don't I give you my e-mail address so you can send the file right now."

"Sure thing." I felt the acid in my stomach churn like a washing machine as he gave me his e-mail address, which I wrote onto a Post-it.

I hung up and sat down before my laptop and composed an e-mail. On the screen was an icon for a file called *FinalDraft.doc*. I placed a pen in my mouth as I opened the document. A cover page appeared in glorious sixteen-point font.

THE ICE CATHEDRAL

By Amanda Anderson

136,134 words

I bit down on the pen as my finger hit the Backspace key and I watched the letters disappear one by one.

When the page was blank, I typed out a new title:

HOUSES MADE OF GLASS

By Jonny Goodsnuff

136,134 words

No, 136,135 words. With its new title, my magnum opus was now one word longer.

As I dragged the manuscript onto the e-mail message to be included as an attachment, it suddenly occurred to me there was no way in Hell that I was going to get away with this. My writing style was nothing like Jonny's, and Stonewall was far too smart not to realize that.

But what else was I supposed to do?

I grabbed the mouse before I had a chance to talk myself out of it and clicked on 'Send.' A cartoon hourglass rotated on my screen. I took a deep breath and squeezed my eyes shut and waited for a bolt to smite me from the heavens. When I opened my eyes, the words 'Send Complete' appeared on the screen.

Though I walk through the valley of the shadow of death...

Those words popped into my mind without warning and I sat there like a statue. Then the phone rang, pealing like a death bell. I contemplated not answering it, and then ultimately decided to get it over with.

"Amanda?" Stonewall said. His voice was tense.

"Yes?" I tapped the pen to steady my nerves.

"I just received Jonny's manuscript."

"Have you had a chance to look it over?"

"It seems as if it's all there. I just need to forward it to Jonny's editor. But we still have to take care of the contract with Jonny's daughters, as well as some other forms." There was a pause. "Jonny and I had a ritual where we'd go to dinner to celebrate. If you'd like, I can bring the contracts with me and you can sign them at the restaurant."

He must have mistaken my silence for hesitation.

"I'd pay, of course."

I let out a nervous laugh. "What? Are you kidding? I'm not going to make you pay for dinner after everything you've done for me! My treat, I insist! Which restaurant did you have in mind?"

"Actually, Jonny chose the restaurants."

"What about Homard's? They make an inspired Lobster Thermidor."

"Homard's is good. Shall I make a seven o'clock reservation?"

"Sounds perfect."

"Will you need for me to pick you up?"

"No, I've got the rental car until tomorrow."

"Great. I'll see you at seven at Homard's."

After I hung up the phone, I did an end-zone dance across the living room.

I'd done it. I'd beaten the system. I'd landed an eight-figure advance and made the big leagues with my very first published novel.

And all it had cost me was my immortal soul.

Part Three
The Sins of the Authors

The remarkable thing about life in Southern California is there is no winter. Sure, the days get shorter, and the leaves fall off some of the trees. But the streets are lined with palm trees and eucalyptus that stay green all year long. There's never any snow, it rarely rains, and every so often a strong wind will blow in from somewhere south of the equator to make the winter days as warm as summer.

Houses Made of Glass debuted on one of those warm December evenings, and I was glad because I wanted to show off my new dress. It was Versace and had gold sequins the size of quarters.

That's right. I got away with it.

Nobody in the publishing industry picked up on my reverse plagiarism—not the editors, not the printers, not the distributors. I felt for sure that when it got to the reviewers someone would cry foul, but it didn't happen. The critics praised *Houses Made of Glass* as "the crown jewel of a long and illustrious career" and wrote that it contained a "poetry and sensitivity that exceeded anything in Jonny Goodsnuff's previous offerings." I thought that should be proof positive that something was amiss, but I guess they didn't know him as well as I did.

I suffered a brief flare-up of anxiety one night when I realized that I'd shown the first ten pages of *The Ice Cathedral* to a number of agents at the conference. But I quickly relaxed. None of them seemed like the type that camped outside the bookstore waiting for the latest selection from the He-Man Woman-Haters Book Club. If by some crazy fluke one of them opened up a copy to see what all of the fuss was about, I'm sure nobody had paid close enough attention to recognize my pages after seven months. And even if they did, I'd just tell everyone that Jonny and I did that as a practical joke, to prove most agents couldn't spot a future best-seller if it bit them on the ass.

I was quickly realizing that when a person is thrust into a situation so illogical that it's virtually impossible, the mind cocoons itself in whatever excuses happen to be close at hand. Certainly no one wanted to be the voice of dissent for what the majority of critics were calling "Jonny Goodsnuff's best read yet." The closer I came to the December release date, the more my worry diminished until it was gone completely and only the thrill of victory remained.

Beyond the occasional splurge on Italian labels, I'd managed my ill-got gains with frugal care. I did freelance makeup for the local television studios and used that money to pick up the check for the weekly dinners where Stonewall and I discussed promotional opportunities for Jonny's work.

I learned a great many interesting and useful things from observing Stonewall, not just about the industry, but also about fine dining. By following his lead, I learned the correct way to hold a pair of chopsticks, how to break open a lobster, the high-class way to eat linguine (it requires a spoon and fork), and how to pair a wine with an entrée without being scoffed at as a barbarian by the *sommelier*.

But try as I might, I couldn't get him to take a look at any of my manuscripts. I told him that by helping Jonny, I learned to mimic the style of his last book. He changed the subject. Every so often, I'd drop a hint into the conversation, which he evaded with the skill of a matador. One afternoon on a seaside terrace that served especially good Mexican food, I flat-out begged him to look at my writing. He heaved a deep sigh, and explained why he'd never (knowingly) take me on as a client.

He told me not to take it personally, but he didn't work with novice writers. His skills and interests didn't involve fine-tuning manuscripts to bring them up to commercial grade, and his reputation and industry connections were of a nature that ran contrary to the cultivation of fledgling talent. Everything he could offer me at this point in my writing career would only stunt my growth. He said we could have this conversation again if I managed to land a contract on my own, but in the meantime, his intervention would do more harm than good.

I asked for a referral to another agent and he changed the subject yet again. So I just sat there and sipped my watermelon margarita and pretended that I didn't think he was full of it.

Little did he know…

Beyond the dresses and those dinners, I pinched my pennies, partly out of habit and partly because I needed money to cover my taxes now that I'd bought the beach house and owned it outright. I'd wheedled the price down to a mere $5.7 million.

The kitchen was still a dungeon, but that gave me an excuse to eat most of my meals over at Lance's place. It became a ritual. He usually wrote all night long and slept during the mornings. I'd come over late in the afternoon with a bottle of wine, and we'd cook together before retiring to the living room to watch whatever movie happened to be on cable. Sometimes he walked me home. Sometimes I spent the night in his guest room.

On weekends, he'd take a break to teach me how to surf. We made out a few times, but he got discouraged when I never let it get past second base. But he never got upset when I pulled away because he thought I was still mourning Jonny. In a way I was. I'd never get over the regret that I couldn't make our marriage work. But my memories were all stained with the realization that I wasn't even a junior partner in our union. I was a fancy pet for him, a pedigreed stray who would give him golden haired babies. Nothing more than a means to an end.

But while Jonny had crossed irrevocably into the past, in the eyes of God and the law, Lance was still married to Lori Anne. For that to change, it had to be his idea, not mine. Otherwise, the next time he saw her there would be nothing to stop him from running back to her bearing tales about how *I made* him get a divorce.

No matter how hard I tried, I couldn't shake the feeling that she was right around the corner, ready to reappear the moment I let my guard down. I kept having a premonition that one night I'd come over to dinner to find Lori Anne sipping cocoa by the fire in a cashmere sweater. "You must be Amanda," she'd say. "Thank you for taking care of my husband, but he doesn't need you anymore"

That line always made me shiver.

Maybe that's why I felt completely unnerved when he refused to come to the industry launch party for *Houses Made of Glass*. So I sat there in the back of the limo, sulking in my shiny new Versace gown, and watched Ivy and Zachary coo at each other like lovebirds. Zachary was in a black tuxedo, Ivy wore a red sari, and I tried not to let them know I was seething with envy at the easy harmony they had found with each other.

At least I wasn't the only one going stag: Stonewall didn't bring a date either. He sat next to me and was so quiet I kept forgetting he was there. When I turned to regard him, he seemed lost in his palm-sized computer. Understandable, since he was one of the hosts for the event. He'd have to make presentations, give speeches, and answer questions about Jonny's writing all night long. As far as anyone knew, I was just the widow.

"So," Zachary said to Ivy as they rubbed noses. "Do you think your publisher is going to throw you a black-tie gala?"

"Given the level of trash they regularly churn out I'm expecting more of a twist-tie gala."

This seemed to bring Stonewall away from his computer.

Ivy smiled at him. "I'm kidding, of course. They're not going to throw me a party."

"Excuse me, but did you just say you're a writer?"

Oh, hell no!

"Well, no, not technically, but I do have a three book deal from Castlegate Books."

"I don't think I've heard of them."

"That doesn't surprise me at all."

I could feel my blood percolating in my veins. For months, Stonewall had made it abundantly clear that he wanted nothing to do with me as an author. Now he was going to proposition my best friend right in front of me? The little agent-stealing tramp? Right now Ivy and Stonewall were two of my favorite people in the world, but if this conversation went where I thought it might be headed, I'd be faced with the uncomfortable dilemma of figuring out which one of them to kill first.

"If you're looking to trade up, this could be your lucky night," Stonewall said. "You and Amanda are going to meet some of the biggest names in the industry. There will be filmmakers as well as representatives from all of the major publishing houses. It will be good for you two young ladies to mingle. A lot of people get their big breaks at parties such as this one."

My shoulders sagged in relief, and a little bit of shame. Ivy was my best friend. I should be happy for her. So why couldn't I stand the thought of her becoming a more successful writer than I was?

"Filmmakers, huh?" Zachary said. "Are they going to make a movie version of *Houses Made of Glass*?"

Stonewall shook his head. "Jonny had a clause stating that none of his books could ever be made into movies."

"Why's that?" I asked.

"He didn't want anyone tampering with his vision. And after seeing what Disney did to *The Little Mermaid*, I can't say that I blamed him."

"What's wrong with the Disney version of *The Little Mermaid*?" Ivy asked in a voice that hinted that Stonewall was venturing into dangerous territory.

"You mean aside from the fact that I find it to be a complete and utter abomination?"

Ivy's mouth flew open in outrage. Clearly, those were fighting words.

She looked to Zachary, who shrugged. "I didn't see the movie or read the book, so I'm not qualified to get in the middle of this."

Ivy smiled. "I know what we're renting next, but in the meantime all you need to know is that in the Disney movie, the mermaid marries her prince and they live happily ever after, while in the original Hans Christian Andersen tale, the prince marries another girl and the mermaid kills herself."

"She didn't kill herself," Stonewall said.

Ivy turned her nose up. "If you say so."

This was interesting: a girl who loves to argue having it out with a man who's paid to argue. My money was on Stonewall.

He turned to Zachary. "What you really need to know is that *The Little Mermaid* is a haunting and tragic tale of unrequited love that the fine people at Disney Studios decided to turn into a musical comedy."

"As well they should have," Ivy said. "The original version is preachy and depressing."

"True," Stonewall said. "But it's a lot more honest than pretending that honor and self-sacrifice are always rewarded in this lifetime."

I had to concede that point. Especially given the nature of my relationship with Lance. Or should I say: the lack thereof. I never gave it much thought, but it suddenly seemed that I was doing all of the work, and all I wanted in return was for him to stop pining for the woman who walked out on him.

Ivy crossed her arms. "And I suppose a story about a suicidal mermaid is more appropriate for little children?"

"Maybe. If it will spare them the misery of thinking that if they try really hard they can make other people fall in love with them."

I winced from that last statement. It hit a little too close to home.

"But don't you see?" Ivy said. "*The Little Mermaid* wasn't a love story at all. Reread it and you'll see that the girl in the Andersen story was a complete masochist. She didn't really want the prince to love her. Her fondest wish was to die like a martyr. She didn't even try to save herself."

Stonewall rolled his eyes, while Ivy's were filled with fire and her cheeks stained with two crimson spots. They seemed to be taking things far too seriously for a pair of adults discussing a fairy tale. Zachary must have thought this as well since his eyes were wide and he tried to hide a smirk behind his hand as Ivy continued her tirade.

"The only sad part of the story was when her sisters sacrificed their beautiful hair to try to save her while she danced like an idiot at her boyfriend's wedding."

"And so you missed that she danced because her heart was breaking?" Stonewall said. "And that she loved him so deeply that she put his happiness above her own?"

Ivy snickered. "Sorry, but I have no sympathy for anyone who is that much of a doormat."

Was I a doormat? Nobody could say that Lance was using me. Not in the traditional sense. But on an emotional level maybe I was making myself too available, and asking for too little in return?

Ivy leaned back. "You know, I'd have cared a lot more for the mermaid if she made even the tiniest effort to save herself. Instead, she just stood back like a fool and let the love of her life marry the wrong person for the wrong reasons."

"You're making a very big assumption," Stonewall said.

"Oh, what's that?"

"You're assuming the prince would have welcomed the advances of a crippled mermaid. Or that he was so noble in spirit that he'd swallow his disgust when he realized that he'd tricked himself into marrying some pathetic, mute, half-fish creature. Maybe it was best for everyone that she died while she still had hope that he wouldn't be utterly repulsed by her true nature."

I felt myself fuming, but cooled down when I realized that Stonewall couldn't possibly know the parallels between the mermaid's story and my own.

Zachary must have noticed my annoyance. "I'd like to know what Amanda thinks of all this."

I sat there with my shoulders tense while they all turned or leaned forward in their seats and waited for me to speak.

"You really want to know what I think?"

They nodded.

I folded my arms across my chest. "I think the mermaid was a complete fool to doom herself over some guy she'd just met! She gave up her life to win him, which is no basis for a healthy relationship. The prince liked her, and she liked him. In time he would have loved her, but she should have just played it cool and kept her tail on until she was certain that he might meet her halfway!"

"Huh," they all said in unison. I expected at least one of them to argue with me, but instead they all settled back into their seats. Nobody said another word for the rest of the ride.

There were no armies of paparazzi waiting outside this party. I guess books aren't that sexy. Still, I couldn't stop smiling. The signs, the music, this was all for me. I'd written my first novel and everyone had heard of it. I wouldn't need to shill my book out—it was already at the top of the best-seller list.

As a writer, I had succeeded beyond my wildest expectations. Nobody knew it, but I knew, and that was enough for me. Of course, I'd cheated and lied my way to the top, but was that really any worse than the dirty marketing tricks I would have had to perform anyway?

"Jeremy!" came a high-pitched squeal as a woman with a perfect manicure and highlights advanced at Stonewall with her arms spread wide. She clasped his shoulders and they kissed the air about a foot from each other's ears.

My first impression was that she was a social climbing phony whose dates were more like job interviews, and who probably cried in the shower because her biological clock was waging a losing war with her frigid libido. However, I had nothing to base that on, so I conceded that she was probably a lovely person.

"Lisa, I'd like you to meet Amanda Anderson and her friends. Amanda is Jonny's widow."

"So sorry for your loss." She grabbed hold of Stonewall's arm. "Will you excuse us? There are some people Jeremy needs to talk to."

I waved. "You go right ahead. I'm sure we can find our way around."

The shortest line for drinks stretched twelve people long. Zachary offered to get them for us, so Ivy and I settled into a tinsel covered table along the far wall where we could get a good view of the other people at the party. Most stood around in their suits and dresses, schmoozing over their cocktails, but a few people sat in the tables and booths and began reading. The sight of it gave me a lump in my throat. This was my greatest dream come true.

"Hey, Amanda," Ivy whispered in my ear, "don't look too quickly, but there's a Mediterranean girl three tables away who hasn't been able to take her eyes off you since we walked in here."

I waited a respectable amount of time before I looked over at the table that Ivy mentioned. At it sat a young man with short red hair and a woman who looked like the Mona Lisa, but with a long Greek nose. A copy of *Houses Made of Glass* sat open on the table, and I couldn't tell who had been reading it. They were holding hands but showed no trace of affection, as if they were actors awaiting a cue. In fact, the man seemed nervous and uncomfortable, like he was afraid that if he showed the slightest interest in his date they might end up in court.

As I watched, she didn't look away but smiled warmly. I swallowed hard as I recognized the significance of her sensible shoes and their conservative haircuts. That pair meant trouble. The absolute giveaway was the ill-fitting outerwear. The woman wore a red satin dress under a black velvet blazer. The heat in the room was almost stifling with all the bright lights and the crowds, but she kept the blazer on. Probably to hide her gun.

I shivered. Zachary returned with a cosmopolitan in each hand and a bottle of beer under his arm. I turned to the others but before I could say anything, Ivy spoke again.

"So where's Lance?"

"He couldn't come. He has a tummy-ache."

Ivy laughed. "He didn't use the word tummy-ache, did he?"

"No, he was just lying on his couch clutching his belly and moaning like a baby until I told him that he didn't have to come here if he didn't want to."

Zachary twisted open his beer. "You don't sound very sympathetic."

"That's because I deliberately left my purse under his coffee table so I'd have to go back for it. Sure enough, he was off the couch and running on his treadmill when I returned."

"Jesus," Ivy said. "So he faked an illness just to blow you off?"

Zachary took a swig of his beer. "That's not a very nice thing to do to a girl you're knocking boots with."

I sighed. "We haven't exactly progressed to the boot-knocking phase of the relationship yet."

Ivy and Zachary lowered their drinks and stared at me in disbelief.

"What? We're taking things slowly."

"Six weeks is taking things slowly," Ivy said. "Six months is a vow of celibacy."

I felt my cheeks color. "I'm not ready to jump in the sack again. I think it's nice that he's willing to wait."

Ivy stirred her cosmopolitan. "And what is it exactly that the two of you are doing while you're waiting?"

"We cook dinner together. We watch movies. We snuggle in front of the fire."

Ivy frowned. "I hate to be the one to break this to you, but your boyfriend is gay."

"Ivy," Zachary said. "You don't know that. He might just have a freakishly low sperm count."

I felt my face go hot. "Need I remind you that he's still married?"

Ivy rolled her eyes. "And what exactly is he doing about that."

"Nothing. If he files for a divorce, she gets half of his money."

"So what?" Zachary said. "If he waits, she still gets half of his money, only there will be more of it."

"What do I care? I have money of my own. The last thing I need right now is to become some rich guy's plaything."

Ivy gave me a sad pout. At that point, the music stopped as the woman named Lisa appeared at the lectern. "Ladies and Gentlemen, can I have your attention?"

She waited for the room to go silent before continuing.

"I'd like to thank each and every one of you for coming out here tonight to celebrate the life and work of the great artist we knew as Jonny Goodsnuff. It has been my great pleasure to work with him in the past, and it was with the greatest of sadness that I learned that the industry had lost one of its greatest legends. I've managed to coerce one of his very best friends to come up here and say a few words in tribute to this great man. So without further ado, I'd like to turn the microphone over to Jonny's agent, Mr. Jeremy 'Stonewall' Kendal."

Ivy grabbed my arm and we screamed out our applause as Stonewall took the podium.

"Hello, everyone, as you all know, I really hate giving speeches."

An anonymous voice shouted out "Liar!" and a few people laughed.

"I first met Jonny five years ago. He was looking for a new agent, and he'd heard of me from another of my clients. I, of course, had heard of him. In fact, when he called, I thought someone was playing a joke on me. But it was no joke. Jonny became my client, and I spent months renegotiating his contracts so he got the money he so richly deserved from some of the unscrupulous rascals here tonight."

Laughter filled the room, some of it mocking, some of it nervous.

"Yes, as I look around I see the faces of many of our friends and former adversaries. Jonny said I was his general. It was he who gave me the hated nickname 'Stonewall' and try as I might, I can't get people to stop calling me that. But I didn't care what Jonny called me. He was my best friend. I'm proud to say that this latest book was the crowning achievement of both of our careers, and I shudder when I stop to think how close we came to losing it forever. And for that we can blame his lovely widow, Amanda."

I felt as if I'd been drenched in ice water. He wasn't going to talk about that. He couldn't be that stupid.

"You see, one night he called to tell me that he'd just fallen for the most amazing girl. He said she was smart and funny—the most beautiful girl alive. Moreover, by some miracle she liked him back. In fact, she'd been receptive to his flirting before she even realized who he was. Where's Amanda? Over there—can we get a spotlight on her?"

A beam of light appeared overhead and my dress lit up like a disco ball. I wished that I could become invisible as I forced a smile and a halfhearted wave.

"Jonny was so very proud of this book. He'd called me in the middle of the night to tell me that he'd just come up with the most amazing idea for his next novel, but no matter how hard I tried to get it out of him he wouldn't tell me anything about it. All I needed to know was that it was going to make history. But first, he told me, he had to go after Amanda Anderson until she fell in love with him.

"Fortunately, she didn't put up too much of a chase. Jonny and Amanda were married about a month later in a private ceremony in Ohio." The room filled with applause.

Don't clap, you fools, I thought. You don't know who you're congratulating. Up until Stonewall took the stage I was congratulating myself for beating the system. But now I realized I'd never be able to look him in the eye again.

"You'd think that Jonny would have taken time off to enjoy being married to the woman of his dreams, but no. Amanda understood how important this book was to her husband. She even agreed to postpone their honeymoon. At a time when many women expect to be the center of attention, she worked tirelessly at her husband's side, transcribing his pages into her computer so that he could release his final book in record time."

The spotlight dimmed and I was glad.

"Unfortunately Jonny was taken from her, and from us, too early. I know he is looking down at us on this magical night, to see us celebrate *Houses*

Made of Glass, the book that Jonny never saw in print, but which was still his greatest pride and joy. So I humbly ask you to bow your heads for a moment of silence to honor this great man."

As I bowed my head, only one thought kept running through my mind: *My God, what have I done?* Jonny always complained that he was surrounded by parasites. Little did he know that he had married the worst parasite of them all.

"Thank you, and I hope you enjoy the rest of the evening."

At long last, the music resumed. I turned my head to the side and nearly spilled my drink as I found myself looking right into the eyes of the woman with the Mona Lisa face.

She attempted a smile. "I see that you're drinking cosmos. Do you mind if I sit down."

Ivy and Zachary scooted over to make room so I spoke quickly. "I'd really rather you didn't. I have a weird thing about sitting next to strangers. No offense."

"None taken," She held out her hand. "I'm Helena."

I took it with reluctance. "Amanda."

"Amanda...?"

"Just Amanda." Did she really expect me to believe she hadn't noticed my moment in the spotlight? My stomach clenched as she moved to the empty chair next to me. I put my handbag on it and then reached for Ivy's and threw that on the chair as well.

"Pardon me, Just Amanda, but I couldn't help but overhear. Right before that last speech, did you say that you have a boyfriend?"

"No," I said. "You must have misunderstood. We were talking about my neighbor. He's a handsome man, so they like to tease me, but I'm a recent widow with no interest in romance."

She leaned on the back of the chair. "That sounds fascinating. So how long have you been neighbors?"

"You know what? I'm going to use the restroom." I stood and grabbed my purse. Ivy was right behind me.

"That was cold, Amanda," she said as soon as we were out of earshot. "She might be a disciple of Sappho, but she was just trying to be friendly."

"When you see Stonewall tell him I wasn't feeling well and decided to take a taxi home."

Ivy chuckled. "You're catching a cab? Wow. You Midwesterners must really have a thing against dykes."

"She's not a dyke, she's a cop."

Ivy stopped walking. "My God, what did you do?"

"Nothing intentional." I looked over at Helena, who had rejoined her date. "It's just that after Jonny died, I–"

At the table, the redheaded man opened his cell phone. As he spoke, his eyes met mine.

Ivy saw it too and she knew what it meant.

"Run," she said.

I pushed through the crowd and made for the doorway. I had to get out of there, now. The thought of Stonewall seeing me arrested for defrauding Jonny's readers after delivering that speech was more than I could bear. Someone opened the door to leave and it framed two squad cars that waited ominously in the alleyway. I turned and ran the other direction.

Two squad cars? Either this party was a beehive of criminal activity or this city took literary matters way too seriously. My panic was so great that I could no longer hear the music blasting over the loudspeakers. I could only feel the bass as it beat through my heels whenever they touched the floor. A woman shouted as I knocked the purse out of her hand, but I couldn't stop. I had to get out.

I reached the front door as it burst open, revealing two uniformed officers. "Amanda Anderson?" One of them said in a voice distorted by my fear to sound like something out of a nightmare.

"Yes?"

"You're under arrest. Stand with your legs apart and your hands against the wall."

There were more cops pouring in, about seven or eight of them. Not counting the two undercover detectives at the table. I blinked and tried to force myself awake. Why were they making such a big deal out of this? As guilty as I felt, it's not like I'd hurt anyone. If anything, I'd made the world a better place by introducing a touch of class to Jonny's junk-pile of literary offerings. So why were they carrying on as if I'd just taken a swing at the pope?

"Now, ma'am."

I stood frozen in place until Stonewall appeared and put his hands on my shoulders.

"Excuse me, officer. Is there a problem here?" His voice had a soothing authoritarian quality that I might have taken comfort in, had I not been more afraid of Stonewall than I was of the cops.

"Sir, this is a police matter, it does not concern you."

"It does concern me. I'm Jeremy Kendal, Ms. Anderson's attorney."

The officer looked at me. "Is that true?"

I nodded, not knowing what else to do.

"Before this goes any further, I'd like to know what my client is charged with."

I bit my lip waiting for the inevitable explosion.

"First degree murder, with special circumstances."

"What?" I screamed. "That's insane! I didn't kill anyone! What the hell is going on?"

Stonewall glanced back at the crowd behind us. "If you must arrest my client, would you mind doing so outside?"

"Mr. Kendal, it is standard procedure in these matters—"

"I've spent ten years as a prosecutor. I'm well aware of what the standard procedure is. However, if you take a good look at the skintight nature of my client's attire, you will see it's quite obvious that she isn't hiding a weapon."

I blushed as the police looked me over, both front and back.

"Very well," said the commanding officer. "You two men follow us. The rest of you meet us in the alley."

Stonewall offered up his arm and I looped my hand around it. "Smile," he whispered to me. "This party is filled with journalists. You have to pretend that nothing's wrong."

I looked at the uniformed officers in front of us and the two behind us. "Oh, I think it's pretty obvious that something is wrong." I forced a smile anyway and nodded at the people who turned to stare. To my horror, some of them were holding up camera-phones.

"Jeremy?" The woman named Lisa said. "What's going on?"

"Serious police business," he said in a loud voice. "I assure everyone that this is not a publicity stunt. This city's police have much better things to do than stage an arrest to promote Jonny Goodsnuff's final book, *Houses Made of Glass,* which is now available at all retail and online booksellers."

I heard a collective groan as people set down their cameras. His voice didn't convince anyone. Not even me, and I knew he was telling the truth. My smile became a little less forced. I guess Stonewall really could talk his way through any situation.

I scanned the crowd for Ivy and saw her pick up a half-finished drink from a table. She then walked over and threw the contents into Helena's face. The detective sputtered and stood dripping, but didn't go after Ivy, who made her way through the crowd. I lost track of her as the police took me through the door and into the alleyway.

Stonewall leaned close one final time before the police led me out. "I'm going to explain the situation to your friends, and then I'm going to take a taxi to the station. It is vitally important that you do not answer any questions until I get there. When they badger you, tell them that you assert your right to remain silent until you have legal representation. Despite what they might tell you, nobody wants to hear your side of the story right now. They're only interested in gathering evidence against you, or tricking you into making a confession."

I nodded as they twisted my wrists around to my back to put the cuffs on me. After all, I was a suspense writer. There wasn't a thing I didn't already know about police procedures and interrogation tactics.

As I sat in the cage in the back of the squad-car with my wrists chained together behind my sparkling Versace gown, I took a small measure of comfort in the fact that I hadn't been arrested for what I'd actually done.

CHAPTER 25

The police led me through the station and into a sparse interrogation chamber with a huge mirror along the wall. A man who resembled a walrus with a huge gut, a thin comb-over, and a thick mustache regarded me as he sat behind the desk. A woman of undeterminable race and age joined us. I knew that she was "the good cop"—they tried to fit those as closely to the suspect's demographic as possible. I wondered if there were additional officers watching us through the mirror, or just a camera.

"I'm Detective Brunston," the Walrus said.

"And I'm Detective Reese, but you can call me Yolanda."

The police released me from my cuffs and directed me to the least comfortable seat, which was a slightly rusted folding metal chair in the far corner. I noticed that one leg of my chair was shorter than the rest. That annoyed me, just like it was supposed to. I clasped my hands over my knees and stared at my thumbs. I'd have to stare at my thumbs every time I spoke. They'd try to read my eyes like a polygraph and even though I was innocent, I knew I couldn't give them anything to work with.

The interrogating officer slid a document to me. "Please read and sign this."

It was the standard form explaining my Miranda rights. I signed it, because I knew that if I didn't, they'd end the interview and begin the booking process.

He tapped his pencil for a few moments on the desk while Yolanda smiled at me. "So...I understand you're a writer?"

"If it's all the same to you, I'd prefer not to talk about that until my attorney arrives."

Her smile vanished. So much for forming a rapport to weaken my defenses. "You don't want to talk to me?"

I stared at my thumbs. I should have said "I prefer to exercise my constitutional right to remain silent," but to be honest, I was a little curious as to how a real interrogation worked. At that point I still believed this was all a horrible misunderstanding and that I didn't have much to fear.

The male detective continued tapping his pencil. "Are you declining the interview?"

I shook my head. "My lawyer knows where I am. He should be here at any moment."

He stopped his tapping. "I must tell you that I hope he is really damn good, since from where I sit, things look pretty bad for you right now. We have a mountain of evidence, and I doubt that a jury will show you much mercy considering the heinous and calculated nature of your crimes."

Yolanda nodded. "We're looking at both premeditation and lying in wait. That makes this a capital offense. You're not from around here, so maybe I should explain that the penalty is death by lethal injection."

They must have seen me as pretty naïve to think I'd fall for such a tactic. "I'd rather not talk about that."

"Suit yourself," Brunston said. "I'm just saying, a pretty young girl marrying a rich old man for his money—I don't think I have to tell you that there are names for girls like that. And then your new husband is brutally murdered only a couple of weeks into the marriage?" He shook his head. "The court and the public don't have a lot of sympathy for people like you. Whatever happens is going to be a damn shame at your age."

So, they thought I'd killed Jonny. That made sense. Standard police protocol was to approach all violent deaths as homicides, and the main suspect in such cases was usually the spouse. It annoyed me that they were tormenting me over a formality, but I was careful not to let it show in my face.

"Maybe she had her reasons," Yolanda said.

"Oh?" Her partner said on cue. "Like what?"

Yolanda stood over me and put her hand on my shoulder. "You know, I think I have a pretty good guess as to what might have happened. I think that Amanda never intended to hurt anyone. She was a good girl, but she didn't know what she was getting herself into."

Brunston nodded. "That makes a lot of sense. I've read some of Jonny Goodsnuff's books. He strikes me as the sort of guy who liked the rough stuff."

Yolanda leaned closer so she was blocking the light. She wanted me to move my head so they could see my eyes, but I didn't. There was nothing I needed to look at.

"What did Jonny do to you, Amanda? Did he hit you? Pull your hair? Make you dirty in places you wanted to keep clean?"

Her partner sounded outraged. "Hell, I wouldn't like that. And I really wouldn't like it if someone did that sort of thing to my daughter."

I risked a glance at his hand, which didn't have a ring. I didn't believe for one minute that he really had a daughter.

Yolanda took her hand off my shoulder. "I have three daughters and I'd like it if my baby girls would come and tell me if something bad was going on, but not every frightened girl can talk to her mama. But you can talk to me if you'd like."

Yeah, I'd bet she'd like that a lot.

I sat there quietly while she stroked my arm in a motherly fashion, but I didn't even flinch. These two were good. They should take their act to vaudeville, but a trick isn't magic once you know how it's done. Yolanda wasn't touching me to offer comfort. She was touching me to prove she could, to establish dominance and to heighten my sense of helplessness and claustrophobia while they wore me down, until I told them everything they wanted to hear, just to get out of that room.

I took a deep breath of the mildew-scented air, and thankfully the door opened and a middle-aged woman in uniform peeked in.

"Ms. Anderson's attorney has just arrived."

Brunston waved his hand. "Send 'im in."

She leaned forward and whispered. "It's Jeremy Kendal."

Brunston's face lit up. "Our Jeremy Kendal?"

"Do you think I would have said anything if it wasn't?"

Brunston nodded at me. "Excuse us for one minute." He got up and darted out of the room like a kid chasing after an ice cream truck while Yolanda followed at a more sedate pace.

Jesus, was there a man in this city who wasn't in love with my husband's agent?

I heard the door lock behind them and actually felt relieved to be sitting there alone in my shimmery Italian gown. On the desk was a cardboard box with a lid over its contents. I forced myself to ignore it. The mirror that took up the far wall was clear on the other side, and I knew I was being watched. This was just as much a part of the interrogation as the questioning.

Despite my best efforts to hide my emotions, I found myself straightening my posture as Stonewall appeared in the doorway flanked by the two detectives. He'd removed his tie, but was still dressed in the same tuxedo he wore at the party. The men were smiling and joking while Yolanda brought another chair in from the outside. She joined detective Brunston behind the table while Stonewall took her old chair. He folded his hands while the detectives tried to look serious again. The oppressive atmosphere they'd worked so hard to achieve was gone in an instant. It felt like we were all settling in for a game of Monopoly.

Brunston looked across the table and sighed dramatically. "Heaven help us, the grandmaster is working for the criminals now."

"Amanda Anderson is not a criminal."

"I'm sorry to disappoint you, but I've got a whole box of evidence that suggests otherwise. Yolanda, you know Jeremy don't you?"

She nodded. "We've met. My promotion came a few weeks before the shooting incident."

Shooting incident?

Brunston must have seen that question in my face. "Jeremy hasn't told you why he stopped being one of this city's most promising and successful prosecutors?"

Yolanda smiled. "One might say that he was too successful."

Brunston nodded. "Some lowlife scumball begged a bleeding-heart judge to let him out early so that he could help young kids turn their lives around. Thing is, he told his cellmate that the real reason he wanted out was to pay a few social calls, starting with Jeremy."

Yolanda sighed and shook her head. "Courthouse security back then wasn't the same as it is now. There were no metal detectors, no checks for concealed weapons…"

"Long story, short," Brunston said. "We got there too late and by that time there was blood everywhere–"

Stonewall cleared his throat. "As much as I applaud your efforts to scare my client and throw me off my game, our taxi is waiting for us outside, so I'm going to have to cut your long story even shorter so that we can focus on the case at hand."

"Our taxi?" Brunston chuckled. "You seem awfully sure of yourself."

"That's because I have a lot more faith in her innocence than I do in your competence."

"Oh, really?" Detective Brunston opened the box. He brought out an enlarged photo of my wedding set and slid it across the table to Stonewall. "Do you know what these are?"

"They look like rings."

"Those are your client's wedding rings, to be exact."

Stonewall shrugged. "So what if they are?"

"We found these in the victim's pocket."

Stonewall gave the detective a blank stare. "And that proves what, exactly?

That he was taking them to be resized? Or that she'd left them on the sink one too many times and he confiscated them to teach her a lesson?"

Brunston wrinkled his nose. "It proves that the rings were off her finger for half a year, and yet the grieving widow never missed them."

"Who said she never missed them?" Stonewall slid the picture back to Brunston. "She just never knew you had them. If they'd fallen down a drain and she'd asked you if you'd pulled any jewelry from her husband's dead body, wouldn't you take that as proof that she's a heartless witch who cared only for her diamonds?"

Brunston's scowl deepened. "Let's move on to the witnesses. We have several eyewitness accounts of Jonny being struck by a car at a speed in excess of thirty mph. They described the driver as a blond woman wearing a baggy tan trench coat. The car had no plates and backed up to hit the victim a second time before driving off."

"Oh? Did you bother to get a composite sketch of this woman?"

Detective Brunston shook his head. "The witnesses didn't get a good enough look. It all happened too fast and she wore dark sunglasses, a neck scarf, and a bucket hat."

Stonewall steepled his fingers. "And you don't find it a bit odd that this mysterious woman took so much trouble to mask her face, her figure, and even her throat, but not her hair?"

"Maybe her hair came loose?" Yolanda offered.

"Or maybe the killer wore a wig and wanted the blond hair to be the only thing for the witnesses to notice. I assume you found the car abandoned somewhere close by?"

"Yes," Brunston said. "We recovered the car from the parking garage of a derelict office building a few blocks away from the crime scene." He slid another photo to us. Stonewall picked it up. I peeked at it and fought to keep all signs of horror from my face when I saw a Jaguar with its front bumper scrunched in and the windshield bloodied and smashed up to resemble a fishing net.

"Look familiar?" Detective Brunston said.

"That's Jonny's car," Stonewall said.

Yolanda nodded. "The very same car that Jonny Goodsnuff insisted that your client took without his permission in the hours leading up to the murder."

Stonewall turned the picture over. "Then please explain how Amanda got home. She didn't own a second car, and the card room is a good three miles away from her house."

Brunston smiled. "This may be news to someone of your diminished lung capacity, but three miles is not an unreasonable sprint for a fit young woman like your client."

"Even when she's anticipating a visit from the police?" He slid the picture across the desk. "Look, as much as I enjoy watching you two fumbling about trying to fit the facts to your theories, I don't have time for these sorts of games. Do you have any real evidence in there? Fingerprints? DNA? Security or traffic light footage offering biometric information about the *actual* perpetrator?"

Brunston brought out a folder. "We have a police report from the victim swearing himself blue in the face that his wife stole his car and he wanted to press charges."

"Except that borrowing a spouse's car is not a crime, and even if it were, Jonny changed his story when the police found signs that the garage door had been forced open from the outside."

Brunston slid some papers to him. "Yes, but if you read the official report, it suggests that the victim changed the story under duress after he and his agent got into a shouting match over his conduct towards the accused."

Uh...what?

Stonewall pushed the papers back with a smile. "Oh, I can assure you that I don't need to read that."

They continued talking and reviewing evidence, but my mind was stuck trying to figure out what those last few words meant. Stonewall had stood up for me? Before I'd saved his life? I searched my memories of my marriage to Jonny, and I couldn't recall a single incident where I wasn't mean or rude or just plain horrible towards Stonewall. Yet he took my side against his best friend and most lucrative client...just minutes before I'd called him a prodigious fop and told him I never wanted to see him again.

Nice, Amanda. You're a real class act.

Detective Yolanda took a sip of water. "Let's talk about the motive, shall we?"

"What motive?" Stonewall said. "Amanda had nothing to gain from her husband's passing."

"Her bank account tells a different story," Brunston said.

"That's only because of the generosity of Jonny's two daughters. She never asked them for a penny."

"Then I'm afraid she's conned them, just like she's conned you." The detective's walrus mustache lifted in a broad smile as he slid over a large manila envelope.

As Stonewall reached in and pulled out ten crisp pages, cleanly cut from a hardcover book, I felt my insides tie themselves into knots.

"Do you recognize those pages?" Yolanda asked.

"Of course I do," Stonewall said. "This is the opening chapter of *Houses Made of Glass.*"

Detective Brunston nodded. "There's more in there."

Stonewall pulled out ten pages of laser printout held together by a paper-clip. I remembered that paperclip. I put it on there while the pages were still warm from the printer.

"Those are pages that your client submitted as a writing sample to the conference where she met her husband," Yolanda said. "The envelope was postmarked from Ohio, four months before the conference."

As the color drained from Stonewall's face, I couldn't help but pray for a miracle—like a meteor strike, or a fire, or a massive earthquake. Anything at all that would keep Stonewall from reading those pages. But read them he did. Side by side. All ten pages. And when he was finished, his face bore the angry and betrayed look of a child who'd just been told that his dog went off to live on a farm. "Where did you get this?"

"I requested her materials from the organizer," Yolanda said. "I'd hoped it would give us some insight into what sort of a girl your client is."

Brunston bared his teeth. "But we all know exactly the sort of girl your client is, don't we, Jeremy?"

Stonewall just sat there, looking angry.

"Well, go on. Let's hear your brilliant explanation for how two different people just happened to be writing the exact same novel at the exact same time. Here, I'll help you: Jonny Goodsnuff ran out of good ideas, so he trolled the local conferences for some sweet young thing he could marry, just so he could steal her work verbatim and pass it off as his next tough-guy novel."

Stonewall's scowl deepened.

"What? Too farfetched?" Brunston said. "Well let's try this one on for size: Your poor, innocent client wanted to get her little book published. But when she arrived at the conference she learned that it wasn't going to be as easy as she thought. Yet here was some clown walking around bragging about how all of his books are instant best-sellers." Brunston put his fist to his chest. "That must have hit her right here. But then she realized she could have her very own best-seller. All she had to do was *take his name.*"

"No!" I said. "That's not what happened!"

Detective Brunston gave me a walrus smile. "Oh really, Amanda? Then why don't you tell us what really did happen."

Stonewall turned toward me. I hoped it was to remind me to be silent, but he just stared as if he wanted to throttle me, and at that moment, I was inclined to let him.

I looked Stonewall in the eyes. "I didn't kill Jonny! I just lost his manuscript." I should have kept quiet. I knew I was supposed to assert my right to remain silent and end the interview now that Stonewall was no longer capable of representing me, but I couldn't. No matter what, I couldn't let him leave the room believing that he'd wired several million dollars to the woman who had killed his best friend.

"I threw it away because I was mad at you and the entire Goodsnuff family, and I didn't think you needed it anymore. When you asked for it, I sent you one of my own. I'm sorry. I wasn't thinking clearly. I didn't know what else to do."

Stonewall just stared. I worried that he couldn't hear me.

"Please say something."

"You lost the manuscript?"

I nodded.

He clenched his teeth as if it hurt to speak. "Amanda, there is only one thing you could have done that would have been worse than losing that manuscript." He rose to his feet and flung the papers from the desk. "And that would be to lose the manuscript—and then *lie about it!*"

Detective Brunston sighed. "Jeremy, calm down."

"No, I'm not going to calm down." He pointed his finger at me. "You don't know what she's like. She hates me! She always has! All she ever did when she was married to Jonny was make snide little comments and mock me behind my back."

I wanted to deny it, but the statement was truer than I cared to admit. I should've known that Jonny was a snitch.

Stonewall buried his face in his hands. "Congratulations, Amanda, you've just ended my career. You've played a cruel joke on millions of people all over the world. And now, in order to save your ass, you're going to have to take the stand and explain how you got Jonny's manuscript—under oath no less. And when you do, there's going to be a mob of very angry people who will want their money back. I don't have that kind of money. Do you?"

I spoke even though I could hear my voice quivering. "Maybe nobody will be upset. The book has been getting rave reviews. Maybe everyone will be impressed that it was written by a first time novelist and the trial publicity will help sales."

Stonewall lowered his hands from his face. "No, Amanda. Nobody is going to be impressed, because nobody likes to be the victim of a hoax."

I knew he was right. This scandal, coupled with the accusation of murder, would end my literary career before it even began. The two detectives tried to hide their smiles. This must have been like an early Christmas. They'd tried to get me to talk and they couldn't, until my own advocate arrived to do their job for them.

I didn't even bother to hide my shame, but that didn't stop Stonewall's rant. "You know what? Jail might be the safest place for you. Jonny wrote his books to appeal to big misogynistic brutes. They're not going to appreciate that the latest was ghostwritten by Gutenberg Barbie."

I shrank in my seat. "The men who wrote all of those reviews seemed to like it."

"Those weren't men, Amanda. Those were critics."

Yolanda stifled a laugh behind her hand and Stonewall gave her an angry look.

Detective Brunston cleared his throat. "Jeremy, if you've finished tormenting your client, I'd like to return to the business at hand."

"Do whatever you want to her. I'm leaving."

"Jeremy, you can't do that."

Stonewall went to the door and yanked it open to illustrate that he in fact could.

Brunston rose from his seat. "Jeremy, think about what you're doing. If you walk out the door, you are willfully disregarding the interests of your client. She'll have you disbarred over this."

"Disbar me then, Amanda. You might as well."

And with that, he slammed the door so hard it made me jump.

"Well that was interesting," Yolanda said.

They both got up and left the room. I couldn't face the mirror, and not just because I was being watched. I stared at my shaking hands for a few minutes until Yolanda returned. She knelt next to me and put her hand on my shoulder.

I pulled away from her. "Don't touch me, and don't talk to me. I want a real lawyer."

"Then I'm going to need you to stand against the wall so I can take some photos."

I looked up at her. "Am I being booked?"

Yolanda nodded. "I'm afraid so."

They took my pictures, my fingerprints, and processed me into their computers before they sent me to jail. There they took my handbag, my high-heeled sandals, and my shimmery gold dress and sealed them up in plastic. They gave me an indigo jumpsuit, a white tank top, a pair of foam slippers, and a plastic tub with stationery and toiletries. The whole ritual made me feel a bit like a nun who was entering a convent. Actually, the analogy was particularly apt in this instance. In days of old, parents shuffled their disgraced and unwanted daughters into the nunnery to prepare their wasted souls for the afterlife.

Between my physical exam and my orientation video, they allowed me to make my one phone call. I dialed Lance's number.

"Pennyroyal promotions, representing Prudy Newcastle. How may we help you?"

I closed my eyes and luxuriated in the sound of his voice. "Lance?"

"Hey, cutie pie, how's the party?"

I tried my hardest not to cry, which made crying inevitable.

"Amanda? What's wrong? Did something happen? Do you need me to come get you?"

"Lance, I'm in jail."

He clucked dramatically. "I let you out of my sight for one evening and look what happens."

I laughed, more out of hysteria than genuine amusement. Still, the laughter calmed my nerves a little, but not nearly as much as hearing Lance's voice.

"So what do they think you've done?"

"They think I killed Jonny."

"That's total bullcrap, Amanda. You couldn't hurt a fly. Should I come over there and raise some hell?"

I sighed. "I don't think that will do a whole lot of good. But I am going to need a good lawyer."

"You don't worry about that. I'm going to get you the best lawyer money can buy. But I take it you might not be coming over for dinner and a movie tomorrow?"

"I don't think I'll be going anywhere for a very long time."

"Don't say that, baby doll. You have to think positive to keep your spirits up. You know what? When you lie in your bed tonight, I want you to imagine I'm right there with you. I want you to close your eyes and pretend that I'm holding you in my arms. And if things get really bad, I'll kiss your forehead and tell you what a good girl you are."

I could already feel his soft skin and smell the fresh scent of his cotton T-shirts. "Thank you."

"I can't wait for you to come home so I can take you into my arms and give you a real bear hug. Then I'll fix you a nice hot bubble bath. Would you like that?"

"I'd like that a whole lot." I had a smile on my face that lasted until I hung up the phone. I forced myself to hold onto the memory of his voice as I took the plastic bin with all of my supplies and followed the guards to my new dormitory.

I think I've watched too many babes behind bars movies, because I expected a tiny cell with a pair of ruthless vixens who would tear me apart like a second grader's Barbie. Instead, I was in a huge room filled with lockers and bunk beds that looked more like shelving units.

A warehouse for wayward women, I thought, as I placed my bin in my locker and settled into the vacant bunk that my jailer assigned to me. There wasn't much in the way of bedding so I placed the folded blanket under my head to use as a pillow. The air-conditioning ran full blast, and the coarse fabric was only a little softer than steel wool. I knew it was going to destroy my hair, but the battered mattress was so thin that I could feel the metal underneath.

It was late and most of the inmates were asleep but the lights were all on as if it were daytime. The whole place stank of urine and vomit, but I knew I'd get used to it. Somewhere, a woman sobbed in Spanish, but nobody seemed to care.

Across from me, a large woman who looked like Oprah's character in *The Color Purple* reclined on the bottom bunk while a woman with long graying hair parted down the middle sat on the top bunk. They seemed nice. I liked them right away for not shanking me or asking for my hand in marriage.

I curled into a ball, ready to slip into my dreams about Lance.

"Hey," the long-haired woman said. "I'm Annalee and this is Jasmine. Jasmine likes to grow pot, and I like to smoke it. Needless to say, we'll keep in touch once we get out of here. Who are you?"

"I'm Amanda."

"Whatcha in for, Amanda?"

"Lying," I said, and turned over on my back.

Annalee whistled. "That must have been some lie."

Tears welled into my eyes again. "I lied to a good man who trusted me, and now his life will be ruined."

This got Jasmine's attention. "Damn, girl, that ain't nothing to be ashamed of! They've been doing that same damned thing to us for nearly six thousand years!"

I couldn't help but laugh.

It wasn't nice, and it certainly wasn't fair. But it did make me feel a lot better.

CHAPTER 26

It took me forever to fall asleep, so I didn't get any real rest before the guards woke us and brought our trays of juice, coffee, and cereal. After we ate, we filed like ants into a common room filled with tables and stools bolted into the floor. I sat with Annalee, Jasmine, and a group of their friends who each read aloud letters that they had received from their children.

I looked around the room of women in matching indigo jumpsuits. There were a few scary characters in the crowd, and some were sizing me up or giving me the evil eye, but they were vastly outnumbered by the legions of women who just minded their own business. From what I could tell, being in jail was a lot like being locked in a roach-infested DMV office, but I thought it would be much worse.

Eventually most of the women went off to their jobs in the jailhouse workshops. I wouldn't be permitted to work until I was tried and convicted, so I went to the commissary to shop for my luxuries out of my jailhouse credit of $120, which was the amount they'd confiscated from my purse at the time of my arrest. The prices and selection reminded me a little of a gas station convenience store. I couldn't find any quality makeup or hair products so I just bought fresh undergarments, a pair of tennis shoes, and a pack of gum. I looked about for reading materials before I realized that I could get books for free at the jail's library. That's where I went next.

My heart soared when I spotted *The Heart of the Scandal,* by Prudy Newcastle. I'd already read it and found its protagonist, Lady Georgina, to be a prissy little narcissistic contrarian, and the hero, Lord Ashingworth to be a smug prick, completely repulsive in every facet of his personality, but that was totally beside the point. In this most desolate of places, I'd found an unexpected treasure-trove filled with words of love written by the man I adored. The book in my hand made me feel a little excited and yet cozy all over. I'd just finished the checkout process when a female correctional officer with a long brown braid appeared behind me. "Inmate Anderson, you have an appointment with your attorney at eleven."

That was quick. Could there be a better boyfriend than Lance Archer? I hadn't even put out for him, and yet here he was, moving Heaven and

Earth to make this situation more bearable. I went back to the common area and continued reading while I waited to meet my new lawyer.

I'd gotten to the part where the headstrong Lady Georgina had spurned the first of Lord Ashingworth's rakish advances when the correctional officer with the long brown braid collected me for my interview. I hid the book under my mattress, and she led me into the visitors' area.

"Arms out," she said as we reached the room and she frisked me through my prison clothes. A male guard stood and watched the pat down without emotion.

"I hope this lawyer likes me a lot more than the last one did," I said.

The female officer gave me a half smile as the male guard opened the door.

I took one step inside and froze in place.

Stonewall was sitting in his suit and tie with his hands folded on the table. He looked up at me and his face bore the same kicked dog expression that he had when he was looking over my writing sample.

"What the hell?" I said in a blind panic.

The officer with the braid held the door. "You don't have to talk to him if you don't want to. You have the right to decline the meeting."

Stonewall sighed. "Right now that would not be a very good idea."

Had I been just a little more of a coward I would have turned and walked away. God knows, I wanted to. Instead, I took the seat at the other side of the table like a little girl preparing to lose a game of chess to a grandmaster.

"Remember the rules, Inmate," the officer with the braid said. "You're each to stay on your own side of the table until your attorney stands to signal that he is ready to leave. No hugs, no footsies, no backrubs, no massages, no straddling or any other form of lewd behavior."

I glanced at her over my shoulder. "I really don't think that's going to be a problem for either one of us."

When she left, I folded my hands together. "Maybe it would be a good idea if you didn't represent me in this case."

He shook his head. "No, it wouldn't be a very good idea. As your attorney I can't be called to the stand to testify against you."

Oh, Jesus.

"Amanda, I want to start by apologizing for my conduct last night. It was totally inexcusable. If you wish to take legal action against me, it is your right to do so."

"No, thanks," I said. "I think I've already harmed you enough for one lifetime."

I expected a sigh of relief from him, but instead he pressed his lips together as if he was in pain. "Amanda, I mean it. What I did to you was unforgivable. It was so inappropriate and unprofessional that Brunston is convinced that it must have been a stunt to render the entire interview inadmissible. In a way, he's right, since I didn't mean a word of it."

"It all sounded about right to me."

"No, Amanda, I just said those things because I was really angry at you. I didn't believe for one instant that you were telling the truth about losing that manuscript. I felt like I'd been used and betrayed by an opportunist," he held up his hand to halt my objection, "because had our situations been reversed, that's exactly the sort of thing I would have done."

"So what makes you think I'm any better than that?"

"When I got back in the taxi, I told myself not to lose any sleep worrying about you. Then I remembered that you had lost sleep worrying about me. Right after you saved my life."

I shook my head. "That wasn't nearly the same thing."

"It was exactly the same thing. We were both forced to decide the fate of someone who offered us nothing but misery. The only difference is that you acted heroically, while I behaved like a spoiled child."

"I think you give me far too much credit."

"Not in the slightest." Stonewall opened a notebook and took out a pen. "What happened to the manuscript was entirely my fault, and now I'm just going to have to take a beating. But that's a worry for another day. Right now, we need to focus on your bail hearing."

"I didn't think that first-degree murder suspects were eligible for bail."

He uncapped the pen. "Normally they aren't, but the prosecution's case is weak enough to argue for it on the basis of lack of evidence. Do I have your permission to act on your behalf?"

"Of course," I said.

He took a form out of his notebook, slid it to me, and laid the pen across it.

"Sign this. It's a contract giving me permission to represent you and act on your behalf." I took the pen. "I feel it's my duty to inform you that it's standard procedure in these cases for the attorney to take a lien against his client's home."

"I don't even know what that means."

"It means if you fail to pay me, I can sell your house and keep some of the money."

My mouth fell open in outrage.

"Don't worry, it probably won't come to that. I just want you to know I have that option. I anticipate this trial is going to cost you upwards of one hundred thousand dollars."

Was he kidding? Why would I pay him that kind of money when I could get a public defender for free?

"If you feel so bad about how you acted yesterday, then why don't you work my case *pro bono?*"

"Because I intend to raise an army of expert witnesses and private investigators, and those people don't work cheap. I'd loan you the money, but since I'm not really sure what I'll be doing for a living once this trial is over–"

"Fine, you've made your point." Tears stung my eyes as I signed the form without reading it and thrust it back at him. "What now?"

"We have to prove that you're not a flight risk. That's going to be tough, seeing as how you're still technically a resident of the State of Ohio. I don't suppose you have a regular job?"

I smiled. "Actually I do. I'm a freelance makeup artist for the local television and movie studios."

"I said a regular job."

I gasped. "That is a regular job. I make over thirty dollars an hour."

"That's not what I meant. We need to show that every day you spend behind bars jeopardizes your ability to remain a productive member of society. Do you report to a boss? Do you have a regular routine where you clock in at the same time every morning? Can you be fired for taking a week off work to sit in a jail cell?"

"No." I said sullenly.

"Can you think of any argument for why you won't just run away if they let you out?"

"I have nowhere to go?"

"Nice try, but that won't work. Let's move on, shall we?" Stonewall tore a page out of his notebook and gave it to me. "I'll need you to write down the names and phone numbers of ten friends who might be willing to vouch for your character."

I stared at the blank page and shook my head. "I probably don't even have ten local numbers in my cell phone."

"They don't have to be friends. They just need to be upstanding members of the community who know you well enough to vouch for your character, such as employers or coworkers."

"I work with a different crew nearly every shift."

"Instructors?"

I shook my head.

"Clergy?"

I shook my head.

"Amanda, you're killing me."

"I mainly hang around with Ivy Joie and Zachary Calvin."

"Is that the couple we brought to the party?"

"Yes."

"Amanda, I really like your friends, so don't take this the wrong way, but would you happen to know anyone with a little less body art?"

"Only Lance Archer."

Stonewall jotted down the names. "I'm a little concerned that bringing in your boyfriend might raise questions about just exactly how broken up you were after Jonny's death."

"Well, then you can introduce him as my neighbor. It's not like we've been intimate."

Stonewall began to write into his notebook and then did a double take. "You haven't been intimate?"

I crossed my arms defensively. "That's correct."

"And *how* long have the two of you been dating?"

I felt my cheeks color. "That's really none of your business. Besides, he's married to another woman. I'm not a homewrecker."

"Evidently not." He glanced down at his notebook. "That leaves your stepdaughters. I know this might be hard for you to believe, but I may be able to convince them to put in a good word for you."

I shook my head. "No way. If I have to deal with Jonny's daughters and their histrionics in a court of law, I'm going to have a complete nervous breakdown."

"You're not giving me much to work with. But don't worry. There is one trick that works miracles in situations like yours."

"Really, what's that?"

"I'll need to call your parents. I'll fly them out here before the hearing. If your mother can convince the judge that you've been a perfect angel who has never given her any trouble, I'll request that you be released into her custody until the trial."

"No."

"Amanda, I have to call your parents. This is your only hope."

"I don't know their phone numbers. And even if I did, they wouldn't help us. And even if they did, it would do more harm than good."

Stonewall looked at me. "I understand what you're going through. I didn't always get along with my mother either. However, you must understand that deep down she did the best she could."

I was happy for him that he was sheltered enough to believe that.

"You're her baby and this is a life and death situation. I think you owe it to yourself to let her help you. Who knows, this may bring about a reconciliation."

I nodded "Yes, it probably would. And possibly a reunion. My mother's in prison."

Stonewall set the pen down. "Please tell me that's a joke."

"It's no joke. She's serving a thirty years sentence for a litany of crimes. Mostly stemming from her heroin addiction."

"And your father?"

"I think it was his embezzling and his subsequent abandoning us that sent her on her downward spiral. I guess the apple doesn't fall very far from the tree, huh?"

I meant that as a joke, but Stonewall didn't look amused. "Then who took care of you?"

"Took care of me? I was sixteen, not four. By that point I was perfectly capable of taking care of myself."

"You lived alone?"

"No. With roommates."

He looked at me as if he didn't believe me. Not right away. "I'm so sorry. I can't begin to imagine how horrible that must have been."

I didn't even want him to try. How do you explain that sort of abandonment to someone who no doubt grew up with nannies and family trips to the Riviera? So instead I tried to make light of it. "It wasn't so bad. I was a popular cheerleader with a job at the mall and no parental supervision whatsoever. If that isn't the America Dream, I don't know what is." I tried to punctuate this with a laugh, but the sound came out more like a sob.

Stonewall closed up the notebook. I knew that he was trying his hardest not to give up, but I also recognized his expression of utter defeat. And for someone as nimble-witted as Stonewall not to find a way out of this, I knew there was no hope.

And I knew why. Even the most liberal of judges would see me as a victim of society, predisposed to evil through no fault of her own. I'd have a better shot at being abducted by aliens than of having a court grant me bail. And if I couldn't even get bail, what hope would I have at the trial?

Detective Yolanda's warning of death by lethal injection was starting to look less like an idle threat and more like a distinct possibility. Stonewall was going to have his work cut out for him trying to convince a jury of my peers not to send me to the executioner, with the whole world laughing at him for even making the attempt.

And then the answer to all of our problems came into my mind like a ray of sunlight burning its way through a storm cloud.

"Stonewall, I know what we need to do!"

He looked nervous. "What?"

"I'm going to plead guilty."

"No, you're not."

"Tell them that I'm willing to make a full confession as long as they take the death penalty off the table."

"You can't be serious."

I smiled. "But I am. Don't you see? That would solve everything. If I confess there won't be a trial. And if there's no trial, then nobody needs to know what happened to Jonny's manuscript."

I waited for him to put two and two together and realize what that meant for his career. Instead, he buried his face in his hands. "You've lost your mind."

My smile vanished. "Why?"

He looked up at me. "Amanda, had the police arrested me instead of you, do you think for one second that I'd plead guilty to keep this business with Jonny's manuscript out of the papers?"

"That's different."

"Is it?"

"You didn't break any laws. You didn't ruin anyone's life."

Stonewall took a deep breath. "Amanda, someone has worked very hard to kill your husband. Are you suggesting that we help that person get away with it?"

I shrugged. "If that's what it takes."

I'm sure that Stonewall wanted to say something, but he couldn't seem to get his mouth closed.

"Look, life isn't fair. There's no real justice in this world, I accepted that a long time ago. The good suffer, and the evil just laugh at us for being so stupid." I smiled. "Don't worry, I got us into this mess. Now I'll just stay here and do my penance."

"Amanda, once you plead guilty you can never take it back. The courts are finished with you. No trial, no appeals. You're stuck serving whatever sentence the judge decides for you."

"It's not so horrible here, and jail is probably the safest place for me. You said so yourself."

"Amanda, you're not going to jail. You're going to prison. It's not the same thing. You're not in hell yet. This is just limbo. This is a place filled with people who did dumb things. Once you're convicted, they'll move you to a place filled with killers and people who've tortured their own children. Many of those inmates have anger control issues. And a lot are fans of Jonny's books."

I swallowed at the full implication of what he was saying.

"Amanda, I've met some of these women. Just take my word for it— you'll be a lamb among wolves. You'll either have to join up with a gang and hope you don't get shivved or punked to badly, or else request protective custody and sit in an eight-by-eight room all by yourself for the next twenty to sixty years."

He narrowed his eyes at me. "Still think it's a good idea to tell everyone that you killed your husband just to protect *my* reputation?"

I sank back in my chair. "Why are you trying to talk me out of this? You said yourself you might lose everything if this goes to trial."

He reached across the table and took my hand. "Amanda, a friend of mine once gave me a bit of advice. I believe it went something like this: Money and things can be replaced, but when you die, you stay dead forever.'"

I smiled. "You've got a smart friend."

"Well, so do you. Are you ready to go back?"

"I have just one more question: would you prefer it if I addressed you as Jeremy or Mr. Kendal."

He thought this over and then smiled. "Actually, I'd prefer it if you called me Stonewall."

"But I thought you said you hated that name?"

He smirked. "You should know by now that you can't trust every word that comes out of my mouth, and that goes double if I'm standing behind a lectern. Are you ready to go back?"

I nodded and he rose to his feet. The door opened behind me and the pair of officers came in to escort us out. The man led Stonewall to the door, while the woman ordered me to hold my arms out again.

"Stonewall?" I said as he reached the door. I felt foolish, but I kept talking anyway. "I'm sorry you got shot."

When he turned around, the smile was gone from his face.

Great. Just when we were starting to get along again, I had to go poking at his old wounds, almost literally. Then I realized that his frown was actually a look of utter bafflement. "I don't know what you're talking about. I've never been shot."

"What about the shooting incident?"

"What shooting incident?"

I should have just left it alone, but he looked so perplexed that I felt compelled to explain. "The thing that the detectives mentioned? The reason why you stopped being a lawyer and went into agenting?"

He smiled in an 'oh, of course' kind of way.

"Amanda, you misunderstood. He didn't shoot me. I shot him."

Chapter 27

Ispent much of the following afternoon lying in my bunk, going over everything I knew about Jonny's death, in the slim hope I might remember something that would prove my innocence. No jury would consider an afternoon nap an acceptable alibi. If anyone thought to ask whose bed I was in while I took that nap, then I'd really be in trouble.

Of course, I could explain that I'd gone to Lance's to hide from my husband's savage cruelty. Or I could simply ask for the syringe and give myself the lethal injection to save everyone a lot of time and trouble.

I was wallowing in despair when the correctional officer with the braid approached. "Inmate Anderson, gather your things and come with me."

I sat up. "What's wrong?"

"Nothing's wrong. You're being released."

I climbed out of the bunk, afraid to believe what I had just heard. "Released? As in, I get to go home?"

"That's correct, ma'am. You weren't brought in for arraignment in the proper timeframe, so you're free to leave. Your ride is waiting for you outside."

I screamed and leapt up and down as if I'd just won the lottery. Only this was better, because people don't get put down like mad dogs for not winning the lottery. Once I'd managed to stop, I gave my few belongings to the other inmates. Like Persephone or the Queen of Sheba, I felt that if I took anything out of this place, it wouldn't bode well for me.

I couldn't stop smiling while they gave me back my shimmery dress, handbag, and sandals, and paid me the balance of my jailhouse credit. I changed in the bathroom, then rummaged through my bag for makeup and painted up my face. My hair was already coarse and lusterless, so I coiled it up and used a stray lock to tie it back before departing.

It was afternoon as I exited the jailhouse. The pink tinge of the early winter sunset was the most beautiful thing I'd ever seen. I breathed in the cool air and then noticed Stonewall leaning up against the wall. He was wearing an exquisitely tailored suit as always. His face was serious and showed no sign of the smugness or conceit that I'm sure I would have expressed if I were him.

I went toward him, with my arms stretched out. "Thank you, thank you! I don't know how you did this, but thank you so much."

His eyes seemed to grow sad as he caught me by the elbows and held me at arm's length. "Let's get one thing clear, Amanda. I had nothing to do with your release. I'm just here to take you home."

I stood there, stunned. "I don't understand. Are you saying they just decided to drop the charges?"

He shook his head. "Nobody is dropping any charges. The prosecution has just decided they need more time to process their case against you. By law, you can't be detained if the formal charges are not filed within forty-eight hours."

"But they can't arrest me a second time, can they? Wouldn't that be double jeopardy?"

"No, that wouldn't be double jeopardy. Yes, they will arrest you a second time."

"You mean I'm going to have to go through this all over again?" I didn't want to break down and start bawling in front of him, but under the circumstances, it was impossible not to.

Stonewall gave me his pocket square and stood there waiting for me to stop crying.

When I was done, I dried my face as best I could.

"Where's your car?"

"I parked all the way around the corner, away from the other cars. I hope you don't mind."

I didn't even bother to answer. After all, who could possibly mind taking a walk of shame across a jailhouse parking lot in a crumpled cocktail dress with a runny face and messy hair? I used the pocket square to catch my fresh tears, until we turned the corner and I saw Stonewall's car.

I took one look at it and forgot that I was supposed to be despondent.

I call it a car only because he called it a car. Really, it was more of a powerful aphrodisiac on wheels. The body resembled a giant scarab beetle carved out of an opaque black-cherry colored glass, as shiny as a piece of hard candy. It had a windshield, windows, and tires, just like any other car, but they blended so seamlessly into the exterior that it took me a while to notice them.

I wasn't a car aficionado, well not until that moment anyway, but I could tell this was the sort of car that didn't get built until after you finished making the payments for it.

For an instant, Stonewall seemed concerned about my radical change in mood, but then he smiled. "You've never seen my car before, have you?"

I shook my head. "Oh, no, I definitely would have remembered. I'll bet you get a lot of tail with a car like this."

"Oh, yes, I do," he said.

Stonewall opened the passenger side door for me and I sighed as the leather of the bucket seats cradled me like a cloud of marshmallow fluff. He took his place in the driver's seat, and we fastened our seatbelts as the instrument panel came to life.

"So did you buy this with your lawyer money or your agent money?"

"I bought this with old money. It takes more than one generation to save up for a toy like this one."

I ran my hand over the seat, which as I suspected, was as soft as lambskin. "So what is this? A $300,000 car?"

He chuckled.

"More?"

"Let me put it this way—I could sell this car, use that money to buy a $300,000 car, and still have a million dollars left over."

I whistled. "I didn't even know they made million-dollar cars."

"They don't make many of them. That's why you don't see these on the road every day. This car makes a statement to publishers that I'm not someone who's easily impressed."

"I'll bet it makes quite a statement to the ladies as well."

"There's that, too."

As we pulled onto the highway, I pulled the compact out of my handbag and used the mirror to inspect my makeup. Sure enough, my face looked like a fright mask. Stonewall's pocket square was still wet from my tears, so I used it to scrub the trails of mascara from my cheeks and the hollows of my eyes before applying a fresh coat. I would have put on eye shadow and powdered my face, but I didn't want to get even the tiniest iota of dust in this car. Therefore, I just touched up my lipstick and eyeliner before closing my handbag.

Stonewall glanced over. "Would you like to stop somewhere to get something to eat?"

"No, thanks. You wouldn't believe how much they overfed me in that place."

I held the square to Stonewall. He took one look at the inky stains and waved for me to keep it.

I looked out the windows at the barren desert scenery. We were out in the middle of nowhere, as jails often are, where the highways are lumpy and pockmarked. Still, our ride was as smooth as glass. The speedometer said we were doing a hundred and ten.

"I can't believe you let this thing out of your garage."

"What's the point of owning a car like this if you don't drive it?"

I sighed. "Jonny's car was a pile of junk compared to this, and he wouldn't even let me touch it."

"I'm glad you were smart enough not to tell that to the police. The DNA they collected during your medical exam matches the blond hair they collected out of Jonny's headrest."

"Oh, then I've been framed." Of course, I'd already suspected as much, but until that moment I couldn't dismiss the one-in-a-trillion chance this was just a long series of unfortunate coincidences. But now I knew there was a sinister hand in all this. Evidence doesn't just plant itself.

"So who would want to frame you?"

"Jonny's daughters, maybe?"

Stonewall shook his head. "They both have alibis. Misty spent the morning at her surgeon's. Lulu was her ride home. There is no way that either one of them could have driven over a hundred miles to steal a car and then use it to hit someone."

"Then I don't know. I haven't been here long enough to have enemies. If I had to guess, I'd say that Jonny was the target and I was just the most convenient person to pin his murder on."

"That's fairly likely. My guess is that it was a deranged fan."

"This doesn't seem like the act of an obsessed stalker."

"You'd be surprised," Stonewall said. "Jonny used to get some fairly disturbing fan mail. At one point, he had the FBI on speed dial, until he realized that most of these people couldn't find their own front doors, let alone his."

I frowned. "The trouble with that theory is that people who kill celebrities don't cover their tracks. They actually want to be caught, to link their names forever with their victims."

"If you say so."

We continued to drive in silence until a rest stop appeared in the distance. Behind a gas station was a set of fast-food restaurants.

I looked down at my sparkly dress and suddenly a perverse idea popped into my head.

"Stonewall, could we stop and get a cheeseburger?"

He didn't say anything, so I assumed that the answer was no, but as we neared the rest stop he pulled off the highway and parked as far from the other cars as we could get.

Walking from that car into the fast food place was like the best after-prom dinner ever. All of the truckers and the vacationing families turned to watch us enter.

I sauntered up to the counter like a femme fatale stopping in for a quick bite before plotting an evening of intrigue.

"I'll have the cheeseburger combo." I said to the girl at the register.

"I'll have that, too," Stonewall said.

She rang us up and Stonewall held out a credit card. I pushed it back and gave the girl a twenty. A minute later, our order was up and we carried our trays to the drink and condiment station.

"Would you like some ketchup?" I asked while he filled his plastic cup with iced tea.

"I haven't liked ketchup since I was eight."

He did grab a few napkins as well as a plastic fork. Probably force of habit, I told myself, as I filled my cup with Diet Coke. But as we sat at a plastic booth, he used the fork to spear a French fry and stared in concern as it wilted like a dead flower.

He set the fork down and opened the cardboard carton that held his burger. "Shouldn't this be wrapped in paper?"

"I guess. I never really noticed."

I opened my own carton and squeezed out two packets of ketchup into the empty side. I dipped a couple of fries and ate them while Stonewall watched in utter bafflement. Then he looked over his shoulder to see what the family at the next table was doing.

"Oh, my God. You've never eaten fast food before, have you?"

He turned back around and shook his head.

"It probably looks weird, but trust me. It's delicious." To prove it I picked up the cheeseburger and took a large bite.

Stonewall mimicked my actions. Almost immediately after tasting it, he made a face and pushed his tray to the side. "You know what? I'm really not that hungry."

I had to swallow quickly to keep from choking with laughter. "You and I come from completely opposite ends of the universe."

"Well, you do a lot better on my side than I do on yours."

"I don't know about that. Did Jonny ever tell you how many different shades of green I turned the first time I ate real French food in Paris?"

"To be perfectly honest, I don't care for it either. If you want some really good European food, you should try the Emilia-Romagna region of Italy."

I tapped the side of my lip. "You've a tiny bit of special sauce near the corner of your mouth."

He scrubbed at the spot with his napkin. "I fail to see what's so special about it."

That did it. I collapsed and buried my face in my arms, sobbing with laughter. Eventually I recovered enough to draw a long sigh and sit up again.

Stonewall looked sullen as he sipped his iced tea.

"I'm sorry. I'm not laughing at you, I swear. I was already half delirious before I came in here. It's just that seeing you try fast food is the most adorable thing ever."

"Adorable isn't much a compliment when you're a man my age."

I tried to force myself to be serious. "Why, how old are you?"

He set down his drink. "How old do you think I am?"

I leaned forward and studied his face. I've dealt with people of all ages at the makeup counter, so I considered myself a good judge, but with Stonewall it was really hard to tell. His forehead was furrowed enough to suggested that he didn't go in for Botox or surgery, but the only lines that could even remotely be considered wrinkles were the fine lines under his eyes, two permanent creases in his forehead above the bridge of his nose, and the tiniest little parentheses right outside the corners of his mouth. I settled back into my seat.

"If I had to guess solely by looking at you, I'd say you're in your very early thirties. But given how accomplished you are, I'd guess you're older than that, maybe thirty-eight or thirty-nine?"

"I'm forty-two."

I smiled. "See, I wasn't that far off."

He smirked. "I thought you were going to tell me that you had no idea that I was so old."

"What? You're not old. You're in your prime. Me? I'm old. I'm twenty-seven and the only thing I've succeeded at is making a complete mess of my life."

Stonewall frowned. "You know what your problem is? You're too hard on yourself."

"You think so?"

"Everyone has strengths and weaknesses, Amanda. People who wish to be successful allow themselves to be defined by the former and not the latter."

"Oh, really? Name three of my best features."

I expected him to mention my straight teeth or my shiny blond hair or something equally superficial.

"Off the top of my head? Very well: You're as brave as a lion, you have a caring heart, and you can admit when you make a mistake."

"Oh," I said.

"Those are all important qualities, especially the last one. Most people just make excuses or look for someone else to shoulder the blame for them."

I shrugged as I sipped my drink. "You're probably right about that. And there's something else about me that you probably don't know."

"What's that?"

"I'm not ordinarily a mean person."

"I've never thought of you as mean."

I laughed. "Oh, come on. You said it yourself. I've been terrible toward you."

"Well, given that I'd introduced myself by breaking into your bedroom while you were sleeping, I would've been concerned if you'd been cordial."

I shook my head. "It wasn't even that. I knew you had your reasons. I was just jealous."

"Jealous?"

"Jealous of you and Jonny. I never thought of you as a housebreaker so much as a home-wrecker." The smile vanished from my face. "Jonny was crazy about you. It was always Stonewall this, and Stonewall that, and Stonewall is so perfect, and I can't wait until Stonewall gets here—It drove me crazy."

I looked down at the table.

"Our marriage was magic, until he got that one phone call from you, and then he couldn't wait to get away from me so he could be with you. Now I realize that it only seemed like magic. Our marriage was doomed from the start. He was never anything but a creepy old man who wanted a Midwestern farmer's daughter with hayseed between her teeth."

I looked up at Stonewall, only to see his mouth in a firm line and a haunted look in those big caramel-colored eyes. I suddenly realized that not only was I speaking ill of the dead, but also that the man that I was bad-mouthing was his dearest friend. A friend that he'd no doubt watched being carted away on a bloody gurney.

"Jonny Goodsnuff had a lot of problems, but he was the first to admit that. He had an enormous amount of contempt for a lot of people, especially himself, but he didn't deserve what happened to him, any more than you deserve what is happening to you."

"I'm sorry...I didn't mean to imply..." I began to say, and then I remembered the prenup, the will, the tale-bearing, the broken promises, the lies of omission, the neglect, the virtual imprisonment, the alienation of my friends, the substandard living conditions, the constant barrage of insults..."No, you know what? I'm not going to apologize! I'm glad you're special enough to be Jonny's golden boy and that you have fond memories of your time together, but after all of the things he did to me, I consider him to have been a very bad man and an even worse husband."

Stonewall looked away from me. "Are you ready to go?"

I got up and we went back to the car without another word.

We were silent on the ride home. I'd long since cooled off, but Stonewall's posture seemed uncomfortable and his face showed a strain that seemed to intensify the closer we got to my house. For a man who was usually so polished to appear so tense told me that either my company had gotten unbearable, or else he no longer considered it worth the trouble to hide his emotions from me.

"What's wrong?" I asked.

"Nothing," he said, just a little too loud and a little too fast.

I wanted to say more, but he looked dangerously close to yelling at me again, and at that moment, I wasn't sure I could bear it.

By the time we reached my house his expression was one of open disgust, and it suddenly occurred to me that maybe Stonewall didn't really like me at all. That the only reason he'd been nice to me and helped me was because he owed me a debt of honor for saving his life. The sooner the trial was over, the sooner the debt would be cancelled and he'd be free to walk away forever.

I wanted to think that I was reading too much into this, but once the car stopped he just kept his eyes straight ahead. I tried leaning forward to force myself into his field of vision, but he turned his head to the side so that he wouldn't have to look at me.

Damn. I knew it.

"Thanks for the ride. I had a great time."

"There's something for you in the back," he said.

I reached behind the seat and found a black plastic box. I thought it was a present and was filled with relief at this show of generosity, until I opened it and saw a dark strap with a blinking red light.

"What's that?"

"It's a GPS monitor. It goes on your ankle"

My heart sank and I shot him a look. So much for my newfound freedom. "Why didn't they put it on me at the jail?"

"I'm an officer of the court, Amanda. In these matters I can pull rank on the police."

I undid the ankle strap of my right shoe and snapped the monitor into place. It looked like a cross between a handcuff and a dog collar with a tiny red light. "Well, I suppose this is better than being cooped up in a jail cell. How does it work?"

Stonewall kept his eyes straight ahead and spoke in a weary voice. "Every fifteen minutes it sends out a signal with your exact location. You can go wherever you want, but you can't take it off, and it's virtually indestructible. In fact, if you try to break it, you will set off a silent alarm that will send out a continuous alert with your precise location that won't shut off until the police arrive."

"Lovely."

"If you feel like playing Houdini, I should inform you that the typical emergency response time for this city is eight minutes. That's eight minutes from the time you start tampering with it, not eight minutes from the time it's off your ankle, so I wouldn't count on having a head start if you decide to make a run for it."

"Oh, don't worry. I think I'm in enough trouble as it is." I reached for the door handle and paused. I expected him to tell me to call him if I needed anything, and I would have told him that I appreciated that, but he didn't even glance in my direction. Instead, he drummed his fingers on the steering wheel as if there was somewhere else he wanted to be.

"Thanks again. For everything. I really mean that."

"Sure," he said tersely.

I got out. As soon as I closed the door, he drove off.

I walked back to my house, determined to have a hot shower and climb into a nice soft bed as quickly as I could. The entrance was sealed off with police tape. I snapped it off and went inside.

The entire place had been searched. That much was clear. The things in the living room had been moved just enough to bother me. I went to check my e-mail only to discover that my laptop was gone. That made sense. The police had a warrant to seize my hard drive, where they would no doubt find six years of research into committing murders, eluding the police, and countless other incriminating details I thought I might need for my writing.

Whoever killed Jonny couldn't have chosen a better patsy.

I made my way up to the bathroom where I ran a hot shower and set about trying to repair the damage to my hair. As I lathered, I looked down at the ankle monitor. I couldn't help but feel a little disconcerted as I heard the drops from the shower echo in the vast emptiness. I was home, but after everything I'd just been through, my dream house felt more like a mausoleum. It was too much house for one person, and as I dried my hair I tried to remember what possessed me to buy it.

Then I remembered that I'd bought it to be near Lance.

I went to the window in the guest room. Sure enough, I could see him on his weight bench, doing his bench presses with his cell phone on a table nearby. I dialed his number. He set the weights back and reached for the phone.

"Pennyroyal Promotions, representing Prudy Newcastle. How may we help you?"

"Hi, Lance."

"Hey, cutie pie. You sound pretty upbeat."

"That's because I'm at home, Lance. I'm watching you pump iron right now."

He sat straight up, and peered up at my window.

"Amanda, that's great! So they've cleared you as a suspect? I told you they would."

I bit my lip. "Not exactly. I'm still the prime suspect, but I guess they need more time to fill out their paperwork."

Lance's shoulders slumped. "Oh, that's rough. But I'm glad you're home anyway."

"So am I, and I'm in dire need of dinner and a movie, so you'd better figure out what we're going to watch before I get there."

Even from this distance, I could see Lance wince.

"What's wrong?"

"I'd really love it if you came over, but I just came down with a nasty case of strep throat. The doctor tells me it's very contagious. It might be better if you waited a day or two."

"Lance. I'll probably be back in jail in a day or two."

"Amanda, I'm really sorry, but this is nothing to mess around with. I'm just looking out for your health."

"Fine. I guess I'll see you later then."

We hung up and Lance went back to his weight bench and resumed his presses. I gasped in outrage. Did he forget that I could see him?

I jabbed my thumb into the redial button.

"Pennyroyal—"

"You know what, Lance Archer? You're a real goddamn warrior working out like that with a hundred and three degree fever."

Lance glowered up at my window. "You listen to me, Amanda. I'm really stressed right now. I didn't want to tell you this, but the police came here with a search warrant yesterday. They asked me a bunch of personal questions about my sex life. They confiscated the sheets from my beds, examined the mattresses with a blue light, and they poked around in my drains with a pair of tweezers. They didn't tell me what they were looking for, but I think I've got a pretty good idea."

I found myself shaking. "Lance, I didn't do anything wrong."

"No, but it looks like you've done something wrong! I know this sounds insensitive, but I just can't handle this right now. There are a lot of very wholesome people who love Prudy Newcastle. They think of her as family. They aren't going to be happy when they find out she's really Lance Archer from Iowa with a slut for a wife and a girlfriend in prison."

I couldn't take this. Not after what I'd just been through. I buried my face in my hand and wept. Over the last few days, my world had been crashing around me, and now Lance pulling this was more than I could bear.

Over the phone, I could hear Lance's voice break up into sobs as well. And Lance wasn't the sort of man who cried easily. "Oh God, I'm sorry. Don't cry. I didn't mean that the way it sounded. It's just that I'm really sick right now. I want to help you, but just give me a day or two to get over this. Okay?"

I forced my voice steady. "Okay."

"I love you, muffin."

"Goodbye." I curled up on the bed and cried. I couldn't see, I could barely breathe, I felt like I was drowning. I grabbed hold of the cell phone and dialed like an automaton.

"Yellow."

I didn't even bother to stop sniveling. "Ivy?"

"Sweetie! Why aren't you calling me collect? Are you out of jail?"

"Yes."

"That's great? So what's wrong?"

"They're going to arrest me again, Ivy. Then they're going to put me on the stand and everyone is going to call me a bitch, and they're going to call me a whore, and when they're done being cruel, they'll strap me to a cot and put a needle in my arm, and everyone will watch me die!"

"Oh, come on. You know I'd never let that happen."

"Please, Ivy. Don't get involved. I destroy the lives of everyone who gets too close."

"That's not true. I've had nothing but good luck since the day we met. If it wasn't for you, I'd have never met Dr. Calvin. I wouldn't have fallen in love with him and we wouldn't have the house with the white picket fence."

"I'm so glad you have a happy life." Then, to my utter disgrace, I broke down and sobbed like a hired mourner.

Ivy waited for me to finish. "Sweetie, are you okay to drive?"

"Sure."

"Good, here's what I want you to do. I want you to pack up a suitcase and drive over here. You'll stay in our guestroom for as long as you need to."

"What if Dr. Calvin comes home and tells you he doesn't want me there."

"Dr. Calvin won't say that. He's cool as hell."

"Thank you, Ivy."

"Just pack your bags and get your butt over here."

CHAPTER 28

I parked my Mini convertible on the magnolia-lined street in front of Ivy and Zachary's suburban cottage and rang the doorbell. Ivy emerged and gave me a brief hug before she grabbed the suitcase out of my hand.

The house looked tiny from the exterior, but the interior had been painted in blocks of rich tan, bronze, and Moroccan reds so that it looked much larger. The art posters and the open layout gave it an upscale lived-in feel.

Ivy led me through the living room with a coffee-colored leather sectional arranged around a medium sized television set. In the far corner was an acoustic guitar that leaned against a faux marble pedestal topped with Jonny's typewriter and a limited edition copy of *Houses Made of Glass*.

Ivy saw me looking at the display. "I can get rid of that if that bothers you."

"No, not at all."

"Good." Ivy set my suitcase against the wall of the guestroom.

We sat on the sectional and ate ice cream while I talked about my adventures of the last forty-eight hours. I told her about being booked, what life in jail was like, and that Stonewall was a former prosecutor. I showed her my ankle monitor and told her that they'd let me out for a reason I was still not clear about, but warned her that it sounded like some sort of bureaucratic screw-up that might be straightened up at any moment.

I didn't disclose any of the embarrassing details. I told her that Stonewall was staging a defense, but I didn't go into the multitude of reasons why this would be a lost cause. I told her that he came and got me out of jail, but I didn't tell her that he probably hated me because I couldn't manage to be nice to him for more than five minutes.

I was just about to get to my conversation with Lance when Zachary came home from work. He wore a blue buttoned-down shirt with his hair parted on the side and combed back. I barely recognized him without his makeup.

"Hello, Amanda," he said as he pulled his cell phone and keys out of the pocket of his Dockers and dumped them into a fishbowl by the door.

"Hi Zachary. Ivy said I could stay here for a few days."

"Yes, she called me at work to tell me." He sniffed the air. "Eggplant Parmesan again?"

Ivy set her ice cream down on the coffee table. "Hey Amanda. Show Dr. Calvin your tether."

I hiked up the cuff of my jeans and he paused to get a good look. "I didn't think they were allowed to put one of those on you if you haven't been formally charged."

"Well, apparently they can," Ivy said.

Zachary went into his room and closed the door. He emerged a few minutes later with his hair mussed and his face painted, wearing a black T-shirt with a skull on it and a pair of distressed jeans. As he passed by us, he grabbed the guitar from the stand.

"See you girls later. Save me some dinner," he said as he walked out to the garage.

"Oh no you don't." Ivy pulled me up and we chased after him.

Ivy caught up to him while he was getting ready to climb into his jeep. "Just where do you think you're going?"

"I have practice at Troy's tonight, remember?"

"Don't be so antisocial, Dr. Calvin. Can't you see we have company?"

"The two of you are eating ice cream right before dinner and talking about boys. That's not a scene anyone with a Y-chromosome should get within fifty feet of. Besides, I told you, we've got a gig next Tuesday night." He strummed out a few chords on his guitar and Ivy crossed her arms in front of her chest.

"Oh, come on. You play rhythm guitar. It's not like anyone's going to miss you."

The guitar made a loud twang. "Ouch, Ivy."

"Yeah, well the truth hurts. Go call Troy and tell him you're a big grown-up physicist with a murder to solve. Amanda won't have to go back to jail if you can use your super-genius IQ to figure out who killed her husband."

"Good thinking, except there's only one problem."

"What's that?"

"I'm not a detective." He went back to strumming his guitar.

Ivy slapped her hand over the strings. "Oh, so what? You're a rocket scientist. That's close enough."

"That's not even nearly the same thing. Detectives solve cases using forensics and complicated profiling and interrogation techniques. I'm just an ordinary kid who's good at math."

"Yes, but don't you remember the last time I got all metaphysical with

you, and you told me that the universe was ruled by physics and that everything can be explained mathematically?"

"So?"

"So, go solve the mathematical equation for who killed Amanda's husband
so she doesn't have to go to prison!"

Zachary looked at her, and then set the guitar on the hood of his jeep.
"You know what? That's not nearly as harebrained as it sounds. Give me a
minute or two to call Troy. I'll meet you in the living room."

We waited until he joined us with a magnetized whiteboard from the
refrigerator and erased the shopping list written on it.

"Now I would like you two ladies to bear in mind that this is just a parlor
game. We're not actually going to accomplish a thing tonight."

"That's still better than doing nothing," Ivy said.

We all sat on the sectional as Zachary placed the whiteboard on his knees.

"Amanda, do you know the mathematical formula for a murder?"

"I didn't even know there was such a thing."

"No problem," Zachary said. "We'll just use the generic formula for just
about any type of event."

He pulled the cap off the dry-erase pen and wrote out: WHO + WHAT +
WHERE + WHEN + WHY + HOW = AMANDA'S GET OUT OF JAIL FREE CARD.

"Of course," I said and felt foolish.

"Now, how many of these questions do we know the answer to for a fact?"

"Jonny died after he was hit by his own Jaguar outside of a card room at
two o'clock on a Wednesday afternoon in May," I said. "That covers what,
where, when and how."

"So those are our constants," Zachary drew a line through each. "So the vari-
ables we need to solve for are: Who and Why."

Ivy stretched out her pint-sized frame on the chaise portion of the
sectional. "That means we need to figure out the suspect and the motive."

"I know the formula for the suspect," I said, getting into the spirit of things.
"It's Motive plus Means plus Opportunity."

Zachary erased the formula and wrote: SUSPECT [MOTIVE + MEANS +
OPPORTUNITY] KILLED JONNY GOODSNUFF OUTSIDE A CARD ROOM AT 2:00PM FOR
[MOTIVE] BY HITTING HIM WITH HIS OWN STOLEN JAGUAR.

Ivy pointed at the board. "I'm seeing motive crop up a lot. Who had the
best motive?"

I didn't even hesitate. "His daughters, Misty and Lulu. But they didn't have the opportunity—Lulu took Misty in to get a face-peel on the day of the murder."

Zachary wrote their names under the column heading SET OF SUSPECTS. "Could Misty have hired somebody and scheduled the procedure to establish an alibi?"

"That's possible," I said, "but she and her sister already ruled the roost. Hiring an assassin to kill a minor celebrity is an awfully big risk just to kill the goose that lays the golden eggs."

Ivy raised one finger. "Didn't you say that any sons you had with Jonny would have gotten most of his estate?"

"Yes, but they could have murdered me just as easily as their father."

Ivy lowered her finger. "Oh, good point."

Zachary looked up from his whiteboard. "Who else stood to inherit?"

"Nobody," I said. "Jonny left his entire fortune to be divided evenly between his daughters."

Zachary drew a square around the two names and put a dollar sign near it. "So that takes care of money. What other common motives are there for murder?"

I thought back to all my research. "Fear, hatred, insanity, revenge, blackmail, sex, obsession..."

"Obsession," Ivy said. "It could be a deranged fan."

"That's what Stonewall said. But people who kill their idols are glory seekers who want to be caught. They don't sneak around in disguises planting evidence."

Zachary raised his eyebrows and added another column labeled EVIDENCE.

I struggled to remember all of the details I'd learned during my interrogation. "The morning of the murder, Jonny's car was stolen. Later, witnesses saw that same car strike and kill Jonny outside a card room. The driver was described as a woman in a baggy raincoat, neck scarf, sunglasses, blond hair, and a bucket hat."

"Then we know the killer was a woman," Zachary said as he drew a tiny sketch.

"Not necessarily," Ivy said. "The neck scarf might be hiding an Adam's apple."

I nodded. "And the bucket hat has got to be the most gender ambiguous garment ever invented. You could put a linebacker in one and people will look twice to be sure it's not their grandmother. Trust me—it takes very little lipstick and blush to create a convincing illusion."

Ivy laughed. "That's so true. You can hide a lot of noggin under one of those things."

Zachary wrote *MALE/FEMALE* on the board. "What other evidence is there?"

"The police recovered my hair from the driver's headrest. I've never driven Jonny's car."

"Aha," Zachary underlined the word *MEANS*. "Who had access to your hair?"

"Everyone, I'm afraid. The laundry hamper is in the garage with the car. The killer could have gathered a few loose hairs from the back of a blouse or a sweater."

"But who knew about the layout of the garage?"

"Jonny and his handyman," I said. "And maybe everyone else. Jonny had a big mouth."

Zachary wrote HANDYMAN under the list of suspects. "I think we can establish that the killer was someone who was familiar with Jonny's life and habits. He or she must have known that Jonny had a blond wife and that he would be at the card room at two. Who knew Jonny best?"

"I'd have to say Stonewall," I said. "But he's defending me. Why would he go to all the trouble of creating an airtight case against me, only to poke holes in it?"

"Maybe he volunteered to be your lawyer to avoid being called to the stand for questioning," Zachary said. "This could all be part of an elaborate con. Let's put Stonewall down under our list of suspects."

Ivy sat up. "No."

Zachary ignored her and wrote *STONEWALL* down on the board.

Ivy reached over and rubbed it out with her fingers. "I said no. He's not a suspect. That's too horrible to even contemplate."

I raised my eyebrows at this. As far as I knew, their only direct contact was a heated argument over a cartoon. So why was she defending him so vehemently? She hadn't even seen his car.

Or had she?

Had he signed her after all? Zachary certainly didn't seem surprised by her reaction. "Ivy, dearest, I know he's your boy, but we can't rule him out as a suspect. You have to keep in mind how manipulative he is. The man's a professional bullshit artist."

"Yeah, well, I've got a built in bullshit detector that tells me that he's as good as gold."

"And who does your bullshit detector tell you isn't as good as gold?"

Ivy gave me a sheepish look.

"What?" I said.

"I'm sorry, Amanda, but I don't like your boyfriend."

I didn't care much for him either at that point, but I was shocked to hear that from Ivy. "You don't like Lance?"

She heaved a sigh. "Not at all. I've known guys like him. They play with women's hearts. I've never trusted him, and when I learned that the two of you haven't even slept together, it made me trust him even less. You're not using him for sex, and yet I don't see what else he's good for."

"Wow," I said. "Why didn't you say anything?"

"Because I was afraid that if I did, you'd never speak to me again."

Zachary wrote Lance on the whiteboard. "Does he have a motive?"

I shook my head. "Jonny disliked Lance, but Lance seemed genuinely fond of Jonny. He was always asking about him and trying to get me to bring him over for dinner. In fact he seemed a little more interested in Jonny than me, until I showed up on Lance's doorstep covered in bruises."

"Whoa," Ivy and Zachary said in unison and sat up straight.

"It's not as bad as it sounds," I said. "Jonny thought I stole his car so he shook me and left finger bruises all over my arms."

Zachary blinked. "Maybe that's the motive. Maybe Lance was so enraged that Jonny hurt you that he had him killed."

"And then planted my hair on Jonny's headrest? Besides, Jonny shook me because his car was already missing. This wasn't a crime of passion."

"Amanda," Zachary said. "I want you to describe everything that happened on the day of the murder."

I thought back. "It all began at about five-fifty in the morning. I woke up because Jonny was yelling at Stonewall over the phone because there was an announcement in the paper for Jonny's new book. Jonny didn't want any publicity."

"Why not?" Zachary said.

I shrugged. "Jonny was just neurotic like that."

Ivy nodded. "So what did the announcement say?"

"I don't know. He didn't let me read it."

She rose from the sectional. "I'll look it up."

"I don't think they have the same ads online," I said.

Ivy sat at the kitchen table and unfolded her laptop. "That's why I'm going to pull it up from the college's microfiche."

"I think he was just crazy," I said to Zachary. "He told me the whole time we were married not to talk about his book. He told Stonewall that he wanted absolutely no publicity of any kind, right before he fired him."

"So they fought?" Zachary looked over his shoulder at Ivy before re-adding Stonewall to the list of suspects.

"Yes, but Jonny called him a few minutes later and apologized."

"We'll get to that. What happened after the initial phone call?"

"I told Jonny that I was going to take a swim. I left the room, changed into my bikini, and heard him throw the phone against the wall. When I left the house, Jonny ran after me and asked me what happened to his car."

"Before you reached the water?"

"Yes," I said.

"The water is only about forty steps from your door," Zachary said. "For Jonny to figure out his car was missing so quickly, he must've run straight to the garage."

"My God. You're right."

"I've seen your garage. Unless it's changed, there's nothing in there but a car and a laundry area. That means that Jonny was either doing a load of wash or else he was planning to go somewhere. Where would Jonny want to go at six in the morning?"

Ivy looked up from her laptop. "Maybe he just wanted to go for a drive to clear his head?"

Zachary pondered this. "Okay, so what happened after Jonny asked you where his car was?"

"I told him that I didn't know and he went crazy and shook me. Then he called Stonewall and told him to get over there."

"And Stonewall drove over there?"

"Yes," I said.

"Why? If someone woke me before six in the morning to barrage me with insults, 'absolutely, I'll be right over' wouldn't be the first words to come out of my mouth."

"Even if that person was your mentally unstable boss? And your next paycheck was for more than a million dollars?"

"Good point. So what happened next?"

"I ran to Lance's house and banged on the door. Lance came to the door and I showed him my bruises and told him that I was leaving Jonny. I saw a fuchsia colored coat draped over a chair, and so I thought he had company. He told me that the coat was his wife's, and he was getting rid of it."

Ivy looked up from the laptop and rolled her eyes.

"He said that he was through with Lori Anne and that I was the girl for him. And then he kissed me."

"And then what happened?" Zachary said.

"He told me to go tell Jonny I was leaving him."

"He did what?" Ivy stood up from the laptop. "He professed his undying love for you and then sent you to confront your abuser? By yourself? And you can't see what a lazy, good for nothing, self-absorbed, loser this guy is?"

I looked to Zachary, who shrugged. "I'm sorry, but I'm with Ivy on this one. If she'd showed up at my doorstep and told me some man had roughed her up, I'd be dead or in jail right now."

"Oh," I said. I'd had to fend for myself for so long it didn't seem all that craven of Lance to send me back to Jonny while he tidied up his closets.

"So what happened after that?" Zachary said.

"While I was at Lance's, the police arrived and Jonny insisted that I'd stolen his car. He wanted to press charges against me, but then Stonewall arrived and they got into an argument about it."

"Right," Ivy said. "Because that's what a man is supposed to do when he sees his friend bullying a woman."

Zachary sighed. "Yes, you've made your point, dear. Go on, Amanda."

"The police noticed that the garage had been broken into, and Jonny retracted his statements against me. Then I came home, barricaded myself in my closet, and packed my bags. When I came out, the house was empty. I later found out that Stonewall had dropped Jonny off at the card room."

Zachary crossed his arms. "So Jonny's car was stolen, his wife was leaving him, and yet he still decided to go off to play poker?"

I shrugged. "Don't ask me. If I understood Jonny, I never would have married him."

"Meanwhile...?"

"Jonny left me a note begging me to call him. I didn't. Instead, I went to Lance's house and took a nap. I woke up at two-fifteen when Stonewall called to tell me that Jonny was dead. Then I freaked out and went home." Zachary looked as if he wanted me to continue, but I couldn't think of anything else to add. "Sorry, I know I haven't given you much to work with, but that's all I know."

Ivy made a sound like a death rattle, and when we turned, her eyes went as wide as saucers.

"Ivy?" Zachary said.

She jumped away from the laptop and pointed at it like she'd seen a ghost. Zachary and I rushed over and we all huddled around the screen.

Jonny Goodsnuff's Got A $10,000,000 Secret
That He Can't Tell Anyone
But In Six Short Months He'll Tell The Whole World
HOUSES MADE OF GLASS
Coming In December To A Bookstore Near You

Zachary whistled. "Ladies, I think we might have just found ourselves a motive."

CHAPTER 29

Zachary went back and reclaimed the whiteboard. "Can we all agree that it's quite a coincidence that Jonny freaked out and died right after this came out in the paper?"

Ivy stretched out on the couch with her arms folded. "I don't know about the rest of you, but I think this is starting to look less like a simple whodunit and more like a mob hit."

Zachary erased the word *MOTIVE* and replaced it with *SECRET*. "I'd like to make an educated guess that Jonny knew something. Maybe about the mob, a drug lord, or a dirty cop. But rather than do the right thing and report it to the authorities, Jonny agreed to keep his mouth shut."

"Coincidentally, or not," I said, "he decided to write a book that he won't even discuss with his agent other than to say that it will, quote: hit the world like the next Krakatoa."

"So let's recap Jonny's final moments, in light of this recent discovery," Zachary said. "The morning begins as Jonny opens the paper and sees it calling him out as a snitch. He freaks and screams bloody murder at his agent and throws the phone at the wall, right before he runs to his car, which is no longer in the garage."

Ivy raised her hand. "Because, it was stolen."

"Because someone was planning to kill him with it." I added.

"No," Zachary said. "I think killing him with it was Plan B. It's more likely they just wanted to keep you and Jonny trapped in the house."

I shivered.

"This drove Jonny completely out of his mind with terror." Zachary said. "The only explanation his panic-stricken mind would accept was that Amanda borrowed it without permission. So he attacked you to get you to admit it. When you denied any involvement, he called his agent and then presumably called the police."

Ivy nodded. "He called the agent first because he knew that the police weren't enough to protect him from what was coming. He needed to get out of that house as fast as he could. I assume Stonewall has a car?"

I sighed. "Oh, yes. Does he ever…"

"Meanwhile," Zachary said. "Amanda fled to see Lance, who made some lame excuses and got the hell out of Dodge himself. Maybe he saw some scary looking character lurking around Jonny's place and knew that trouble was brewing?"

"Or maybe a sixth sense told him that something was going down, and he didn't want to be involved," Ivy said.

"There's no such thing as a sixth sense." Zachary said, which caused Ivy's nose to wrinkle in annoyance, but he continued. "So Jonny drove around with his agent. Who, after being screamed at, fired, and dragged out of bed, was probably none too fond of Jonny at this point. Jonny asked to be dropped off at the card room, where he'd be surrounded by witnesses in case anything was to happen."

"Then why did Jonny leave the card room at two o'clock?" I asked.

Zachary looked at me. "Maybe he was in the habit of leaving the card room at two every day. Did you ever go there with Jonny?"

"No."

"Then I hate to say this, but maybe the card room was just a front for him to go off and do something he didn't want you to know about."

Ivy rose from the couch. "You know what? Let's find out. What's the name of the card room, Amanda?"

"I think it was *Lucky Aces.*"

Ivy did some typing on her laptop and then picked up the phone. "I'll put it on speaker."

After the third ring, a female voice answered. "Lucky Aces."

"Hello," Ivy said with an English accent. "Could I please speak to a manager?"

"Just a moment," she said.

Ivy gave us a thumbs-up as we waited.

"This is Gary," A male voice said.

"Hello, Gary," Ivy said in her accent. "I'm Elizabeth Marvin, a claims investigator with *Pagoda Life and Casualty.* I'm calling to clarify some details concerning the casework for Jonny Goodsnuff."

"We had nothing to do with that, and we accept no liability."

"Yes, yes, we're well aware of that. You'll find that our investigative techniques are a little more exacting than those of your local police. You can be sure that anything you divulge will be held in the strictest of confidences. We just need to know why Jonny Goodsnuff chose to leave your premises at the time that he did."

"I have no idea."

"So Jonny Goodsnuff was not in the habit of leaving the card room in the afternoon?"

"No ma'am. He usually played right through until closing."

"Did he leave with anyone or by himself?"

"By himself. We've already explained all of this to the police."

Ivy bit her finger in contemplation.

"Is that all you needed, Ma'am."W

Ivy gave us an imploring look, but I didn't have any ideas, and apparently, neither did Zachary. She sighed. "What can you tell me about the phone call?"

"What phone call?"

"Jonny's phone call right before the accident." Ivy winced and twisted her eyes shut, until Gary spoke again.

"Yes, which one?"

I clamped my hands over my mouth and Zachary grabbed the whiteboard.

"Give me everything you've got," Ivy said, dropping the accent in her excitement.

"Well as I remember it, Jonny was at the table, when someone called to say they had a message for him."

"Was this a man calling, or a woman?"

"A man."

Ivy pumped the air with her fist. "Do you think you'd remember his voice if you heard it again?"

"It was six months ago."

"Yes, of course. So what happened after that?"

"I called Jonny to the phone, but almost as soon as he put it to his ear, he tossed the phone away. He opened his cell phone and said 'I need you to come back here and get me, now' as he ran out the back. And that's when the car hit him."

"Did you see it?" Ivy asked.

"Shit, we all saw it! One second he was running like his pants were on fire and then some crazy blond chick in a Jaguar slammed into him a couple times and sped off."

"Did you get a good look at her?"

"Hell no, we were watching Jonny fly around like a pinball. The police asked us these same questions. It should be in their report."

"Is there anything else that might be of interest to us?"

"Nothing that I can think of."

"Thank you, Gary. You've been most helpful."

"No problem."

She hung up and Zachary smiled. "I wonder why the police didn't assign more importance to the phone call."

Ivy rolled her eyes. "Maybe it's because the police are a bunch of pigs, dead set on blaming Amanda."

Zachary smirked. "The police are our friends. It's not their fault that you couldn't drive within the speed limit or find a legal place to park."

"Yeah, well I'll bet if I had boobs like Amanda's they would have let me keep my license."

Zachary patted her knee. "Your boobs are fantastic, pumpkin-butt. However, behind the wheel you're a danger to yourself and others. But you're a good little detective, since we've cracked the case."

"Huh?" Clearly, I missed something. "What do you mean we've cracked the case?"

Zachary held up the board. "Everything we've learned about this case fits in with our theory. Jonny tried to cash in on a dirty little secret, but was snuffed out over an unfortunately worded advertisement in the Times."

"Yes, but even if we've guessed correctly, we're still not any closer to knowing who did it."

Zachary put down the board. "*Au contraire.* The answer to that question is right at our fingertips." He picked up *Houses made of Glass* from the pedestal and flourished like a game show hostess. "All we need to do is read this until we find Jonny's ten million dollar secret."

Oh...crap.

"Guys, we've got a big problem. Jonny didn't write that book. I did."

They stared at me in complete incomprehension, so I told them the whole sordid tale from the beginning. When I finished, the book dropped from Zachary's hand.

Ivy winced. "I guess I'd better serve dinner."

We ate in silence. Or I should say they ate in silence. I'd just taken the tiniest slice of Eggplant Parmesan and moved it around with my fork. Even if I hadn't lost my appetite, it seemed as if I'd done nothing but eat for the past two days. Ivy looked at me then covered her mouth to hide her laughter.

"What, Ivy?" Zachary said.

"I was just thinking that if Amanda goes to next year's conference, her story would be perfect for the 'If I can make it, so can you' speech."

"That's not even remotely funny," Zachary said.

I mashed my food with my fork. "I thought it was."

All at once, the three of us began laughing. When we were done, Zachary shook his head sadly, but he was still smiling. "We had the answer right in our grasp."

"You don't know that," I said, "You said it yourself, this was all just a parlor game. For all we know, we were wrong about everything."

Ivy sighed. "The important thing is we gave it our best shot instead of just doing nothing."

Zachary shook his head. "I'm not giving up. There must be something we've overlooked."

Ivy patted his hand. "Maybe we'll get some ideas while we're watching the news. Amanda, do you want to watch some TV with us?"

"No, thanks," I said. "I couldn't get much sleep in jail so I think I'll turn in early."

Ivy stood, "I guess we'd better get your room ready then."

We all went into a home office, with a sofa bed along one wall and a computer hutch in the opposite corner. Zachary pulled out the bed while Ivy carried out an easel with a half-completed painting and came back in with a stack of blue flannel sheets. I offered to help, but they shooed me away so I reached into my suitcase and got out my cotton pajamas. They were Pepto-Bismol pink, printed with huge lavender and white 60's-inspired daisies. I'd packed them because I didn't think that Ivy would appreciate me hanging around her One True Love in my silky sleepwear with my panties and cleavage peeking out, but when she saw the pattern, she made a face.

So did Zachary. "I'm sorry, Amanda, but that has got to be the ugliest pattern I've ever seen in my life."

"No kidding," Ivy said. "That looks like something the Easter Bunny threw up on."

I shrugged. "That was my first thought when I saw these in the clearance bin, but I know what looks good on me."

"If you say so," Zachary said without the slightest conviction.

I changed in the bathroom and came out in my pajamas as Ivy and Zachary finished making up the bed. Ivy saw me and smiled, then tapped Zachary on the shoulder.

He looked at me and blinked. "You weren't kidding. That looks great on you."

Ivy sighed. "You look like a cupcake. I'm so jealous. I've always wanted to wear pink, but it makes me look like a deranged little monkey."

"What's so special about the color pink?" Zachary said.

As those words echoed in my mind, I let out a gasp.

"I'm sorry. Did I say something wrong?"

I sank onto the bed. "Not at all. I had a nightmare where I asked myself that same question. It was right about the time Jonny died."

Ivy shivered. "That's called an omen."

"No," Zachary said. "It's called a coincidence. There is no such thing as an omen."

Ivy fluffed a pillow. "Yes, well there are more things on heaven or earth than are dreamt of in Dr. Calvin's philosophy. I have premonitions all the time."

Zachary tweaked her nose. "That's because you're a silly girl, and these so called premonitions are the only way your underutilized logic centers can get you to take anything seriously."

That got me thinking. "Agatha Christie once wrote that what people call 'women's intuition' is really the summation of observations made at the subconscious levels."

Zachary nodded. "I totally agree."

I drew my knees to my chin. "So maybe there really is something significant about the color pink."

"Or maybe it was a premonition," Ivy said.

"Or maybe it was a coincidence. Let's go, Ivy, I'm sure that Amanda's looking forward to a good night's sleep."

I tucked myself in as Ivy flipped off the light. "Nightie-night."

I nestled in the dark, but no matter how hard I tried, I couldn't get to sleep. My mind had too many thoughts running through it.

What was so significant about the color pink? Lance had a pink rose on his computer. Was that what bothered me? I thought back to the nightmare and replayed it in my mind. I saw the skeletal remains of an arm and the word pink carved into the wall. Then I turned and saw Jonny reaching for me, with his agent and his handyman at his back.

I sat up in bed. That image was even more horrifying now that I knew Jonny was dead. I stared in the direction of Zachary and Ivy's computer and noticed it had a tiny red light glowing, just like the damn red light winking at me from my ankle.

I switched on the light and returned to bed, where I stared up at the ceiling and tried to focus my thoughts, but my mind was racing.

"I can't wear pink. It makes me look like a deranged little monkey," Ivy had said.

What's so special about the color pink?"

I broke into a cold sweat. Something was trying to claw its way out of my subconscious. But what? I felt the answer was something terrible, but I had to know. My life depended on it. Was it a premonition? Intuition? An omen? I told my subconscious mind that if it had something to say, then it had better just say it and get this over with.

I closed my eyes and I saw myself standing in Lance's house. He grabbed hold of me and tried to kiss me passionately. "I'm not even attracted to you," Lance had said.

"I can't wear pink," said Ivy.

The fuchsia coat draped over the couch.

"I don't want you talking to the neighbor, Amanda. Not even to tell him that you can't talk to him. Especially not to tell him that you can't talk to him. His wife went missing and if you're not careful you'll go missing too."

"Why don't you call the police?"

"No police."

"Amanda, where the hell is my car?"

Now the images were coming into my mind like a slideshow in fast motion. Lance talking to me on the phone, begging me not to leave his house. Lance kissing me, the desperate act of a desperate man. Lance coming to the shower to tell me that he just wanted to be friends. Lance kissing me with my red wig on. Lance following me to the restaurant to talk me out of leaving Jonny. Lance meeting me in the shower and asking me where Jonny had gone. "Come into my house, Amanda. How's Jonny? When's he coming to dinner? How's he doing with his book? How far along is he? What's it about? What's it about? What's it about!"

I opened my eyes. When I sat up again, I was hyperventilating and my heart was racing a mile a minute.

I ran out of bed and into the living room where Ivy and Zachary were curled up together, watching the evening news. Ivy sat up and muted the television.

"Sweetie, what's wrong."

"It was Lance. Lance killed Jonny. What's more, I can prove it."

CHAPTER 30

Ivy and Zachary leaned forward on the couch, their eyes opened wide. "Sweetie, are you sure about that?"

"Yes, I'm sure. I should have seen what was happening. When I met Jonny he was staying at the same hotel I was. Despite the fact that he had a huge beach house only a few miles away. I asked him why, and he didn't have a ready answer. Now I know. He was hiding from Lance."

I tried to organize the thoughts racing through my mind. "He was terrified of him. I asked him why and he said something about Lance's wife disappearing. Yet he took it all back when I suggested he phone the police. You see, he couldn't tip off the police. Not without spoiling the premise for his ten million dollar tell-all—which wasn't due to come out for another six months at least. He only came back to the beach house when I told him it would look a little funny if he decided to stay away."

"Go on," Zachary said.

"We returned to the house, and what's the first thing he does? He hires some greasy-haired mouth-breathing gawker to install a kitchen—in a rental!" I spread my fingers wide. "Why? Because Jonny was madly in love and wanted me to be happy? No. Because he was using that shifty-eyed troll as a lookout while he barricaded himself at his writing desk with his revolver."

Ivy and Zachary both nodded, though I wasn't sure whether that was in agreement or to let me know they were still listening.

"Meanwhile, Lance tried to sweet-talk me into arranging a meeting with Jonny, or at least revealing what he was working on. Lance couldn't be sure that Jonny actually saw anything. Otherwise, he would have found a way to kill him sooner. Since the police hadn't broken down his door, Lance probably assumed he was safe. Until the ad cropped up in the paper to rekindle his darkest fears. So he stole Jonny's car in preparation for their final showdown. Here was a guy, after all, who'd already put a good deal of thought into how to get away with murder. When Jonny refused to take his call at the card room, that must have been the final nail in the coffin. Jonny Goodsnuff had to die, and quickly, before he had a chance to run to the police."

Ivy swayed her head. "I told you I didn't like that guy."

Zachary looked up at me. "Amanda, you mentioned that you can prove this."

"I can. It's the color pink. Lance didn't want to let me into his house, and the reason was because he had a bright fuchsia coat draped over his couch. He insisted the coat belonged to Lori Anne. But the coat couldn't have belonged to her. I didn't know it at the time, but Lori Anne was a *redhead*!"

I waited for the significance to dawn on them, but they just stared at me.

"Don't you see? Lori Anne had dark red hair. She wouldn't have been caught dead in a neon bright purple-pink color like fuchsia."

Ivy blinked. "Except, everyone knows it's a myth that redheads can't wear pink."

Zachary nodded. "Ivy's friend Becca is a redhead and she looks great in fuchsia. She wears it all the time."

I crossed my arms. "But is she a natural redhead?"

Zachary turned to Ivy who shook her head.

"I don't see what difference that makes," he said.

"It makes all the difference in the world. There are two types of red hair. There's orange-red, which looks bad with pink, and there is blue-red, which clashes with orange. Blue-reds, like burgundies, come out of a bottle. They don't really occur in nature. Lori Anne's color was natural."

Ivy opened her mouth to say something, but I raised my hand.

"Now some of the less flamboyant shades look angelic with pastels like pink, but really, those girls are auburns or strawberry blondes. True redheads, like Lori Anne, tend to have complex color with coppery highlights, as well as pale or ruddy skin that doesn't hold a tan. They look best in blues, greens, or browns to tone down all of the different reds they have going on. As a pageant girl, she'd have sense enough to know what she looked good in. A fuchsia coat on Lori Anne Archer would look like a strawberry milkshake that someone covered with barbecue sauce."

Zachary sat up straight. "So then Lance had a female accomplice?"

I shook my head. "Not at all. I think Lance bought that coat for himself, so he could wear it while he murdered Jonny."

"But you said the killer wore a tan coat," Ivy said.

"Of course he did. He couldn't very well commit the murder in that coat, not after I'd already seen it in his living room."

Zachary curled his lip. "Wait a minute. The mysterious femme fatale in the neck scarf and the bucket hat—was Lance?"

Ivy and I both nodded.

"I'm sorry, but there is no way in Hell that I could ever mistake Lance Archer for a woman."

"Right. I'm sure Lance probably thought that, too—until I taught him all about the rudiments of facial contouring. Which is also known as *Drag Makeup* in some circles."

Ivy gasped, but Zachary just sat there with an incredulous frown on his face.

"I wear makeup and I don't look like a girl."

"You wear manly pirate makeup. There's more to drag than just ruby lipstick and false eyelashes. A dark border drawn along the jaw to give the face a more oval appearance. Bronzer, to slim the cheeks and nose. Lip pencil, to turn the mouth into a cupid's bow. Once you'd laid the foundation, just shade in with appropriately girly colors and away you go. In a speeding car, there is no way anyone would know they were looking at a man."

Zachary still didn't look convinced.

"Go to Ivy's laptop and do a search for *Drag Queen Contouring* if you don't believe me."

He shook his head. "I think I'll take your word for it."

I did my best Perry Mason impression. "And with that, I rest my case in the matter of Anderson v. Archer. But before you dismiss my theory as the ranting of a color-obsessed cosmetologist," I flourished at the pedestal with the novel and the typewriter. "I ask you to consider the *literal* relevance of the title Jonny picked for his final book."

"*Houses Made of Glass.*" Zachary said under his breath.

Ivy lowered her voice dramatically. "Two glass houses, side by side, one overlooking the other with a bird's-eye view of all sorts of things a nosy neighbor is not supposed to see."

"Good job, Amanda," Zachary said. "But you said you had proof."

I felt a sinking feeling in my gut. "I already told you. The proof is the fuchsia coat."

Zachary shook his head. "This is a murder trial, not an Encyclopedia Brown story. The police aren't going to drop the charges, just because the prime suspect *claims* she saw a pink coat instead of a blue one."

I sank onto the sectional and buried my face in my hands. My dear God, he was right. I was one hundred percent sure Lance was guilty—but I couldn't prove a damn thing.

Ivy came over to put her hand on my shoulder. "Hey, we're a lot further than we were before. There must be a way to prove he did it. Are you sure that Jonny didn't keep a backup of his manuscript?"

I looked up. "He couldn't have. He wrote it on a typewriter."

Zachary knelt on the other side of me. "Perhaps he made a photocopy. He couldn't have been such a Luddite that he wouldn't use a Xerox machine."

I shook my head. "Why would he make a copy? He wasn't even halfway finished. And before you ask, he didn't use any carbon paper."

Zachary squinted. "What do you mean he didn't use carbon paper? Isn't all paper made out of carbon?"

Ivy's mouth fell open. "Holy crap, Dr. Calvin, you don't know what carbon paper is?"

He shrugged. "Apparently not."

Ivy sputtered. "How can you have a PhD in nuclear physics and an IQ of a zillion and not know what carbon paper is?"

He shook his head. "Gee, Ivy, I guess I missed that lecture at MIT."

I might have smiled if I didn't suddenly feel really old.

Ivy reached into her purse, pulled out her checkbook, and tore out a slip of inky black paper.

"This is carbon paper. Hence, the term *carbon copy.*"

I nodded. "Back in the olden days, writers used to sandwich it between two pieces of paper so that they could type out two copies at a time instead of one. Actually you get three copies, since the letters appear on the back of the carbon paper like a negative."

"It's kind of like having a second typewriter ribbon," Ivy said.

Zachary cupped his hand over his nose as he bowed his head to absorb all this. "So carbon paper works somewhat like a second typewriter ribbon."

"It works exactly like a typewriter ribbon." As the full implication of those words dawned on me, I rose to my feet. "Which means, according to the symmetric property of equality, that a typewriter ribbon should work exactly like carbon paper!"

I gave him a moment to let my words sink in before we both dove for the pedestal. We reached the typewriter at the same time and our hands collided as we both grabbed for the ribbon.

"I don't think that's going to work," Ivy said. "I saw an experiment like this on TV, and as I recall the typewriter kept typing over the ribbon multiple times until all you could see was a jumble of letters—"

I did my best not to listen to her as we unwound a bit of each spool then held the ribbon up to the light. The ribbon held a continuous stream of letters. But it quickly became apparent that those letters spelled out entire sentences. Some or all of Jonny Goodsnuff's final novel had to be on that typewriter ribbon.

"Now let's just hope that Jonny was superstitious enough to start each novel with a fresh ribbon," Zachary glanced at Ivy. "Cupie, we need the Scotch Tape and the scissors."

Ivy scurried away without a word and returned with a big purple tape dispenser

"Look at this," he placed his thumb and forefinger on the ribbon around letters LanceArcher. "Isn't it against the law to put your neighbor in a novel?"

"Not if it's true."

Once we'd wound the ribbon back to its beginning, Zachary carried it to a floor lamp and used the scissors to cut away at the pleated burgundy fabric of the lampshade.

"What are you doing?" I asked.

"He's creating a viewing surface," Ivy said.

He tore away fabric revealing flat white plastic, then held the beginning of the ribbon to the top of the lampshade and secured it in place with several pieces of tape. He looped the ribbon around the shade and applied more tape so that the ribbon wrapped in a spiral. Ivy came over and rotated the lampshade so that Zachary could concentrate on keeping the ribbon straight. When he'd covered the entire shade they taped the ribbon into place at the bottom of the shade. "Ready?"

Ivy reached down and flicked on the lamp. The letters on the lampshade seemed to come to life like black-light artwork.

Zachary looked up at the top of the lampshade. "Amanda, did you read any of Jonny's manuscript?"

"Only the first sentence."

"By any chance was it: *People in glass houses shouldn't stow bones*?"

"Oh my dear God, yes."

After Ivy and I managed to stop screaming, Zachary looked at us. "I'm not sure how well this will work, or how long it will take to copy the entire manuscript. It's good that there are three of us. One of us is going to have to read this ribbon out loud, one of us is going to have to type, and one of us is going to have to sleep."

"I can read or sleep," Ivy said. "But I think that we all know that I can't type."

That's when I agreed to type, because there was no way on earth that I'd be able to sleep.

Ivy and I spent the night transcribing the contents of the ribbon into a document on her laptop while we sent Zachary off to bed. After all, he was the only one of us who had to go to work the next morning, and the last thing I needed was a missile crisis on top of everything else that had gone wrong.

Ivy read aloud from the lampshade while I typed. I was able to follow along until the end of the prologue, but soon the words didn't even register any more except through my fingers on the keyboard. After what seemed like only a couple of hours, Zachary reemerged from the bedroom, looking tousled and sleepy-eyed. "How's it going?"

"Pretty good," I said. "You should go back to bed."

"No I shouldn't," he said. "It's eight in the morning."

I didn't believe him so I looked out a window. The sun was up and there was a wren chirping at me from a tree branch.

"We're up to the third chapter." Ivy said.

He came over and peered at what I was typing. "Any clues?"

Ivy shook her head. "Well, there's plenty in the prologue, but after that it's just a bunch of expository crap about how much of a jerk Lance is, and speculation as to how any man could be content with such a flat-chested shrew for a wife."

I glanced at the page I'd just transcribed. Lance tried to work as Lori Anne nagged at him from across the living room in a tank top and thong panties. Jonny confessed a slight bias against her because of her lack of a bust, or a waist, or an ass, or anything else that he considered a feminine curve.

Zachary ran his hand through his hair. "Nothing so far that suggests how, when, or where Lance killed his wife?"

"No," Ivy said. "But plenty of reasons as to why he might have been tempted."

"I was afraid you'd say that." He went to the phone.

"Who are you calling now," she asked.

"Work. I'm calling in sick so I can take over at the keyboard."

"You don't have to do that," I said. "I'm not even close to being tired yet."

He hung up the phone. "In that case, you should probably rest your eyes for a few minutes. Why don't you go lie down with your eyes closed and count to one hundred?"

I couldn't fault his logic so I went into the guestroom and stretched out on the comforter. I looked at the alarm clock, which read 8:14AM. The pillow felt soft and fluffy. I regretted placing my head on it because it was going to make it that much harder to get up. I remember getting as far as thirty before it became too much effort.

I closed my eyes. When I woke, the clock read 8:08PM.

I sat up. That couldn't be right. But when I looked out the window the night sky was filled with stars. Damn. I rose from the bed, changed into a T-shirt and jeans, and went into the living room.

Ivy was still at the lamp, but she was sitting in a folding chair, with her shoulders sloped and her lids at half-mast. The bags under her eyes were dark, as though she'd rubbed them with charcoal. As she read, the words warbled as if she'd had too much to drink. I realized with alarm that she'd been reading aloud for an entire day.

Zachary looked up from his typing.

"Get her to bed," I told him

She shambled to her room. "It's okay. I know where it is."

"Why didn't one of you wake me?"

"Because you looked far worse than that. Coffee?" He pointing to a perco-lator and a collection of mugs on the counter.

I poured myself a mug. "So have you gotten to the good parts yet?"

"Sure," Zachary spun around in his seat. "Take a look at this."

I peered over his shoulder and read the text on the screen:

```
     Lori Anne waited for her husband to set
out on his errands before returning to her
house to collect her belongings. She had never
returned from work this early before. The
dirty gray sand of the beach extended to the
driveway, where the wheels of a large suitcase
whirled and snatched up twigs and pebbles as
Lori Anne marched back into her marital home.
She was defiant, yet terrified. She nearly
turned back from the edge of her doorstep, but
summoned her courage and entered.
```

"You might want to brace yourself," Zachary said. "It gets pretty graphic."

She opened the trunk on the living room
couch, and darted up the steps, descending with
armloads of clothing and jewels that writhed
from her clinging arms like fish dropping from a
net. She might have retrieved these treasures
from the splendid staircase, had her husband
not returned unexpectedly. He stood waiting at
the landing with his steel-muscled arms crossed
after witnessing what would be her final trip
down those stairs.

It was hard for me to motion for Zachary to scroll further. I already knew
how this turned out, but that didn't stop me from biting my nails and
hoping I was wrong.

The girl staggered as if struck by a sword
but swallowed her bitter fear, and bombarded
her husband with angry words. Lance's wrath
matched her own and his anger only seemed
to goad her on. She raised the volume of her
litany as they shouted at one another, their
faces red and their chins so close that they
nearly touched. When she realized that she
couldn't silence her husband, she pushed him
away from her and he balled up his fist and
struck her, for maybe the first time in all of
the years they'd been married. She fell and
lay there as if she were dead, until her body
convulsed violently and a puddle of sticky red
fluid seeped out of her mouth to pool on the
granite tile.

Oh, my God, I thought. No wonder he couldn't bear to see her pictures
in color anymore.

Lance knelt over her, and at first it
was concern that glittered in his eyes. Then

```
he hazarded a glance towards the table and
retrieved his wife's note.
Lori Anne awoke and clutched at her cheek as
she felt a flash of pain, but before she could
arise, her handsome young husband gazed at her
with cold eyes, and crouched over her like a
tiger poised to strike. Lowering her gaze, she
wept and pleaded for her life. Lance knelt
and listened without pity until she was done
speaking, then his powerful fist descended again
and again into the center of her skull like a
blacksmith's hammer, until the floor tiles were
every bit as crimson as her blood-red hair.
```

I jabbed the screen. "There's our evidence right there. Lance would have bleached away all the DNA evidence he could get to, but his floor has no grouting. Lori Anne's blood must have soaked between the tiles and into the foundation."

"Except that blood is hidden somewhere below a couple hundred square feet of granite flooring. I'm guessing that the police will need something a little more precise before they'll show up at Lance's door with a warrant and a jackhammer."

I scrolled about with the mouse, unsure of what I was looking for. "Why didn't anyone notice that Lori Anne was missing?"

"Her family in Iowa probably assumes she's in California. Her friends from California probably think she's gone back to Iowa. Anyone who knows enough to worry must assume that she's hiding from her husband and doesn't want to be found."

"But what about her boyfriend? Why didn't he go to the police after Lori Anne disappeared?"

"Maybe there was no boyfriend. Or maybe he has a wife and kids, and didn't want to get into trouble?"

"Lance said he was married, but he was also her boss. He didn't have to tell the police everything."

But the more I thought about this I realized that Zachary had a point. People talk, and few things are as damaging to a man's family life and career as a dead mistress.

"There is still some manuscript to get through," Zachary said. "I assume the rest of the book describes how Lance covered up the murder, so it's reasonable to expect that Jonny's furnished us with a few more clues, or better yet, the name of the cemetery in the prologue where Lance hid Lori Anne's remains."

"Have I ever told you that you and Ivy are the most amazing friends ever?"

"Ah, you'd do the same for us and you know it."

I smiled, and then I heard my cell phone ring. "And right on cue, this must be Stonewall. It's about time he called. I can't wait to tell him how we've not only solved Jonny's murder but also recovered his manuscript." I pulled the phone from my purse.

"Hi, there." I said.

"Hi, yourself, cutie pie."

I froze and fought to keep the terror out of my voice as the blood in my veins turned to slush.

"Hey, Lance. How's it going?"

CHAPTER 31

Zachary's face went pale and he rushed over to stand next to me. I turned the phone to the side so he could hear.

"Where are you? I just came by your house and tried your intercom, but you didn't answer."

Zachary raised his hand for some sort of pantomime, but I looked away because I didn't need help with this. "I'm staying at a hotel."

"Really? Which one?"

I forced a laugh. "This is going to sound crazy, but I'm not even sure what city I'm in. After we hung up, I didn't know where to go, so I just kept driving."

"Ah, I'm so sorry about that, honeybee. I'm all better now so why don't you jump in your car and come on home."

"Alright. I'll leave right now."

Zachary shook his head vigorously.

"Look, I just remembered that I can't make it tonight. I have a doctor's appointment."

"At night?"

"No, not tonight. First thing in the morning. I've got a scratchy throat and a fever, so I think it would be better if we wait until tomorrow so we don't pass it back and forth to each other."

"Ah…well, okay, but you call me as soon as you can and let me know that you're on your way. I miss you and love you so much, baby doll."

"Aw, I miss you too. Oh, and Lance?"

"Yes, cutie pie?"

"There's something I think you should know." I took a deep breath and Zachary gave me a worried look. He was right to worry, because what I had to say bordered dangerously close to tempting fate. But if I was going to be instrumental in sending an ex-boyfriend to prison, I'd sleep better if I eradicated any tattered remains of my affection for him first. "I spoke to a lawyer. There's a real possibility that I'm going to plead guilty."

I hoped I wasn't being too obvious. Zachary leaned closer as we listened for Lance's reaction.

"Wow…That's…pretty serious. You…didn't really kill him, did you?"

"No, but my lawyer said that if I try to fight this, I'll end up making things worse for myself."

Those words were harder to say than I thought they'd be, but I couldn't let him hear the pain and anguish in my voice, because that would give Lance an excuse to say all the right things to me. Whatever he said next, it had to come from the heart.

There was a long silence.

"So do you think I should plead guilty?"

Lance spoke slowly, as if trying to convince me that he was giving the matter his full consideration. "That's a pretty tough call, Amanda. I…I can't make this sort of decision for you. This is something you're going to have to figure out for yourself. But I'll stand by you no matter what you decide."

"Thank you, Lance. That sure is good to know." Zachary placed a reassuring hand on my back as tears filled my eyes.

"Don't forget to call me from the doctor's office. I can't wait to see you again."

"Likewise."

I couldn't hang up fast enough.

I turned to Zachary. "He never cared. Never! This whole time I've just been a stupid little pawn in his sick little game!"

"Bear in mind we are talking about a deranged wife-killing fruitcake."

"Well, Jonny thought I was a worthless bimbo as well."

Zachary rolled his eyes., "Yeah, because *he* was much more normal."

I had to smile at that. "I sure know how to pick them, don't I?"

"Don't worry, everyone's entitled to a couple of psycho exes in their past."

"Thanks. You know, you really should let me go over there tonight. If I look carefully enough I may spot a trace of blood or something else we can take to the police. If they show up here tomorrow with an arrest warrant, we might not get another chance."

All traces of humor vanished from Zachary's face. "Amanda, you do realize that if you go to Lance's tonight, it will be the last thing you ever do."

"Oh, come on, I have enough sense to be careful."

"This isn't a matter of being careful. I'm pretty sure that the only reason Lance wants you over there is because he thinks he's only one staged-suicide away from pulling off three perfect murders."

"Okay, now I'm scared. We need to go to the police."

"Really? And who do you think they'll be most inclined to listen to—the all-American boy? Or the tattooed punk, the juvenile delinquent, and the alleged black widow killer in the ankle monitor?"

I pointed at the lampshade. "They'll listen to Jonny Goodsnuff and his hundred and fifty pages of reasonable doubt."

"Assuming that the police believe that Jonny actually wrote it."

"So what if they don't? When they go to investigate, they'll figure out that it's all true."

"But it's not all true."

I sat down because I felt like a freight train had slammed right into my gut. "What do you mean by that?"

"I mean your husband obviously had to make up some of it. He describes Lance and Lori Anne's thoughts and feeling, as well as many details he couldn't possibly have witnessed. Not to mention the artistic liberties he took to spice things up a bit."

"What do you mean by spiced things up?"

Zachary took a deep breath. "There is no polite way to say this, but somewhere about page seventy Jonny reverted back to his standard formula and gave Lori Anne huge coconut-sized breasts."

I bowed my head and clutched at my hair. "Oh, that pig. If he wasn't already dead, I'd kill him."

"It's okay Amanda, we've gotten this far. We just need to figure out what our next move is going to be."

"I already know what the next move is going to be." I went to the laptop. "When did Lance kill his wife?"

"It must have been a few days before you met your husband at the conference. Back in May."

"That's what I thought."

Zachary peered over my shoulder. "What are you doing?"

"It's about time we found out what happened to the two months before she went missing."

I pulled up Facebook.

Name: Lori Anne Archer.

Relationship status: It's complicated.

I'll say.

Zachary watched as I scrolled to the list of her friends on Facebook. "What are the odds that someone will want to talk to us at this hour?"

He pointed to a buxom blonde in pale pink lipstick, a sequined tube dress, and cascades of platinum curls. "This one probably would, for a price. Candy Stacks. Something tells me it's not the name her parents chose for her."

I gave a wry smile. "Or him."

He wrinkled his nose. "If that's a man, I want his autograph."

I clicked on the link. "Look, she's even got a fan club, and according to her events, she's dancing at Club Peaches tonight. Care for a little late night reconnaissance?"

He pointed at the bedroom. "Sorry, but I've got a girlfriend, and I'm not going any place that might screw that up."

I sighed dramatically. "Oh, well, I guess that means more Peaches for me."

Club Peaches turned out to be a raunchy dive in the middle of a strip mall in the lower-middle class end of town, and despite the colorful name, the building was Darth Vader black. The sign looked like a trucker's mud flap and advertised live dancers and XXX Entertainment with a free cheeseburger dinner and a two-drink minimum.

The men who staggered out the side door looked like they'd had a lot more than that.

I didn't go in. I couldn't. If I couldn't avoid jail, at least I could say that I made it a point to stay out of that place. So I sat on the hood of my car, under the glow of a streetlight, and mentally kicked myself for not coming up with this genius idea of *not actually going in* while I still had a chance to drag Zachary along.

Not that I was worried for my safety. The men who pulled up their collars and averted their gazes as they darted past looked like they were more afraid of me than I should be of them. And with good reason. If any of those filthy animals so much as gave me a "hi, there" I was prepared to unleash the full force of my wrath.

Normally, I wasn't this judgemental. Even as a fourteen year old virgin, I never bought into the myth that a girl's sexuality was some sacred treasure to be surrendered only to that one special guy who can lie the most convincingly. But it was high time I got serious. From now on, I wasn't going to roll around with a guy until I was sure I was in love with him, and that certainly wouldn't be the sort of man who hung out at in a place like Club Peaches.

He'd have to care just as much about me, and I wouldn't settle for anything less than the total package: looks, brains, class, humor, a kind and loving heart, etc…He wouldn't have to be rich, in fact, I'd prefer it if he wasn't, but he'd still have to be hot. I wasn't *that* evolved.

I glanced at the building as a pockmarked woman emerged out the side door. Her crispy white-tipped hair was up in a Scrunchie and she'd dressed down in a pair of dowdy jeans and a leopard print coat. She hoisted her hobo-bag under her arm and walked right past me into the parking lot. It took me a minute to realize that I was looking at the undoctored image of the woman from Facebook. I leapt off the car and strode after her.

"Candy? Candy Stacks?"

She looked back at me and walked faster.

I chased after her. "Candy, wait, I need to ask you some questions."

She stopped and turned. "Are you a journalist, or a cop?"

"Neither."

"All right." She counted off on her fingers. "I don't do movies, I didn't screw your boyfriend, and I've already accepted Jesus Christ as my personal savior and he's cool with what I do for a living. Does that answer any of your questions?"

"No. I need to know about Lori Anne Archer."

"Who?"

Damn it. I hadn't considered that a lot of people have never met their Facebook friends. "Red hair, slim build, she married a good-looking romance novelist—"

"Oh, her, Trish's friend." Candy unlocked her car door. "Look, I'd love to stay and chat, but right now my ten year old is watching my two year old, so I really should get home."

I reached into my purse and held out a fifty. "If you could just give me five minutes, maybe you could apply this toward a proper nanny."

Candy snatched the bill out of my hand and buried it in her bra. "Five minutes. What do you want to know?"

"I need to find out what happened to Lori Anne. It's a matter of life and death. I'll give you more than fifty if you can help me find out what happened to her."

"Sorry, haven't heard from her since she left her husband."

"So you knew about that?"

Candy nodded. "She hated his guts. The only reason she hung with us was to get away from him."

"But do you know why she hated him?"

She pushed one finger against the side of her nose and snorted dramatically. I thought she had allergies, until I realized it was pantomime. "Lori Anne was an addict?"

"Not Lori Anne, her husband."

She had to be kidding. I'd been over at Lance's nearly every day for six months and had never seen any sign of drug use. Believe me, I knew the signs. I had a feeling that Candy Stacks didn't know a damn thing and was playing a joke at my expense.

She must've read something from my expression. "You didn't know that about him? She used to call him Lemon Doughnut because he was always in the powder. Funny thing was he didn't want to hit the clubs, he'd just stay home with his big bag of snow. He said he needed it to meet his deadlines. Eventually she made him quit, so he'd work out with his weights all day long instead."

Okay, we were talking about the same guy. Candy took out a half roll of breath mints and popped one in her mouth.

"I think her husband killed her when she tried to leave him," I said.

"Then the bitch probably got what she deserved."

"Meaning what, exactly?" I said over her sucking sounds.

"Meaning she was a bitch, and she probably got what she deserved." Candy slid the mint over into her cheek. "I never did like her. I used to feel sorry for her, but last Saint Paddy's day I invited her to my party and she called me a nasty skank and an unfit mother before she hung up on me. Like she's got any right to bring up my kids. Screw her."

As I listened to the mint crunch between her teeth, I decided to change course. "Do you think it's possible that Lori Anne cheated on her husband?"

"No, I don't think that's possible. Cheating implies she had boundaries. Let just say that this guy didn't care where she got her appetite from, as long as she came home and gave him his dinner." She glanced at her wrist. "I think it's been five minutes, don't you?"

"Wait, one more question, do you know anything about the rumor that Lori Anne was having an affair with her boss?"

She shook her head. "Not a thing. Go talk to Trish."

"Could you give me Trish's number?"

She opened her car door and climbed inside. "Yeah, right. Like I'm going to give out a friend's number for fifty dollars. I'd head over to Jolly Joe's if

I were you."

"Jolly Joe's?"

"Jolly Joe is Trish's boss. He used to be Lori Anne's boss." She slammed the door shut and started the engine.

"Wait, what's Joe's last name?"

She gave me a piercing look. "Does he even have one?"

"How do I–"

"Google it."

She peeled out of the park lot and did an illegal left turn through a double yellow line.

I heaved a sigh and called Zachary, who Googled the address for Jolly Joe's Pimptasic All-Night Used Car Lot.

CHAPTER 32

You'd think that the car dealership would be a little more refined than the strip joint. In the case of Jolly Joe's, you'd be wrong. The salesgirls milled about dressed like French prostitutes. I'm not being judgmental here. They really were dressed like old time French prostitutes: in berets, striped tops, fishnet stockings, and miniskirts slit very high up the side.

I parked on the street and approached the lot. Although it was night, there were so many lights that I could see my shadow as if it were noon. I walked straight to the most expensive car on the lot and stared at it until I heard footsteps.

"Howdy, Creampuff," a jovial voice said.

I turned and saw a man in a purple cape and hat leaning against a walking stick with a huge glass gem at the top. He was supposed to look like a pimp, but with his huge gut and his bushy black beard, he looked more like Henry VIII.

"You must be Jolly Joe," I said.

"And you must be looking for a job."

"Actually I'm looking for a car."

"Well howdy-ho-ho, I like that even better. Are you looking for an automatic or a manual, because if you don't mind my saying so, you seem like a girl who really knows how to handle a stick."

Oh, so it was going to be like that then?

"Actually, I just need something with child locks. You know, so my kids can't play around with the doors while I'm driving?"

Jolly Joe sucked a deep breath through his molars. "Oh...how about this one over here, ma'am?" He pointed to a dark blue four-door sedan.

"Good enough."

I took the driver's seat while he buckled up as a passenger. "I think I'll forgo my usual spiel about keeping your hands off the sales staff." Joe wagged his eyebrows suggestively.

I fastened my seatbelt. "I'll try to control myself."

We left the lot and he told me where to drive, and I steered through the deserted streets past empty office buildings and fast food restaurants. When we were at a particularly remote street, Joe began his pitch: "Darling, I'm not even going to beat around your bush. It's late in the year, and it's late in the day. Tell me what I'd need to do to sell you this car tonight."

I turned the steering wheel until we were parallel-parked, and turned to face him. "You could start by answering some questions about one of your former salesgirls."

"What the hell is this?" He grabbed for the door handle, so I hit the lock button.

"I'm sorry, Joe. But I really need this information tonight."

Joe was jerking at the door like a girl in a B-rate slasher film. "Please don't kill me. Look, if it's about the pimp thing, it's all in good fun. I'm all bark and no bite. I take good care of my girls and I keep them in school. I'm a devout feminist, I swear. I've got a wife and kids."

"Does the name Lori Anne Archer mean anything to you?"

His eyes became big and frightened. "I never touched her! I swear on my mother's grave!"

"I heard that you were lovers and she planned on leaving her husband so you could be together."

He slumped against the door. "I knew it, my wife hired you. She found out about that red-haired succubus and she's going to leave me over one stupid mistake. She'll take the kids back east to her parents' and I'll never see them again!"

I rolled my eyes while he collapsed into sobs. Some player. I let him cry a bit before I heaved an audible sigh at him.

"Joe, I have no intention of ruining your marriage. But I think Lance Archer killed his wife, and if we don't stop him, I'm going to be his next victim."

Joe sniffled and slumped back in his seat. "You know what? That doesn't surprise me at all."

"Can you help me?"

He nodded. "Let's go back to the dealership. We can go into one of the sales rooms and have a cup of coffee. What I have to tell you is going to take a while."

Joe poured coffee into two Styrofoam cups while I slid into the chair across from him. He took off his purple hat and set it on the far end of the table.

"Lori Anne and I met though Trish. Trish is one of my best salesgirls and she came to me and said that her friend needed a job so she could get out of the house and away from her psychotic husband. I trusted Trish, so I said okay."

He looked down at his coffee. "I wished I hadn't. Lori Anne was supposed to be hot stuff, but she was the type that only seems hot to other girls. You know, tall and skinny with thick hair and great big feet? Some guys like that, but not the guys who shop at Jolly Joe's."

"Go on." I took a sip of my coffee.

"I put her in an office and had her do loan approvals but even there, she was a disaster. Lori Anne was one of those girls who could never be quiet. She had no work ethic and was always calling my girls off the lot just to gab it up for hours. I had the paperwork all ready to fire her. Then her husband called and said she needed a month off because they had big plans for Valentine's Day."

Big plans for Valentine's Day? Now we were getting somewhere. "I assume you didn't have the heart to ruin their vacation?"

He tore open three sugar packets and let the grains trickle into his coffee. "What can I say? I'm a romantic. I figured I'd just fire her when she got back." Joe looked up. "The trouble is, when she came back, she'd been supersized."

"Supersized?"

Joe smile at the memory. "She was sporting the biggest pair of jugs I'd ever seen in my life."

I felt my pulse quicken. "Lori Anne Archer got breast implants?"

Joe's eyes sparkled. "They were so magnificent I don't even know how to describe them."

"Would you say that they were the size of coconuts?"

"Yes, exactly the size of coconuts. So you've seen them?"

"No, but they're pretty easy for me to imagine." I took another sip. So Jonny hadn't embellished after all. This was excellent. I was tempted to call Zachary, but first I needed to hear the rest of the story.

"Not only that, she stopped talking. She'd wish me a good morning of course, but then she did her work with great efficiency, and then went home without saying a word. I promoted her to sales, and in her first week, she was selling more cars than all of the other girls put together."

"That must have been wonderful for you."

"No kidding! I thought I was dreaming. Then one day, I was walking through the waiting area and I heard her bawling in the ladies room. I walked in and peeked over the top of the stall to see if she was okay. She was just sitting on the toilet in her salesgirl costume and crying her eyes out. I asked her what was wrong. She told me that she was going to kill herself."

"Did she say why?"

"Turns out she never wanted implants. Lori Anne was perfectly happy as a flat-chested freak, but she'd promised her husband that if he went to rehab and stayed clean for six months, she'd get a boob-job, just as big as he wanted. She didn't think far enough ahead to realize she'd have to go through with it."

He took a sip and then reached for another pack of sugar. "Trish advised Lori Anne to pretend that she wanted the implants, but then to get the doctor alone and beg him to make an excuse for why Lori Anne wasn't a candidate." Jolly Joe heaved a sigh. "It might have worked with most doctors, but not the one Lance chose. He just told her she was flat and unattractive and her new implants would give her an armload more confidence. Personally, I think he made a good case, but Lori Anne only agreed because she was afraid of what would happen to her if she didn't."

The poor girl. No wonder she withdrew completely from her social circle. She must have felt completely violated and disfigured.

Joe continued his tale. "She went on and on about how her husband had turned her into a circus freak, and I stood there draped over the stall and listened intently, mainly because from my perch I had a bird's-eye view of those tantalizing gazanagas. It hurt me to see those precious love pillows being so cruelly disparaged, but when I looked into her eyes, I saw she was dead inside. So, in a moment of weakness, I promised I'd pay to have the implants removed."

He ran his hand over his beard and shook his head sadly. "I regretted those words as soon as they were out of my mouth, but her eyes lit up and she gave me the hottest sidelong look. My heart melted. She told me to get down and she'd open the door for me. I had to wait a minute or two before she slid the latch, but when the door opened, she had on nothing but her fishnet stockings.

"Believe me, up until that point I was a happily married man who would have never thought of doing the sorts of things Lori Anne and I did in the stall that day, and every day afterwards, but a sight like that, it makes a man's brain stop working."

Wow. This really was a Jonny Goodsnuff novel. No wonder my husband tried to make ten million off this tragedy instead of going straight to the police like any sane human being with a soul might have done.

Then Joe's face became somber. "I never intended to have the implants removed, of course. I figured I'd just constantly tell her how beautiful she was and treat her like a queen, and in time, she'd grow to love them as much as I did. It seemed to work. Lori Anne made me rent her a condo so that she could leave her husband. It was tough, because my wife watches the money like a hawk, but I finally scratched together enough to make a deposit on a nice loft near the college. Lori Anne just had to wait until her husband was gone, pack a few bags and leave. She was back to being a pain in the ass again, but I was so whipped that I had caviar and champagne chilled and waiting by the bed to celebrate."

"But she never showed up."

"That's right. She left me. She didn't go to the loft, and she didn't come to work. I really thought we had something special, but that whole time she was just using me."

I blinked in wonderment at how anyone could be so dense. "And you never suspected foul play? You said her husband frightened her. You knew he wouldn't just let her go. You said you aren't surprised he's killed her. So why didn't you go to the police when she went missing?"

He looked up and met my eyes. "How am I supposed to know she'd gone missing? I haven't seen her since the night she broke up with me."

I felt my mouth go dry. "She...broke up with you?"

"She told me she was going home to get her stuff but it turned out that was all a lie. She left me a voicemail because she didn't even have the balls to tell me to my face it was over. She'd found someone else. Someone who loved her for her mind and wasn't just going to use her like a piece of meat."

That didn't mean anything, I assured myself. Lance must have dragged her to the phone and forced her to call, right before he killed her. "When did she call?"

"You mean the first time or the last time?"

I felt like I was sinking. "She called you more than once?"

"She drunk-dials my voice mail at least once a month to tell me what a loser the guy turned out to be, and that she's sorry, and she wants to get back together. The first call was on the day she was supposed to move in the apartment. The last call was a week ago."

I set the cup down. My hand shook so much that I was afraid I'd slosh coffee all over the desk. "Are you sure it's her, and not just someone pretending to be her?"

"It's her, alright. Lori Anne's got a funny colloquial way of talking and this distinctive nasally whistle to her voice. Add in a drunken slur, as fast as a hummingbird. Sorry, no actress could pull that off. Not even Meryl Streep. It's her voice, and voicemail shows it's her cell number." He gave me an imploring look. "But you say her husband found her and killed her, so I guess the calls are going to stop now, right?"

Son of a bitch!

"Lori Anne is alive."

Ivy and Zachary sat on the sectional and watched as I paced across their living room like a caged jungle cat. "Lance didn't kill his wife, and since that is the lynchpin of our entire theory that means we've been wrong about everything."

"Then how do you explain the pink coat?" Zachary said.

Ivy nodded. "Not to mention the douche bag non-answer he gave when you asked if you should go to prison?"

"I don't know," I sank into a seat with my face in my hands. "But give me ten minutes and I'll come up with something."

Zachary frowned. "If Lance isn't the killer, then why does Jonny's ground-breaking novel have his name written all over it?"

I ran my hands through my hair. "Because it was obviously a work of fantasy, and he intended to change the names in the final draft."

Zachary shook his head. "No way. The Archers are far too recognizable. Either Jonny knew for a fact that he'd be able to impugn them without legal consequence, or what we've been looking at isn't the real manuscript."

For the merest of moments, those words gave me hope, but then I buried my face in my hands. "It's the right manuscript. There's just too much detailed information for this to be a ruse."

Ivy jumped up from the sectional and clapped her hands together. "I've got it! Lance killed a hooker!"

I groaned. "Ivy, please, I'm too tired to grasp at straws right now."

"No, think about it! After Lori Anne left, Lance brought home a redhead for a night of kinky role-playing, but he got carried away, and killed her. Jonny watched it happen but he didn't know that Lori Anne wasn't the girl being murdered!"

I curled into a ball. "I appreciate what you're trying to do, but the whole thing was a fool's errand to begin with. We can spend all night hammering and shoehorning the facts, but since we don't have any evidence, this is all a waste of time."

Zachary eyes went wide. "Wait a minute. We absolutely do have evidence. We have a body!"

Ivy squealed and clapped her hands together but I wasn't getting my hopes up that easily.

"I mean, come on. Do you really believe a cowardly weasel like Jonny would have tracked a killer like Lance all the way to a cemetery, without Lance noticing the headlights of the slick Jaguar tailing him?"

Ivy thought about this. "Jonny must've hid in Lance's suv while he was burning up his wife's remains."

I turned my head to her. "Brilliant, Ivy. Because whenever I watch someone kill the love of his life with his bare fists, I know my first instinct is to trap myself in a closely confined space with him."

Zachary rose from the sectional. "Hey, if there was a perfectly logical explanation for Lori Anne's horizontal growth spurt, there's probably an explanation for this as well. Ivy, let's see if we can find an address for the cemetery."

I crossed my arms over my chest. "Oh, so Jonny finally disclosed the name of the place?"

Ivy peeked at me from around the laptop. "No, but he did say that it was right on the coast. How many cemeteries could there be right at the shoreline?"

I rolled over onto my belly. "I'd guess zero. The groundwater would seep in and flood the graves."

Zachary tutted. "You're failing to factor in the elevation. Ivy, check the cliffs."

Ivy pointed at the laptop. "Right here. Look at the pictures. Willows and roses along the far gate, and it's only about four miles from Amanda's place."

Zachary gave her a nudge. "Lance strikes me as the sort of guy who likes to stay close to home. Print out some maps and Jonny's prologue and we'll go check it out."

"Oh, no we won't." I said, but they ignored me as the printer buzzed to life. Zachary and Ivy headed off to their room and emerged a few minutes later dressed from head to toe in black like chimneysweeps. Ivy went outside, while Zachary grabbed a coat and a satchel and carried them into the kitchen.

"You're not actually going out there, are you?"

Zachary flicked on a flashlight and tested the beam. "If there really is a pile of evidence out there, we need to find out exactly where it is so we can show it to the police."

"Assuming the police don't find you first."

Zachary didn't say a word as he placed another flashlight, a pair of rubber gloves, some dishrags, and a few bottles of drinking water into the satchel.

Ivy reappeared and leaned a shovel against the open doorway.

"I didn't know we had a shovel," Zachary said as he put on his coat.

"We don't, I borrowed it from the neighbors."

Zachary paused his buttoning. "Do the neighbors know you borrowed it?"

She shrugged. "It'll be back in their shed before they need it."

Oh, great. There wasn't anything that could possibly go wrong in this scenario. I propped my chin up on one arm.

"So let see if I've got this straight—you two are going to a cemetery in the dead of the night to dig for human remains?"

Zachary frowned as he hoisted the satchel onto his shoulder. "When you put it that way it just sounds so wrong."

"It sounds wrong because it is wrong! In the best case you're tampering with evidence. The worst case involves handcuffs, jail time, and parole hearings. And that's assuming you're not shot, bludgeoned, or torn apart by police dogs."

Ivy clapped her hands together. "I know, isn't it exciting? I can't wait until we get there."

"Well have fun, you two," I said, "because I'm not going. There's no way I'm vandalizing a cemetery in the dead of night on some wild goose chase."

Zachary carried the shovel out to the car and Ivy tossed me a black hooded sweatshirt. "Put this on. I know you haven't been in So-Cal long enough to need a jacket, but it tends to get chilly over the water."

I caught the sweatshirt with one hand and set it on the table. "I told you. I'm not going."

"Suit yourself. After all, it's your funeral," Ivy sighed. "Well, yours and Stonewall's, but we don't really care about that, now do we?"

I grabbed the sweatshirt from the table and stood up. "You can be a real bitch, you know that?"

"Yes, but I like to think of myself as a bitch with a heart of gold."

I pulled on the sweatshirt. "You know something, Ivy? I've got a really bad feeling in my gut. You do realize the police are monitoring my every move?"

She waved it off. "Good, that will just lead them to the body sooner.

It'll be fine, trust me."

I joined Ivy at the door, but as she reached for the light switch, my misgivings got the better of me. "Wait, before I end up back in jail, there's something I need to take care of. Can I borrow your laptop for two minutes?"

"Sure thing," Ivy said. "Lock up when you're done. We'll wait in the car."

I went to her laptop and logged into my e-mail account. No new messages, but that was hardly surprising.

I composed a message of my own.

Dear Stonewall,
I know there are still plenty of shopping days left until Christmas, but how often does a girl like me find the perfect gift for the man who has everything? Attached you'll find a copy of Jonny's final manuscript. We were able to read the ribbon in Jonny's typewriter so Ivy, Zachary, and I spent the last couple of days transcribing it into this file. I know it's too little, too late, but at least it's something.
Thanks for everything you've done for me. You're an amazing human being.
Hugs,
Amanda

I attached Jonny's manuscript and hit send. I felt myself blush, as a deep stirring within my ribcage spread over me like the warmth of a summer day.

Now where the hell did that come from?

CHAPTER 33

I slept on the way to the cemetery and dreamt of Stonewall. In my dream, we were at the fast food place, but rather than point out that he had a dab of sauce under his lip, I leaned forward and kissed it away. Then I kissed him again, because his skin tasted fresh and exotic, like a blend of mint and white nectarine.

When I pulled away, he was frowning.

I rested my cheek on my arm and glowered at him as he picked up his napkin and scrubbed the spot where my lips had been.

"Let me give you some friendly advice, Amanda—Men like me don't kiss trash."

My eyes fluttered open and I stretched out in the back of Zachary's jeep. Ivy turned her head and looked down at me. "Hey, sweetie. Are you okay back there?"

"Stonewall said I was trash."

"It's okay, you just had a bad dream."

"How did you know I was talking about a nightmare?"

"Because, Stonewall would never say something like that."

I yawned and sat up. "I think I like him."

Ivy smiled at me. "Of course you do."

"No, I didn't mean that in a platonic way."

Ivy nodded. "We knew what you meant, dear."

I just stared at her because I didn't know that was possible.

"Sweetie, I don't know if you realize this, but you get pissy jealous whenever you see him talk to another woman, and that includes me."

Oh, my God, she was right. I was a Lady Georgina. But at least Stonewall was no Lord Ashingworth.

"I think the next time we go to dinner, I'll let him pick up the check, and after he walks me to the car, I'll steal a goodnight kiss."

Ivy nodded and settled back into her seat without saying anything.

"So do you think I have a shot?"

Ivy and Zachary exchanged glances before they threw back their heads and burst into laughter.

"Is that an *Amanda is an idiot* – yes or an *Amanda is an idiot* – no?"

Ivy turned back around. "Oh my God, you don't see the way he looks at you?"

"Of course not," Zachary said. "She must assume he looks that dopey all the time."

"Stonewall doesn't look dopey," I said.

Zachary chuckled. "Oh, he looked like the devil himself after they arrested you."

Ivy leaned over the headrest. "He's crazy in love with you, Amanda. Why do you think I like him so much?"

"So he's not your agent?"

"Dear God, no. Do you really think he'd take the time to write up a contract for some small-fry cartoonist while he's moving heaven and earth to spring you out of jail?"

"He told me he didn't have anything to do with that."

Ivy sputtered. "And you believed him? You don't think he got on the phone with his old boss and called in a few favors?"

Zachary sighed. "Not everything is a conspiracy, Ivy. The DA's office probably doesn't set suspected murderers loose after cocktails and a few rounds of golf."

"Hey," Ivy said. "It wouldn't surprise me."

I raised my eyebrows. "So you two figured this out after only knowing him for one day?"

She shook her head. "Oh, please, I figured it out after knowing him for five minutes. You two are crazy about each other and it's blatantly obvious to everyone but the two of you. You really have never given it any serious thought?"

"No, of course not. He's way out of my league."

Zachary looked back for a moment. "That's funny, because he feels the same way about you."

"Really?"

Ivy nodded. "You do realize that when we were talking about *The Little Mermaid*, we weren't really talking about *The Little Mermaid*."

"I suspected as much but I thought Lance was the Prince and I was the mermaid."

"No, you're the Prince. Stonewall's the mermaid." Ivy turned around in her seat so that she could face me. "Here is how I remember it. We were sitting in the back of the limo. Stonewall just sat there and moped until the topic of *The Little Mermaid* came up and he used that as an excuse to bitch about what exquisite torture unrequited love is."

I shook my head. "I don't remember that."

"So I said he needs to let you know how he feels, and then he implied that it was a lost cause since you could never like him that way."

Zachary glanced at me in the rearview mirror. "So then I said I wanted to hear your thoughts on the matter."

"And what did I say?" I wasn't sure I wanted to know the answer.

Zachary smiled. "You told him to be patient."

I gasped. "Oh, my God, I was right!"

Ivy sat back. "Well I'm glad it's all sorted out now. You know, Amanda, wouldn't it be funny if this whole mess occurred because it was the one way the Universe could get the two of you together?"

Zachary rolled his eyes. "That would *really* suck for Jonny, Lance, and whoever's buried under the rosebush."

Then I remembered the last time I saw Stonewall, and how he couldn't even stand to look at me. He wasn't being shy. I knew loathing when I saw it. I didn't have the heart to tell them that if he ever did have feelings for me, they had long since soured. Once this was all over, I was going to have to work pretty damn hard just to make him like me again.

We'd entered the road through the cemetery. Row after row of tombstones glistened white among the cypress trees. The flashlights wouldn't be necessary. There were lampposts every few feet, lending support to the full moon beaming through the faint mist of the night sky. I'd been half-afraid that it would be a scene out of a ghost story with owls and wild dogs staring at me with glowing eyes. It all seemed so quiet and normal, as if we were spending a day at the park instead of exhuming the dead.

"Where are the roses?" Zachary asked Ivy and she unfolded a map.

"Take that winding path and keep driving. The roses border the whole south side."

Zachary drove until the path ended and then punched the steering wheel and swore under his breath.

"What's wrong?" I asked.

He pointed and we looked out to see a patch of dirt around the willows, out of which jutted at least a couple hundred thorny bushes, all of which were brown and leafless and cut back for the winter.

"Would either of you ladies care to guess which one of those is our pink rosebush?"

We all got out of the car and surveyed the seemingly herculean task before us. I wandered along the border of the rose garden. All of the bushes looked alike, with their dried skeletal arms stretching outward.

"This is hopeless," Zachary said. "Absolutely hopeless. We could dig for weeks and never find anything."

Ivy smiled weakly. "My granny grows roses. There are little plastic tags on the bottom that say what breed they are."

He snarled. "Well that's just great, if you have the colors of all of the breeds memorized."

Ivy turned on a flashlight and flipped through some papers. "Let me see if I can find anything in the prologue that will give us a clue as to where exactly this rosebush is."

Zachary bent and examined the closest tag. "Ivy, my sweet, I know I'm asking the obvious, but where exactly in the rainbow would I find a color like *Home Run*?"

Ivy didn't even look up from her reading. "Don't think I won't smack you in front of Amanda."

I entered the rose bed and used a flashlight to inspect around the willows hoping to find some incriminating depression or any other clue that an evil deed had been done nearby. When I'd circled the last of the trees without finding anything, I called out to the others. "Anything?"

"Nothing," Ivy said and folded up her printout.

I turned off my flashlight. "Can we go home now?"

Zachary sighed dramatically. "I guess so."

I cut through the rose bed to leave, but as I was halfway through I saw a plant whose thorn-covered branches seemed spread in a particular snowflake formation.

Something about it told me that it bore further investigation. I called Ivy and Zachary over and pointed. "There. That's the one."

"How do you know?" Zachary asked.

"I just do."

He knelt and inspected the tag with his flashlight. He raised his eyebrows. "*Pink Promise*."

"I'll get the shovel," Ivy said.

She gave the spade to Zachary and we both stood back as he placed it at the base of the rosebush and dug into the ground. When he uprooted the plant, I stepped forward to place it to one side while he continued digging.

Then the shovel hit something solid with a clunk.

Ivy hugged herself. "We found something."

"It might be a rock," Zachary said. He pulled on a pair of dishwashing gloves from the satchel and reached into the pit, but after he wiped away most of the dirt, he looked up in disappointment. "It's just an old trowel someone left here."

Ivy gasped. "According to the prologue, a trowel was the last object Lance placed in the pit before it was covered up. Right below it should be his clothing."

Zachary paused a bit to take that in, then probed the pit with the butt end of the shovel. When he raised it, there was a sucking noise as he pulled up a length of denim caked with soil.

Ivy hopped about and clapped her hands together. "Busted!"

That was it. We did it. We had found enough evidence to clear my name so there wouldn't be a trial. I was so relieved that I found myself laughing and crying at the same time.

Zachary pulled off the gloves and tossed them in the bag. "Now all we have to do is call the police and have them exhume whatever else is down there." He turned to me. "But first I need to know how on earth you knew where to dig."

"I don't know," I said.

Ivy smiled. "It must have been déjà vu."

"Except there's no such thing as déjà vu," Zachary said.

Ivy clapped her hands over his cheeks. "Why do you need a scientific explanation for everything? Sometimes things happen just because they're supposed to."

I tried to smile, but the trouble was, I agreed with Zachary. How *did* I know where to dig? It couldn't be luck—my luck was never that good. I looked at the rosebush, lying on the grass with its roots exposed and its branches stretched out as if it was pleading for something. Then an ice-cold chill went through me when I remembered I'd seen it before.

"Both of you. Get back in the car. Now."

"What?" Ivy said. She seemed more afraid of the tone of my voice than by what I was saying.

I backed away from the rose bed and pulled the others by their sleeves like small children. Then I shushed them and I turned on my flashlight and searched the branches of the willow trees above us. I didn't see anything until I shined the beam at the wrought-iron fence behind us and saw the glint of a lens blink at me like the eyes of a feral rat. And its cord, like a tail, snaked down along a post where it was camouflaged with electricians tape.

"I need you to go to the car, now. I know how Jonny knew where the body was buried. Lance set up a camera to watch this spot. But he made the mistake of setting it up before the burial and not afterwards. Jonny could watch Lance, using Lance's own computer."

"Well that's great that you figured that out, isn't it?" Ivy said weakly.

"No, it's not! Lance can see us! He's probably already on his way over here!"

Thankfully, they listened to me that time, and hurried to the car. But they stopped when Ivy looked back while I knelt on the grass, hiked up my pant leg, and tried my hardest to pry the monitor from my ankle. "What are you doing?"

"Get in the car. You two need to go straight to the police, and not leave until you know for a fact that Lance is in custody."

"We can't just leave you here," Zachary said.

"You can and you will." I pushed as hard as I could until I could feel the metal bite into my skin. I hoped it would be enough.

"I don't think that's going to come off," Zachary said. "Those things are engineered to be virtually indestructible."

"Yes, I'm aware of that. They just need to know I made the attempt."

The red light on the monitor flashed like a distress call, but just to be safe I pried at it some more.

"Forget that," Zachary said, and to my horror, they began walking away from the car. "You need to come with us. I have a cell phone. You can call 911 right now and lead them to this exact spot."

"Don't you understand? I've set off an alarm. I'm a fugitive now. If I go with you, you'll be aiding and abetting." I waved toward the car. "Go! Don't worry about me. In less than ten minutes, a swarm of police cars will be at my precise GPS location to arrest me, and when they do, they need to see this shallow grave and take it seriously. If Lance removes the evidence, this will all have been for nothing."

"No," Zachary said. "If Lance wrings your neck, this will all have been for nothing."

I was going to scream at them one last time but my mouth went dry as the beams from a pair of headlights winded down the path. I lowered my pant leg to hide the rapidly flashing anklet. I prayed it was the police, but as I've said, my luck has never been that good.

Ivy and Zachary turned just in time to see Lance's suv pull up. They backed away as he slammed the car door behind him.

"Well, look what we have here," he said as he advanced on us with a hunting rifle slung over one shoulder.

CHAPTER 34

I glanced at my watch just long enough to note that the big hand was on the two. In *The 1,001 Arabian Nights*, Princess Scheherazade had to keep talking for three years to stop her man from doing murder. I just had to stall Lance for eight minutes.

He was rocking on his heels. As he stood illuminated by the headlights of his suv a few beads of sweat dripped from his forehead and slid down his upper lip. I thought back to the last time I kissed those lips, and the memory felt like snails crawling across my face.

The night was cold, so his sweat was from adrenaline. If I had only myself to worry about I probably would have fainted, but my fury completely over-ruled my sense of self-preservation. I was afraid, but I could see past my fear because I had to keep my wits about me. I spoke to get his attention.

"This isn't what it looks like," I said in a bored drawl, hoping to interject some levity into the situation.

"I should hope not," Lance said. "Because it looks like you lured your friends up here so you could shoot them, before you turn the gun on yourself."

Ivy shook as Zachary held her, his own face was white with terror. Why did I let them come here? They were young and successful, with everything to live for. But then they got too close and now they might die for it.

Lance looked over at them. "Oh, does this gun scare you? Don't worry, I just use it for hunting. I thought I might see a couple of cute little bunnies scampering across the grass. But I'm not going to see any scampering, now am I?"

I picked up the shovel. "I suppose you want us to put everything back the way we found it?"

"No, as a matter of fact, I want you to keep digging."

I walked over to the pit and lifted out shovelfuls of dirt, scraping at the sides and pretending that the earth was a lot harder than it was. I had to dig as slowly as possible to give the police time to arrive. As I worked, Lance wandered across the clearing between the roses and cemetery to the north of us. He came to a stop midway between me and the line of huge cypress trees that separated us from the moss covered tombs. The tree closest to Lance had a hollow that gave it a subtle jack o' lantern appearance.

He stood with his hunting rifle in his arms while he watched me work. Even from a distance, he stank like a mixture of skunk and goat. Ivy and Zachary huddled together and every so often he'd glance in their direction. If only I could make him forget they were there, but Ivy was making whimpering noises. Lance looked as if it was giving him a headache.

He waved the gun at Zachary. "You! Make her shut up before I really give her something to cry about."

"Don't do anything stupid," I said. "They're not a threat to you."

"Oh, really? Then why were they digging in the exact spot where I buried my wife's remains?"

I used that question as an excuse to stop digging. "I don't know what you're talking about. Lori Anne's alive. I met someone who spoke to her just a week ago."

"Really? I wonder if it sounded something like this," he pulled a digital recorder out of his pocket and a woman's slurred cries filled the air.

"I'm sorry. He means nothing to me. Please, give me one more chance. I love you so much. I'll do anything for you."

Lance clicked it off and then tapped it with his finger. "You should get one of these, Amanda. As a writer, you never know when inspiration will strike while you're sitting in traffic. And it's amazing how much fun you can have with a cell phone, the proper audio editing software, and a cheating wife's last words."

"You sick bastard."

He put the device back in his pocket.

"Don't feel sorry for Lori Anne. She had it coming. I gave her everything—money, love, complete and total freedom to do whatever she wanted. But the moment I wanted something from her, she threatened to take half of everything I worked for and share it with some fat idiot."

He shook his head. "I never should have let her hang out with those friends of hers. She was such a good girl. This place ruined her."

No, you ruined her, I thought.

He shifted his gun. "So how did you figure this out?"

"I'll tell you tomorrow." As I resumed digging, I tried not to look at the items of odd shape and texture that rolled off with the soil. I had to keep this up to buy time. I looked down the winding path. I didn't see any headlights, but I was growing tired so I was sure that I'd been working for nearly eight minutes. I glanced at my watch.

The big hand was past the five.

It had been over fifteen minutes, twice the time it should have taken for the police to arrive. Heartsick, I forced myself to keep digging. The police weren't coming. They could send a dozen officers to arrest me in front of half of the publishing industry, but they weren't coming to save us. I was sure I'd tampered with the anklet enough to set off the alarm, but for all I knew, it was going off in some empty office where nobody could hear it. Maybe they thought I wouldn't get far and they could just pick me up in the morning.

"That's good enough." Lance turned to Zachary and Ivy. "I need you two to go over there next to Amanda. I want you to stand about five feet apart."

I'd hoped they would take that as their cue to run as fast as they could in opposite directions before Lance had a chance to raise his gun, but instead they came over and did as he said.

"Now turn around so I can't see your faces."

They did that too, and I wanted to scream at them for making this so easy for him.

"You too, Amanda."

Oh, no. It was not going to end like this. Not with us dead and Lance telling reporters that I'd always seemed like such a nice girl—maybe a little odd—but he certainly didn't think I was capable of doing something like *that*.

I threw down the shovel and marched toward him. "You go to hell, Lance Archer. I'm not going to make this easy for you. If you're going to shoot me, just shoot me in the face."

"Oh, you think I won't?"

Ivy began screaming in hysterics. "No! Don't shoot her! She didn't want to come here! She tried to talk us out of it! I made her do it!"

I paused in midstep. My God. She was right. I didn't want to come to the graveyard.

Good for you, Ivy! Her outburst might have bought us a few more crucial minutes. "Listen to her, Lance. She's telling the truth. I didn't want to come here."

Lance let out a laugh. "So what are you saying? That I should kill your friends and let you go?"

"I'm saying you don't have to kill anyone. Think about it. You got lucky by killing Lori Anne at a time when nobody would realize she was gone. If I were to vanish, nobody would miss me either. But these two," I pointed back at Ivy and Zachary. "They'll be missed! Leave them out of this and you'll get away with everything. Killing Lori Anne, killing Jonny, framing me for the murder. Everything."

"And how's that?"

"Because I wasn't joking when I offered to plead guilty."

Lance chuckled. "You must think I'm really stupid. The only reason you were going to plead guilty was because you couldn't prove your innocence. Why would you confess to a murder you didn't commit except to save your own neck."

His mocking got the better of me so I spoke without thinking. "I never offered to plead guilty to save my own neck—I did it to protect the man I love!"

I stood shaking as all the walls I'd built around my heart came crashing away. It was true. I loved Stonewall. I loved him and I'd probably never see him again. Maybe it was better that way. If he still had feelings for me, maybe it would be better if they stayed clean and pure before I had a chance to screw that up, too.

I looked away, but not before I caught the smile of surprise on Lance's face. "You really mean that?"

My voice broke and I blushed all the way to the roots of my hair.

"God help me, I mean it with all my heart."

Lance seemed genuinely touched. "What a good girl you are. Why couldn't my wife have been more like you?"

I thought about the monitor on my ankle and forced myself to look him in the eyes. "Lance, let's run away together. There is nothing keeping us here. We can be in Mexico in less than three hours. I don't care where we go, as long as you're with me."

Lance shook his head. "You're wanted for murder. We'll be arrested at the border, and those two will come forward and tell the police everything they know."

"The border patrol doesn't have to know I'm in the car. I'll hide in the back seat—they're only concerned with humans being trafficked in the other direction. Once we're across, I'll have my bank wire us all my money, and we can take a flight to wherever you want before the police realize we're gone. Ivy and Zachary won't say anything. They know I'll be better off if they don't talk to the police."

I never thought he'd give my words any serious consideration. I wanted to buy some more time for the police to arrive. But to my surprise, Lance tossed the rifle onto the grass.

"You know what? I want to believe you, but I'm afraid I'll just have my heart broken again. So we're going to compromise: we'll drive down to Mexico, but I'm afraid you're going to be bound and gagged."

Even better! I couldn't wait to see the look on everyone's face when the police finally tracked down the ankle monitor. Assuming, of course, they managed to find us before Lance strangled me and tossed my body in a dumpster.

"I think that sounds perfectly reasonable," I said.

"Great. Then I just need you to turn around, get down on your knees and cross your wrists behind your back. You two sit on the grass and don't turn around until we're gone. I don't want to have to do anything rash because one of you decided to be a hero."

He needn't have worried. Even without the gun, none of us stood a chance. I'm deceptively strong for my size, but I wasn't delusional enough to believe that I could survive more than a minute of hand-to-hand combat with a bruiser like Lance. Zachary might last another five, but Ivy's heart would explode from sheer terror before Lance even touched her.

I began to turn, but when I looked at Lance, he had murder in his eyes. He wasn't going to tie me up. He didn't even have anything to tie me up with. He just wanted me to turn around so he wouldn't be haunted by the look in my eyes as he killed me.

If there was any way to come back as a ghost, I was going to haunt him day and night to make sure he never had a moment's peace. It's not like I'd have anything better to do. At least I could take some comfort in the fact that there was no way Lance would get away with this. Stonewall would make sure of that. Maybe he had every reason to hate me for everything I've ever said or done to him, but my death would wipe the slate clean.

Thank goodness I had the foresight to send him Jonny's manuscript. When he woke and saw my e-mail, and the news of my premature death, he would put the pieces together and come after Lance like the wrath of heaven.

Suddenly, a feeling of peace came over me. I'm not sure if it was a premonition, intuition, or most likely, something purely logical—a shadow or a sound that I detected somewhere in the periphery of my senses—but something told me that what was about to happen was meant to be.

I looked at Ivy who sat shaking with her shoulders hunched. I glanced at Zachary who reached over and took Ivy's hand. I turned my back to Lance and knelt on the grass, and as I did, Ivy looked back over her shoulder and screamed in a voice tight with terror.

"Amanda! No, he's got another gun!"

I turned my head and saw Lance raise his shirt just enough to reveal the pistol that was tucked into his waistband. I turned back around and closed my eyes. There was nothing I could do about that.

Though I walk through the valley of the shadow of death…

In my mind's eye I saw the card that Gertrude Hastings had dropped on the floor. Three gray-skinned corpses reaching up from their shallow graves. Amanda, Ivy, and Zachary all off to meet a bad end together.

Then I heard the two shots ring out, one right after the other.

I waited to fall down, but it didn't happen. I'd always imagined that if I were shot I would collapse instantly with a tearing, searing pain. Instead, I felt cramped and cold, as if I was freezing to death from the inside out.

I couldn't hear Ivy screaming anymore. I opened my eyes and she sat paralyzed, staring past me. But she didn't look frightened, she looked baffled. Zachary turned and looked at me, and then Ivy, and then patted his head and stared down at the back of his own jacket.

Even though I was so cold that my teeth were chattering and my vision had been narrowed to a tightly focused haze, my mind worked just well enough to know what that meant.

I hadn't been shot. I had no idea how it was possible for Lance to miss me at this range, but he had. I turned and saw that his pistol hung from one finger as his arm dangled at his side. Then he dropped his gun with tears in his eyes, like a man gripped by a profound despair. "God damn it," he sobbed. "God fucking damn it."

For a moment, I entertained the fantasy that he cared too much to shoot me, but that delusion quickly faded as he staggered around a bit as if drunk.

I leapt back as he dropped straight down like a tree being felled, revealing a sniper next to the wall of a tomb near the cypress tree, holding a pistol with both hands in a James Bond pose. Only this guy was a lot hotter than James Bond. He was tall with big brown eyes, and wore a pair of slacks and a loose fitting gray sweater that went nicely with his slim build and tousled dark blond hair. My first thought was that he looked a lot like Stonewall.

Then I realized he was Stonewall.

I didn't recognize him at first because I'd only ever seen him looking all corporate in his tailored suits and hair gel. But a disheveled Stonewall was a hot Stonewall. He looked incredible, maybe not in the empirical sense, the way Lance used to, but he was exactly my type. It was as if I had gone to God with a blueprint and said "build me one of these" and God ripped it up and said "Your imagination isn't good enough. Let me make you something better."

By some miracle he must have read Jonny's manuscript already and came here to check things out for himself. Either that or he was really an angel. When I didn't move, his smile vanished and he put his gun back in its holster and slowly approached me.

A voice in my mind screamed to stop being such an idiot and run to him. I rushed over and he caught me and held me close and reached for his phone.

"Brunston, you'd better get over here quickly. I had to shoot the bastard." He hung up and stroked my hair. "Amanda, you were not making it easy to get a clean shot."

I turned and saw Lance staring at us with a cranberry-colored stain near his shoulder and his mouth hanging open in outrage. Ivy and Zachary were back on their feet and had moved the gun out of Lance's reach. They seemed to have the situation under control so I shuddered and buried my face against Stonewall's chest.

He looked down at me with concern. "Are you alright?"

"I'm okay if you're okay."

"Me? I'm fine," he said. "And just so you know: if you were to vanish, I would miss you."

I blushed. "Oh, so you heard all of that?"

He held up his PDA. "Heard it and recorded it for posterity. You don't mind if I play this back to a few of my friends working for the prosecution, do you?"

I gazed up. Those warm caramel eyes went so nicely with the faint trace of stubble. "You go right ahead."

He gave me a sly smile. "So how much of that was true?"

I sighed and ran my hand over his tousled hair. "Every last word of it."

He went red around the ears and looked down. "I know I look like a mess right now, but this time you really did get me out of bed."

"Has anyone ever told you that you look really good with a bit of scruff to you?"

Stonewall smirked. "It's the gun."

"It's most certainly not the gun." I brought my hand up to caress his jaw. The stubble felt so good against my hand that I had to know what it felt like against my lips so I kissed him on the cheek. Then, by reflex, I kissed him on the mouth.

Stonewall turned away. That's not to say that he recoiled. He just ignored the kiss altogether like it never happened.

Oh, well. So much for that theory. I sighed and tried to step away, but his arm across my back held me in place like the safety bar on an amusement park ride.

"Ivy," he said without releasing me.

"Yes?" I looked over and saw that Zachary crouched behind her. She had Lance's gun in her hand and was pointing it at Lance, who looked as if he'd a crawled a couple of feet in our direction.

"Have you ever used a gun before?"

"I can't say that I have."

"Then there are three things I want you to know. One: Every gun is a loaded gun, even when you know it's not. Two: Never assume that you can shoot at someone and not kill him. And Three: always keep your finger outside the trigger guard until you're ready to fire. Got that?"

She winked. "Sure. Everything over here is under control."

"Good," Stonewall said. Right before he pulled me closer, and drew me into a kiss. I'm not sure how to put that kiss into words, other than to say that it felt completely familiar, and oh so perfect. It was as if we'd kissed a million times before, in a hundred different lifetimes, and every kiss had been better than the one before it.

I heard sirens and could see the red and blue flashing of a half dozen squad cars.

Oh, great, *now* the police arrive.

CHAPTER 35

Stonewall held me as the police swarmed the scene. Brunston and Yolanda emerged from an unmarked car.

"It's good to see that you two have finally patched up your differences," Brunston said as he held up a pair of handcuffs and walked to Lance. "Okay, Prince Charming, these nice officers are going to keep you company until your ambulance arrives."

Lance flung his good arm in our direction. "He shot me! That coward shot me in the back! You have to arrest him."

"No we don't," Brunston said as he clamped the cuffs into place. "I gave him permission. He asked if he could use lethal force if his princess was in danger and I told him to go right ahead."

The detectives took my eyewitness testimony first, then Stonewall's, which I appreciated, since that meant we wouldn't have to be kept apart while they talked to Ivy and Zachary.

A few of the uniformed officers spread crime tape and took photos of the crime scene before the paramedics came to collect Lance. Stonewall and I started walking back toward the tombs, but we stopped when we heard Lance shouting.

"Amanda! You're dead! When I get out, I'm going to gut your boyfriend! I'm going to make you watch, you two-timing slut!"

"Like I haven't heard anything like that before." Stonewall tried to put his arm around me, but I turned around.

"Lance? There's something you need to know." I pointed to Stonewall. "This is the guy I was willing to go to prison for."

It took three cops to shove him onto the gurney and strap him down after that. I knew it was petty of me to enjoy that, but I did.

There was a bench on the other side of the cypress trees so we sat there as the crime scene was processed. I let myself relax a little, and Stonewall reached over and held my hand. I'm sure that was all he intended to do, but soon I was making out with him again. I worried that I was coming on too strong, but I couldn't help myself. If the police hadn't been there, I would have done a lot more than that.

He indulged me for a few seconds before he pulled back. "Amanda," he whispered. "Is this a dream, or do you really like me a little?"

"I like you more than a little," I said. "I like you a whole lot."

"And I like you far too much." He reached over and held my hand in both of his, as if he had something serious to tell me and needed to soften the blow. "Amanda, I'm completely obsessed with you. I fell for you on the day we met, and since then I haven't been able to think about anything else."

I shrugged. "I fail to see why that's a bad thing."

The look of anxiety didn't leave his face. "Amanda, I'm no saint. I've plotted and schemed to find ways to be near you. You had every reason not to like me in the past. I didn't realize how inappropriate it was until it had gone too far."

Poor Stonewall, he looked so worried. I caressed his face and resumed kissing him until I heard Brunston and Yolanda approaching.

"Okay, knock it off you two troublemakers," Brunston said. "Jeremy Kendal, you are a pain in my ass. You couldn't have resolved this without resorting to lethal force?"

"No, I don't think I could have."

Yolanda held open a plastic Ziploc bag. "I'm going to need for you to surrender your weapon."

We stood up and Stonewall removed the holster from his belt and dropped it into the bag. Yolanda turned to me and smiled. "Amanda, your friends said that they had to leave, and you'll need to get a ride from someone."

I sniffed in mock outrage. "Some friends they are. Why I bet that I could go missing for hours, or even days, and they wouldn't show the slightest bit of concern."

"Well, I suppose there's one way to find out," Stonewall said.

"Hey, don't reward her, Jeremy," Brunston said. "She's been a very reckless girl."

Stonewall put his arms around me and rested his chin on my shoulder. "You're only saying that because she's a better detective than you are."

"Well, so are you," I said. "Seeing as how quickly you managed to piece the whole thing together just based on Jonny's manuscript."

Stonewall looked startled. "The lost manuscript?"

"Yes, the one I e-mailed you about an hour ago."

Stonewall released me and browsed to his e-mail. On the list of messages, I could see mine at the top, unread.

"Wait, a minute," I said. "If you didn't get my message, then how did you get here before the police?"

"Well, to be fair, their cars don't have a top speed of over two hundred and fifty miles per hour."

Brunston went red in the face. "Jeremy, you're lucky that I didn't hear a word you just said."

"No, Stonewall, I meant how did you know to come here at all?"

Stonewall looked away and Brunston cocked his head.

"Look, all I know is that we got a frantic call from Jeremy saying you were in danger. We would have been here sooner but I could barely understand a word he was saying. Fortunately he called again when he had a better handle on the situation."

I sighed and stared down at my ankle. "Then I guess the alarm never went off after all. And here I was, thinking I was brilliant for tampering with the ankle monitor."

"What ankle monitor?" Yolanda asked.

I wondered if she was playing a game with me but her face looked deadly serious. As did Brunston's.

"The ankle monitor they gave me when they released me from jail." The two detectives just looked at me as if I was making the whole thing up so I hiked up the leg of my jeans. "This ankle monitor."

Brunston looked grave. "They weren't allowed to put that on you."

Yolanda nodded. "In the eyes of the law you're a free woman. That is a complete violation of your constitutional rights." She leaned over to get a better look. "You say they put that on you in the jail?"

"Yes…" I thought back and realized that wasn't exactly true. I looked over my shoulder at Stonewall, who was holding up a key.

"For the record, I never told her that she had to wear that."

Oh, so *this* was what he was worried about. And with good reason! I snatched the key from him. "You were *stalking* me?"

"It's just a red dot on a map. It's not like I tapped your phone or installed cameras in your house." The detectives snickered. "I didn't."

I unlocked the tether and gave it to Yolanda, who said. "Are you sure you want to get in a car with this degenerate?"

"That's an excellent question. Stonewall, do you have any idea how many different types of wrong it was to put that thing on me?"

"Of course I do. Why do you think I couldn't look you in the eye when I gave it to you?"

I thought back to our big falling out. Which I now realized wasn't even a falling out at all. "So it wasn't because you despised me?"

"I could never despise you, Amanda. I needed to keep an eye on you and give you a way to let me know if you were in trouble. "

Brunston shook his head sadly. "Sorry Jeremy, but you're still a pathetic wanker."

"I knew this was going to make you hate me forever, but I'd rather be hated by you than risk never seeing you again. There, are you sufficiently disgusted now?"

I looked over at Brunston and Yolanda who grinned like jackals. I'm sure they would have turned a blind eye if I decided to punch him a few times, but to tell the truth, all I could feel was profound relief that he had never hated me. I put my arms around his neck and smiled. "Disgusted, yes. Sufficiently? Not even close."

Brunston cleared his throat. "We'll let you two sort this out by yourselves. Amanda, we'll try to get your computer back to you as quickly as we can. Jeremy, you need to come by the station tomorrow." He glanced at me. "Late in the afternoon would be fine."

After they left, we walked past the tombs and the cypress trees into the field of grave markers. In the past, it might have appeared somber to me, but in my euphoria the air smelled cleaner, the stars shone brighter, even the tombstones glowed with a pearly sheen. I watched Stonewall and studied his face as he gazed into his PDA.

"What are you looking at?"

"The document you sent me. I would have never guessed that Jonny kept a diary."

"No, that's Jonny's final manuscript."

"You must be mistaken. Jonny's final manuscript was recently published and is already available in bookstores."

"What? How can you not remember—" I stopped talking when I noticed Stonewall's Cheshire Cat smile. "Oh, right, what am I saying? It must be his diary. His recently found, incomplete, and as of yet *unpublished* diary."

Stonewall nodded. "I was thinking for this particular project, we could shop it as a posthumous Goodsnuff journal, as completed by his widow. It really is the best solution for everyone—Jonny's final wishes are honored, his fans will get to read his final novel, the publishers will make a bundle— all while I get to establish you as Jonny's apprentice and the heir to the

Goodsnuff literary dynasty—which should make it a lot easier to justify the similarities between your work and Jonny's, should anyone happen to notice them."

I looked up at him.

"Wait a minute. Did you just offer me representation?"

"Only if you're interested."

"Oh, I'm interested. But I thought you only took on established writers as clients?"

"Well, you did write a bestselling novel, and nobody could deny that your debut was an unprecedented critical and commercial success, even if you only managed to get it published by the most unconventional and perverted means imaginable."

"Ah, thank you. Coming from the master, that's high praise indeed."

"Except there is one caveat that you may not like—you can't change a single word of what Jonny has written."

"You've got to be kidding me. That means I have to write around his noxious, cringe-inducing style."

"Sorry, but we have to honor the man's work, not bury it."

I let out a mock whimper and kicked at some gravel. "I suppose it's the least I can do."

As we neared the parking lot, I could see his car glistening like a flawless ruby in the moonlight.

I looked up at Stonewall. "Can I drive?"

I meant it as a joke, but he pulled his arm away from mine.

Then he reached into his pocket and dropped his keys into my hand.

All I could do was stare at them while he walked over to the passenger side.

In case you're still wondering, this guy is a keeper.

About the Author

Ellie Burmeister is a native Californian and a graduate of SDSU. She has worked and traveled extensively in Europe. She's also done some acting for movies and television, and would do more, if she could find the time. Her hobbies include reading, travel, hanging out at the beach, and fine dining. She's a vegetarian who eats fish, but if she says she's a pescetarian, people assume it's a religion and offer her carrot-shaving sandwiches instead of halibut. Beyond that, she leads a fairly simple life.